THE EGYPTIAN PROPHECY

Gil Winkelman

ISBN: 979-8-9858867-0-2

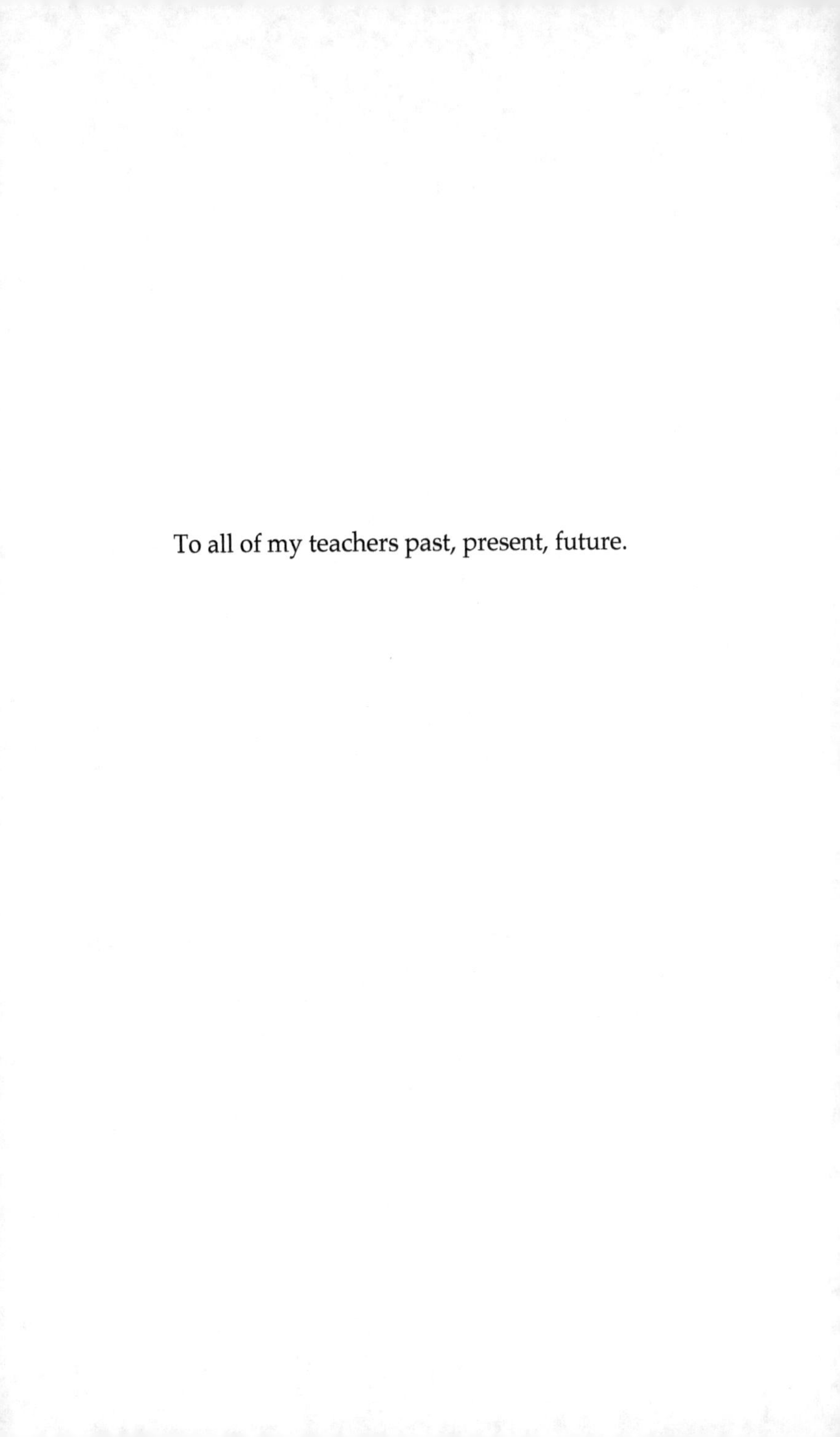

To all of my teachers past, present, future.

Characters, Places, and Terms

Main Characters

Ramose: Egyptian name for Moses
Miriam: Biological sister of Ramose
Ahmose: Pharaoh of Egypt and adopted father of Ramose
Nefertari: Adopted Mother of Moses who has the following titles: Queen of Egypt, Pharaoh's Daughter, God Wife of Amun-Re
Ramose-Ankh: Oldest son of Pharaoh; adopted brother of Moses
Siamun: Second oldest son of Pharaoh
Amenhotep: Youngest son of Pharaoh
Meritamen: Oldest Daughter of Pharaoh
Sitamen: Youngest Daughter of Pharaoh
Harwa: Teacher of Ramose
Rekhmire: Teacher of Ramose and advisor to Pharaoh
Balaam: Advisor to Pharaoh
Iyov: Advisor to Pharaoh
Zipporah: Wife of Moses
Paser: Attendant to Ramose

Minor Characters

Joseph: One of Jacob's twelve sons who became Vizier of

Egypt.
Jacob: Father of the twelve tribes of Israel
Apepi: Former Pharaoh of Lower Egypt
Khamudi: Last Pharaoh of Lower Egypt who Ahmose killed to end the war of unification
Teta: Noble and father of Maiherpri
Ankhu: Son of noble and friend of Amenhotep
Maiherpri: Son of noble and friend of Amenhotep
Jochebed: Mother of Moses
Amran: Father of Moses
Hannu: Son of noble and friend of Amenhotep
Serah: Granddaughter of Jacob who is an elder at the time of Ramose
Merneferre Ay: Last Pharaoh of the 12th Dynasty and ending of the Middle Kingdom.

Terms

Habirus: the older more technical name for the Hebrews
Hyksos: The term used to represent the non-Egyptian people living in Egypt. Technically, this is a Greek word, shortened from a longer Egyptian term.
El Shaddai: The Habiru name for God.
Sebou: Ritual of welcoming a new baby into a family.
Wepet-Renpet: Egyptian New Years. It corresponds to the rising of the Nile River.
Akhet: First season of Egyptian year. It corresponds to the time of flooding. Roughly June through September.
Peret: The planting season in Egypt after the flooding subsides. It corresponds to October through January.
Shemu: The harvest season in Egypt that corresponds to February through May.
Ma'at: Both a goddess and a concept. Ma'at is the ideal of balance, ethics, righteousness, rolled into one.

Places

NB: The Kingdom of Egypt is viewed upside-down in that the

Nile River flows South to North but is viewed the opposite on a map.

Lower Kingdom: The Northern Kingdom

Upper Kingdom: The Southern Kingdom

Kush: Also called Nubia. It is directly South of Egypt

Strongili: An island in the Mediterranean Sea that was the seat of an advanced civilization. Only Santorini is left from the volcanic destruction.

Akortiri: A port city on the island of Strongili.

Avaris: The former capital of the Lower Kingdom.

Waset: The former capital of the Upper Kingdom and the unified kingdom. It lies within modern day city of Luxor. It was called Thebes by the Greco-Romans.

Buhen: An outpost city/military installation on the Southern Edge of the Egyptian Empire near Nubia. Currently, it is underwater as a result of the Aswan Dam

Northern Desert: The Sinai Peninsula

Great Sea: The name for the Mediterranean Sea

Bitter Lakes: A series of Lakes Near the Suez Gulf. The sea receded leaving salt water lakes inland.

Gods of Egypt

NB: This is not a complete list.

Hapi

Seth

Osiris

Amun-Re

Nut

Hathor

Khepri

Geb

Heqet

Atum: Another name for Amun-Re

Prologue

When he first told me of his childhood, I dismissed my father's tale. I knew fratricide and incest to be commonplace in Egypt. Many pharaohs rose to power by killing their older brothers. And all Pharaohs marry their oldest sister, but few have sex with the others without marriage. After hearing about my father's encounter with Sitamen, I suspected why he may have banned sibling marriage. For that matter, his upbringing in Egypt is why he forbade many things including the use of magic, though he was a great magician. Possibly the greatest ever.

Until a few years before my father's passing, I knew nothing of his involvement in the royal's palace politics. His story's outlandishness contrasted with what I knew of my friends' parents' upbringing. They told little of their early days other than to say, "We were slaves in Egypt." Their stories are buried with them.

I knew only that for many years, Habirus toiled in the dirt, making bricks for one or another of Pharaoh's construction projects. They built his tomb and temples to their gods. At Pharaoh's behest, my people opened the canal that would lead to their freedom.

But my father's story was distinct. I learned of the contrast from other Habirus when he sat me down late in his life. The day he did so dawned like most of the others had as we wandered the desert. We collected manna and ate our simple breakfast. We drank water from the well my aunt found. Nothing my father did prepared me for his announcement.

"Gershom," he said. "Another will lead the people."

The abruptness of his pronouncement stunned me for a moment. "But Father," I protested. "You have prepared me…"

He waved me off. "Your path differs from mine for the Holy One has another role for you."

The Holy One. My father spent the last forty years trying to instill the belief in one God in our people. They missed his message. Years of living in polytheistic Egypt corrupted any notion of one all-pervading deity. Egypt's pantheon contained hundreds if not thousands of different gods, each with his or her purpose. As a result, the Habirus failed to grasp the abstract idea that all is unified. That beneath the surface of form lay a cohesion one could discern, but not with the five senses. Did I understand this because I was Moses' son? Or had my proximity to him given me access to this understanding? To be fair, my father failed to understand this concept for many years, even after his direct encounter with the Holy One at the burning bush.

I looked down at my feet as tried to soften the blow. "Your task requires more subtlety, more finesse."

Curious, I asked, "What is it?"

"You are to tell my story, our story. The story of how we came here."

"Your story? Why?"

"Everything that has happened was shaped by the people in my early childhood."

" I know nothing of your life before I was born."

He nodded his head in agreement. "Do you not know why I left Egypt?" he asked.

"I only know rumors. That you struck down a task master who beat Habiru slaves. I do not understand why a prince would need to run for killing a cruel taskmaster."

"That is all you know?"

I nodded.

"We must remedy this," he said. "For I killed cruel men, and innocent ones too. But that is not the reason I left Egypt. I left because of my role in my brothers' deaths. And to stay would have brought more pain to our people."

"How did that happen?" I asked.

Here lies the tale he told me.

PART ONE

1

Contradictions shaped my early childhood. Though my family and I lived in poverty inside Avaris, the capital of the former Lower Kingdom, a rich tapestry of love and adventure flowed through my life. My parents came from minor noble families of Lower Egypt, but faced a drastic change in their lives with aplomb and grace. Pharaoh Ahmose had occupied Avaris after he conquered his Northern neighbor, the Hyksos, in a bloody and devastating war. Pharaoh removed families from their homes and forced them into work camps. Mine was no exception. We moved downstream to a place where danger came yearly as the Nile flooded.

When the water was not too high, the river beckoned exploration and experience. While my parents slaved for the Pharaoh, my older sister, Miriam raised me. Miriam and I spent most of our days basking in the Nile's luxury, playing along the shoreline, watching dragonflies flit from white lotus petals to papyrus stalks, wings iridescent and gossamer over the shimmering water. Little troubled us. If we were hungry, there was ample fruit for us to eat. We did not understand our poverty, for we spent our days surrounded by beauty and richness.

An illness I developed as a five-year-old shattered this dreamlike childhood. It would be many years before I learned the true nature of the illness. After fainting and falling, I became bedridden for several days. Miriam fussed over me, the only interruption being a visit by an Egyptian official. Miriam returned, and I felt her tension. She did not reveal the reason for his call. Later, I overheard her crying to my parents, mentioning an Egyptian prophecy and my imminent presentation to the Pharaoh.

Sobbing, Miriam asked, "Is he actually a prophet, Mother?"

I did not hear my mother's answer, only her gentle hushing. That evening, Mother sat on the floor beside my straw bed. As she came closer, I smelled her toil in the fields: raw oats, barley, sweat, distilled into her own perfume. The annual fragrance of harvest season.

"Why did the Egyptian man come to our house, Mother?"

She gave me a surprised look. "This is not your concern, my son," she said, with tightness around her eyes, as though she might cry. "Your only goal is to get well."

***

"Where was your brother Aaron?" I asked my father. "Is he not older than you?"

"He came later," my father snapped. His nostrils flared, looking impatient. "Stop interrupting, Gershom. The tale is long, and I will reveal all in time."

"Forgive me, Father," I said, and he continued in his story.

Had I known what my recovery would lead to, I may have lingered in my illness. But I recuperated, and my parents informed me I would go to the palace the very next morning. We would venture to the area that excluded Habirus, my birth-people, and those conquered by Egypt's current rulers.

"Why must we heed the call of a pompous ass?" I overheard Father ask.

"Because he is Pharaoh," Mother replied. "What will we do? Flee to the desert?"

"Why not?"

"With Pharaoh's army chasing us?" Mother rebuked. "You would not be speaking thus if Khamudi summoned us."

"He was a good man. He would not bother us over some stupid prophecy."

"Balaam's visions proved accurate," Mother said.

"Do not use that traitor's name in my house!"

Mother laughed, a tinkly chorus. "House? We live in a hut."

Rather than respond, my father stormed out, without a door

to slam.

The next morning, I prepared for the day. My presentation at the court of the Pharaoh required formal attire. Rather than my usual short tunic and sandals, on this extraordinary day, I wore a long, white robe paired with heavy boots, which caused discomfort in the warm sun. Never had I worn such finery. As I followed my parents down the dusty road, I wondered why the Pharaoh wanted to meet me.

The dirt path gave way to a stone road. Shemu, the harvest season had ended, but the ground waited for the floods of Akhet. Dust and dryness lingered along the smooth, worn path. Small rocks and dried mud had collected between the gaps of the stones. The road opened to a broad public area, which transformed daily into a makeshift market. Smells of meat cooking, mostly waterfowl, rose into the air. Vendors hawked grain, fruit, clay pots, clothing, small ivory wands to ward off evil spirits, and the ubiquitous statues of Egyptian gods. Un-dyed linen hung on posts covering each cart. The stalls were packed so close together that the entire ensemble appeared as though shaded by one large canopy.

My parents led me on a direct route from one end of the market to the other, but as we passed, the shouts and conversations of the marketplace became gradually inaudible, and a stillness enveloped us. Villagers stopped what they were doing and stared as we approached. Whispers followed in our wake. But by the time we arrived at the other end, the market's usual cacophony had resumed.

We reached a large gate that blocked the route into the palace district. Bronze bars stood in the portal. Hinges attached to the stones allowed the gate to swing open towards us, as we waited on the more impoverished side of the city. Two guards halted our entry into the wealthy neighborhood. My father showed them the papyrus scrap, evidence of our permission to enter. Crossing into the exclusive part of town, I noticed how quiet the place was. Fewer people walked along the road. As we continued through the streets, unfriendly glares and looks of surprise met us along the way. New laws forbade Habirus from entering this part of the city. Some shouted unkind words at us, but I did not speak Egyptian well, and I did not know what they were saying. But my parents understood and retreated into themselves. Later, I would learn that they hurled vile insults—insults that would follow me into my exile.

As we drew closer to the palace, the homes became more massive and grander. Shade cast from palm tree branches planted inside the walls cooled small areas on the street. Through gates, I saw entryway gardens with elaborate fountains. My mother criticized the exploitation of water, the lifeblood of the desert, to grow decorative plants.

The houses were massive stone structures surrounded by high walls to keep out us undesirables. Caretakers busied themselves readying homes for the owners' seasonal use. Typically painted white to keep out the heat, in our former neighborhood commissioned artists painted the exterior walls in vivid colors and hieroglyphs that depicted scenes of family heroism. These etchings showcased each family's history. As we drew closer to the palace, these scenes increased in number.

"Why do they glorify themselves as if they are gods?" my father asked no one in particular.

As we walked, he explained that before my birth, this neighborhood had belonged to my ancestors' home. Several families lived in each house. Most were painted white then, without all the etchings and showy colors. Now, our people lived in much smaller homes closer to the river, outside of rebuilt walls, and just one Nile inundation away from death.

Akhet began the annual flooding season when the river swelled and flooded the land with the southern rains. With enough elevation, living near the water was desirable year-round. The wealthy dwelt in raised homes that protected them from the river, without fear that the Nile would sweep them away while they slept. Beautiful terraces overlooked the water, and stairs allowed them easy access for bathing or swimming. Our Habiru clay huts possessed no such luxuries. Rapidly rising water could kill many of us unexpectedly. Father explained how lucky we were to live perched on a raised mound, protected from the floods.

"Why did we leave this neighborhood?" I asked.

"When Ahmose conquered the land," my father began, "he moved many Egyptians from the south here. To punish those who fought against him, he took their homes away."

"Did you fight against him, Father?"

"I worked in the justice system for the Pharaoh of the Lower Kingdom but was not a soldier."

"Oh," I said, disappointed, hoping my father could tell me stories of heroic deeds and bravery. "Why did Ahmose conquer the land at all?"

"There was one kingdom," my mother explained. "Then there were two kingdoms. And now there is one again." I looked at her, feeling confused.

Though I remember her answer, I have only a vague memory of the way my mother looked. Miriam once told me she and Mother mirrored one another. Both had long, wavy hair, always covered out of modesty. Their hard-driving Egyptian masters caused their hands to become calloused. Mother's long nose curved to the left, and Miriam's mouth was rounder than Mother's. But my sister's soft, deep-set gray eyes reminded me of my mother's. Reflected in their gray eyes, the first women in my life, Miriam and my mother had shaped my sense of right and wrong.

"Many, many years ago, Egypt was one large empire," my mother further explained. "Famine in other lands caused more Northerners to settle in Egypt. The Pharaohs welcomed the foreigners, who worked for little money performing animal farming and other tasks that some Egyptians felt was beneath their abilities. But over the years, the foreigners became the majority in the Northern part of the lands. When Merneferre Ay, the last Pharaoh of his dynasty, died with no heirs, the kingdom splintered into two. The Northern or Lower Kingdom was ruled by one Pharaoh while the Southern or Upper Kingdom was ruled by another."

My mother told me that "Hyksos" was a derogatory term invented by Ahmose's relatives, who looked down upon their northern neighbors as uncultured farmers.

"Ahmose does not like foreigners though they helped build his country," my father said. "He will try to erase any evidence of rule by non-Egyptians."

Whether my young age or the lack of comprehension of why Pharaoh would wish to erase another culture, I could not say. But I did not appreciate his reluctance to give others credit.

We arrived at the palace, pausing for a moment before continuing towards the front. My mother gazed at me, making me shift in my boots. Her gray eyes were trying to tell me something, staring at me with liquid coolness. I broke away from her stare. Tilting my head back, I looked up instead at the sheer, high walls of the building in amazement.

Etchings depicted Set, the storm god, a god of the Hyksos and Egyptians. The vibrant blue, red, and green had crumbled in spots, revealing the yellow sandstone beneath. Lowering my head, I spied sphinxes resting on either side of the stairs at the bottom, painted with detailed facial expressions. Yellowish bodies extended towards heads covered with traditional Egyptian headdresses and decorated with thick black and white stripes. The human faces of each statue differed, for the one on the left frowned while the one on the right smiled. They painted the face on the left a dark color, almost black, while the one on the right was white. Little did I know how the sphinxes reflected the two-faced nature of most of the palace's inhabitants.

I climbed the stairs and felt how the rise of each step was so substantial for my small legs. I gaped as I walked, trying to take in all the sights and sounds while being careful not to trip.

"Close your mouth," my mother scolded. "Pharaoh does not want a wide-mouthed boy in his presence." Immediately, I shut my mouth and continued my ascent towards the giant double doors that waited at the top. Expecting our arrival, two guards opened the doors, and a servant led us through ornate halls decorated with shining gold and copper. Columns lined the sides of the corridor, dividing the large area into three parallel hallways. Beyond the columns, decorated walls depicted scenes of men fishing on the Nile and hunting in the swamps. Minoan artists had painted these pictures—so very different from the typical hieroglyphs seen in other Egyptian artwork.

But now, different artisans painted over an original mural of a Hyksos victory against the Egyptians. Ahmose would remove all Hyksos artwork for, as my father said, he wished to erase all things not Egyptian. All signs of a different civilization were to disappear.

At the end of the long corridor stood two large double doors matching those at the palace entrance in size and decoration. I guess they stood around fifteen cubits tall and each eight cubits wide, with few markings on them, plated in gold. Guards opened the double doors in unison. My legs were tired, and I wanted to rest, but the herald called out our names as we entered the audience chamber.

***

"Amram and Jochebed! Approach the mighty Pharaoh Ahmose, Uniter of Egypt," the herald bellowed, pronouncing my parents' names without a problem though foreign to the Egyptian saying them. Nobles and courtiers sat in chairs against the unadored walls on either side of the ample open space. Mother and Father led me across the massive chamber towards a pair of looming thrones. Hundreds of eyes stared at us as we traversed the area between the doors and the royals. I was so nervous, I felt I might faint at any moment.

Pharaoh's ornate throne comprised gold inlaid wood, with the heads of lions carved into the ends of the arms and lion's feet on its four legs. The back comprised a red velvety material, though I could not see it with Pharaoh sitting on it. On a matching throne next to him sat a woman whose long black hair had hundreds of tiny beaded braids falling past her shoulders. Her almond-shaped eyes watched me with a kind visage. Their countenances mirrored those of the sphinxes at the palace front. I found the graciousness of the woman's face more comfortable to view than Pharaoh's stern expression.

We stopped five cubits from the thrones, and my parents bowed their heads in homage to the Pharaoh, as was the custom of the day.

"Do you like the palace as I have rebuilt it?" Pharaoh said, looking at my father, waving his hands in a gesture of the surroundings.

"It is very nice, your Majesty," my father mumbled.

"Yes, it is turning out well. I must remove the artwork the Hyksos left." My father said nothing, so Pharaoh continued, "It was a shame to destroy some of it, but your people gave us a good fight?"

"Yes, your Majesty."

"Do not be too sad, Ah...Am...ran." Pharaoh tripped over my father's foreign-sounding name. "Everyone knew Egypt would unite again, as the prophets told us. You could be on my throne. After all, you were a former noble of the Hyksos court."

"True, your Majesty. But it is not your people who are enslaved and subjugated."

"Had Khamudi and his father not been such weak rulers, it might have been otherwise," Ahmose scowled. "I am glad to be rid of him, for he was deceitful and weak, which is not a good combination. My one regret was not thanking Khamudi before I ran my spear through his chest and snuffed out his miserable life. If he had not tried poisoning the Egyptians in the Upper Kingdom, my father would never have been able to unite our people against the Lower Kingdom."

My father's face did not betray shock at Pharaoh's cruel comments. Instead, he replied, "The deaths of your people from the grain were not his fault, your Majesty. None of us in the Lower Kingdom knew the grain had gone bad. Many of our people died, too."

"So you say," Pharaoh retorted. "Both my father and brother died during the war because of that chieftain." He chose a derogatory term instead of king or Pharaoh. Ahmose glared at my father for a few moments before changing the subject.

"You have brought this child to us, Ah...Maram and Jochee..ebed?"

My father grimaced at the second mispronunciation of his name. There were snickers, and muffled laughter from the nobles gathered in the hall. I wondered if perhaps Pharaoh did this on purpose, to insult my father.

"Yes, your Majesty," said my father, Amram. "Though we do not know what need you have of a small child."

"He is a subject of the Pharaoh, Ahmaram." More muffled laughter. "As are you! We believe he is the child foretold by our seers as the one to help..."

Pharaoh stopped and cleared his throat. I was too young to wonder how a five-year-old could help the most powerful ruler in the known world. Confused, I looked at my parents for some sign of understanding, but their blank faces revealed nothing.

"He will help avert a disaster," Pharaoh continued changing his words. "We shall raise him in the ways of the Egyptians, teaching him about our gods. My sister-wife, Nefertari," he motioned to the beautiful woman seated next to him, "thought it would be wise to have one of the Habirus raised by us. I agree, and I have consented to her wishes in this matter."

My parents looked at one another in shock, not expecting this. I was so overwhelmed by the grandeur of the castle, and the pomp and circumstance of the court, I did not follow the discussion. I sensed my mother's surprise and concern, though, and edged myself closer to her.

"But, your majesty, he..." my father stuttered.

"It will be good for your son to live at the palace, Amram and Jochebed," Nefertari interrupted, looking kindly towards my parents. She had no trouble pronouncing my parents' names. "It will forge a new bond between our people and allow you to better integrate into our society. Pharaoh Ahmose and I will care for him as one of our own. We will teach him the ways of Egypt. Ours are the right ways. We will raise him as our son, fourth in line to the throne."

There was murmuring amongst the nobles with that statement. I overhead snippets of comments reminiscent of the insults hurled at us as we walked into the palace.

"Sacrilege...allowing a half-breed that close to the throne," one said.

Pharaoh raised his staff to quiet the room. I did not yet understand how this decision would alter my life.

"We appreciate your kindness, your Majesty," my father said. "We thought our son might be at the palace for a short time. But he is Habiru. It would not do to teach him the ways of the Egyptians."

"With all due respect," Ahmose sneered, "we have had enough of the ways of the Shepherd Kings, of your filthy animals, and your backward beliefs. It is time to restore Egypt to its greatness. We will restore our public buildings, our temples, and the libraries you and your people neglected for so long. Your people destroyed the vegetation in this region, cutting into your most profitable crop, papyrus. What kind of idiot does that?" Ahmose glared at my father implying that my father destroyed the land himself.

"That may be, your Majesty, but the Habirus are not the Hyksos. We are just a small minority in the region," Amram responded.

"It matters not!" Pharaoh shouted. Then lowering his voice.

"In Egypt, all are responsible if one is guilty." He referred to Ma'at, a concept that would drive me from Egypt.

"But it is no matter now. We have dealt with your people and the other tribes of the Hyksos justly. You, however," he said, pointing at me, "will be fed, clothed, and sheltered. You will learn our ways, and in time, understand our superior ways."

Then, turning back to my parents, he continued, "You and many of your brethren will enjoy these policies. You will gain special privileges for giving us your son. Our gods will reward you. You will have no need for animal sacrifices. Our priests do that in the temples. It is good to have them open again."

"I am Habiru, your Majesty. We only believe in El Shaddai." My father held his head high as he spoke the Habiru name of God, his loud voice carrying to the far corners of the great room.

"Pfft! One God! I have heard of this idea of one god," Pharaoh said with disdain. "I do not mean to insult you Ah, Amamram. It is just so…" Ahmose searched for the word, "… foreign to me. How can one deity contain all that power? How does one deity do all of those different things?"

My father replied, "El Shaddai knows all, and can do all."

"Right! He must, if there is only one of him," Pharaoh said flippantly, evoking more laughs in the room. "Still, your son needs proper instruction. Just in case…" Pharaoh said as he turned towards me. He stood from his throne to look down at me. His eyes were not kind like Nefertari's, but ruthless and battle-hardened. My soon to be adopted father's gaze bore down upon me as he asked, "What is your name?"

Nervously, I mumbled my Habiru name, followed by "your majesty," as my parents had instructed me to say to him.

"That will not do," Ahmose said. "It sounds so, well… so strange. I think making it more Egyptian would be good for me, and for you, child. We cannot have the other boys teasing you because your name is so different. But not to make it too confusing, what sounds similar in Egyptian?"

One of the Pharaoh's advisors whispered into his ear.

"An excellent idea, Balaam," he said. "We shall call you Ramose, which means Son of the Sun God, Ra. Nefertari and I shall raise you as one of our own, with our children. You will study with their teachers, the best in Egypt, to learn our ways. My son, Amenhotep, is only a year older than you. You two will learn from my trusted advisor, Rekhmire. I hope that someday you will be good friends. And who knows? Maybe you can be a good influence on one another."

"A better influence than his brother Siamun, your Majesty," a voice said, more audibly than intended. Ahmose shot a stern look in the direction the comment came from, but said nothing.

Pharaoh motioned to a guard to remove me from the audience chamber. At that moment, I understood what the adults had already agreed upon and tried to cling to my parents, who just stood there doing nothing, as the guards took me away. Screaming, I looked back at my parents, tears streaming from my eyes.

"A sensitive one, eh?" Pharaoh said. "Well, that is all right, my son. We do not have to worry about you trying to take the throne from the older boys!" He laughed. He would die with a different opinion of me.

The guard led me out of the audience chamber, and towards the private royal living quarters. As we walked through the halls, we came upon a young boy about my age, though slightly larger, followed by a small group of other boys. An older, taller boy whispered something to the boy in front as I approached. The boy in front said, "Here comes the crying Habiru! Your god, Habiru, will not hear your tears!"

The guard admonished him, "Amenhotep, this is Ramose. He is your adopted brother now. Brothers help. They do not criticize each other."

"He is not my brother! And I will never, ever need the Habiru's help!" the boy yelled at the guard while glaring at me. Then my new adopted brother turned his back on me and strolled off laughing with his friends.

2

Amenhotep's enmity upon my arrival at the palace conditioned me to avoid anyone my age, exacerbating my loneliness. Every day I would put on a brave face, while at night I cried myself to sleep. Like most children, I felt little control over my life. Forces more significant than my parents controlled my existence now. I struggled to comprehend how I had ended up at the palace. Other children must have had visions such as mine. "Why me?" I wondered, and not for the last time. My self-pity continued long after I left Egypt.

Moving south with the royal family to a palace in Waset exacerbated my despair. I felt isolated, for my biological relatives remained in Avaris. I spent my days locked in my room, avoiding everyone. I refused to leave for meals and ate little. Nefertari intervened a few weeks later. Returning from the temple, she and her daughters, Meritamen and Sitamen arrived at my quarters to invite me to an excursion. Meritamen, several years, my senior, was older than my sister Miriam. Meritamen's small nose and soft lips resembled her mother's. Only her almond-shaped eyes hinted that Ahmose could be her father. Sitamen and I were almost the same age. She too favored her mother, and yet she had a visage different from either parent.

"Where do you wish to take me?" I pouted.

"To the river. You must learn to swim."

"Swim?"

"All Egyptian children receive instruction," she responded, her kindness apparent. "Though not from the queen at the terrace of the Pharaoh."

She instructed a servant to change me into something suitable for swimming. The day was warm already, and though I still felt sorry for myself, the thought of swimming enticed me to leave my room. I rose from my giant bed of simple wood construction, inlaid with intricate paintings on the head and the footboard. Painted on the interior footboard was a baby in a reed basket. In the center of the room lay a stone table with four legs. Two wooden chairs surrounded the table. Tapestries hung on the walls depicting the many gods of Egypt.

"What did you do at the temple?" I asked as I changed my clothes.

"Performed a ritual to return the sun to the sky," Meritamen replied. "Mother is teaching me."

"How do you do that?" I wondered, looking out the window to see the sun high in the sky.

"Mother possesses the title God's Wife of Amun-Re. When I get old enough, that will be one of mine too."

"And your sister's too," Nefertari added.

"The ritual honors the God that brought about the unification of Egypt, Ramose," Meritamen explained. "When Father conquered the Lower Kingdom, he felt obligated to give thanks to the God Amun-Re. For it was the Sun God who guided him to victory. He rededicated a temple to the God in Avaris and is building a new one in Karnak."

"That is true, Meritamen, but it also provided an opportunity for Ahmose to give wealth to his daughters and take power away from the priesthood."

"But how do you raise the sun?" I asked, confused.

A soft laugh emitted from Nefertari's mouth. "The sun rises on its own just fine, Ramose. But my husband believes we must appear powerful, so the people worship us."

Leaving my room, Meritamen and Nefertari described the ritual of waking the spirit of the Sun God through offerings at his statue in the temple near the palace. Nefertari and Ahmose were siblings, and like her mother, Meritamen would marry whichever of her brothers became Pharaoh. Nefertari's multiple titles, including Queen, Pharaoh's Daughter, and God's Wife of Amun-Re, confused me. Which was she? All of them, she explained.

"How can one have so many names?" I asked. Nefertari laughed in response.

As we walked, I noticed the lavish furnishings, colorfully painted walls, ornate sculptures, and in some places, hanging tapestries. Servants, some of them Habirus, moved to the side and bowed as we passed. A few weeks before, I would have stood aside for the people who now accompanied me.

We arrived at paired double doors that opened to a stone patio adorned with tables and lounge chairs. To my left, a wall of the palace adjoined the terrace; to my right rose a small stone wall. The closest end abutted the castle, while the far side became stairs leading away from the patio.

"The stairs lead down to a small beach, Ramose," Nefertari explained. "We can swim until the river rises. After that, the current will be too much for you."

We walked down the steps, and she showed me the beach. Servants carried umbrellas for shade and offered snacks of dates, figs, sweet barley cakes, and other delicacies I had never seen before. Aware of my hunger, I devoured the offerings. Watching me, Nefertari and Meritamen smiled at each other. After I had my fill, Nefertari explained that this place was always available. Pharaoh, when he was at the palace, would bathe here every morning surrounded by courtiers. When he was away fighting the Nubians, we could use this place. She wanted me to learn to swim and would teach me over the next several seasons. But on this first day, I placed only my feet into the water while Nefertari pleaded for me to take care.

For the next several weeks, after performing her daily ritual to awaken the sun, Nefertari would bring me to the terrace to play in the river and learn to swim, never venturing far because of my lack of skill. Each time I entered the water, she would warn me to be careful. For each day, the water level swelled higher in response to the rains in Nubia. Nefertari explained that Ahmose would soon return, for battle became more difficult in the torrential rains of the South.

The day before Ahmose's return, we walked down to the water, and Nefertari told me to be wary, as was our ritual. "The marble stairs get slick when wet, Ramose," she said as she had for the previous days. Just as she said this, my foot slipped, and I fell headfirst into the swift current. Nefertari dove into the river, pulling me out. As she pushed on my chest, water arose from my mouth, and I coughed.

"Are you all right?" she asked, fear in her voice.

I nodded as I caught my breath between coughs. Nefertari ordered a servant to carry me back to the terrace. She followed and had me placed on a lounge chair. Sitting next to me, she said, "I will name you Moses. For I have drawn you from the water."

It did not occur to me when I was so young, why my adopted mother would give me a name derived from a Habiru word. Moses meant something very different in her native Egyptian language. Many years would pass before someone other than Nefertari, or the Voice would call me by that name.

***

While Nefertari's and Meritamen's kindness deflected the pain of missing my family, it incited Amenhotep's jealousy. He did not pass up any chance to insult me. I spent those early days avoiding my brother, returning to my room to cry and console myself, feeling the sharp division between my Habiru heritage and living with the royal family.

One evening before my third moon living at the palace, Nefertari came to my room, interrupting my brooding. She sat down on the plush blue satin divan next to me. "Ramose," she said sweetly. "I spoke with the high priest at the temple of Amun-re about your today. To help you feel more Egyptian, and to help your brothers accept you like one, we will perform a birth ritual for you."

"What do I have to do?" I murmured.

"Nothing," Nefertari said, and then described the ritual.

"This is the ritual Egyptians do when a baby reaches seven days," I said. "I am too old. And I have lived with you longer than seven days."

"That is true, Ramose. But ceremonies are powerful tools that sometimes change the attitudes of people and the gods."

The next morning a servant woke me to prepare for the day. He bathed me, then anointed me with various scented oils. Next, he dressed me in a beautiful linen tunic made just for me.

He brought me to my adopted parents waiting at the front of the palace. A large group of nobles and servants gathered for the occasion. But their numbers paled compared to the crowds of commoners, slaves, and Hyksos that assembled for the celebration for Pharaoh provided free food for all holidays.

Nefertari lifted me to her shoulders, then carried me down the stairs and into the road towards the temple complex. Rekhmire stood to my right with a big smile on his face while Balaam and Iyov walked to my left with indiscernible expressions. Behind my parents walked my two adopted sisters, Meritamen and Sitamen, and one of my adopted brothers, Ahmose-Ankh. Each smiled as they pounded the mortar and pestle together with exuberance in sync with others in the procession. I heard Siamun and Amenhotep, complaining to their friends while walking empty-handed behind us about what a baby I must be to need the ritual of Sebou.

Sitting on Nefertari's shoulders, I could see above the heads of the crowd. The red walls of the temple complex loomed large ahead of us. Outside the walls lay a white chapel that paled in comparison. The limestone building appeared to be twelve cubits on each side and half as high. Three large openings dominated each wall of the structure. Wide ramps extended from the central opening on the front and back sides with stairs on either side of the ramp. Deep etchings decorated the exterior walls as did the interior and on the interior columns telling stories of Senusret, his devotion to Amun-Re and the beautiful canal he built eons ago. Many baskets of fruit and flowers rested on the sills of the openings.

In front of the chapel, priests cleared the way for the royal family and the statue of Amun-Re that rested on a cart at the bottom of a ramp. This statue was small compared to the others I had seen. But its size made it easy to transport for celebrations.

A priest signaled to Nefertari to hand me over, but she refused, choosing to carry me into the main complex. Forty or fifty cubits high shot the high red walls making the chapel look tiny in comparison. Etched into the surfaces stood a Pharaoh in the pose of Osiris, the god of the underworld, the same Pharaoh as the one carved into the walls of the white chapel.

I gazed up towards the high walls, trying to decipher the hieroglyphic etchings. The noise of the crowd and the banging sounds distracted me. We came to an opening in the wall measuring about twenty-five cubits high and fifteen cubits in width. We passed through the ten cubits thick walls to enter a wide but short yard filled with statues of Egyptian gods. On the other side of this courtyard lay another wall, mirroring the one we just passed through.

We passed through the second wall to find a nearly identical courtyard as the first. Past the third entrance, lay a much larger courtyard covered with smooth, white stones. This one was triple the size of the others. A chapel mirroring the one outside stood in front of a massive white temple. Different Egyptian gods carved into the tall columns looked down upon me, and the assembled giving me the feeling of being smaller than I already was at my young age.

Ahmose had ordered the rededication of the temple after his victory over the Hyksos and Nubians. Miriam would later tell me later that Habiru slaves refurbished it.

The ritual continued in the courtyard, a mass of people cheering while banging their mortar and pestle instruments. Then the high priest raised his hands to quiet the crowd. Nefertari put me down next to Ahmose-Ankh before joining the priest. As the priest began speaking, Nefertari dismissed him.

"Thank you all for welcoming, Ramose, fourth prince of Ahmose, to our family," she began. "We give thanks to all the gods of Egypt, but particularly Amun-Re, god of the Sun, for the fortune we have in finding such a gentle soul."

The crowd cheered, and Nefertari waited for everyone to quiet down before continuing.

"Why does mother speak instead of the high priest speaking?" Sitamen asked Ahmose-Ankh.

"Father is trying to take power away from the priesthood," Ahmose-Ankh whispered. "It is why you and Meritamen are learning the ritual of bringing the sun up."

"Praise is Amun-Re," Nefertari cried out, then chanted in a language I did not understand. The crowd repeated the chant. Nefertari and the assembled crowd continued singing hymns in this responsive manner. I watched mesmerized by the call and response that continued for nearly an hour. The chanting completed, Nefertari descended the stairs to join me once again.

The high priest said a few prayers to the different gods of Egypt, giving thanks to Hapi, Heqet, Geb, Khepri, Hathor, Isis, Nut, Seth, Osiris, and Pharaoh, also considered a deity.

The gathered people praised the gods, and the festivities began. People left small baskets of fruit, sweetbreads, and baked goods along the stairs of the temple. Servants arrived with food for everyone. Nefertari took my hand in hers and led me up the stairs. A makeshift throne at the top allowed me to sit and enjoy the offered treats. Various nobles approached the dais to introduce themselves; most were cordial, though more than a few gave me disapproving looks before departing.

Teta, the father of a mutual friend of Siamun and Amenhotep, Maiherpri, approached the dais and asked, "What is the meaning of performing the ritual for an Egyptian baby on this Habiru?"

Nefertari glared at Teta, her nearly black eyes ablaze. "You dare question God's Wife of Amun-Re?"

"He is a foreigner, your Majesty," Teta replied coldly. "Why defile the royals? He will try to usurp the thrones from your real sons."

"He will not," Ahmose said, stepping in trying to defuse the situation. "Ramose is but a simple boy."

"Suit yourself, Pharaoh," Teta responded. "But we must not ignore the words of the prophets."

"Who is ignoring the words of the prophets? Prophets give warnings, and we are heeding their vision."

"This is a dangerous way to heed the warnings of the prophets," Teta said, and then withdrew as Nefertari glared at his back for a few moments. The next noble ascended the dais, and her anger abated as she greeted him.

The celebration continued for many hours, and for me at such a young age, this was very tiresome. Nobles made speeches and greeted me after the pronouncements ended. I returned to my room, exhausted. But the excitement of the day and remembering Nefertari and Ahmose arguing about Teta made sleep difficult.

"Why did you not condemn him?" Nefertari yelled.

"He is a powerful noble," Ahmose responded.

"He has always challenged my authority. One day he will question your rule."

"Possibly, but he will need help from the other nobles."

"Do not doubt his desire to make his son Maiherpri Pharaoh."

"I agree that he is dangerous, but we cannot confront him. Not yet."

I thought about the prophecy that Teta and Ahmose discussed. "Were there one or two prophecies?" I wondered. "Why would I want the throne of Egypt?" Their voices quieted, and finally, unable to hear their conversation, I fell fast asleep.

3

Though meant to integrate me into the family, the Sebou ritual increased Amenhotep's jealousy. He continued to taunt me, barely restraining himself in front of Nefertari. While she reprimanded him when he said something rude in her presence, she missed the dirty looks he gave me behind her back.

Amenhotep's anger towards me paled compared to the torment I received at the hands of Siamun, second son of Ahmose and Nefertari. Though he would perform many dangerous pranks against me during my early years at the palace, Siamun's peculiarity came to light a few weeks after the adoption celebration.

On a warm mid-Akhet day, the Nile rose quickly, spreading moisture and silt on the land, flowing too fast for us to play anywhere near the water. My swimming lessons postponed until the flooding ceased, the entire family constellation gathered in the private royal chambers, - rare though it was for all of us to be there, together.

Plush furnishings adorned the room, and the walls shone with opulence. Velvety and satin chairs, loungers, and settees provided more than enough places to sit or recline. Intricate tapestries depicted battles, life on the Nile, and journeys to the Underworld. In time, Nefertari would tell me many of the myths behind these scenes.

Siamun and Amenhotep huddled in the corner of the large room near a window. Meritamen combed the hair of her younger sister, Sitamen, as they listened to the conversation between Ahmose-Ankh, Nefertari, and Ahmose. I sat near my oldest brother while he argued with his father about the rights of the Habirus.

Ahmose-Ankh looked more like his mother than his father. He possessed similar eyes and mouth. His nose, however, looked different from either of his parents, as though someone had grabbed it off a statue and placed on his face.

Ahmose-Ankh's benevolence shone through as he and Ahmose discussed "the Habiru problem." Ahmose-Ankh defended the rights of my people.

"The Habirus work hard, Father," he said. "That was true when the Hyksos ruled too."

"They are lazy people," Ahmose retorted.

"Ahmose!" Nefertari said, admonishing her husband-brother. "That is a terrible thing to say! Particularly in front of our newly adopted son!"

"Habirus are not all bad people," Ahmose said to Nefertari. "Ramose comes from a good family, and you feel better having him here."

He spoke about me as if I was not in the room. I knew I was small for my age, but I felt invisible.

"Father, your words shame Ramose for not being Egyptian," Meritamen kindly said to her father as though appealing to an invisible compassionate side of Ahmose.

"True. It is not your fault you were not born one of us, Ramose," he chided. Apparently he knew I sat in his presence. "But you must learn the ways of Egypt, for that is what will help unite Egypt. We must erase all records of the Habirus and all foreign things!"

"But father," Ahmose-Ankh said, "That will just create more resentment."

"Leadership requires making unpopular decisions, Ahmose-Ankh. The nobles do not care about equity. Greed drives them, not justice. My brother promised gold to the nobles for their help in the war."

"Yes, Father, the nobles require placation. But what advantage does subjugation of the Hyksos give them or us? It only brings greater dissent and foments rebellion. Cooperation work better, does it not?"

"Subjugating foreigners," Siamun said without emotion and in a low voice, "detracts from the suffering of the Egyptians who are poor. Pitting them against an outside enemy empowers us as rulers."

"Well said, Siamun," Ahmose exclaimed, beaming at him.

If Nefertari's graciousness sprouted in the form of her eldest son and daughter, Ahmose's hardness exuded from their second son, Siamun. He appeared to have budded from his father as the harsh angular features of their faces mirrored one another. None of his mother's kind features shone on Siamun's face.

Then, turning to his eldest child, Ahmose said, "The nobles could create problems for us. Many people will kill me, or all of you if they do not get what they want. We could descend into civil war again."

"We could descend into civil war anyway," Ahmose-Ankh snapped back defensively. "Rebellion foments even now."

"The Hyksos deserved their fate," Ahmose interrupted.

"What harm did they do, Father?" Ahmose-Ankh argued. "The Hyksos are Egyptian, too; many lived here for generations. Why should they not get the same rights as any other Egyptian?"

"Why, indeed? Why should they stay at all?" Ahmose became agitated. "They do not follow our ways, nor do they try to learn them. They interrupt the homogeneity of Egyptian culture."

"Homogeneity of Egyptian culture?" Ahmose-Ankh seethed. "That is a myth! Half our gods belong to pantheons of other religions!"

Ignoring the comment, Ahmose took a deep breath and told us the story of how the Hyksos came to live in Egypt. Different tribes arrived bit by bit over a long period, including the people of my birth, the Habirus. Ahmose outlawed the Habiru use of the names of the tribes, for he believed the ban quelled rebellion.

"I invited none of the tribes here, and I cannot send them back. They arrived because they were hungry. Famine ravaged their lands. For a time, they provided cheap labor, helping with farming, developing canals, and overflow systems. But they never integrated into our society. They introduced their gods and ideas of the desert into Egypt. They worship Set, the storm god, instead of Hapi, God of the Nile, or Amun-Re, Deity of the Sun! When they finally got control of the government, they destroyed huge swaths of papyrus groves to plant grass for their animals to eat. Idiots!"

"Ahmose!" Nefertari exclaimed. "What did I say about insulting Ramose's heritage!"

Ahmose looked at her but said nothing. Then Ahmose-Ankh spoke.

"Father, we used their services to manage the animals, for Egyptians did not wish to have those jobs. What harm comes from them keeping their ways?"

Nefertari beamed at her oldest child.

"How would you do that?" Ahmose hissed, missing the sweet moment between mother and son. "The nobles lost sons and fathers during the unification war. They have no desire to allow it. If it were up to them, the Hyksos would have no rights at all and forced from the land."

"As mother says, this disturbs Ma'at," Ahmose-Ankh replied.

Ma'at, the Egyptian goddess, depicted in hieroglyphs as a feather, represented order, truth, balance, and justice all wrapped together. Ma'at provided a template for living one's daily life. To enter the Underworld, a soul must weigh less than a feather. Symbolism I came to appreciate later in life.

Simultaneous to his saying this, another scene unfolded in the room. While Ahmose-Ankh turned to look at his mother for confirmation, she paid no attention, distracted by Siamun's movements near the window.

Suddenly, Nefertari shouted, "Siamun? What are you doing?"

I turned to look. His actions were incomprehensible to my young mind at first. A dragonfly he had trapped squirmed to get away while he ripped the wings off one by one, his face twisted with a distorted smile. Amenhotep, sitting near him, only watched while the three other children gasped.

"How awful!!" Meritamen exclaimed.

"Come away from there!" Nefertari said. "Hurting animals

disturbs Ma'at!"

Ahmose, having missed Siamun's actions, only focused on the discussion. Responding to Ahmose-Ankh's last comment, he scoffed, "Pah! You have listened to the priests too much. Ma'at? What of it? Ma'at is how the priests control the population. Who believes that one's heart can weigh less than a feather? We all will get to the Underworld; you can be sure of that. Take what you can in this lifetime; build a monument to yourself. No one else will do it for you, and if you do not, your memory will perish."

Later I learned that Siamun took Ahmose's comments about Ma'at to refer to his own actions and not Ahmose-Ankh's comment. Siamun lived his life as though Ma'at applied to others. In that moment, Nefertari instructed Siamun to clean up the dragonfly. Though she lectured her son about the importance of Ma'at and repentance to the gods, no remorse registered on his face. Amenhotep listened to this conversation while the Pharaoh and his eldest son continued their discourse.

"Monuments do not serve anyone," Ahmose-Ankh retorted.

"We can serve many people," Ahmose said. "But they need not be in our country. Your great, great, grand Uncle, Pharaoh of the Upper Kingdom for many years, ruled with a strong fist and considered attacking the Lower Kingdom to unite the lands again. Before he could do that, famine beset the land of Nubian, causing their people to stream across the border. A lesser man would have sent troops to kill these invading hordes, while a weak man would have allowed them in. But this savvy leader chose a different path. He sent bread, meat, and beer to the Nubians to stop them from coming to his land. Sending aid proved to be more fruitful than having them come north. Egyptian culture might have completely disappeared had he not done that. He learned the mistake of our forbearers who invited foreigners to come to Egypt when there was a famine, and eventually, they took over."

"It costs us nothing to help others, for we have more than enough food. It is the Egyptian way to help others."

"You speak of Ma'at!" Ahmose yelled at my older brother.

"Calm down, Ahmose," Nefertari said, tuning into their paralleled discussion. "He is only a boy."

"Your son must know this if he is to rule!" Ahmose

exclaimed. "Neither the Hyksos nor the Nubians possess a worldview of Ma'at! How would you be able to serve people? We would lose our values and culture. The entire kingdom would dissolve into chaos! We should be able to choose who we help for reasons of our own. And we must preserve our values at all costs!"

Ahmose paused. Everyone was quiet after he yelled. Tension and heat hung in the room. "Ma'at is a tool of the priesthood to control people," Ahmose hissed, straining to remain calm. "I dislike the priesthood because they have too much power. But they preserve our ways. We can use them to centralize power back in Waset. We can exact tribute from the Great Sea to Nubia. And the priests keep people in line, particularly the nobles."

Suddenly Ahmose gave a quick, dry laugh. "It may be the only thing keeping the nobles from attacking us. Their belief in Ma'at and magic."

"Do you believe in magic, Father?" Amenhotep asked incredulously.

"I believe in my power, Son."

"But Father," Ahmose-Ankh insisted, "we can create policies that satisfy the nobles and the Hyksos. You could put forth laws that give them incentives to learn our ways. You..."

"Yes, Ahmose-Ankh," Father interrupted. "That is why Ramose is here. I exchanged tax breaks and better housing for Ramose with Amram and Jochebed." In private, Ahmose had no trouble pronouncing my parents names. "I give privileges to some tribes, but not others. It aids them, but it also helps us. We have a Habiru in the royal family, and that makes Habirus feel as though they are one of us. But as your younger brother has observed, it divides the people who might otherwise unite against us."

Hearing Ahmose's words caused my chest to tighten. Several tears escaped my eyes, trickling down my young cheeks. I missed my family more than ever, though it gladdened me to know they had moved from the dangers of the rising river. I wanted to lash out, angry about the exploitation of my family. But my survival depended upon civility and wits. Later, much later, I would get my revenge.

My face must have betrayed my emotion for Ahmose-Ankh

came over and put his arm around me. "Well, Father, it pleases me to have Ramose in our family. He is a gentle soul, and I am proud to call him my brother."

I noticed Amenhotep scowl, and he moved closer to Siamun in reaction to Ahmose-Ankh's kind gesture. My oldest brother walked away from me after Meritamen asked him to help her untangle the brush from Sitamen's hair.

Ahmose ignored his oldest son's comment as he moved closer to his sister-wife, whispering to her as they drifted away from their children. They did not notice me nearby. "Ahmose-Ankh may be too kind to rule," he whispered to her.

"He will be ready when the time comes," she whispered back.

"The nobles are ruthless..."

She interrupted him. "Yours is not the only way to handle the nobles. He manages his brothers well."

"We still need the nobles' help," he whispered. "I believe one of them may know where the staff is. Kamose was certain the Hyksos had it."

"Why are you obsessed with this staff, Husband-Brother? You have claimed that it is just a piece of wood with a jewel on it," Nefertari said.

"It is an Egyptian symbol," Ahmose snapped. "The staff belongs to the Pharaoh. Father and brother both lost their lives trying to recover it."

"Is that how our brother lost his life?" she said. Ahmose grimaced at her sarcasm, but she continued. "Besides, I thought you did not believe Rekhmire's prophecy? Why not just make a new one?"

"Why indeed?" he replied, looking out the window. "I could, but I am uncertain of its appearance. If someone had seen it and could describe it, maybe I could do that. But the prophecy that Balaam and Rekhmire saw about the boy..." He trailed off as though she knew to what he referred.

"What if they are wrong? What if he is just a simple Habiru boy?"

I wondered what she meant. Did I have a purpose for them?

Ahmose looked off into the distance, distracted by his thoughts as if he had not heard Nefertari's last comment. Then, looking towards me, he said, "There is someone who might know the staff's true appearance. And it is possible that one of my sons can talk to him and discover the truth about the staff."

"You can figure that out by yourself," Nefertari said, rising. "I must go purify the family for Siamun's actions."

"What did he do?" Ahmose replied in wonder.

Nefertari glared at Ahmose, and I noticed all three of my brothers gazing at me. Amenhotep scowled at me, eyes smoldering, while my other two brothers wore very different smiles towards me. Ahmose-Ankh's gaze revealed kindness, but Siamun's face distorted as when he pulled the dragonfly's wings off of its body. At that moment, I felt the same as the insect, twisting under Siamun's gaze. Ahmose missed Siamun's cruelty towards the dragonfly, and my brother's hostility aimed at me.

"He killed a dragonfly," Nefertari said to her husband-brother and took Siamun to the temple to purify both for his actions. Nefertari disciplined my adopted brother, but Siamun's cruelty would not stop with dragonflies.

4

The flooding of Akhet subsided, producing a fertile and black soil for the planting activity of Peret. As the waters receded, my swimming lessons with Nefertari resumed. Our time by the Nile continued as Peret yielded to the harvest of Shemu. The fighting in Nubian required Ahmose and my oldest brother to be absent. They would return at the start of the year in Akhet, when fighting ceased for the rainy season.

My swimming lessons allowed me to avoid Amenhotep and Siamun, for each continued to taunt me despite Nefertari's admonishment. Given the discord my presence created, I did not understand Nefertari's reasons for adopting me. When I asked her, she told me that her superstitions about numbers incited her actions. She and Ahmose had five children together, three sons and two daughters. Nefertari considered five to be unlucky, so I became the sixth child, a better number that brought balance into the family system. Later, I would learn the real reason for my adoption.

Towards the end of my first year at the palace, Nefertari gave me permission to wander Pharaoh's private grounds. Surrounding the backside of the castle along the river lay a vast swath of land set aside for Pharaoh. Manicured gardens and walking paths led to a rectangular pond. Even when Pharaoh ventured south for battle, this area teemed with nobles attempting to gain favor at court. Servants came and went, ready to attend to the whims of the privileged.

Further afield from the royal residence beyond the demands of nobles, and the ears of servants lay wild areas. The lush landscape contained pomegranate and palm trees, giving ripe fruit to anyone who could reach them. Papyrus grew wild on the banks, as it did in most places along the Nile. While Pharaoh owned the land, nature ruled here. Unkempt foliage grew as it wished, as branches and trees strewn the sandy shores.

Few ventured there, allowing me a respite from the barbs of the other boys and my two vicious brothers. I would spend many hours wading, digging and observing the ways of the water and the subtleties of the river and swamp. I learned the rhythm of the Nile. The gurgling of the water sounded like whispers, a voice, as though the water told me the story of its existence, speaking of its connection to the desert and how it lovingly gave moisture to the land. Sometimes, it seemed to call me, and frequently, I thought I heard it call me by the pet name my adopted mother gave me, "Moses, Moses." I never responded for I knew not what to say.

My trips to the river served another purpose; in secret, by the water, I met my sister, Miriam. My unhappiness spurred Nefertari to arrange these meetings, having Miriam transferred to Waset on some pretense. At first, my adopted mother joined us, asking that neither Miriam nor I mention it to anyone. Later, I learned that Nefertari had someone perform Miriam's work while she and I played by the river. It was a luxury afforded few Habirus.

Miriam and I met outside the city where the land was lush, thick with palm trees and papyrus growing tall, concealing us from sight. I would walk through a forest of scattered palms, cedars and junipers to arrive at the bank of the river. Sometimes I wandered past the boundary of the private lands of Pharaoh and the city. It seemed a short distance, charged with anticipation each time I went to meet Miriam. Though Nefertari encouraged this interaction, my actions felt like a minor act of rebellion against the nobles and Pharaoh, for my sister taught me about the ways of the Habirus. Ahmose and my teachers shamed me for asking about my biological ancestors. I told no one other than Nefertari about those rendezvous, and I felt a rush of exhilaration as I descended the small hill that dropped towards the water.

For the next year, the rhythm of my life remained the same. I spent mornings swimming with my adopted sisters, and the afternoon with my biological one. This continued without incident. But in my third year of living at the palace, something unexpected occurred. As I listened to the river waiting for Miriam, I heard a rustling behind me. Expecting my sister, it surprised me to see a tall man with a dark complexion appear from the thicket. He seemed startled by my presence too, though the scraggly beard on his face made his expression challenging to discern. He wore a simple skirt, patched in several places and of a style from a time long before my birth. His shirt was tight, dirty, and ripped in a few places, exposing a sinewy yet muscular frame. Over one shoulder, he carried a pack and over the other a longbow.

For some time, we looked at each other, neither of us moving or speaking. Then the man broke our silent standoff. "You are not afraid of me," taking off his pack and longbow to sit beside me on the large log I sat while I waited.

"Should I be? Who you are?"

"I am one of the 'swamp people,'" he said as though I should understand his meaning.

"What is a swamp person?" I asked.

"Who are you, boy?" he answered as a way of response.

"I am Ramose."

"The adopted son of Pharaoh," he said without surprise.

"What are you doing here? Are you meeting a friend too?"

"I live here."

"In the swamp? Why? Did you do something wrong?"

He laughed. "No! I did something right!"

"Do you get lonely being by yourself?" I asked.

"Not at all," he replied. "For there are many creatures and plants who keep me company."

The man explained that he and others like him left civilization, removing themselves from politics, fiendish palace plots, farming, and taxes. He disliked how areas and resources would enrich a few people.

"I no longer wish to partake in the violence of slavery and exploitation. Long ago, I helped govern the Lower Kingdom. I enjoyed being of service to a king who believed in helping many people, not just a few of his friends. I cared not where I was or who I worked for, so long as I was helping others," he said.

"I ended up in jail one time, but I think it helped toughen me up. There are others like me, who despise Ahmose's wars and how he treats people. We live in the swamps, living off the land, fishing, and hunting."

"But it is good we collect food and share with others in need," I said. "That is what my oldest brother Ahmose-Ankh says. He is not afraid to invite foreigners to the land like Ahmose is."

The man looked at me perplexed, maybe confused that I did not identify Ahmose as my father. "Your brother sounds sensible, and if he becomes Pharaoh, maybe I will come out of retirement and work for him. Your father only seems to be interested in gold, even if men die in war. Greed is not a cause worthy of my commitment."

The man pulled something out of his bag and put it in his mouth. "Do you want some?" he asked, offering me a piece of something that appeared reddish-brown with ruffles, almost like a piece of bark. "I dried the fish myself."

"Thank you," I said, taking some. It was salty, chewy, and delicious.

"Things are changing though," he said. "Your father is creating problems, not just for the swamp people but for everyone."

"What do you mean?"

"Do you know about the island that exploded?"

"How would an island explode?" I asked, perplexed.

He took another bite of his dried fish, chewing it while looking out into the distance as if peering into the interval of time and space. "Ask your mother about Strongili. The island that exploded left something on the land that will create problems if Pharaoh does not take care."

"Are you a prophet? Some people around me are prophets."

A sly smile spread across the man's face. "I am just telling you what I see."

"What is the difference?"

"Prophets fail if their predictions come true," he responded.

How true his words are! To the people who adopted me, I

am a failed prophet, even though the people of my birth revere me as a great seer today! But at the moment with the man, I did not understand, so I changed the subject. "Are you allowed to be here? This is Pharaoh's private land."

"Someone invited me," he replied. "Anyway, Pharaoh can afford to relinquish a few fowl."

He rose from the log we shared, grabbing his pack and throwing it over his back. "I will see you again sometime, young Ramose." He walked upstream, away from the palace.

***

Miriam arrived moments later.

"Hello," I said.

"I need to tell you something," she blurted. Her face contorted with grief, as though someone had just died. I utterly forgot about the man.

"What is wrong?"

"I am being sent back to Avaris."

"Why?" I cried.

"Someone must have discovered our meetings."

"That is unfair! You are the only good thing about being here."

"I know," she said calming herself down and coming over to hug me. "It will only be temporary. Nefertari will find an excuse to bring me back," Miriam assured me as tears ran down my cheeks.

"Are you sure?" I asked.

"She told me herself. Ahmose requires Father elsewhere to help build a new temple. Why must they build them at all?"

"Ahmose say it appeases the gods."

"Pwaf!" Miriam spat. "The true God needs no appeasement. Only love. For that is Its true existence."

Her argument did not take my thoughts away from her news. The day was warm, but not too hot. Like so many other days when I was little, Miriam and I sat looking at the river. She grabbed a pomegranate from a tree and opened it to share.

"I want you to stay here, Miriam," I cried.

"I do not want to leave either," she said, hugging me. "You must be careful at the palace."

"Why?" I asked.

"There are people there who want to hurt you. I think you

can trust Nefertari. She seems to have your interests at heart. Listen to her. But trust no one else."

"I will, Miriam," I agreed, without realized that doing so nearly got me killed. Had I trusted others, I might have avoided an unfortunate incident.

We talked more, enjoying our time by the river. We parted before the sun settled in the West. When I returned to the palace, I sought Nefertari to ask her about Miriam's departure.

"I am so sorry, Ramose. This was not my idea," she explained. "But when Ahmose found out about your visits, he ordered your family removed from the area. I will find a reason to bring her back here. She is learning midwifery, and there is a need for her skills here."

Nefertari hugged me and told me that everything would be fine. She instructed me to continue to go down to the river. For one day, Miriam would return. "You seem so much happier since you have been able to go to the river. I think it may be more than just seeing Miriam. But you must be careful."

"Why?"

"Some people want to hurt you. The same people who want to hurt me, too."

"Cannot Pharaoh protect us?"

Nefertari forced a sardonic laugh. "He protects what suits his purpose."

"I will protect you, Mother," I said and noted the surprised look on her face, for it was the first time I had used that term with her. She hugged me again. Then I asked her, "Why are there so many prophecies about me?"

"What do you mean, Dear?" she asked.

"I heard you and Ahmose discussing a prophecy about me. Something that Rekhmire and Balaam foresaw. And Teta mentioned a prophecy that seemed to concern me."

"It is one prophecy," she said blandly. "But you are too young to know them yet, Moses, but one day you will."

"Am I only a simple boy?"

Nefertari gave me a compassionate look. "Is that what this is about?"

"Some prophecy landed me in the palace as though I am important. But then people say I am but a simple boy."

"Both may be true. Today you are a boy. But what tomorrow

will bring none know."

"Will you tell me about the prophecies?"

"If it is appropriate. Remember, though, that it may not be talking about you."

She gave me another hug, then kissed me goodnight. As my deep-seated loneliness returned, I cried myself to sleep.

5

If the Name that is the breath of life was an actor in my early childhood, I did not feel Its presence living in the palace, for Amenhotep and his friends made my day-to-day existence miserable. The seasons turned again, and my formal instruction began during my fifth year living in Waset. Avoiding Amenhotep proved difficult for our instructor, Rekhmire taught us at the same time. Days that Rekhmire's other duties made him late became an invitation for Amenhotep to taunt me. Ankhu, Maiherpri, Hannu and other sons of nobles befriended my brother, hoping for future favors. They contributed to the insults I received, and Amenhotep liked their attention. Though I learned to remove myself from the situation to avoid their teasing, their actions would lead to my leaving Egypt. I would not learn their involvement until my return many years later.

Waiting for Rekhmire's arrival one day, I sat by myself while Amenhotep gathered with his friends, laughing and boasting of their hunting prowess. Maiherpri said he had killed a boar the size of a calf.

"I threw a spear right at it, hitting it between the eyes," he declared.

His story astounded the other boys. Even Amenhotep showed admiration.

"Sounds like quite the kill," Hannu said.

"Did your father help at all?" Ankhu asked a hint of doubt

in the story.

"A little," Maiherpri admitted. "He injured the boar first. But it was my spear that finished him."

"Where was the hunt?" Hannu asked.

"In the new area on Pharaoh's grounds," Maiherpri responded. "Pharaoh invited us. Your brother Siamun was there."

Even from my position in the corner, I could see Amenhotep looked unhappy. Not seeing or caring about his friend's pain, Ankhu continued "I heard that area is beautiful now."

"Very," Maiherpri agreed. "There are a lot of boars there. Siamun said he killed one too, though who knows."

The other boys gave sharp glances at Maiherpri. While they all knew Siamun exagerrated, it was not something that one said about a royal.

As Rekhmire arrived, he said, "Boys, it is time for Their Highnesses to have their lessons, so I bid you depart now."

The children rose to leave, and as they did, I asked a question of Rekhmire that had been bothering me since my first day at the palace. "How did things change so fast for the Habirus, from freedom to slavery almost overnight?" I regretted my query as soon as the words left my lips.

"Your people are defective," Maiherpri snorted. "You do not understand the value of making money, you are terrible fighters, and you stink because you loiter with filthy animals!" The other boys snickered.

"That is no way to speak to a member of the Royal Family," Rekhmire snapped at Maiherpri. "Apologize immediately!"

Maiherpri mumbled an apology as he looked down at my feet.

"Since you boys need a lesson," Rekhmire said. "I will change the plan for today, and you will join their Highnesses. It is important to understand the past so as not to repeat the same mistakes."

The noble sons gave me evil looks, blaming me for their detention. We filed into Rekhmire's office, its clay walls absorbing the heat of the morning, leaving a crisp, musky interior. My teacher's suite comprised several rooms. The large central antechamber contained three long tables with benches for pupils to sit. Alcoves on the sides provided small spaces for quiet contemplation, reading of scrolls, or creation of potions. A wooden door at the back of the suite hid Rekhmire's private study where he practiced magic. Our teacher forbade us from entering that room, our first day of study.

The other boys sat down on several benches around the primary table. I chose the furthest spot away from them I could. Rekhmire began his tale.

"Fortunes can change because of events beyond our control. We plan, we pray, and we sacrifice to gods. But who knows why things happen for individuals or kingdoms?

"Seers foresaw Egypt's reunification, though a veil obscured the prophets' visions. They could not foresee if a war, marriage, or a peace treaty would bring them back together. Or where the capital would be, Waset or Avaris. A giant sea swell brought about this prophecy, not poor rulership."

"What's a giant sea swell?" queried Hannu. I was glad someone else asked, for I feared being teased again.

"It is a wave so big and so forceful that you have seen nothing like it in your life. For if you had, you would not have lived to tell anyone of its power. Harmless does it seem at first as the waters of the sea disappear. For many leagues, the sea floor reveals itself, unveiling the wet sands and rocks that lay beneath the water. Treasures abound as people walk through the mud to reach ships lost at sea. People ventured out to recover the items, gold, and jewels buried underneath the deep waters, believing them to be a gift from the gods."

Rekhmire paused for dramatic effect as I imagined walking along the seafloor, my feet sinking into the wet earth.

Then he continued. "Nun, god of the sea, thwarted the robbing of his treasures, bringing vengeance upon the people as the waters returned with a fierceness rarely seen. A fifteen cubits tall wave hit the shore leading a path of destruction far inland, sweeping away people, animals, houses, and buildings. Whole towns disappeared forever! One person's failure did not bring the fall of the kingdom. Rather, the sea wiping out most of the coastal settlements in the North weakened the kingdom."

"What caused the giant wave?" Maiherpri asked. "I think the gods were punishing the Habirus for taking over the Lower Kingdom."

Rekhmire looked off into the distance. He possessed an incredible talent for bringing stories to life. On this day, he graced us with this gift, for all of us sat captivated by his tale.

"North of Egypt in the Great Sea lay a tiny island with a vibrant civilization named Strongili."

At the mention of Strongili, I remembered meeting the man in the swamp, but said nothing, for I feared being banned from my refuge. Instead, I focused on Rekhmire's story.

"An inlet on the southern tip of the island protected ships as they unloaded cargo. On the land around the harbor, the beautiful city of Akrotiri stood, with multistory buildings rising from the hillside. Hot and cold water came to the upper levels of these structures. But unlike Egyptian structures, the pipes lay inside the walls. Some building had three or four floors. Terraced gardens climbed between the houses, providing foods that grew in the fertile soil on the island. They had different gods — or I should say — goddesses, for their primary deities, were female. Skilled artisans crafted gold statues of fertility goddesses so beautiful that one could weep with joy upon seeing them. Women often ruled there.

"As a boy, I visited this land, awed by what I saw. The lines on the buildings embraced grace as they blended into the surrounding landscape. Fantastic artwork on interior walls contained exquisite and vibrant colors unseen in Egyptian paintings. The walls of the temple depicted women collecting saffron flowers used in rituals, to dye cloth, and for seasoning food. I remember one picture of the Nile with blue monkeys jumping in trees. I do not know why they were blue. I loved being there and wanted to return. It never happened, though, for the mountain that gave the island its birth would also be its destroyer. Omens of its destruction came, as the ground shook sometimes. This happened when I visited."

"How do you mean, Rekhmire?" Amenhotep asked.

"The earth moves under your feet, slowly, barely perceptible. At first, you think you are imagining it. Then the shaking and rolling grows more substantial, causing the wood and stones of the buildings to groan as the ground rumbles. Just before you think the world might burst open, everything stops, and quiet ensues.

"It felt as though some god grabbed the building and shook

it with his hand. When I left the building, I saw cracks on the stairs that ran along the terraced gardens. Fractures in the wall's plaster surfaced. The high priestess told my father that the mountain goddess stirred from her slumber and would destroy the island when she fully awoke."

"The High Priestess' vision proved true," Rekhmire continued, "for the tremors increased. People readied to leave the island, packing their valuables and sailing for the island of Minos to the south. My father and I returned to Egypt, his mission complete.

"The mountain formed the island, bursting hot molten earth that cools in the sea. But a day arrived when the crater consumed itself and the island, erupting with such fury I heard the blast here in Egypt. Smoke and ash reached high in the sky. The explosion caused the sea to ripple and waves to form. Less than a day later, the great wave hit the Egyptian coast, followed by so much ash falling from the sky, the sun barely shone for several weeks. Then a wind came, blowing the ash east of Avaris where it accumulated around Bitter Lakes. That year proved to be colder than any in my life. All the crops failed too."

"Why did the mountain goddess destroy the island?" Hannu asked.

"Who knows what motivates the actions of the divine? I have stopped asking that question."

"Do they not have magicians there to stop the explosion?" Hannu asked.

"Their magicians must not be as powerful as Egyptians," Ankhu declared.

"I cannot say boys. I only know the great wave destroyed all in its path, including most of the Minoan ships. Losing most of their coastal cities and their trading partner to the North weakened the Hyksos. But it did something I did not foresee."

Rekhmire paused for a moment, again trying to pierce the veil guarding the past. "Misfortune can strike any person or kingdom, but great leaders handle a crisis with grace. Apepi, the King of Lower Egypt, did not in this one, though he did in others. Maybe his advisors panicked, given his old age. At the time the great swell destroyed much of the land, he had reigned for over forty years. He needed to maintain a steady amount of trade to both keep the wealthy nobles pleased and to repair the towns lost on the coast. His advisors suggested rebuilding the destroyed ports and sending aid ships to Minos."

"That weakened them," Hannu declared. "We must take what we can from our neighbors, even by force."

"Is that what you believe, Hannu?" Rekhmire asked.

"My father says Ahmose-Ankh is too soft for his beliefs."

"That is what Apepi's new and young advisor believed as well. He argued that the Minoans could not rebuild and sending aid would prove futile. His advice to Apepi was to leverage his large standing army to focus on trade by land."

"That makes sense to me," Ankhu agreed.

"The Minoans proved to be more resilient than the advisor knew. Their destroyed ports were rebuilt quickly. And the ash that accumulated in the western half of Minos enriched the soil instead of causing problems. Likely most of the ash blew beyond Minos to Egypt. But that is not part of our story."

"Can the ash cause problems for Egypt?" I asked.

"It is unlikely, Ramose," he responded. "I suspect issues would have arisen before now if it were a problem."

Though my teacher answered surely, the ash would cause problems for Egypt.

"Apepi sent this advisor to Nubia and the Upper Kingdom to suggest subtly that each of those realms threatened the other, producing false 'evidence' of such. Ahmose's father agreed to a deal of protection but wanted grain in exchange."

Here Rekhmire paused. The boys knew about the grain exchange, as all Egyptian children learned from a young age how the Hyksos poisoned the Egyptians. "None of the seers foresaw the danger in the grain. Ultimately, the grain caused the war."

"How?" I asked for I had not received the same indoctrination.

"They traded the cereal for the transport of gold from Nubia to the North. But the grain caused anyone who ate it to die, killing many Egyptians. Ahmose believed Apepi poisoned his people, and declared war, rallying the Egyptians of the Upper Kingdom behind his cause."

"They did not do it on purpose, did they?" I asked.

"They did," said Maiherpri. "Your people are sneaky."

"Though your father may have taught you that, Maiherpri," Rekhmire cautioned, "he is incorrect."

"Why was the grain tainted?" I asked.

"We do not know. But the great wave led to the grain exchange. Now you know about the Strongili eruption and how it relates to the war of reunification."

Rekhmire said this to all of us while looking at me. He knew that Strongili's destruction ruled my past. Even at a young age, I sensed it would dictate my future.

6

Neither Rekhmire's story nor Nefertari's mild discipline of my brothers changed my life in the next year. My teacher's lecture did not stop the taunts of Amenhotep and his friends. In fact, this only increased their jeers. They called me a murderer as though I had poisoned the grain myself. And the pranks continued. I might find a frog in my bed from time to time or be victim to many harmless tricks. But the day I pulled back the sheets to discover a scorpion hissing and waving its pincers at me, I was on edge.

When Rekhmire was not teaching me about magic, I spent time at the river, enjoying my alone time, tuning in to the water, watching dragonflies and studying the plants further. One Shemu day, sitting on a log listening to the water gurgle slowly by, the man I met two years before sat on the log next to me.

"Good day, Swamp Person," I said.

"Good day, Ramose," he replied, smiling.

"I realized I do not know your name."

"That is true. They once called me Harwa."

The name sounded familiar, and I realized why. "You were the court magician for King Apepi."

"That is right, Ramose," Harwa replied.

"You must be ancient. How old are you?"

He laughed, then answered, "I am too old to remember. Over 100 seasons of flooding."

"Goodness! That is old! You must be a magician! Rekhmire says you were one of the most powerful men in Egypt until you disappeared after Strongili erupted."

"You learned about the island."

I summarized the tale that Rekhmire told us. "Rekhmire said Strongili was the most beautiful place he had ever seen."

"He did, did he?"

I described the paintings as Rekhmire had. Then Harwa said, "Glad Rekhmire told you the story. But did you know he never went to Strongili?"

I stood there slack-jawed.

"The story is true," Harwa continued. "And the poisoned grain resulted from the flood caused by the great wave. But he withheld information, Ramose. Not that he was hiding anything from you, but he lived in the Upper Kingdom. He observed nothing that happened."

"Why did he tell me he did?"

"Because of the man associated with these plans, I suspect. I was the one who had once been to Strongili, not Rekhmire. I told him that story, and what we thought happened to the grain." Harwa shared with me what they believed to be the issue with the grain.

"Could you have done anything about it?"

Harwa thought for a moment. "We could have waited. We would have seen the effects of the flooding. Balaam convinced the king of the plan to use the army."

"Balaam? Siamun's teacher and advisor to Ahmose?"

"Yes," Harwa replied. "He came from the West, working his way into Apepi's inner circle. When he convinced Apepi of this terrible idea instead of rebuilding and sending aid, I resigned."

"Does this have to do with the prophecies?" I blurted.

Harwa gave me a quizzical look. "What do you know about prophecies?" he asked.

"Not much. I overheard Ahmose and Nefertari discussing it one time. They were talking about some staff, a symbol of the Pharaoh. Another time, a noble named Teta accused my father of playing with fire regarding a prophecy. But they mentioned no details."

"You are a perceptive child, Ramose."

"I tried to ask Nefertari about it," I sulked, "but she told me nothing."

He looked off in the distance, stroking his beard as he thought about what to tell me. Then he said, "Maybe, for now, Ramose, it is best."

"But I want to know."

Harwa smiled, offering me some of his delicious dried fish. "If that is your destiny, you will find out when the time is right. There is no need to rush things. And sometimes telling people what will happen makes them try to change the plans, leading to chaos."

Harwa changed the subject, and even at such a young age, I knew he would say nothing more on the matter.

***

My visits with Harwa continued with the change of seasons from Shemu, to Akhet and then to Peret. He continued to teach me more about the history of my people in Egypt. One day, Nefertari surprised me with the news of Miriam's return. I ventured to the river to meet her. Farmers worked planting in the fertile black silt left by the deluge. But I took no notice of their activities, so excited I was to see Miriam. Harwa arrived before Miriam, and as he and I spoke, my sister walked up.

"Why are you speaking to this strange man!" she implored as she approached.

"This is Harwa, Miriam," I responded.

She glared at him before turning to me, "Everyone knows you must not speak to strange men, particularly swamp people."

"Everyone," Harwa responded, laughing, "except your brother."

"He may be in the service of a noble who wants to kill you."

"Sit, Miriam," Harwa said. "The boy has enough to worry about without such nonsense."

"You deny the truth," Miriam accused.

"I deny that I would try to harm him."

"How do we know?"

"Because, Miriam, I made a promise to your great, great Uncle to protect his family after he died. Let me tell you of your ancestors."

"Why would I want to know about other slaves?"

"Though your Great, Great Uncle Joseph started as a slave,

he became much more than that."

Though I had not seen my sister in some time, I knew her well enough to perceive her skepticism. "You could not have possibly known him. He died long ago."

"As I told your brother, I am old. Joseph and I met in jail," Harwa responded.

"Jail?" Miriam asked. My sister gave Harwa a dubious look.

"They imprisoned him, falsely accused by the wife of the captain of the palace guard. But we helped each other get released."

"How did you do that?" I asked.

"Joseph possessed the remarkable ability to interpret dreams."

Miriam shot Harwa a caustic look. "How would dream interpretation get you out of jail?"

"Let me tell you the story," he said. Taking a deep breath, he paused before revealing his tale. "To say my position was dangerous would be an understatement. As the Royal Butler, I selected wines, arranged meals for feasts and managed the palace staff. Then to ensure Pharaoh's safe from poisons, I taste everything before he does."

"Wow!" Miriam exclaimed. "That would be dangerous."

"Indeed, it was. The season before Pharaoh's birthday celebratory feast, he became ill. At first, the royal physicians believed demons had invaded his body. As his condition deteriorated, others who shared the same meal mirrored his illness.

"The doctors found poison in the cakes that caused the illness. They arrested me and the royal baker. I did not understand it, for I had sampled everything, the cakes, the wines, the food. But Potiphar, the captain of the guard, gave Pharaoh an antidote, and he recovered. Obviously, a poison caused the illness, but I did not know which."

"Did you get sick too?" Miriam asked.

"I did not. The baker knew I resisted most poisons. That was why I suspected him, though we were friends up to that point."

"How did you know someone poisoned something?" I asked.

"Most poisons change the flavor of the food. I have a

sensitive palate, allowing me to detect the subtlest variations in the flavor of food and drink. Blue lotus masks the flavor, but hallucinations affect the poisoned person. I neither detected the poison nor did I have visions."

Harwa paused for a moment, looking at each of us, assessing our mood before continuing. "Joseph lived in the place of our imprisonment when we arrived, for our prison provided plush surroundings of house arrest by Potiphar. Joseph, the baker, and I became friendly. Joseph's beauty and grace amazed those who met him. He possessed the charisma and qualities of a great leader. I suspected he possessed a layer of vanity that his arrest tempered.

"One night I dreamt of a vine that sprouted with three tendrils and flowered to provide grapes. Suddenly, Pharaoh's cup appeared in my hand, and I squeezed the juice of the grapes into that vessel. I handed Pharaoh the cup. He drank from the goblet and smiled. I awoke perplexed, unable to comprehend the meaning. Joseph, seeing my confusion, asked what was wrong.

"'I do not understand my dream.' I told him.

"'Tell me your dream, friend,' he said, 'for the interpretations belong to El Shaddai.'

"I told Joseph my dream, which he interpreted to mean that in three days, Pharaoh would release me and restore me to my previous position. Hearing this, the baker came over and told Joseph his dream. 'I dreamed that three baskets were on my head filled with loaves of bread for Pharaoh. But birds kept eating from the basket.'

"Joseph grimaced at the man. 'After your hanging, the birds will eat your dead flesh.' Joseph always was blunt." Harwa gave a wry smile.

Then he continued, "Three days passed and because we were in jail, we forgot that Pharaoh's birthday had arrived. On that third morning, a guard came to release me as Pharaoh restored me to my previous position. But they hanged the baker that day."

"We know this story," Miriam said. She gave Harwa a skeptical glace. "You want us to believe you were Pharaoh's cupbearer?"

He bowed with an exaggerated motion and accent. "At your

service, my lady." I laughed at the gesture and speech.

"I do not believe you knew our Uncle Joseph," Miriam declared.

"I have never heard about Joseph," I said.

"Because Pharaoh is raising you and hates all things about our people," Miriam responded.

"We can agree about that, Miriam," Harwa said. "Ahmose uses fear and hate to unite the nobles. Oddly, it both endangers and protects our young friend here."

"How do you mean?" Miriam asked.

"Without creating an outside enemy, the nobles might unite against the royal family to take power. But by bringing hate into the palace, it endangers your brother."

"Ahmose believes that," I said, briefly repeating the conversation that happened in my parent's bedroom a few years before.

Miriam eyed Harwa for a moment. "Tell us something about Uncle Joseph we do not know."

"Joseph was a brilliant man," he continued. "He saved many, many people's lives by interpreting Pharaoh's dream. And you may have heard the story, Miriam, of how that got him from jail, but that was not entirely true."

"I want to hear this story," I said.

"Pharaoh dreamt that seven thin cows ate seven fat cows," Harwa explained. "Joseph interpreted that to mean seven years of plenty would precede seven years of famine. He created a plan to save surplus harvests and store it for seven years. Seven years! Do you have any idea how difficult that is? For so many people?"

"Everyone knows about that," Miriam challenged him. "How do we know you knew him? You can fool my little brother."

Harwa smiled. "Do not underestimate your little brother, young Miriam, for greatness appears to be in both your destinies!"

"Stop putting foolish ideas into his head! He has enough bad influences from the palace."

Harwa gave her a look I could not interpret. I wanted him to say more about my future and to tell me of the prophecy, but he focused on Joseph.

"After my pardon," he continued, "Pharaoh had a different dream whereby he walked in the desert. The king came upon carrion crows eating a boy hanging from a tree. As he stood looking in horror at the dead child, he saw men of his cabinet behind him laughing.

"Pharaoh asked about his nightmare the next morning, and I told him of Joseph's ability to interpret dreams. The Pharaoh did not summon him for another week and in that time other dreams, including the ones I already told you, disturbed Pharaoh's sleep. But this dream of the child frightened him more than the others."

"What did the dream mean?" I asked.

Harwa smiled before explaining that Joseph interpreted the dream to mean that his advisor, the vizier Pairy, plotted to kill the Pharaoh and blame Harwa and the baker.

"The innocent child represented the baler. When confronted, Pairy confessed. Pharaoh executed him and the other conspirators. After Joseph interpreted the other dreams, Pharaoh promoted him to Vizier of the land."

Harwa paused for a moment, staring into space as if penetrating time. "Though he saved many, he lived with regrets; regrets of his vanity and conceit."

"Joseph was not vain," Miriam argued.

"His conceit provoked his brothers to sell him into slavery."

"What!" Miriam exclaimed. "Why would they have done that?"

"How do you think Joseph landed in Egypt without his brothers?"

"I guess I had not thought of that," Miriam conceded. "What happened?"

"Like his father, the All spoke to Joseph through dreams."

"Jacob interpreted dreams too?" I asked.

"It is how he received the name Israel."

"Israel?" Miriam interrupted. "I have not heard that name."

"Jacob was the name given to him by his parents, Rebekah and Isaac. But El Shaddai gave him a new one."

Miriam's expression changed. That Harwa knew the name of the God worshipped by Habirus impressed Miriam. She listened with rapt attention to Harwa's tale of how Jacob became Israel. Running from his twin brother Esau, Jacob lay his head on a rock to sleep. A ladder appeared before him in a dream that extended to heaven. There he could see the magnificence of God. The All promised to protect Jacob on his journey from the land of Canaan.

"Jacob sojourned with his mother's brother Laban, marrying both of Laban's daughters. When Jacob returned, he came to the same spot of his encounter with El Shaddai, but this time a man guarded the rock. Jacob wrestled with the man all night, prevailing over this stranger as morning came. He demanded the man bless him before he released this stranger. The man turned into an angel, and upon blessing Jacob, gave him his new name, Israel, meaning, 'one who wrestles with God.' Israel would walk with a limp for the rest of his life.

"You are the Children of Israel," Harwa explained.

"I like that!" Miriam exclaimed with a smile on her face for the first time since meeting Harwa. "Did Joseph tell you the story about Israel?"

"Jacob did."

"You met Jacob?" Miriam gaped.

"Yes, and his other sons. Joseph's brothers filled in many of the gaps in the story. Over time, I pieced everything together, but discovering the tale prevented a grave injustice from happening. After Jacob died, the brothers feared retribution for their mistreatment of Joseph in his youth. And Joseph may have if not for my intervening."

"You intervened," Miriam asked. "How?"

"We were great friends by then. We taught one another many things. But his pride got in the way sometimes. Israel experienced God face-to-face, and God blessed him. He had many sons, cattle, and other wealth beyond compare. He made peace with his brother Esau too. But he did not understand how to be a good father, or how to be in a relationship with his wives."

"Mother told me Jacob would have been better off had Rebekah chosen a wife for Jacob rather than having him fall in love with Rachel," Miriam confessed.

"Your mother may have been right, for Jacob played favorites. He loved Rachel and the two sons she bore him more than the others. As a result, he showered favors on them even before they earned them. Jacob tried teaching the secret of the

All to each of his children, but Joseph alone showed aptitude."

"Is that why Jacob gave him the coat of many colors?" Miriam asked.

"Is that what you heard?" Harwa laughed. "Jacob did not give Joseph an actual coat. What I mean is Joseph knew the many aspects of El Shaddai to be of the same cloth. He saw the many in one and the one in many."

Miriam nodded, understanding something that I was too young to know.

"Joseph flaunted his knowledge, making his brothers jealous. The final straw came when he shared a dream he had with the family one morning. Joseph went to the breakfast table, exclaiming that he saw twelve sheaves of wheat, and eleven sheaves bowed to one. His brothers were not happy with him.

"'Do you mean you will rule over us?' they said to him.

"Another time he had a dream that the sun, the moon, and eleven stars bowed to him too. His father also berated him. 'How can you say that? You think you are better than all of us?'

"Tired of Joseph's arrogance, his brothers plotted to kill him, but Reuben stopped them. Instead, they threw Joseph into a pit and sold him to Midianite slave traders. Joseph came to Egypt as a slave. After I assisted his release from jail, he became Vizier of Egypt, second only to Pharaoh in power."

"Were his dreams prophetic?" I asked.

"In a manner of speaking," Harwa replied. "Remember, I mentioned that he planned for seven years of famine?"

Miriam and I nodded.

"We cut into the swamps to plant grass for the cattle to ensure enough feed for them. The Nile Delta flowed and could sustain grass for the animals, though it rained little in Lower Egypt."

"Ahmose criticized the Hyksos for doing that." I said.

"Hyksos is a derogatory term, Ramose. But you probably do not know that as your education begins at the palace. I imagine Ahmose thought it terrible that we did that. But it was our only choice to prepare."

"It is a problem now," Miriam asked.

"How do you know?" Harwa asked.

"The river speaks to me," she replied.

Harwa nodded, saying nothing of Miriam's admission. "It could be," he warned. "If Ahmose goes through with his plans without restoration, many people might die."

Before Harwa could say anything further, a slave girl came running over to find Miriam. A woman had gone into labor, and she needed Miriam's midwifery skills. We all departed in separate directions. Harwa said he would see us again soon.

I did not understand yet the connection between Joseph's actions and Strongili. The Holy One brought this together to lead to our people's salvation. But that remained far in the future yet.

7

For several years I thought Amenhotep channeled his hatred for me into pranks, leaving various creatures in my bed. But an encounter with both Siamun and Amenhotep the week following Miriam's return changed my mind about the dynamic at the palace. Walking near the place where Miriam and I would meet, uneasiness gripped me as I approached the river. Despite the calm rustling of grass, papyrus and palm trees, that Shemu morning, my anxiety increased as I roamed through the underbrush.

When the apprehension first came over me, I thought it was because of the warning that Harwa gave Miriam and me the last time we spoke. Could some unseen impending doom be causing this tightness in my chest, I wondered? My breathing became difficult when I spied Amenhotep crouched behind a bush.

Though frightened by his presence, curiosity compelled me forward as I crept slowly towards him, trying to determine his actions. He turned and put a single finger over his mouth, motioning me to be quiet. Turning back around, he peered through the fronds of the fern. I crouched beside him as he pointed through the stalks. Ahead of us, I saw Siamun, back toward us, bent over a log. One hand lay on top of the trunk. Something appeared to move underneath it, while in Siamun's other first, he held a small hammer that jumped up and down onto the log, a pinging sound emitting with each downward strike. Over and over, this pattern repeated. Ping, Ping, Ping. Wanting to get a better look, Amenhotep motioned for us to crawl forward. The intermittent pinging sound continued. As we settled quietly behind a different bush, me behind Amenhotep, the hammering stopped. Upon seeing what Siamun had on the log, Amenhotep turn around, wide-eyed, the color drained from his face. I watched Amenhotep run past me, double over and vomit. Then I looked to see the results of the hammering.

A frog lay on a log. There were nails in every one of the frog's limbs as each struggled independently to free itself from the bondage that Siamun had imposed. Amenhotep's retching sounds caused Siamun to look up. He saw the two of us behind the foliage.

Twisting our way, he revealed the characteristic crooked smile on his face, no sign of remorse. He laughed, mocking Amenhotep's reaction. "Come see my masterpiece!" he exclaimed.

Amenhotep recovered and walked forward, pulling me with him. Scowling at his older brother, Amenhotep asked, "What are you doing Siamun?"

"Practicing my torture techniques for you guys." He took a dagger out and split open the abdomen of the frog blood spurting from the soon to be fatal wound. Siamun peeled back the flesh of the near-dead animal to expose the chest and beating heart. Amenhotep and I stood there frozen, our sensibilities offended. But we were powerless to stop the horror in front of us.

"You are both turning the color of the frog," Siamun laughed.

***

The spell broken, Amenhotep and I fled. Siamun laughed, harshly hurling insults our way as we ran away from the river. In our haste we cut through the trees, branches clipping us as we passed. We reached the place where the path to the river met the side road leading to town. We stopped, for here we felt safe enough. Both of us hunched over, hands on our knees as we tried to catch our breath.

"Are you all right?" I asked Amenhotep, panting.

He nodded, still unable to speak.

"We must tell Mother and Father," I said. Immediately, I regretted my words because I remembered my planned rendezvous with Miriam. I needed to warn her, but this would require me to reveal my secret to Amenhotep. Or I would need to lie to him.

"We must go to Rekhmire," Amenhotep said, now able to speak.

"Why not just tell Father?" I asked.

"Because he will not believe us."

"What do you mean?!" I said confused. I assumed Ahmose would believe his biological son, even if he would not believe me, the Habiru.

"Siamun is Father's favorite," he said. "He can do no wrong in Father's eyes. You must know that? Remember the dragonfly incident? Father will never punish him, and he is blind to the effects of his behavior. Mother talks to him, but Siamun's behavior does not change. Once he put a scorpion in Ahmose-Ankh's bed. Our older brother did not like that and punched Siamun for such a dangerous act. They punished Ahmose-Ankh, but not Siamun. Balaam defended Siamun, explaining his behavior away. He said he was too young to understand the dangers of that specific scorpion."

"Siamun put the scorpion in my bed? I thought you did that!"

"I would not have done something that perilous!" he protested, looking a little hurt.

Was he remorseful? Before I could consider, my legs weakened, and I felt faint. A whooshing sound filled my ears as though I held a giant shell against both at the same time. I leaned against a nearby cedar tree to steady myself and closed my eyes. I breathed slowly as a quiet voice arose in my mind, similar to the one I often heard by the river. It was almost silent, so soft that had I not quieted my mind and closed my eyes, I might have missed it.

The Voice whispered, "You can tell Amenhotep of Miriam, for he already knows."

At that moment I understood that Amenhotep's emulation of Siamun was not flattery. Amenhotep assumed mimicking his enemies' behaviors would protect him. Amenhotep recognized the dangers of the palace and surrounded himself with people who might defend him. Since Ahmose had not reprimanded Siamun's behavior for treating the Habirus poorly, Amenhotep did the same. But Siamun's behavior today shattered any illusion of solidarity.

"You know about Miriam," I said.

"Yes," Amenhotep replied nonchalantly. "I came to the river to spy on you two."

"We need to warn her about Siamun before talking to Rekhmire."

Continuing along the road to intercept her, we spotted Miriam on her way to the river, and waved to her. Almost to her full height, a young woman, she wore a long gown that deftly revealed the curves of her body; she wound her hair into a loose bun exposing her neck and shoulders. I looked at Amenhotep, who stared at my beautiful sister. I introduced her to Amenhotep, who became tongue-tied, unable to look away from Miriam. My chest tightened as I wondered about Amenhotep's character. I knew Siamun's cruelty would not stop at animals. By this time, he would defile slaves and servant girls should they come his way. Even my personal attendant, Paser, feared Siamun, and avoided my adopted brother. Was Amenhotep any different in that way?

Miriam did not notice his reaction, for she appeared to look off into the distance. Then her eyes rolled back in their sockets, momentarily only showing the whites of her eyes. A moment later, she spoke in a throaty voice different from her own. "Pharaoh, your heart shall harden, though I show signs of wonder to you! It is no worry. My first born shall be plucked from you. And know the hardships that have faced the Children of Israel."

Amenhotep and I caught Miriam as she fell and settled her on the ground. She lay there motionless for a few minutes, looking glassy-eyed. Coming to, she appeared confused. "What happened?" she said, unsure why she lay in the grass.

I helped her sit up as Amenhotep said, "You had a vision."

"Like Ramose?" she asked. "What did I say?"

I repeated back what she said. She looked at each of us. "You do not remember what you said?" I asked her.

"Do you remember your vision?" she replied.

"What vision?"

"No one told you?" Miriam responded incredulously. "The one that made you leave home years ago for the palace? You said, 'the rivers will run with blood, and at that moment, I shall lead the Children of Israel out of Egypt!' It was cute until you fell and hit your head on the ground."

"That makes no sense," Amenhotep said. "Who are the Children of Israel?"

Miriam and I looked at each other. Recalling what Harwa recounted to us the previous week, I realized the significance of this prophecy. Knowing we could not tell Amenhotep about Harwa, Miriam lied and said that she did not understand it either. Then she continued with her story.

"I thought Ramose was emulating me for I had visions before his incident. Then Pharaoh sent advisors to the house. I overheard two of the advisors discussing an Egyptian prophecy similar to yours. They spoke in hushed tones about a canal. One advisor wanted construction to start right away, but the other believed there was something out of balance that meant that we should wait."

"I have heard father speak of reopening a canal," Amenhotep said. "But he is waiting to finish subduing the people in the Northeastern part of the empire before starting the project."

Was this the prophecy that everyone was discussing? Did Harwa know about the canal? Is that what he wanted to tell us last week? I pondered these questions until Amenhotep broke the silence.

"Does everyone in your family have visions?" he wondered.

"Mother says," Miriam explained, "our family can hear El Shaddai's words though other Habirus heed the voice too."

Amenhotep looked at her in disbelief. "El Shaddai? That is your god?"

"It is the only God!" Miriam fumed, jumping to her feet. She was ready to fight my adopted brother. Her hand clenched, preparing to strike him. Amenhotep readied himself in defense.

Worried that Miriam would get herself into serious trouble, I stepped in between the two, grabbing my sister's arms while speaking to Amenhotep. "We need to speak to Rekhmire!"

"Yes, we do!" he agreed.

"About what?" Miriam asked.

Their anger abated. We walked back towards town. Amenhotep and I told Miriam of the encounter with Siamun. Miriam's expression morphed from disbelief to disgust. "What sort of person does such a thing?" Miriam exclaimed. "He must never become Pharaoh!"

We parted ways with Miriam as we approached the town. Amenhotep and I continued to search for Rekhmire, finding our teacher in his private study, the door ajar. Inside, a trickle of sunshine bled from a tiny window high in the wall close to the ceiling, revealing the accumulated dust in the room and air. Rekhmire stood at his desk, bent over something we could not discern. Scrolls, sheets of papyrus, a sword, a chalice, some coins, and a wand lay scattered in front of him. Feathers, dried leaves and flowers, and several species of dead insects collected along the long table.

"Master Rekhmire," Amenhotep's tentative voice asked as we entered the chamber.

Rekhmire continued rocking back and forth rhythmically, chanting something incomprehensible. We moved closer, and we saw him stirring the contents of a small pot on the desk. A puff of smoke rose from the container. Cantillating louder, Rekhmire swayed forward and back vigorously. The room seemed to darken for a moment as a chill air entered the room.

Rekhmire stopped, the darkness fading, heat returning to the place. Turning around, he barked, "Fools! What are you doing here? I told you never to enter without knocking unless it is imperative."

"Apologies, Master Rekhmire!" Amenhotep said. "The door was open, and we thought you were reading. We have something important to tell you."

"What could be so urgent that you interrupted my work?" he snapped.

"What were you doing?" I asked, forgetting our mission because of my curiosity.

"Working on a potion from some notes I found in Avaris. Magical spells lost in the Upper Kingdom, but preserved by the Hyksos. Never mind that, what brings you here?"

Stammering, Amenhotep told Rekhmire about what we had witnessed by the river.

"You also saw this, Ramose?" His voice was full of concern.

"Master Rekhmire, it is true," my voice squeaked. I stopped, cleared my throat and then continued. "Amenhotep tells the truth. Siamun tortured and killed a frog."

Rekhmire looked at us sideways. "A perfectly good magical potion ruined, thanks to you boys," he grumbled, still angered over the interruption. "I must go back to the northern swamps to find the ingredients again. Show me where this occurred."

I wondered if Rekhmire believed our story. We took him to the scene of Siamun's cruelty, only to find most of the evidence gone. Though Siamun cleaned the mess as best he could, clues remained. Blood stains and four tiny holes revealed the accuracy of our tale. Rekhmire groaned and sat on the log. He placed his hands on it, closing his eyes. Though I hoped Rekhmire would witness the monster's blasphemous act, my teacher possessed other ways to uncover the truth. Producing a short, curved, ivory rod with hieroglyphs on it, he began a series of chants, closing his eyes, rocking back and forth as he did earlier. Every so often he waved the wand in the air as if trying to swat away invisible foes. A quarter of an hour later, he stopped chanting and opened his eyes.

"He will bring ruin to the royal family!" he exclaimed. "You cannot torture a messenger of a goddess! He disturbs Ma'at, and his violent acts linger in the wood. Boys, sit by me and place your hands on the log."

We did as our teacher instructed, sitting on the log while resting our hands on it and eyes closed. The sun slowly descended in the west past the other side of the river, the warmth dwindling with it. Focusing on the log, I tried to sense what Rekhmire described. At first, I thought I imagined it. I felt subtle sensations, a series of tiny vibrations followed by a slight tug in the wood. The log remembered the fear and pain of the frog.

Rekhmire sensed my awareness. "You feel it. All things remain. The violence, the joys, the patterns. You can find your way, lost in the desert, by sensing the emotions of the beings who have passed through." His words I would remember when I fled Egypt later in my life.

"I feel nothing," Amenhotep said.

"You may feel it one day, though I suspect you have other

gifts, Amenhotep."

Both of us opened our eyes and removed our hands from the log. If Amenhotep seemed distraught about this, it did not show. He only looked impatient.

"Something needs to be done about that child," Rekhmire muttered under his breath, standing from the log.

"Yes," Amenhotep said vehemently. "Siamun must be stopped!"

Rekhmire shot Amenhotep a stern look. But he knew Siamun to be a problem that Ahmose could ill afford to ignore any longer.

"You must tell the Pharaoh about this. In front of everyone."

"Master Rekhmire," Amenhotep cried. "Siamun will turn this around against us. Father loves him best. He always gets his way!"

"How will he squirm out of this?" Rekhmire responded. "You both saw him torturing a frog. You have proof, and I have seen it with my own eyes. Felt it go through my being. Let us return and have dinner together."

We sat together for a meal before Rekhmire went to discuss Siamun's behavior with Ahmose. Little did I know that tomorrow I too would come face to face with Pharaoh of Egypt.

8

Paser, my attendant, woke me early the next morning. He was a little older than Ahmose-Ankh, but about a foot taller. Several months would pass before I would consider asking this person so intimate in my life about anything in his life. Though he served me daily for several years by this time, I knew nothing of him. His heritage, beliefs, and hopes were all a mystery to me.

Paser informed me I was to present myself to Ahmose in the throne room. My brothers often attended hearings in front of Pharaoh. As a son of Pharaoh, I should have too, but until now they had never invited me.

"Your summons," Paser explained, "is to tell the events of yesterday."

"You heard what occurred?" I asked.

He placed a bowl of fruit and some freshly baked goods at the small table in my room. I pulled a chair up and sat. Though my stomach rumbled some, Paser's pronouncement disquieted me. I no longer felt I could eat, for I felt sick to my stomach. I had not been to a formal visit with Pharaoh since the day I arrived at the palace in Avaris.

"Of course," he replied. "The servants know of all that occurs at the palace."

"What do I say?"

"Tell them what happened. Nothing more, nothing less."

I nodded as though I understood, but Paser knew me well

enough to know I did not take his meaning. "Pharaoh does not want to punish Siamun for his actions. He may try to uncover inconsistencies in your or Amenhotep's stories to give Siamun an out."

"Oh," I said. "I guess that makes sense."

"Balaam wanted you and Amenhotep to present separately, but Rekhmire somehow discouraged Pharaoh of that action."

"Why would Balaam?"

"It is easier to confuse you if you present your findings separately," Paser interrupted. "Often, when two people witness an event, their views differ slightly. Balaam and Rekhmire both know this. Balaam wishes to bewilder both of you. Be careful of him."

"What will he do?"

"I am told he can cast spells."

"Spells?" I said. "Would not someone see his motions? Or a wand?"

"I know nothing of magic. I only know that Balaam convinces Pharaoh of many things that others cannot comprehend."

"Why does Balaam care if Siamun gets punished or not?"

"He is Balaam's favorite student."

Though Paser said the words, I could not fathom them. Siamun was the least talented of Ahmose's sons. Why did Balaam favor him? I knew little of Balaam having seen him a few times around the palace.

"They will punish Siamun today. Unless Balaam's spells work on Pharaoh."

"What do you mean?"

"I do not know if I can explain it. Observe Balaam today. But whatever the outcome, beware of Siamun."

"Why is today different?"

"If they reprimand him, he will become more dangerous," Paser replied, sounding more like a prophet than a servant.

After I forced down some food, Paser bathed and dressed me. I could dress myself, but as a royal, I would not do so on momentous occasions. Paser placed a simple, yet fine robe on me, then strapped new sandals upon my feet.

When finished, Paser escorted me towards the throne room. But instead of turning down the main staircase towards the main entrance to the audience chamber, we descended a staircase I seldom used. From there, we followed a hallway to a door with a guard standing beside it. Without a word from Paser, the soldier opened the door, motioning me to be quiet. Inside, I heard Rekhmire and Ahmose discussing something about a canal. I do not remember the details of that discussion, only that the project would increase trade and make moving products easier for many nobles and merchants.

My eyes needed a moment to adjust to the darkness of the room. Wood paneling covered the walls except for one area to the left that appeared to be a screen. Chairs faced this spot. Walking into the chamber further, I could see we were parallel to and slightly behind the throne. The mesh screen allowed those on my side to observe without being seen. All the chairs remained empty, save one. Amenhotep turned around when I arrived and whispered, "Glad you made it."

"The canal planning will continue Your Majesty," I could hear Rekhmire saying.

"Excellent, Rekhmire," Ahmose said. "You have a concern you wanted brought to my attention."

"My Lord," Rekhmire replied, stepping to the front of the throne. "Amenhotep and Ramose both witnessed something of grave importance to the Kingdom."

"Please tell us about this matter.," Pharaoh said.

"The younger princes observed Siamun performing an abomination. He nailed a frog to a log!"

Gasps escaped many in the audience. Even Nefertari winced before quickly regaining her regal countenance.

Ahmose sat on his throne, stone-faced, staring at Rekhmire. "This is a serious charge, Rekhmire," Pharaoh said. "The torturing of animals is a serious breach of Ma'at and could bring ruin to the land and the royal family."

Did I hear a tone of doubt in his voice? My stomach tightened, and I felt that the little I ate earlier might empty from my stomach.

"Yes, my Lord. I think both Amenhotep and Ramose have concerns."

"Let me hear the story from the boys," Ahmose said.

Rekhmire motioned us to come forward. Amenhotep led me towards a door on the side on the wall to the right of the screen, opposite the door I had entered the room. We walked out behind the thrones and around them to be standing to the right of Pharaoh and Queen. Siamun came forward from the audience as though a lowly peasant approaching the Pharaoh. Balaam walked over to stand beside my demented brother. Rekhmire looked dismayed, but said nothing.

Taller than the average Egyptian, but shorter than a typical Habiru, Balaam wore his beard like neither group. Egyptians shave most of their faces, leaving a long, thin, braided strand hanging from their chins. Habirus and other people of the Northeastern regions do not shave their faces much at all. Their beards are bushy and unkept. Balaam, however, kept his beard close to his face as though he grew it for only one week. Where Balaam came from, none knew.

I looked around the room feeling sicker seeing the stern looks from the people in the audience. But one face shone as a beacon of light that settled me. Miriam sat quietly by herself in the back of the chamber. How did she get in? I wondered.

Voice shaking at first, Amenhotep described the events of the previous day. He explained how we spied upon Siamun at the log, hammering for some time and see the frog pinned by all of his limbs struggling to free itself.

"With a knife, Siamun sliced through the chest and stomach of the frog," he cried. I could see tears glistening in his eyes.

While Amenhotep found the behavior revolting, I did not think he was this upset. Was he playing to the audience? I could not tell, but once again, the nobles voiced their disapproval, shocked by the violence. Pharaoh stamped his staff several times to quiet the assembled.

"Go on, Amenhotep," Ahmose commanded.

"Then Siamun told us he was practicing his torture techniques to use on us."

I think shocked murmurs came from the audience, but my focus was on the tightness in my stomach rising to my chest, making breathing difficult. Struggling for air, I emitted an inaudible gasp as a whooshing sound rose in my ears, then cleared.

Balaam cut off Siamun, who defended his actions. Pharaoh's advisor spoke with a thick and powerful voice, and as he talked, the whooshing sound in my head became more pronounced.

"Your Majesty," Balaam began. "These are serious charges against my student, your son. I am sure there is another explanation other than torture. We could argue that we kill animals to eat, though they are messengers of a god. Is a frog a messenger if a small child catches it?"

Part of me felt compelled to agree with Balaam. His words made sense to me. What was the big deal about Siamun's behavior, I thought? Others in the room murmured agreement with Balaam.

As quickly as the compulsion to forgive Siamun came, it left as though waved away. Siamun was not a "small child" — he neared adulthood. And I would never treat an animal in such a manner. Looking around the room, I saw the same change appear on the faces of the audience. Peering over at Rekhmire, I could see his hands were behind his back, and in one of them, he concealed a small ivory wand. This hand subtly moved.

As Pharaoh pondered Balaam's words, a wave of dizziness overcame me once again. My stomach and chest tightened, and my knees became weak. I felt I might vomit right in front of the Pharaoh. But instead of bile coming out of my mouth, words formed as if by a force that existed outside of me. They burst out of my mouth in a voice I didn't recognize.

"Pharaoh! Even now, your son plots to poison you and your house!"

And as soon as the words left me, the sense of foreboding disappeared. My chest relaxed, and I felt faint. I might have fallen if not for Amenhotep catching me. I felt everyone's intense stares. Some openly gaped while others shook their heads in disbelief. Later I would learn that not everyone believed that I spoke from another voice. Rather some thought I was trying to bring attention to myself.

I could hear Rekhmire speaking quietly to Ahmose. "He states a prophecy again, my Lord. It is as we have foreseen. Ramose may be a great seer though he is slow-witted and speaks in riddles."

"This appears to be so," Ahmose whispered. "But I do not see how that helps us. His prophecy is not clear; how do we solve the current problem?"

Though Amenhotep steadied me, I still felt nauseated and

that I might vomit at any moment. Pharaoh's summons required me to stay.

Ahmose turned to his second son and asked, "What do you have to say for yourself, Siamun?"

Siamun stood up and looked over at Balaam, who appeared shaken. But he nodded in response, revealing he coached Siamun for this audience. "Father. I think my brothers misinterpret my actions, for I came upon an injured frog. I acted in mercy to ease its suffering."

Murmurs broke out about this comment. Once again, Pharaoh stamped his staff to quiet everyone.

My father looked at Siamun. "And what of the comment you made to Amenhotep and Ramose?"

"And of the hammering?" Rekhmire whispered, but Pharaoh ignored it.

"I was only teasing them, Father," he said with a smile on his face and a wave of his hand.

The room quieted as Ahmose considered the situation. "These are serious charges. While I do not doubt what Amenhotep and Ramose saw, I think they may have misinterpreted Siamun's intention. I do not believe Siamun requires punishment for torture. But Siamun must make amends with Heqet by performing her dance in front of all."

The steps of this adoration are ones we learn as little children, maybe four or five floods of age. Someone who is Siamun's age would not typically perform this dance. Siamun slunk to the front and dance. He performed it with small steps, unsure of the moves, exuding shame. Whether it was real embarrassment or pretense, I could not tell. The adults laughed and clapped when he finished, and Ahmose dismissed his sons from the audience chamber.

As he walked by me, Siamun whispered, "I will kill you, Habiru." Then he moved past us. I looked around for Miriam, but she no longer sat in the audience chamber. Had I just imagined she was there? Siamun walked through the front doors well ahead of Amenhotep and I as we left the audience chamber side by side.

9

Almost imperceptibly, the tension between Amenhotep and I decreased. Amenhotep's snide remarks towards me curtailed as he showed first civility, and then warmth, towards me. While Amenhotep's hostility diminished, Siamun's anger escalated. He missed no opportunities to scowl or bump me in the halls of the palace if we encountered one another. Following the audience for Siamun's actions, Rekhmire left on a mission for Ahmose. Still shaken from the incident with Siamun, I feared to venture to the river alone. I sensed that Amenhotep had the same reservations too, though he said nothing. Nefertari offered to take us there together to help us resolve our fears.

The warmth of the morning foretold the coming of Akhet and the flooding season, heralding the start of Wepet-Renpet, the festival to mark the New Year. Amenhotep and I lingered by the river while Nefertari watched. As we explored the area together, a servant arrived to inform the Queen that something required her presence inside. At first, Nefertari insisted we return with her, but as Amenhotep and I both enjoyed the time by the river, we mastered our anxiety, and pleaded with her to allow us to stay.

"It will be fine, Mother," Amenhotep said. "Ramose and I can look after each other." And for the first time, he gave me a warm smile.

"It will be fine," I echoed.

Nefertari agreed, leaving with the servant. My adopted brother and I continued to explore the riverside for some time. Hearing footsteps, both of us froze, fearing Siamun's approach. Amenhotep motioned me behind a log. As we crouched down, watching for the intruder, we saw Miriam burst through the bushes. Relieved, we stood to greet her. She wore a simple midwife's tunic with stains suggesting she had just arrived from delivering another baby. Seeing her, I wondered about her appearance in the throne room the other day, but her face looked troubled, causing me to forget to ask her.

"You seem upset about something," I said as she walked over to our position by the river.

"Your father goes too far this time, Amenhotep!"

"What did he do now?" Amenhotep asked, mildly surprised.

"He wants to make all Habiru sacrifices illegal. Only Egyptian priests can make animal sacrifices now! Why would Ahmose do that?"

"Ahmose struck a deal with Thuty, the High Priest of Amun, last week for not punishing Siamun for killing the frog," Amenhotep explained.

"Do you mean to tell me that Habirus are losing rights because Ahmose cannot control his spoiled child?" Miriam raged. "How is this fair to my people?"

Amenhotep started to defend his father, but stopped. Then he said, "You are right Miriam, it is not fair. Not only did he concede the rights of Habirus, but next week's festival at the temple will exclude most Egyptians. If I become Pharaoh, as you predicted last week, I will not sacrifice the rights of many to save one."

Miriam assessed my adopted brother, as though trying to determine if he was being truthful. "What you say may be true, Amenhotep. But what about the Pharaoh after you?"

"That is always true, and for all Egyptians," Amenhotep said. "Someone could change any law whenever they want. There is nothing that would allow me to take away titles from nobles given by my father."

"I guess that is true," Miriam responded.

"Do all the Habirus see the sacrifice ban as a problem?"

Amenhotep asked.

"No," Miriam admitted. "The tribes of Reuben, Benjamin, Gad, Asher, and Ephraim do not care. They are too busy profiting from Ahmose's policies."

"It is not all bad," Amenhotep said, smiling.

"It is bad. Pharaoh's system favors exploitation."

"Every system creates winners and losers, Miriam, for not all are equal."

Miriam thought for a moment before replying. "But everyone comes from the one God and can find that beauty within their hearts."

"That may be, but that does not mean they will not be slaves."

"What do you mean?" Miriam said, her eyes ablaze. "People deserve proper respect and civility. Egyptians treat frogs and fleas with more reverence than Habirus!"

"That is untrue!" Amenhotep protested.

"You have rules for animal sacrifices, but you do not care how hard you work my people! Most receive no money!"

"Someone pays them!" Amenhotep snapped back at her.

"Pays? What are you talking about?"

"Many people are making money," Amenhotep said, "if they follow Ahmose's rules and do not fight our authority."

"Few of the people within any of the tribes earn money. Habirus are slaves. And taskmasters overburden Egyptians too! Your policies encourage overwork. Taskmasters refuse to give water to pregnant mothers who are working."

"Some taskmasters are cruel," Amenhotep admitted. "But most give workers shelter, food, and water. They can work outside or inside depending on the season."

"No rules govern the treatment of Habiru workers," Miriam responded. "The large stones of buildings have crushed Habiru slaves."

"Many jobs are dangerous," he responded. "Life at the palace is a risk." He laughed a dry, sardonic laugh.

"Risk? We have no choices of our jobs or even where to live."

"I do not have choices either. I must do as my father tells me."

Miriam sighed. "We have lost something bigger."

"What is that?" Amenhotep asked.

"Ourselves," she said. "We have lost the knowledge that say we are working towards something we believe in and are making Egypt a better place for everyone."

Amenhotep did not answer right away. He thought for a moment, then asked me about my thoughts of the discussion.

"I do not know. I had no choice about living that the palace. But I think my life is better."

"How so?" he asked.

"I eat three wonderful meals a day," I said.

"There is food available for everyone," Amenhotep defended.

"No, there is not," Miriam said. "Many people go hungry because their masters do not feed them."

"Why? There is more than enough," he responded.

Waving his arms for emphasis, Amenhotep pointed out the date and pomegranate trees growing by the Nile. Though not ready yet, they would be laden with fruit in a few months' time.

"Some landowners stop slaves from taking food from their holdings."

"That is absurd!"

"Many landowners would rather the food go to waste than provide for others," Miriam reported.

"That makes no sense."

"Ahmose's policies encourage this waste, Amenhotep. Hate has a way of spiraling in unintended ways. People become obsessed with ideas that do not serve their interests. Slavery takes many forms."

"That is what I am trying to say," Amenhotep replied.

"How do we create a society that allows for people to reach their potential then?" Miriam asked.

Neither Amenhotep nor I had an answer for Miriam.

***

We talked for a few more hours, floating from subject to subject, much like the dragonflies and bees around us. It gladdened me that Miriam and Amenhotep did not argue about everything. And for the first time since I met Amenhotep, he and I behaved like friends. Still, I felt vulnerable at the palace, especially after Siamun's treatment of the frog. His actions impressed upon me a feeling of powerlessness. While both Nefertari and Ahmose-Ankh warned me at different times of the dangers lurking there, I never felt unsafe in my quarters. Though I knew he would strike at me, what I found in my room upon returning from the day shocked me. I darted into the hallway and almost ran into Ahmose-Ankh.

"What is wrong, Ramose?" he asked, having just returned from Buhen.

Blood dripping from my hands, I was too upset to speak. I motioned for him to follow. We walked through the lavish second-floor corridor, past the chambers of the other royal family members, and back to my room. I could not enter, so frightened was I. As I waited at the threshold, I pointed to my bed in terror. The horror of what I found earlier. Ahmose-Ankh approached it and pulling back the covers revealed a severed calf's leg with a knife lodged near the top. The dismembered limb dripped blood on my sheets and blanket, leaving a sticky ooze in the center of the sleeping surface. Ahmose-Ankh gasped, his face stricken with horror. Recovering, determination replaced disgust.

"Siamun goes too far!" Ahmose-Ankh spat walking out of the room. "We must tell Father."

Turning towards Ahmose's private chamber, my brother instructed his servant to clean my room and replace my bed. The servant nodded assent as we continued in search of Ahmose. Approaching the chamber, we found the door ajar.

"You cannot change a prophecy, your Majesty," someone said standing in the doorway.

"I can with the staff. Make him ready to receive it," we heard Ahmose say. I wondered to whom he referred.

Rekhmire stepped through the doorway, surprised to see us. "Good day, your highnesses," he said, surprised to see us. "Is your father expecting you?" Rekhmire moved side to side and looked back as though hiding something.

"No. But that is no matter, Rekhmire," Ahmose-Ankh replied, pushing past my teacher.

"Hello Ahmose-Ankh and Ramose," Ahmose said as we entered the room. "How are you two this evening?"

"Not well, Father," Ahmose-Ankh responded curtly,

proceeding to explain the situation in my room. Ahmose listened to the tale, betraying no emotion.

"Siamun's actions are tiresome, Father. Ramose feels unsafe in the palace. He is our brother, regardless of his heritage."

"It is troubling, your Majesty," Rekhmire agreed.

"This is unacceptable, and Ramose must feel comfortable here. Do you have proof Siamun did this act?"

"Father! Do not be blind! Siamun threatened Ramose a few weeks ago, and his attitude towards Ramose and foreigners is well known. You have not liked foreigners in the past, but you have been willing to set aside your prejudice to improve the kingdom. Siamun does not understand this."

"Ahmose-Ankh," father admonished. "I think this discussion is inappropriate in front of Ramose. Perhaps we should continue in private."

"I think Ramose deserves to learn what he faces."

Grimacing, Pharaoh asked Rekhmire to take me back to my quarters. Walking away, I heard Ahmose and my brother yelling at one another. Though jumbled, I could pick up a few words and phrases here and there.

Now clean, I still did not want to sleep in my bed, traces of the violence remained, defiling my personal space. I lay awake, terrified to fall asleep, but also waiting for Ahmose-Ankh's return from his argument with Ahmose.

A little while later, I heard him whisper, "Ramose? Are you still awake?"

"I am," I said sitting up in my bed.

He walked into the room and sat down at the foot of my bed, quiet for a moment. "I spoke to father about what happened," he said.

"I know, I heard the yelling."

Ahmose-Ankh smiled embarassed. I knew he wanted to tell me everything. Though he could scarcely protect himself, he wished to shield me from the terrors at the palace. He told me about their conversation, avoiding the disparaging terms I had heard earlier.

"You know the story of the Hyksos and the Egyptians and how father reunited all of Egypt?"

I nodded.

"Father's prejudice against the Hyksos stems from his father and brother dying in the war. He finished what they had started, though I think he forgot that both sides were to blame for the war. That he allowed you into the family at all is amazing.

"The feuds between the Habirus and Egyptians and the Nubians and Egyptians will continue because no group wishes to be subjugated. Egyptians must understand that we need to work together with the Hyksos and Nubians. But that is likely a long way away, and until that happens, things will be dangerous for you. Your Habiru birth outweighs your Egyptian upbringing."

Ahmose-Ankh paused for a moment. He was right about my Habiru origins. But after my conversation with Miriam and Amenhotep, I realized how little I knew about the lives of my birth people. I enjoy comforts most of my brethren know little about.

Embarrassed, I changed the subject. "Do you know what Rekhmire and Ahmose were discussing? Something about a staff and a prophecy?" I asked.

"I wondered that too," he replied. "There are many prophecies, Ramose. Rekhmire and Balaam have predicted many things that have never happened. One time they predicted that the Nile would turn red like blood, signaling the coming of a revolution within the country. How ridiculous is that? How would the water turn into blood?"

I said nothing to Ahmose-Ankh about the prediction I gave as a small child.

"Ignore these sorts of things, Ramose. Otherwise, you cannot sense the surrounding danger."

"Is that why you are such a good fighter?" I asked.

"I suppose, in part. Iyov does not pay much attention to magic and seeing the future like Rekhmire and Balaam. He prefers direct action, though I do not mean to discount what the others teach."

"Maybe I should learn from Iyov?" I said.

"You likely will someday. You must learn to fight as all the sons of Pharaoh do. Soon, I will leave Waset to rule Buhen. Iyov and Balaam will teach Amenhotep and Siamun. Then you will have a turn with both those teachers.

"I have tried protecting your from the dangers here—some

that you do not know you have faced. Father is blind to Siamun's evil ways, though mother sees it. You can trust my friends, Mahu, Djau, Unas, and Rekhmire. Talk to them if you have a problem and they can introduce you to others who are closer to your age."

"Yes, Ammi." That was my nickname for Ahmose-Ankh.

"Develop a friendship with Amenhotep. I do not know if that is possible or not, but I will talk to him. I am concerned...." He trailed off.

"What are you concerned about Ammi?"

"Oh, it is probably nothing. But I wondered about Amenhotep and Siamun plotting together. Though Siamun seems to dislike everyone."

"Siamun seems to have been born angry," I said. I told Ahmose-Ankh of my day with Amenhotep and Miriam. We talked about different things after that, including what he would do in Buhen. We planned that I would visit him, though we could not know at the time that this would never happen.

10

Rekhmire's return from his travels meant my lessons continued the next day. A mixture of emotions ran through me that morning. I found myself reluctant to work. At first, I thought finding the severed leg in my bed still bothered me. But as I strolled towards Rekhmire's office to begin my studies, I realized something else bothered me.

Rekhmire's comment about me being slow-witted still festered, and his disbelief about my vision heightened my resentment. Not that he disagreed with my prediction, for he had said the same thing about Siamun himself. When I arrived that morning, instead of showing kindness about the lamb's leg, Rekhmire tested me, interrogated me, trying to determine if I was acting or if I possessed the gift of prophecy.

"Did you think about what you would say?" my teacher asked about the day in the audience chamber.

"The words just came forth," I defended.

"You thought nothing of them?" he chided.

"I do not even remember what I said."

Just then Amenhotep joined us.

"Do the voice?" Rekhmire demanded.

"What are you doing?" Amenhotep yelled. "He does not remember what happened! If I had not of caught him, he would have fallen."

"So he says!"

"Why would he fake it?"

"To punish Siamun. To make Pharaoh's son look bad."

"Why do you not believe in his prophetic abilities? His..." Amenhotep stopped. I knew he was about to say something about everyone in my family being prophets, but he could not reveal that he knew Miriam. Calming himself he said, "He came to the palace because you thought he is a prophet."

"What makes you believe you know something of this?" Rekhmire snapped.

"Everyone in the palace knows!" Amenhotep retorted.

Grabbing Amenhotep's wrist, Rekhmire lead my adopted brother out of the office while I followed. He dragged him along back the long outdoor walkway while various people watched Pharaoh's top advisor man handle a prince of Egypt. People gawked in our wake. Arriving at Nefertari's office, Rekhmire spun Amenhotep around and thrust him towards Nefertari.

"Your Majesty," Rekhmire stated. "I am done teaching your son." Then turning to me, he said, "Let us go, Ramose."

He walked past me expecting me to follow. I looked back at Amenhotep, who stood there stunned. But a sly smile flashed across Nefertari's face.

***

The Wepet-Renpet festival began with the rising waters of the Nile. It celebrates the start of the New Year. At my young age, I could not partake in the ritual fast the first day, but they canceled my lessons. In the evening, I feasted with the royal family at various events. When the celebration ended, I bid Ahmose-Ankh farewell as he departed for Buhen. Amenhotep started work with Balaam, and Siamun continued with Iyov.

Already upset by Ahmose-Ankh's departure, I confronted Rekhmire about his behavior.

"Why do you not believe my vision from the other day?"

"Why do you say such a thing?"

"You kept asking questions as though you did not believe me!"

"That is not the case." Then he paused. "Have you had these visions other times?"

"I do not know, Rekhmire. I know that I one came to me when I was younger, which is why I came to the palace. You thought me capable of such a thing when you had me come here."

He admonished me, and I mumbled an apology. "You think I am slow-witted, and I am not sure why that is."

"I think no such thing," he denied. "Quite the contrary. You are one of the brightest people I have worked with."

"Why did you tell Ahmose, otherwise?" I asked.

"Ah! Now I understand your concern. I thought you were lying about something because you could not speak the other day about the incident." Rekhmire smiled, pausing for a moment. "Hiding your power from your enemies is sometimes necessary. The purpose of my words was to throw others off, not you. If your enemies knew your true gifts, you would be in grave danger. Ahmose might banish you from the kingdom. Or worse."

"How do you mean?" I asked.

"My observations of you suggest you show great promise as a magician. Maybe as a leader. But we cannot let others know this. Ahmose believes you to be a simpleton. Do nothing to make him believe otherwise."

"Yes, Rekhmire." Hearing that Rekhmire believed my story, I felt a wave of relief. Softening towards him, I told him about the voice I heard.

"You hear a voice too?!" he exclaimed. "How long has this gone on?"

"As long as I can remember. Mostly by the river."

Rekhmire pondered what I had said for a moment and then asked more questions about this voice. He wondered when I heard it, what it meant. But I had few answers for him, as I ignored the voice. Until he pressed me, the sound of the river and the voice that came from my mouth seemed to be unrelated. Rekhmire told me he believed the voice I heard was Heqet or Hapi.

"Who is Hapi?" I asked.

"That you ask such a question tells me I have neglected teaching you properly," he responded. "In the beginning, Amun created himself out of the vast primordial nothingness."

"Do you mean Atum?" I asked.

With a suspicious glance, Rekhmire asked, "Where did you hear about Atum?"

"I overheard a discussion when in Avaris," I lied, not

wanting him to know about my discussions with Harwa.

"Do not let Ahmose hear you say that. He may not like the priesthood, but he believes in their god. Atum is an older story belonging to Heliopolis. The stories are similar enough, but I will use the names Ahmose prefers."

I asked him why it mattered if both groups referred to the same god. To Egyptians, he explained, a name is everything. Knowing the name of something gives you power over that being.

"It is the basis of magic. Amun imbued everything with magic. Like the wind, Amun permeates everything. Amun used a sound to create form out of the shapeless. That frequency is what we control when we do magic."

"What does this have to do with Hapi?" I asked.

"I am getting to that," he replied with impatience. "Amun created all the gods, but from where Hapi came, few agree. Some believe he sprung from Nun, the primordial waters, just as Amun did."

Rekhmire rose and walked towards the window facing the Nile. He stared at the river in silence for some time. Then he turned around and walked out the front door of his office, motioning me to follow. Stopping at the doorstep, he pointed to a clay statue beside the door that stood about two cubits tall. It depicted a man with breasts wearing a headdress of papyrus plants rising from his head. In each hand he held a water jug that pointed downwards. The man knelt with one knee on the ground; his legs bent at the knee to ninety degrees.

"For centuries, Egyptians have worshiped Hapi, bringer of floods. Every year, rains in the South inundate the river. Too little brings famine. Too much causes houses to flood and people to drown. Increased water takes longer to recede, delaying planting of crops. Balance is the key. Fifteen cubits are perfect. We pay homage to the god to bring the right amount of flooding. That in part is why we celebrate Wepet-Renpet. In a year or two you will partake in the ritual and better understand its meaning."

Rekhmire explained that this area of the Nile River floods when the days are longest. Sopdet reaches its highest point in the sky, telling Hapi to bring more water to the region. The flooding lasts for several months. Shortening days coincided with receding waters, leaving a dark, fertile soil, perfect for growing crops that farmers seeded with grains and greens. Planting occurred around the autumn equinox, near the full moon, providing foods to eat throughout the seasons. Barley and flax ripened earlier than wheat and emmer. Because they mature at different times, only one crop of the four might fail if the flooding was off. The only time all four crops failed was after the Strongili eruption caused changes in the weather patterns. With the growing season disrupted, the grains tainted, people starved, and war ensued. Failure of all four crops would come again later in my life, during the redemption.

Rekhmire anthropomorphized the land, sun, water, and plants as though Hapi watched over them as a parent does for a child. The god infused the papyrus plant with the wisdom to grow both on land and in water, creating space for us to walk in the swamps on the rhizomes of the plants that buried themselves in mud. Otherwise, much of the land would be impassable.

As Rekhmire explained, "But the papyrus plant also filters the water, making it drinkable for us. Without it, the river would become silted and tainted," he said. "I do not fault the Hyksos for cutting into the papyrus as Ahmose does. The Hyksos' gods mirror most of the Egyptian gods with similar traits and qualities. But they have no god for Hapi and therefore know little about the importance of papyrus. The statue kneels on the ground to remind us how the papyrus plant grows, and the headdress mirrors the plume of the papyrus stalks."

Even at this young age, Rekhmire's explanation troubled me. He caressed the statue as one might a lover. I believed in the interconnectedness of all things and understood how he could want to give powers to natural forces. The symbolism is important in shaping the ideas of a society. Icons, though, puzzled me. My biological mother had told of how Abraham, our father, smashed all the idols in his father's workshop. Having no life of their own, they could not protect themselves from his hand.

How could an inanimate object do what Rekhmire stated? How could torturing a small animal bring destruction on the perpetrator? Ahmose-Ankh was correct; I was caught between two worlds and knew not how to reconcile the different beliefs. I pondered these thoughts as Rekhmire studied me.

"What purpose does the statue provide?" I asked.

"The statue contains the Ka of Hapi."

"Ka?" I asked.

"The Ka is a part of the soul along with the Ba, the shadow, your name, and your body. For now, the Ka and Ba are the important parts. The statue provides a place for the Ka and Ba of the god to perform magical acts. Did you notice the small statuette of the goddess Serqet on my table? She is the goddess of magic. I used the figurine to invoke her power, calling her soul to it."

He paused for a moment, looking me over. "I find it hard to believe it is Hapi that speaks to you. Though I believe less that it may have been Heqet."

"Why is that? She comes as a frog sometimes and lives by the river. Maybe it is she who speaks to me."

"Because she is a goddess and rarely speaks through men."

"I did not know that. Tell me about Heqet," I said.

Rekhmire went into detail about how the fertility goddess brings life to all things and brings the floods to the Nile. We finished that day discussing Heqet.

Throughout the flooding season, I learned about each of the gods of the Egyptian pantheon, as Rekhmire revealed ancient mysteries of Egyptian magic found in the scrolls he poured over. He obsessed with finding the god that showed himself through me, and he studied each in his free time, sharing with me some secrets he learned.

"The basis of magic," Rekhmire said one Akhet day, "is to know an object so well, that it reveals its mysteries to you. Then you can change the state of an object. By focusing on your breath, you calm yourself, find Ma'at within yourself, bringing clarity to the true nature of the subject. Clear your thoughts, allowing them to rise without a struggle as if you are watching a twig float in the Nile. Never forget, magic permeates you!"

I practiced the breathing exercises he taught me to quiet my thoughts. Later, he would regret teaching me this technique. At that time, he hoped some divinity would burst forth revealing to him at last who I carried within me. Each day I disappointed him when nothing revealed itself to either of us. And though I felt I had failed my teacher, I enjoyed our lessons, for they gave me time away from the palace and the cruel children of nobles who taunted me daily. I wished that one day I would become a great magician and be able to sweep these tiny demons from the Earth. That day would come soon enough.

Most days, Rekhmire had me breathe as I watched something, a candle, a statue, a stone for nearly an hour. When I first started this practice, my mind raced, remembering humiliations handed to me by one of my cohorts. I envisioned plans for revenge. But over the course of a moon or two, my mind calmed. I no longer thought of such things, or if I did, I let the thought go.

After each session, I would prepare dinner. Rekhmire taught me practical skills, such as how to cook. All my life I enjoyed cooking, for it provided me an opportunity to focus on something other than thoughts of revenge.

Focusing on a candle one day in early Peret, I watched my breath, noticing the rise and release of thoughts. This day started much the same as the others. My mind drifted. Then I caught myself hanging onto ideas before releasing them into the stream. I closed my eyes instead of watching the candle. At first, I heard sounds outside, children playing, birds singing, the wind rustling leaves until those sounds slid away and everything became still. And then I heard a voice—no, a whisper—and felt a presence. I thought when I opened my eyes, I would see someone standing beside me. But my eyes would not open.

"Moses!" something whispered.

I strained to listen, and felt so still and quiet that my head was empty. Darkness surrounded me, and I thought it could swallow me at any moment. Feeling as though I might fall into a deep abyss, my eyes popped open as I gasped for air.

Rekhmire, noticing that I was panting, asked me, "Is something wrong?"

Not understanding what had just happened, I said nothing. I grappled to comprehend this experience, which only caused it to slip away from my awareness. Breathing gently to steady myself, I assured Rekhmire I was fine.

I continued to breathe, but instead of focusing on the object before me, I wondered why the expanse of the abyss caused me to recoil and why did the voice call me Moses?

I knew Rekhmire would not understand. While he showered kindness on me in private, his focus on individual gods blocked his ability to see the truth of my experience, for though I had only completed my tenth flooding season, I knew this was not a local god. And I mistrusted his association with Ahmose. Someone older and wiser would need to explain this to me, someone not employed by Pharaoh.

11

For three consecutive days after my experience in Rekhmire's study, I ventured to the river hoping to see Harwa, but not finding him. My studies with Rekhmire towards the end of Akhet combined with spending time with Amenhotep prevented me from finding him. It was not until the water of the Nile receded and the planting season of Peret came that I sought for Harwa. Early in the season, I ventured to the Nile again to find Harwa sitting on the log he and I often shared by the water.

"Ho, Ramose!" he called as I approached. "It has been some time."

"Hello, Harwa," I replied, sitting next to him. "It is good to see you. Where have you been?"

The papyrus grew tall in this location. Thick stalks reached at least fifteen cubits skyward, sprouting into fuzzy plumes high above our heads. The fallen trunk lay near the water with a small clearing of space for us to watch for anyone coming through the foliage.

"I could ask you the same," Harwa said, smiling. "I needed to visit a friend in the East. The journey was long and arduous. I only returned yesterday."

"Did you hear what happened with my brother, Siamun?"

"You mean the frog incident?" he asked. "I heard about that abomination. I do not even believe in Heqet, yet I find his actions very disturbing. You must be careful of him."

Ignoring his comment, I asked, "Do you believe in Hapi?"

"God of the Nile? What makes you ask?"

I told him about my experience after Rekhmire taught me the breathing technique.

"Why did he show you that technique at such a young age?" he asked.

I told Harwa about hearing a voice by the river. He asked me a few questions about what I meant about hearing the voice, the circumstances, and what it said. Then he asked me what I learned from the swamps.

"What do you mean?" I responded.

"The river talks to you. What is it telling you?"

I quieted my mind, listening intently. I had never tried this intentionally, and I struggled at first. Previously, I just sat playing by the river and heard something whispering. When I looked around, there was no one there. This would go on for some time until I realized that whatever spoke did not have a body.

Today, I strained to listen. I realized I was trying to force the hearing. I quieted myself and sat and waited. At first, I imagined what amounted to the sound of whispers before I discerned the words. I thought I heard the river telling me a story, one I was not sure I believed. Slowly, the murmurs became more audible, more engaging. Some voices only described their rush to the sea. But a story emerged from what now became a cacophony of sounds.

Turning to Harwa, I declared, "The waters hurry to the sea. But there are problems. Uncle Joseph damaged the swamps. Removing the papyrus endangered the river. It speaks of contamination from the lake. I do not understand that."

"You do hear the river!" Harwa replied, sounding surprised. "How long have you heard the river?"

"Miriam taught me to listen when I was younger."

"I wonder what possessed her to do that. It must run in your family! The swamps act as a filtration system, cleaning animal and human waste, run-off from building projects, and extra silt from further upstream. Before Jacob and his sons brought their families, and flocks to the Nile Delta, the areas to the north flourished with papyrus, reeds, cattail. But now there are more people in the region than this area can handle. And if Ahmose reopens the canal…" He trailed off.

"Rekhmire believes that praying to Hapi…"

"Praying will do nothing," Harwa interrupted me with a half-laugh. "Something contaminated the lake."

"It is a saltwater lake," I said.

"Bitter Lake's name derives from that. The Red Sea once came this far north before receding, leaving the lakes landlocked, with stagnant, salty water. Nothing comes to cleanse the water. But what I am talking about is more than that. When Strongili spread ash and rock miles and miles away, much of that ash settled in and around the lake, causing it to sour and fester like an unclean wound. The water changed and reeked. Fish died, plants decayed."

"How do you know this?"

"I stopped there on my return journey. I have watched it change over the years. But I feel it. In my body, and in my spirit."

"Can you teach me how to do that too?"

"I think you already know how to do this, Ramose," he said. "You hear the water of the river talk to you. You listen to it. You become the water."

"I guess that is true," I replied.

"You touched the All," he said.

"The All? You mean Atum?"

"When you practiced the breathing technique, you touched a darkness. What did you call it? An 'abyss'? That is the All, the void from which everything springs. Maybe it is Atum or Amun. But whatever it is, you cannot build a statue to represent it. The All is formless. All things come from the One, and by adaptation become many. All forms are one, but we perceive them to be separate."

"Why was it so scary to me?" I asked.

For the first time, I realized I felt panic when I touched it. Harwa explained. "We recoil from anything that reminds us we are not distinct.

"People view gods as different powers because it makes it easier to understand. We can create an idol to represent Hapi, or Set, or any god you want. Giving qualities to the river as the god Hapi makes it easier to explain what is happening. But everything including you, Ramose, comes from the One. It flows through all things as water does."

"As water?"

"Not water that flows in front of us now," he suggested, pointing to the river. "It is a vitality possessing the quality of water, flowing through you, me, the papyrus, the log, the sand, and the water too."

"You mean Ka?"

"Not quite. Ka implies something personal. It is the part of your soul. It contains the essence of the One. Your ancestors are imbued into your Ka, too. But I am talking about something different. It is as though you took the Ka and Ba of all things and put them into a soup. There is nothing distinct about the ingredients. Imagine taking one rain drop. By itself it is distinct. But can you decipher an individual drop in the ocean?"

"No," I replied.

"This essence gives life to everything regardless of the form that life takes. It gives us life. When you know this in your heart," he pointed to his chest, "then you know how to transform anything. You can see the world from the perspective of another person, animal, or thing. I have become the lake, become the swamp, become the Nile. That is how I know rebuilding the canal is a bad idea."

"How do I do this? How do I sense this too?" I pleaded.

"You touched this power when you fell towards that void. Close your eyes for a moment and cover them too."

I did as Harwa instructed. "What do you see?"

"Nothing," I responded.

"Relax and breathe as you did the other day with Rekhmire."

I closed my eyes and did as he instructed, but still, I saw nothing. As I calmed myself, focusing only on my breath, I noticed an undulation around me. "I see things moving, vibrating more."

"Yes! Everything flows out and in; all things rise and fall; all things have rhythm."

"Slaves will build the canal," I said, uncovering my eyes and opening them.

"That is probably true; maybe even some of your blood relatives. Slaves build most civilizations," Harwa glowered, looking out over the river.

"But you know there is something not right with the lakes?" I asked him.

"I do. One day, you will go there, and you will feel it too."

***

Before I could ask Harwa more about Bitter Lakes, Miriam appeared.

"Ho, Miriam," Harwa said as she approached.

"I remember our story was interrupted," she said in greeting.

"Our story?" Harwa questioned.

"About Joseph," Miriam replied. "They called me away before you answered my question. Did his dreams come true? Did his brothers bow down to him? I have not forgotten."

"No, you have not," he laughed. "You have an excellent memory, Miriam. Mine is not as good as it once was. I have journeyed much since our last meeting. But I must ask you something first. How long have you heard the river speak to you?"

When she stared blankly without saying a word, he added, "I know it does. Ramose hears it too. What does it say to you?"

"I do not remember the first time it spoke to me. Maybe when Ramose was a baby. When we ventured to the river, the river told me where danger lurked."

"And you told no one about this?"

She shook her head.

"Why did you teach Ramose?"

"In case he ever needed to find water in the desert," she answered. "I know it is odd. There is always water in the desert. I do not know why I had such a thought." Later though it would save my life in the desert.

"Very well," Harwa said after a few moments. "Joseph's story. Where were we?"

He thought for a moment. "When I left off, Pharaoh had released Joseph from jail and made him vizier of the land of Egypt, second in power only to Pharaoh. After the seven years of plenty, seven years of famine hit the entire region, just as Pharaoh's dream foretold. Joseph's plan required swamp removal to create land for cattle to graze. As a result, people came from around the region to buy food from the Egyptians.

For the famine not only affected Egypt, it hit the surrounding regions. In fact, because most of the areas around Egypt had no water, it was much worse."

Harwa told of a group of ten men arriving from the Land of Canaan asking to purchase food. This was not unusual, for many people came seeking grain. But something about these men caught the attention of the magistrate in charge of rationing food. He called Joseph over to see the men. Joseph recognized the men at once.

"It was then he asked me for my advice," Harwa explained.

"'My brothers are here in Egypt,' Joseph told me.

"'Your brothers?' I responded. 'The ones who sold you into slavery? What brings them here?'

"'Famine, I suppose, like everyone else. I do not know what to do.'

"We devised a plan. Joseph met his brothers, but they did not recognize him. Twenty years had passed, and Joseph wore the traditional Egyptian chin beard. His brothers bowed down to Joseph, Vizier of Egypt, their faces to the ground."

"His dream came true," Miriam exclaimed.

Harwa nodded. "And Joseph remembered not only his dreams, but the mistreatment he suffered at their hands. He accused them of being spies, which they denied.

"'There were twelve of us,' Reuben explained. 'One is no more, and the youngest stayed at home with our father.'

"Joseph replied, 'I will test you, then. One of you will remain here until the others return with your youngest brother. This way I will know you are not spies.'

"The brothers, unsure how to handle the situation, asked to convene privately. Joseph, however, observed them, listening to their conversation. The brothers lamented selling Joseph into slavery. Reuben cried, 'You are being punished for this. Did I not say do not hurt him? Now we will pay for the spilling of his blood!'

"Joseph wept hearing his brothers speak and questioned our plan. Still, he sent Simeon to jail while the others returned to Canaan. He gave them food for their journey and covertly placed the silver they used to purchase the food back in the grain sacks.

"Even before unpacking their bags of grain, Jacob did not

want to send Benjamin, his youngest son, back to Egypt in exchange for Simeon. Once they emptied the sacks, the brothers found the silver Joseph replaced. Jacob feared they had sold Simeon and did not wish to send anyone else back to Egypt.

"But as their grain supplies dwindled, the brothers pleaded with Jacob to allow them to go back to Egypt with Benjamin. Reuben said he would kill his own sons if Benjamin did not return; Jacob would not consent. Judah offered to be cursed forever if he returned without Benjamin."

"Cursed forever?" I said. "Is that not extreme?"

"It is a trait of your family. Even Jacob spoke rashly sometimes, with no thought to the consequences of his words. Remember, words have power."

"Did they take Benjamin to Egypt?" I asked.

"Patience, my friend. I am getting to that. All the brothers departed for Egypt, but Jacob had them bring a tribute of balm, honey, and almonds. And he doubled the silver they produced the first time.

"Upon seeing Benjamin, when his brothers arrived, Joseph ordered a feast prepared. Judah told Joseph's administrator he and his brothers brought double the money this time as they found the original silver in their bags. The servant waived it off, saying he had received his money. They released Simeon from jail and returned him to his brothers. To the brothers' surprise, the Vizier invited them into his home for a feast.

"The men bowed to Joseph again, who responded by asking how their father fared. The brothers told Joseph that Jacob still lived. Then Joseph turned to Benjamin, his full brother, and said, 'May God treat you well,' before grief overcame him. Joseph left, refreshed himself, and returned to start the meal."

Harwa looked into the distance as if piercing the veils of time. The day warmed and dragonflies and bees buzzed nearby from time to time.

"Joseph gave them their grain and sent them away. But as they readied to leave the city, the guards stopped the brothers to search their belongings for the silver Joseph hid in their bags. The guards found a silver goblet in Benjamin's sacks. Joseph demanded whoever stole the cup should become his slave.

"Then, Judah stepped forward exclaiming, 'Take me instead! Benjamin is the only surviving brother of our old father's favorite wife! It would kill him if we returned without him.'

"Hearing this, Joseph sent his servants away and revealed to his brothers his identity."

"Why did he not tell them when he first met them?" I asked.

"Joseph's brothers humiliated him when he was younger, and he wanted revenge. When I saw his heart hardening, I convinced him to forsake his original plan and test them instead. His vanity almost prevented him from forgiving his brothers. Once the brothers showed remorse for their actions, he forgave them."

"Just like that?" I asked. I thought about the hurt I had felt over the years. I would not hesitate to torment Siamun or Maiherpri if given the chance.

"Just like that. Revenge is a bitter pill, Ramose." Harwa gazed at me with steely eyes. "Joseph had punished his brothers enough. He understood continuing to do so only brought hatred to himself.

"After they knew who he was, Joseph invited them to return with their father to Egypt. 'The famine will continue for more years,' he told them. All of Jacob's animals and household moved to the land of Egypt. And they cleared more swampland to make room for their flocks along the former route of the canal, because it was unused land. The people settled there and remained until Ahmose's victory."

"This was the tale my mother shared with me," Miriam said. "Great Aunt Serah told her the story."

Harwa smiled. "I knew Serah. She was a fine woman."

"She is alive!" Miriam said.

"Still alive!" Harwa exclaimed. "How can that be?"

But Miriam ignored the question. "What was Jacob like?" she asked.

Harwa paused for a moment to consider his response. "I spent only a short amount of time with him because of his advanced age. Jacob was a remarkable man, touched by the divine. Though physically blind, he pierced the veil to the spiritual realm.

"He had his faults, to be sure, playing favorites even later in life, though in his older age, there was wisdom behind those acts. He taught me about the All, about El Shaddai."

Miriam asked what I was too young to know to ask. "Did Joseph have a direct experience of El Shaddai as Jacob did?"

"I do not believe he did, Miriam," Harwa responded. "Jacob shone like the sun, with a beauty and grace like no one I have ever met. Joseph possessed charisma but his view of the All was as the full moon reflects off the still waters of the Nile."

"What do you mean?" she asked.

"Most people cannot tolerate a direct encounter with the All. It overwhelms them. One must prepare for the experience. Joseph was a righteous man reflecting the divine. But he did not have the face-to-face experience as Jacob did."

Harwa looked at me when he said this for it related to our earlier conversation. Before I could form a question about how one prepares to experience the divine, Miriam asked, "Did Joseph's brother tell you this story?"

"They filled in gaps. After Jacob died, they feared retaliation for how they treated Joseph in his youth. But he forgave their past actions. We mummified Jacob to preserve his body for travel and buried him with his fathers in the Land of Canaan, as he requested. Joseph led the expedition and invited his brothers to return to Egypt."

"The Egyptians mummified Joseph when he died too," Miriam exclaimed. "Serah told me the Egyptians put Joseph's mummified body in a metal casket and placed him in the Nile River."

"I remember that day," Harwa said.

"When the redeemer comes to take us back to the land of Canaan, the Children of Israel are to bring his body with them. That seems odd to me."

"Joseph asked his children to return his body to the land of his fathers as Jacob had been. Instead, Pharaoh mummified the body, placing the casket in the water to bless the Nile. An Egyptian prophecy provided the impetus to do so."

Once again, the specter of prophecy raised its head in relation to me and my ancestors. Before I could ask about it, Miriam chimed in, "Serah says the time comes soon for us to leave Egypt. She told me she had not heard the term Children of Israel for many years, so it must be soon."

Harwa eyed her, then me. "It may come soon," he said. "Or it may not. I guess it depends upon the redeemer and those to be redeemed."

He smiled at her quizzical look. "A leader cannot appear and say, 'follow me' unless the people will follow."

"I guess that is true," Miriam responded. "Thank you for telling us about our people. Ramose and I appreciate knowing our history."

Miriam excused herself, saying she needed to check on a pregnant Egyptian woman. Harwa and I both left shortly after. As I walked home, I wondered about Miriam's last comment. Our people? Did we live in the same group? I lived at the palace while she and most Habirus lived in huts. Our people served me, catering to my every need. I knew more about Egyptian history than I knew of my immediate biological family. Were we the same? That day, I did not know to which people I belonged. Though I understood more of my ancestors, I did not see how it connected to my future.

12

For the next several weeks, I reflected on what Harwa told me about the history of my people and the different prophecies. What type of vision would make someone put a casket in the river? Who was the redeemer Harwa mentioned?

My duties with Rekhmire made me forget about these questions as the weeks continued, and the seasons turned. He showed me ancient scrolls, teaching me about magic and spells. My mind filled with thoughts about magic forced other ideas from my mind.

And I began spending more time with Amenhotep. As he now thought of me as a person and not just a Habiru, our interactions transitioned from cordial to friendly. But Amenhotep's need to appease his noble-born friends delayed this process. He still laughed at me in front of his friends sometimes. But the cutting remarks ceased. An incident in late Peret began a trajectory of events that changed my status amongst this group of kids.

The weather was cold, and our military training began. Arriving the first day of my combat training, I saw Amenhotep, Hannu, Maiherpri, and Ankhu talking in a group. Amenhotep acknowledged me when I entered the room, then ignored me, mimicking the others' rude behavior. Iyov and an assistant showed us spear maneuvers using blunt sticks, then paired us. Maiherpri and I ended up together. Because he knew most of these poses, his face betrayed boredom with the slowness of the lesson. Later in the day, we sparred, our sticks clashing back and forth with increasing vigor.

We jousted until Maiherpri knocked the spear from my hands with such force that everyone else stopped and Iyov came over. "Our goal is not to maim an Egyptian Prince, Maiherpri," Iyov scolded, towering over him, dismissing my sparring partner for the day.

Over the next couple of weeks, I did not spar with Maiherpri. Instead, I found myself paired with Amenhotep or Hannu. While Iyov did not want to see me get hurt in mock combat, he also did not provide me with the instruction I needed to protect myself. While he worked with the other boys, showing them the intricate maneuvers and correcting them, he spent little time with me. As a result, none of my cohorts wished to be my partner because I was so clumsy.

After being humiliated in class for a few weeks, I sought Harwa to ask him for advice. I found him by the river and told him what had been occurring in my combat training class.

"Let me see your form," he said.

I grabbed a stick off the ground, assuming an attack position as if ready to battle.

"Your form is off," he said, walking over to where I stood. "Move your hands lower like this," he commented as he adjusted my hands. "And bend your knees more. This will prepare you for all threats."

"This differs from what Iyov showed me," I commented.

"That is because Iyov does not know Tahtib."

"Tahtib? Dancing with sticks?"

"Now we consider it entertainment, but Tahtib is an ancient form of Egyptian martial arts. Some hieroglyphs show the forms of the movement and postures. Rekhmire may have a scroll containing the poses."

"I have only seen scrolls containing magic spells," I responded.

"That is good for you to learn, too. But Tahtib helps you learn to focus your thoughts and power."

Harwa showed me a series of motions, correcting my form while I repeated each movement. I practiced most of the morning before needing a break. Sweating in the heat, I sat next to Harwa on a log by the shore. He offered me dried fish.

I ate almost out of his hand.

"Hard work," he smiled. "Tahtib training is not just about the postures. It is a mental exercise too. You must breathe and focus your thoughts as you move."

"Is the breathing the same that Rekhmire showed me?" I asked.

"It is slightly different. And I will teach you the method when you are old enough. For now, you must understand the core of the discipline is experiencing the connection of all things, flowing with the stream of life. Then you can know your enemy and overcome him. But to do that, you must first know yourself."

"How do I flow with the stream of life?" I asked.

"Do you remember the day you experienced the flowing motion of the surrounding energy?"

"I do," I replied thinking back to the day I closed my eyes and felt the swirling energy around me.

"The movements of Tahtib mimic the flow of energy. As you realize this, you can harness this power."

"Why am I not learning about this?" I asked.

"Tahtib arose as a spiritual practice in the Old Kingdom. During the Middle Kingdom, it became associated with entertainment, but in secret some teachers taught the underlying truth behind the moves. As the Hyksos came, Egyptians adopted the new technology brought by their invaders, including chariots and the longbow. They forgot about the importance of Tahtib and its ways."

Over the next few months, I became proficient not only in Tahtib, but with the longbow. I gained more physical balance, mental equanimity, manual dexterity. But my tentativeness and insecurity slowed my learning. Harwa lost patience with me sometimes, which only exacerbated my anxiety. But I made progress and felt more comfortable with the movements.

"As you become proficient with it, as you steady your thoughts, you can kill a man with one strike," Harwa told me one day during my lesson. " Your breathing comes naturally to you, Ramose, but your movements are too indefinite. If you strike an opponent, do it without hesitation."

That Peret, almost a year to the day I jousted with Maiherpri for the first time, I learned the power of Tahtib fighting him.

Believing we needed to know how to defend ourselves against a real enemy, Iyov paired us to battle one-on-one until only one fighter remained. Two at a time, we would enter a ring to square off against one another, with the winners meeting until only one of us was undefeated.

Hannu knocked down Ankhu. Then Maiherpri and I fought each other while others watched. He came at me hard as though trying to kill me. I parried his thrusts and blocked the swing of his stick as best I could, losing ground in the face of his hurried blows aimed at my head and feet. Losing my balance, he knocked me to the floor with his stick, momentarily knocking the wind out of me.

"Ramose. Let someone else fight," I heard Iyov saying.

But instead of yielding, something within me took over. I rolled away from Maiherpri's downward thrust and rose to my feet in one motion. I slammed my stick into his side, knocking the wind from him. Maiherpri fell to the ground, but having lost control, I kept coming at him. I hit him several times as he lay there defenseless, cutting his face, arms, and chest until Iyov hauled me off of him.

"Ramose!" I heard Iyov yelling. "You must stop. This is not to the death!"

After he pulled me away from our makeshift arena, I realized he must have been screaming for a few moments before dragging me away. Breathing in the method that Rekhmire taught me, I calmed myself. Iyov ended the tournament for the day while he sought a healer to help Maiherpri.

***

After beating Maiherpri, I ventured to the river to find Harwa proud of my victory. Sensing he would arrive soon, I waited for him and listened to the water. Quiet at first, I only heard it speak my pet name, "Moses, Moses." I thought I heard it say it will run with blood, unsure if I heard that or if I imagined it as I had discussed this of late.

Harwa walked up moments later. I told Harwa about what the fight with Maiherpri. Though pleased I battled well, disappointment showed on his face. "You must learn to contain yourself and control your feelings. Going crazy in combat can be very dangerous, as you can tell."

The mistreatment I had experienced overwhelmed me. "Maiherpri humiliated me so often over the years, Harwa! He deserves punishment," I screamed, anger exploding from me in tears and shouts.

Harwa said nothing for a few moments before calmly saying. "Only the All can punish someone, Ramose. Revenge is not the same as dispensing justice, for it only serves your purpose. A society cannot function when vendetta replaces the rule of law."

I breathed to stop my sobbing. I churned the anger and hate that arose in me, not wanting to accept Harwa's words. Noticing this, Harwa challenged me to redirect my feelings. "You are not a victim, Ramose!"

"They pulled me from my parents and forced me with the crazy people at the palace," I argued.

"That is one perspective, but from a different perspective, an opportunity presented to take you away from a life of servitude."

"And placed me in the hands of a demented step-brother who wants to torture me as he does the animals."

"Siamun is a disturbed child, to be sure. But you allow him to persecute you. You have power. Even if your only act of defiance is to know his actions do not change your behavior or thoughts!"

"Should I allow Siamun to continue to torment me?" I asked with sarcasm.

"You can defend yourself, as you showed Maiherpri. More than anything you shook his confidence."

I believed what he was saying just long enough to stop feeling sorry for myself for a moment. Maybe he was correct. I am powerful. "Mother said the same."

"And your relationship with Amenhotep is improving. You have one disturbed brother, but Amenhotep and Ahmose-Ankh are good brothers. You did not have a brother when you lived with Miriam and your parents."

"That is true," I conceded.

We sat in silence for some time as I steadied myself. I was still feeling hurt, but not as acutely. Then changing the subject I asked, "How many prophecies are there?"

He laughed. "As many as there are grains of sand in the

desert, my young friend! Which prophecy do you refer? There is one that Rekhmire, Iyov, and Balaam share. Maybe it refers to you, maybe it does not."

"Yes, that one."

He stopped for a moment, quieting himself, though he was communicating with some unseen presence to get permission to tell me what he knew.

"Yes, he is old enough to know," he mumbled to something unseen. Then turning to me, he said, "Each of Ahmose's three advisors saw the birth of a child exceeding all men in virtue, glorified as a great leader through the ages. At first, Pharaoh believed this child to be an Egyptian and to be the most famous Pharaoh ever because Rekhmire told him so. Balaam and Iyov disagreed with him. They said, 'Nay, Your Majesty. The child we see is of Habiru origin and will lead them from the land.'

"Iyov recommended drowning all Habiru males in the Nile. And Pharaoh might have given the order to do that, had Rekhmire not whispered about the staff to Ahmose."

"I heard Ahmose discuss a staff from time to time," I said.

"From what I have heard, it is an obsession of Pharaoh's. But it saved the Habirus if nothing else."

"For now," I replied.

Harwa nodded his head in agreement. "Things may get worse for your people before they improve."

"What is the staff?"

"Pharaoh believes it to be an artifact of power, one that can give him immortality."

"Can it? If he finds it, I mean."

"That is unknown. It might work for the right person wielding it, someone who can discover the source of its power. But the same power could destroy the wrong person."

"Is Ahmose the right person?"

"He has to find it first," Harwa said with a sly smile. "Shall we practice? We have spent too much time talking, and not enough time in action. You have more to learn, including controlling your temper in battle."

I sensed he knew more than he was telling me, but I did not press further. Instead, I focused on receiving the instruction he provided.

***

In the following weeks Maiherpri recovered, but the tension between us grew. One day, as he passed me on the street, his father spat in my direction. A great insult. I stopped, not knowing how to respond. He was an adult of high status, and though I was a prince in name, I felt beneath his station. I stared at him, seething as my fists clenched and unclenched. He met my gaze with a smirk, waiting for me to strike, hoping he would have an excuse to punish me. Or beat me senseless. We glared at one another, with others looking on. I wanted to hit him. But I remembered my conversation with Harwa, and instead of fighting, I turned and walked away.

I went back to the royal chambers, continuing to seethe when I ran into Nefertari. "You seem upset, Ramose," she said.

When she heard of the incident, Nefertari became outraged. "We must go tell Ahmose immediately," she said, and she took me to his quarters. Listening to the story, Ahmose showed more concern about taking power away from Teta than for any insult towards me. Still, he acted the next day.

Paser led me to the observation chamber next to the throne room to observe the proceedings the next day. Several years had passed since I took part in any actions in the official audience chamber. That day, the hearings were about Siamun's torture of a frog. But on this day, Siamun stood there, looking disinterested while he fidgeted. His expression registered a slight change when Ahmose punished Maiherpri's father by stripping him of several of his minor titles.

Then my demented adopted brother turned towards me and said, "You will pay for this, Habiru," and left the room.

After that, Maiherpri and the other son of nobles avoided Amenhotep altogether, choosing to associate with Siamun instead. At first Amenhotep blamed me for his isolation, reverting to his former hostile behavior. But with Nefertari's encouragement, he and I spent more time together.

***

Several days later, Iyov combined the older and younger students to begin sword training to complement our spear skills. I found myself in a different training group, this time with Siamun, Amenhotep, and other sons of nobles. As we waited for our instructor to arrive, Siamun boasted that he would teach us a lesson today, especially me, the Habiru.

Amenhotep stepped forward to defend me against our brother.

"He is a better brother than you," Amenhotep chided.

"Amenhotep," I said. "You need not defend me."

But Amenhotep already drew one of the wooden swords we used to practice. I stepped in front of Amenhotep to stop him from assaulting Siamun. For the first time, I understood Amenhotep's rage at our demented sibling. I sensed that Siamun would severely hurt the younger brother should they spar.

Then I turned to Siamun. "Let us see if you can beat me," I said.

Siamun's face contorted with his twisted smile. "Since you asked."

Both of us drew wooden swords used for sparring and began our contest. The clank of wood sounded throughout the room as we clashed the implements back and forth. Siamun struck down at my head. Deftly, I blocked the attack. He swung at my legs, but found no opening in my defense. He seemed surprised by my skill, as my long arms and Harwa's lessons helped me. None of the boys knew of my Tahtib training with hands, stick, and sword. Siamun came at me, and I blocked each thrust and swipe.

As sweat dripped down each of us, Siamun became more frustrated. Rage in his eyes, he lunged at me as I repelled his clumsy assaults. His lack of discipline caused him to fatigue and left him open to my counterattacks. I whacked him with the blunt side of the sword, the wood smacking against his unguarded body, angering him further. We continued in this manner for some time until I knocked him down to the mat, winning. He turned bright red with embarrassment while the others stood around, stunned. Siamun rose and walked out.

"I will soon dispose of you, dirty shepherd, once and for all."

My cohorts stood stunned, as much from my victory as from Siamun's outburst. Maiherpri glared at me, remembering how I had drubbed him months ago. He turned away, disappointed that I did not receive the same treatment as he.

After this, Amenhotep's respect for me increased. He no longer saw me as the weak person I still felt myself to be. More often than not, he wanted to spend time with me rather than the nobles. For the next few weeks, he and I ventured to the Nile together. While I enjoyed this new friendship with my brother who had hated me for so long, I knew I would not be seeing Harwa while Amenhotep was with me. I longed to tell Harwa about how I had bested Siamun and kept my poise, thinking he would be proud of me.

Before I figured out how to solve this dilemma, I felt ill. At first, I believed I had eaten bad meat, but after a few days of stomach upset, I was no longer sure. When I asked Nefertari about it, she said it could take time to feel better. She gave me some horrible tasting herbs mixed with burnt charcoal. My health improved the next day, and I thought of it no more.

But I awoke a few days later with my head pounding and feeling sick to my stomach again. As I had nothing scheduled that day, I considered staying in bed, until Amenhotep arrived, intent upon going to the river with me. Paser brought a tray of breakfast fruits and baked goods. My heart rate increased as I rose from the bed, then subsided after a few moments. Thinking eating might help, I had a few bites of breakfast.

"Are you unwell, Ramose?" Amenhotep asked. "You look pale, almost ashen."

"I do not feel right," I replied as waves of nausea hit me.

I sat down to steady myself. Perhaps because I was moving too fast, I vomited on the floor, and continued to do so for about ten minutes. My breath shortened, and my heart raced. I observed a halo around Amenhotep. Then I saw it around every object I saw. When I looked back at Amenhotep, I saw he wore a headdress of papyrus. (Where did he get that?) The plumes of the leaves reached high into the air. Amenhotep sprouted breasts and knelt before me.

"Ramose," Amenhotep said. "Are you all right? Ramose?"

Amenhotep tried to help me to my bed, but I struggled, feeling agitated.

"Go get Nefertari," I thought I heard my adopted brother say. But when I looked up, Amenhotep vanished. The god Hapi knelt before me.

"Ramose," the god said. "You must save me!"

"Save you? I am but a child, and you a god."

Feeling light-headed, dizzy, I thought I might vomit again.

The room swayed as though I were on the water.

"You are the child of the prophecy," he said. "As a tool of my Father, you can stop my destruction and the death of all within my waters."

"Your father?" I asked, confused.

"The All, the father and mother of everything including the gods, wants to prove to Pharaoh that it is the only God, the one true God. Fix the swamps before Ahmose reopens the canal. Otherwise, my waters will become infested, killing everything within them."

Before I could protest that I did not know what to do, Hapi transformed into Heqet, the frog goddess. "You must stop, Siamun from torturing me," she said. "It is your doing that he comes to harm me."

"How is it my doing?" I wondered. Heqet transformed from a frog into a man with a bird on his head, claiming I would harm the earth. "How would I do that?"

Without answering, the figure changed as the face of the man morphed into a grotesque and giant head of a fly. Stunned, I did not comprehend this creature's warning, for its voice came out as a buzzing, as if a thousand flies buzzed around me. I covered my ears, for the sound overwhelmed me.

Again, a transformation occurred, and this time it changed into a beautiful woman. She approached me, undulating her hips in a seductive dance that my near-adolescent mind struggled to understand. The woman's head transformed into one of a cow before my eyes. For a moment, Amenhotep returned to my vision. He held me to the side as I continued to wretch my empty stomach. Another woman approached, saying, "This is madness. Go find the servant girl, Miriam. Tell her to find our mutual friend and bring him here!"

My vision blurred, and a buzz came to my ears, making it hard to hear her. I saw a different beautiful woman coming closer, with kind eyes and a peaceful demeanor. She wore a pure white gown and a throne-shaped headdress. "You can stop this madness, my son," she said. "You can become the greatest Pharaoh in the history of Egypt. It is yours to take."

"But I am Habiru," I cried out. "How can I become Pharaoh?"

The woman faded from my vision, replaced by another

woman carrying a large jug on her head. Though I thought I saw her lips move, the roaring in my ears prevented me from hearing her words. Then she waved her arms, and the sky darkened as clouds rolled overhead. Lightning flashed and shook the ground I lay on. I blinked my eyes, clearing my vision. I saw that I remained in my bedroom.

"Prop him up," I heard a man's voice say. "The vomiting should cease. I would like to get some of these herbs into him."

Hands lifted me into an upright position with my head tilted back. The man poured herbs into my mouth. But then he was not a man but a man with the head of a jackal.

"All right, Ramose," the jackal-headed man said. "Drink up before the chaos descends upon you."

The roaring returned to my ears, and I could hear nothing he said. A booming voice came through the din as the jackal-headed man disappeared. In his place, stood a handsome man with a sun disk adorned on his head. He shone brighter and brighter, causing me to shield my eyes from the intense light. The light dimmed, and Ahmose stood before me.

"Why did you not bring me the staff?" he demanded.

"What staff?" I asked, confused.

"Do not play tricks on me, Ramose! You found it. I want it! Did you think I would not find out about your betrayal?"

Before I could answer, Ahmose drew a sword and raised it to strike me. I threw my arms up, attempting to block the deadly blow.

"Stop him from flailing," I heard someone say.

"No!" I screamed, struggling as I felt my arms being held down. As I felt a warm liquid in my mouth, Ahmose's sword plunged into my belly. I felt the blood rising from my throat as a burning sensation went from my mouth to my gut. I looked down to see my entrails splayed on the floor, and I wondered about their meaning.

"You will go on a long journey, Ramose," a male voice said. "A trip that will transform you into a new man. One that never existed before now."

Looking up, I saw a woman's face. I thought I should know whose countenance it was, but I could not place it. Then the face blended into white light. "Sleep my son," the voice said sweetly before the light faded and the world became black.

PART TWO

13

"You are awake." Though the voice sounded familiar, I found it difficult to place. I struggled to focus my eyes. "We thought we might lose you."

Pillows propped me up, though I did not recognize where I lay. As my vision cleared, I saw a tall, muscular humanoid wearing the headdress of Pharaoh on his canine head standing over me.

"Be still," said the dog-headed being.

"Am I dead?" I asked the man-dog.

"Dead?" he asked, staring intently. "Why would you ask that?"

"I assumed you only come for dead people." Somehow I knew I should recognize the voice that spoke.

"Who do you think I am?"

"Anubis, god of the dead," I responded.

"You are very much alive and in your bedroom at the palace, Ramose. Though someone poisoned you. Had I not been helping you build a tolerance to the particular toxin, Anubis might be before you! The blue lotus mixed with the poison you ingested causes hallucinations."

"Poisoned?" I said, now bewildered. "How?"

He poured white liquid from a breast-shaped vase into a breast-shaped glass. Then handing me the smaller glass the dog-man commanded, "Drink this."

I drank the contents. It tasted foul. For a few moments, I

closed my eyes, trying to take in all the dog-man said.

"The usual way, I suspect," he said answering my question. "Someone placed it in your food. They used the blue lotus to mask the bitter taste of the poison. Whoever did the job was skilled at mixing the poison, less so with the masking agent."

"I thought I heard you chanting in a strange language," I said.

"A healing incantation I learned in Strongili and of their dialect."

Opening my eyes, I regained my focus. Instead of seeing Anubis, I made out the face of Harwa, his long beard cut. Still, his soft brown eyes shone with mischief. Harwa, my unofficial teacher, teller of forbidden stories, stood by my bed. He was the "swamp person" who dropped out of society before the war of reunification. He learned his skill with poisons and their cures, serving as an advisor and cupbearer to the Pharaoh of the Lower Kingdom, ruled by the non-Egyptian rulers.

Looking around, I saw the intricate design of a baby in a reed basket painted into the footboard of the bed. A stone table with four legs beyond the bed, surrounded by two wooden chairs, came into focus. To my right, a window allowed for the view to the outdoors. Tapestries hung on the wall, depicting the gods of Egypt, with Amun-Re most prominent.

Wrapped around my wrist was an amulet inscribed with pictures of snakes and scorpions. Before I could ask, Harwa explained. "That is a healing amulet. Nefertari placed it on you prior to sending for me."

"How did you get to my room in the palace?" I asked.

"I walked," he joked. Then, with a stern expression, he said, "Nefertari recognized that your illness was not usual. She had Miriam find me, and I came right away."

"Does Ahmose…" I asked, but my hurting head welcomed Harwa's interruption.

"No one knows I am here. Nefertari made sure of that. Hence, my shaved beard. Pharaoh would not welcome me, as far as I know. Nefertari disguised me as your manservant."

"Why did she think to summon you? Did Rekhmire not know of an antidote?" I asked. "Not that I am unhappy you are here."

Before Harwa could answer, we heard voices beyond the

door of my room. "I will see my son when I want to see him," bellowed Ahmose.

"Now he is your son?" a woman's voice replied. "Because you think he can provide a service to you?"

"This is not the place to have this discussion, Nefertari!"

Harwa motioned for me to be quiet. "Pretend you are asleep," he whispered as he moved away from the bed towards an alcove hidden by tapestries.

Just as he settled into his hiding place, my adopted parents entered the room. Ahmose, Pharaoh of Egypt and his sister-wife, Nefertari, stood in the doorway.

"Do not wake him," Nefertari whispered as they approached me.

"I need to know if he is well," Ahmose whispered back.

"He is not ready to do your deed just yet, regardless," my adopted mother replied.

"You are sure it was poison?" Ahmose asked.

"Yes, Ahmose," she said exasperated. "He is showing many signs of a toxin, including the yellowing of his fingernails."

"Who poisoned him?" Ahmose asked.

"Are you blind?" Nefertari responded.

"Anyone could have done it," Ahmose defended.

"Not anyone," another voice came through the doorway. Pharaoh and his wife must have motioned for him to be quiet, as he did not speak anymore. I only heard him walking towards the bed.

"Ramose ingested a very rare combination of herbs that can overwhelm the mixer of them," whispered the other person. "Only someone proficient in crafting poisons could make this concoction."

I recognized the voice of my teacher, Rekhmire, who served as one of the top three advisors to Ahmose, Pharaoh of Egypt. Balaam and Iyov also held positions as advisors and taught my other brothers. Iyov primarily taught fighting, though he did not teach me well. I had not yet had Balaam for a teacher.

"Rekhmire, you were once my cupbearer. Could you have done this?" Ahmose asked.

"Nay, my lord. My knowledge is limited to plants from the Upper Kingdom. It is in part why we had Nebamun succeed me in those duties. He has more knowledge of the poisons offered by the Northern Kingdom. Besides, I have no reason to kill Ramose."

"Rekhmire did not know how to treat this poison, Ahmose," Nefertari added.

"So he says," Ahmose said suspiciously. "How did you find a cure then?"

"A Habiru midwife," Nefertari responded. "Though she did not identify the particular poison, she is adept with healing herbs. She had several mixtures that work on many ailments."

"Who else knows how to make these poisons?" Ahmose asked.

"Only a few people I know, your Majesty," Rekhmire responded. "We lost most of the knowledge of poisons and distillations when the kingdoms split. I found allusions to poisonings of this type in the texts we found in the Hyksos temples. There may be more people who know this art than we suspect. I know Balaam has skills, for he came from the Northern Kingdom."

"Why would Balaam want to murder Ramose? That makes less sense than imagining that you were the one."

"True, your Majesty. But he could have taught one of his students the methods."

"You believe Siamun would poison his brother, Rekhmire?"

"I believe it to be a possibility, my Lord. It would not be the first case of fratricide in an Egyptian royal family. And there was a clumsiness to the potion, to be sure. Ramose's hallucinations suggest too much blue lotus in the mixture. An expert apothecary would not have made that mistake."

"What are you implying?" Ahmose asked.

"Nothing, your Majesty," Rekhmire replied. "Other than poisonings amongst brothers has been commonplace in our history."

"Ramose is the youngest son, however. Siamun gains nothing by his death."

"Other than avenging his embarrassment," Nefertari responded. "Siamun was not pleased that Ramose bested him in combat."

"How did he do that?" Ahmose asked in quiet amazement, "with so little training."

"You can ask him when he feels better," Nefertari

suggested. "We can return when he is awake. In the meantime, to be safe, we should devise a plan to separate Siamun and Ramose. Assuming Siamun did the poisoning, I do not want Siamun to have another chance to kill him."

I heard them close the door behind themselves as they left. Harwa then stepped forward from the alcove as I sat up.

"That answers that question," Harwa said.

"What question was that?"

"Rekhmire knows how to make poisons. Nefertari called me because she was not sure of Rekhmire's involvement."

"Was he?" I asked. Now I feared that my trusted teacher may have tried to kill me.

"Rekhmire has little to gain from your death, and I doubt he would have shared information about the scrolls he found had it involved him." Harwa paused for a moment, looking off into the distance as he did when he pondered something, as though his gaze could pierce an invisible veil of time.

"Rekhmire is correct. Someone taught your poisoner the craft, but their clumsiness reveals them to be a neophyte. Otherwise, you would not have had so many visions alerting Amenhotep to find your mother."

"Why me?"

"You keep asking that question, Ramose, as though you have no control over the situation."

"I did not poison myself!" I exclaimed.

Harwa laughed. "I hope not, though you would not be the first person to do that. Nor the last."

"Why would someone want to kill me?"

"You ask that question? Remember how you lost control with Maiherpri? He desires revenge. And I heard about how you toyed with Siamun. You play a dangerous game, Ramose."

"I only defend myself."

"That is one way to look at it. Every action has an opposite reaction with equal force."

"They hated me before I beat them."

"True. But your actions created more fear in both boys; something neither is accustomed to, nor likes."

"Still, you seem to believe it is my fault."

"This is not about blame, Ramose, or victimhood.

Everything that happens to you and around you reflects something within you."

"What does that mean?"

"The hostility you face reflects the bitterness within you."

"Since I was little, animosity has met me everywhere I have turned," I argued. "I did nothing to bring that upon myself!"

"Keep your voice down." He listened if anyone heard. Then whispered, "That may be. Each of us carries within us the past of our ancestors. All of their actions affect you, just as all of your actions will influence future generations."

I thought about this for a moment, then asked, "How?"

"Remember the vibrations you sensed in the water, rocks, and trees?" he asked. When I nodded, he continued. "The frequencies stay with us. Everyone vibrates at a different rate and maybe multiple rates in different areas of their lives. When you touched the abyss while breathing, you slowed your rate down to see it."

"Is that why I flinched? It was uncomfortable?"

"You are learning," Harwa smiled. "That is exactly what occurred. Keep at it. Over time, it will become more comfortable and you can clear the vibrations of your ancestors."

"What ancestor shapes my actions?"

"Are you not a Levite?" he asked rhetorically. He had told me of my origins. "Levi and Simeon committed an act so heinous that Jacob cursed the brothers on his deathbed instead of giving them a blessing."

"What did they do?" I asked.

"They had incited violence under the pretense of peace and murdered innocent people."

"Why?"

"Jacob and his sons lived near a town in Canaan. Remember that Abraham insisted that Isaac not marry a woman from the local area. Isaac insisted that of Jacob and Esau too. Jacob tried to instill the same on his sons, but the younger ones married Canaanite women."

Harwa continued the story explaining how Dinah, Jacob's only daughter, ventured to town to meet with the women there. Dinah's beauty struck the magistrate's son, Shechem, who wished to lie with her. As she was not to marry a

Canaanite, she refused, so he raped her. Shechem's father, Hamor, approached Jacob to plead for forgiveness. Hamor suggested the two children marry. Jacob realized Hamor outnumbered his clan and wanted to plan an effective response to this outrage.

"Does not Hamor mean 'ass' in Hittite?" I asked.

Harwa smiled. "I am glad your lessons are teaching you something. Jacob used that name when he told me the story."

Though my jaw hurt doing so, I smiled.

"Jacob's sons devised a plan, asking Hamor and his clan to become circumcised to allow Shechem to marry Dinah. They agreed and while they recuperated, Levi and Simeon slaughtered everyone in the village. Outraged, Jacob rebuked his sons for killing everyone under the circumstances."

"Why?" I asked, perplexed. "Shechem raped his daughter. Ma'at teaches his family deserves punishment for his actions too."

"I am amazed how someone so young has the wisdom to discern who deserves punishment."

"Shechem raped Dinah. That justifies revenge!"

"You sound like Miriam," Harwa replied. "Unlike you and your sister, I do not pretend to understand God's view of justice. And neither did Jacob. His encounter with the divine shook him to the core. No rule of law existed in that part of Canaan. Hamor ruled the town where Jacob and his sons lived. While he felt justified in punishing Shechem, he was waiting for inspiration before acting."

"What do you mean?"

"Each of us carries the memories of our family. Those memories can incite us to action, but it is not necessarily the right approach. Waiting for inspiration from the divine requires patience. Jacob rebuked his sons on his deathbed because his sons acted for selfish reasons. He knew the sons of Levi and the sons of Simeon would carry the impulse for violence. He wanted them scattered amongst the Children of Israel to avoid them inciting disorder within the country."

"How do I know if I am being inspired by the divine or by a memory?"

"You know only after you act," Harwa responded. My confused look made him add, "It is why we purify ourselves every moment. Focusing on the divine, on El Shaddai. You must become pure presence, breathing at the moment as it unfolds. Over time, you learn to just know."

Because I still felt light-headed from the poison, its remedy, or having vomited my dinner, I could not grasp Harwa's explanation. "What day is it?" I asked.

"Forgive me. Here I am trying to teach you something when you have not eaten for two days."

Rising, he walked to the door, peaked into the hallway, rang a tiny bell, then closed the door to return to my bedside. "Someone will bring you food in a few moments. Now, where were we? I remember, everything you see reflects something within you."

"How?"

"Because you are the only thing in the universe; I am the only thing in the universe."

***

A rhythmic knock at the door interrupted Harwa again. He walked to the door and tapped it three times in rapid succession. Two quick beats came in response. Harwa opened the door, revealing Nefertari holding a tray of food. She entered the room while he closed the door behind her. He pulled a small table to my bedside as my adopted mother placed the tray on it.

"You are awake," Nefertari stated.

In between bites, I told her I had been awake when she and Ahmose entered the room. She smiled in response and told me she was glad I waited to speak to Ahmose until we could talk.

"You know your life is in danger," she said.

"Siamun wants to kill me," I responded.

"I only want Ahmose to believe I think it was Siamun. I do not know who is trying to murder you, but I intend to find out."

"Who else would want to kill me?"

"There are Teta and his son, Maiherpri. Not to mention Balaam, though he possesses the skills to make a poison without causing hallucinations. And your presence at the palace terrifies several noble families."

Nefertari sat on the bed next to me, throwing her arms around me and hugging me. "What am I to do with you,

120

Ramose?" she said before releasing me. "You are almost of age of marriage. Soon, Ahmose will find a role for you in the government. Many nobles fear your retaliation."

"Why?" I asked.

"Because you bested Siamun and Maiherpri in mock battles. They fear the Habiru prowess in combat and that you learned so fast. There is talk amongst the nobles that you will teach other Habirus how to fight, leading to a revolt against the legal Egyptian rule."

"That is ridiculous," I argued.

"I know dear," she said. "But they do not. We must be careful about what role you have going forward."

"Do you know which families fear me, mother?" I asked.

"Most. Why do you ask?"

"I had the strangest vision before I awoke in my bed."

"The blue lotus causes hallucinations, Ramose," Harwa explained. "Pay them no heed."

Ignoring Harwa, I explained that I saw a parade of strange beings. "First a man wearing a headdress with papyrus growing out of it approached me. Then a woman that looked like a frog. I recognized them as Hapi and Heqet. I was not sure if the other visions were gods or symbols of noble families."

"Who else approached you?"

"After Heqet, a man with a goose on his head and a snake around his neck."

"Geb," Harwa mused.

"Then a man with the head of a fly," I continued. "Followed by a beautiful woman wearing a headdress with a red solar disk on her head and the horns of a bull."

"Khepri and Hathor," Harwa interjected.

"Another beautiful woman appeared with a jug on her head. When I did not follow her instructions, the room darkened, and it rained. Telling you this now seems odd, but at the time it frightened me. Especially when the woman disappeared, and a man with a jackal head appeared."

"Nut, the sky goddess, and her consort, Seth, the storm god," Harwa explained.

"Then Siamun dressed as Pharaoh attacked me with a sword. I think he killed me. What does this all mean?"

Harwa and Nefertari gave one another concerned looks but

said nothing.

"Siamun will not become Pharaoh," Nefertari said. "He would destroy the kingdom."

"But were the other people I saw representations of the noble families?" I asked.

"If I had the skills of dream interpretation as your great Uncle Joseph did," Harwa said, "I could decipher your visions. But I do not think they were the families of the nobles. They seemed too much like the different gods. As you know, the people consider Pharaoh a deity."

"What does each god represent?" I asked.

"You know Hapi is the god of the Nile and Heqet the frog goddess," Harwa said. He told me about each god in my vision.

As I ate, Nefertari said, "Odd that your hallucinations would be that clear about each deity."

"It seemed less like a hallucination and more like a vision. Each of the gods pleaded with me to stop their destruction."

"What did you mean, Ramose?" Harwa asked.

"It sounds too brash."

"Tell us."

"Some gods wanted me to become Pharaoh. As though I could stop the destruction coming to Egypt. Otherwise a series of plagues will afflict the land and the people."

"That does not sound brash," Harwa whispered. "Remember when you asked me about a prophecy? This vision is like that prophecy."

"Harwa!" Nefertari exclaimed. "This is not the time to discuss this!"

"I agree," Harwa said. "I need to go. But the time nears, Nefertari."

"I know," she conceded. "I am just not ready for Ramose to grow up just yet."

"That may be. But we may want him to leave Waset for a while. Can you send him to the Northeastern desert to gain leadership and combat experience? Let us get him away from Siamun and convince the nobles about his loyalty fighting desert tribes."

"I do not want to fight my people," I protested.

"It is unlikely you will. Only a small group of Habirus ran

back to Canaan. Some made it. Various tribes and wanderers still populate the desert."

"An excellent idea, Harwa!" Nefertari said. "I will suggest this to Ahmose."

"You need to send him with someone you trust. Someone who will not betray him."

"I know just the person," Nefertari said.

14

For the next month, I spent my time confined to my chamber recovering. Rekhmire visited me daily, bringing a small ivory wand with hieroglyphics inscribed on the surface. While waving it over me as I lay in my bed, he chanted unfamiliar words. Towards the end of that month, I asked him about his actions.

"What is that?" I asked.

"It is a healing wand," Rekhmire responded.

"I thought you were a magician," I said.

"I am. Physicians and magicians perform both roles. Most magicians heal people when not working in the temples. I have other roles in the kingdom. But many temple priests spend their time casting healing spells as I am right now for you. People hire them to create or lift curses, too. My early training included the healing arts."

"What is inscribed on the wand?"

"Each wand differs by what you wish to accomplish. This one calls upon Isis for protection against demons and enemies."

"How does waving the wand protect me?"

Rekhmire smiled. "That question exposes your Habiru heritage. Are we to debate the power of idols again?"

"I do not believe it necessary," I smiled. Ever since learning about my forefather, Abraham, smashing idols, I wondered about any form of idolatry.

"Even if there is only one God as your Habiru ancestors suggest, I do not see why it could not have divided itself into many forms?"

"Possibly," I conceded. Then changing the subject, "Is something specific written on the wand?"

"It is how the wand works."

"How would words written on a piece of ivory heal someone?"

"Words have power, Ramose," he replied. "Combined with intent, words carry potency to change anything."

"How?"

"Amun-Re imbued everything around us with magic. Our thoughts affect everything, regardless of the intent of our Ba. Most people are unaware of their thoughts and feelings which creates unintended consequences. This is one thing that makes you unusual with your peers."

"What do you mean?"

"You can quiet your mind to hear what is around you. You know what you feel. Your ability to focus intention, to learn, to strike with power—it is very unusual, Ramose. A gift. And a curse."

"How is it a curse?"

"With power comes responsibility. Most people prefer to wallow in their own sense of victimhood rather than embrace the burden of inner strength."

Harwa said something similar earlier that month. As I grew older, I learned the wisdom of their teaching. But in that moment, I ignored his comment and asked, "And the wand?"

"The writing reinforces the ideas. I use the device to help focus on my goal. I see the symbols as I chant, which allows me to manifest the intended desire."

Using idols perplexed me, but the wand as a concentration device made some sense.

He continued his incantation for the better part of an hour. When he finished, he handed me something to drink.

"Is this one of those foul-tasting brews?"

"Drink it," he demanded, and I did as requested. "It is the last you will need for you are better. Tomorrow we shall continue your lessons."

"Can I leave my room today?" I asked.

"I do not see why not."

***

As Rekhmire left, I rose to dress myself. While doing so, my servant Paser entered the room, informing me that Nefertari misjudged Ahmose's willingness to send me to the desert. Pharaoh flat-out refused to let me command troops. He believed Siamun and Amenhotep deserved the honor first. Ahmose dispatched Siamun to the East to fight escaped Habiru slaves, remnants of Hyksos forces, and Midianites, the people who lived in that region.

Though angry, I said nothing to Paser. Instead, I ran to the river. Late Shemu, the driest time of the year in Egypt, made the ground hard and cracked. The soil waited for the inundation of Akhet to renew it and be ready for the planting season of Peret.

I followed my typical path past palm and pomegranate trees. The papyrus plumes were small, longing for the water to bring their glory out. I failed to notice the vegetation, though, in my search for Harwa, who often waited in an isolated region of Pharaoh's private land knowing I alone could find him. That day, he was there and greeted me as I walked up.

"How are you feeling, Ramose?"

"Angry!" I replied. I told him of Ahmose's decision.

He considered my statement for a moment, then said, "It is the right choice."

"But–" I began.

Harwa interrupted me. "Our goal was to separate you two. Away from here, Siamun cannot poison you. Let him leave. Commanding others is not all that easy and maybe Ahmose will see his shortcomings. Besides, Ahmose is right. Going out of order will only confuse the men serving under your command. They may not follow your commands if they believe you are trying to usurp your brothers."

"It is unfair!" I complained.

"Many things in life are. They just are. You can accept what is or fight it."

As I still felt the injustice of the situation, Harwa led me through some Tahtib exercises to help me channel my anger. For over an hour, I swung a rod through the air, striking at imaginary opponents. It felt good to move after my long confinement. But my convalescence showed as I tired easily from the exertion. Sweat streamed down my body, for the day was hot.

In a matter of days, the Nile would flood, marking Wepet-Renpet, the celebration of the New Year. Ahmose-Ankh, my oldest brother, would return from Buhen in the South as fighting against the Nubians stopped for the rainy season.

Sitting next to Harwa, he handed me some water to drink and dried fish to eat. "Ahmose and Nefertari decided together to send Siamun away, for reasons that have nothing to do with you."

"Which are?"

"He tried to defile Meritamen." Harwa spoke gravely. "They save her for Ahmose-Ankh."

"That does not surprise me. Siamun assaults many of the palace servants, male or female. Paser avoids him as much as possible. Why is it you have heard about this when I have not?"

Harwa winked at me. "Maybe you should try to talk to your servants about something other than your desires."

"What do you mean?" I defended.

"As someone who feels victimized living with the royal family, you have isolated yourself from the people of your birth. Did you know Paser is Habiru?"

I shook my head.

"I thought not," Harwa continued. "Nefertari found you a servant you could be comfortable around. He is from the tribe of Dan."

"Why does he possess an Egyptian name?"

"Most Habirus have them, Ramose! They have adapted to the ways of Egypt to fit with the culture. The servants know what is happening at the palace. Unless you get to know them, you will not learn of what occurs."

"How would they know?"

"This question reveals how little you pay attention to what is around you. Servants surround you. They observe your every move, and you pay them no heed. One may have poisoned you. Or seen your poisoner!"

"I had not thought of that," I admitted.

"Your survival depends upon your powers of observation,

Ramose. And creating allies for yourself in the palace may keep you alive."

"I have befriended Amenhotep," I defended.

"That is good," Harwa interrupted. "But he too ignores those around him." Harwa paused for a moment. "You are being raised to view yourself as above others. Most Egyptians consider you a deity."

"They do?" Knowing all of my faults, I did not understand how anyone would see me that way.

"Setting yourself apart from the rest of the people only weakens you in the long run."

"How do I get to know them?" I wondered.

"Ask them about their lives. Get to know them as people, not someone who answers your requests. Start with Paser. He will introduce you to others you can trust. Eventually, you may determine who poisoned you."

"I thought it was Siamun."

"Maybe it was Siamun. But whoever was behind it, someone knows something."

"Did you or Nefertari ask the workers?"

"We did, but we learned little. Most do not know me, and Nefertari is a royal, feared by most Egyptians. The Habiru servants at the palace see you as their champion."

"Me? Why?"

"That is becoming a familiar refrain for you," Harwa laughed. "Because you are Habiru and you are being groomed for an influential role in the Egyptian government. Even if you never become Pharaoh, you will shape policy to help the Habiru people. They know that. But you will need to gain their trust."

"By talking to them?"

"Yes, just get to know the workers as people, not as servants. Pharaoh took a significant risk in welcoming you into the family. Other besides Siamun wish you dead. Possibly, Siamun mixed the poison at the behest of another. If you want to know what happens at the palace, who Siamun meets, ask Paser."

"How do I know that Paser did not poison me?" I asked.

"I spoke to him."

"What did he say?"

"It was less what he said, but how he said it. What happened to you and that he missed the poison embarrassed him greatly. Back to work!"

Harwa ran me through another hour of Tahtib practice before sending me back to the palace. I arrived at my room to find Paser drawing a bath for me. Paser's appearance defied his age. Though I knew he only lived several inundations longer than my oldest brother, Ahmose-Ankh, he looked older because of hard work and living in adverse conditions for much of his life. Now that I knew of his Habiru heritage, Paser's height made sense. He was a full head taller than my brother with long muscular arms. Paser wore a dull sand-colored tunic similar to all the house staff at the palace. His long nose extended from his clean-shaven face softened by his kind eyes. How did I not notice he was Habiru?

Greeting him, I asked about his day. Giving me a suspicious glance, he replied it was fine.

"Thank you for taking care of me when I was ill," I said.

Stiffening, he replied, "It is my job, My Lord."

I smiled. "You did more than required."

"Thank you, my Lord." The curtness to his tone remained.

I struggled against my bias and inexperience in speaking to servants. Though I had known Paser most of my life, I did not know how to talk to him. I undressed and climbed into the tub. "You are from the tribe of Dan?"

"Yes, my Lord."

"Do you know Jacob's blessing to Dan?"

"I do not, My Lord."

"Paser, please call me Ramose when we are in private. All these 'My Lords' are cumbersome."

Paser smiled. "Thank you, my... Ramose. What did Jacob say to my grandfather?"

"'Dan shall judge his people, as a tribe of Israel. Dan shall be a serpent in the way, a horned snake in the path, that bites the horse's heels, so that his rider falls backward. I wait for Thy salvation, O Lord!'"

"What in the name of Re does that mean?"

"I hoped you might know." We both laughed and joked how Harwa would tell us something obscure without explaining. I told him the other blessings including the ones for Reuben, Levi, and Simeon which sounded more like curses than blessings.

"Come to think about it," he said, "the words sound familiar. My grandmother told me a rhyme about the tribes of Jacob."

"Did she know the meaning?" I asked.

"Not that I recall. You are from the tribe of Levi?"

"I am. Harwa explained that causes my recklessness."

Paser smiled. "I think you are brave, Ramose. You stand up to the bullies. Maybe if more of our brethren did that..." He left the thought hanging, then looked away, ashamed for his boldness. His words highlighted a problem within the Habiru community. Not everyone disagreed with Ahmose's policies. The divisions between the Habiru tribes would be the major stumbling block to my saving the Egyptians from the fate of the plagues. But that was many years away.

"Paser is not a Habiru name," I asked trying to change the subject to help him feel at ease.

"No, it is not," he answered, his anger still showing. "When I moved to the palace, the Vizier gave me the name."

"I understand. Ramose is not my birth name either."

We shared our Habiru names with one another, chatting while I finished bathing. Paser handed me a towel as I stepped out of the tub.

I said, "I know you had nothing to do with my being poisoned."

"I am sorry I allowed it to happen, Ramose."

"It is not your fault."

"My carelessness permitted the person to gain access to your food."

"Because you did not stand by my food the entire time? That sounds ridiculous."

"Maybe so. But we knew someone was trying to kill you. I will not make the same mistake."

"Do you think it was Siamun?"

"He may have mixed the poison, Ramose, and asked one of his trusted servants to place it in the food. But there is no way he could have placed the poison in the food himself. One of my friends would have seen him. I have learned nothing else, however. I told Harwa that I will let you know if I learn anything."

"Thank you, Paser."

"You should know there is a division between the servants at the palace," he warned.

"Oh?" I said, looking up from dressing to see the distress on his face.

"Ahmose's policies favoring Egyptians cause the lowliest servant to look down upon Habirus. They view dirt better than us!"

"How preposterous! They too are subjugated!"

"Maybe so, but it does not change things for you. It means that resentment towards you foments amongst the non-Habiru servants."

"Any of them could have delivered the poison."

"That is correct."

"I will discuss this with my mother."

Paser smiled. If nothing else, she might transfer the servants harboring resentment from the palace. We discussed Ahmose-Ankh's return for Wepet-Renpet, and my excitement to see my oldest brother. Paser liked my oldest brother, Ahmose-Ankh, for the same reason I did. He accepted the Habirus as people worthy of citizenship within Egyptian society and not just defeated foes to enslave. Ahmose-Ankh welcomed me to the family readily when I first came to the palace.

"You arrived at the palace around this time this time of the year?" Paser asked me.

"I did. This will be my seventh year here."

"Soon you will come of age, maybe this year or next."

I shrugged, not knowing what to say. My coming of age would create problems I wished to ignore for the moment. The possibility existed that until I reached maturity, more attempts on my life were possible.

When I said nothing, Paser spoke. "Ahmose-Ankh wished to meet my Aunt Serah. Would you like to join us?"

"Serah is your aunt?"

"You know of her?"

"Harwa mentioned her," I said. "I thought she was Asher's daughter."

"She is the daughter of Asher and not from my tribe. But she adopted the children of Dan because the rest of Jacob's children viewed us as outsiders. She is not my aunt, but that is what they call her. I love hearing her stories about Jacob, Joseph, and the family. And she holds hope for our redemption."

"Redemption?" I said naively.

"When Joseph died, he instructed us to stay until the right time. A leader or prophet would reveal himself as the one to lead us out of Egypt."

"Has anyone proclaimed himself leader?" I asked.

"Two false prophets did so. Serah saw right through both and denounced each of them."

"Serah must be a powerful woman."

"She is very unusual," Paser admitted with admiration.

***

Amenhotep's knock on the door interrupted us. Standing in the doorway, I saw he looked different since my illness began. In the last month, he appeared to have lost his baby fat, giving his face a more angular appearance. His eyes seemed broader and more pronounced, like both his parents, Ahmose and Nefertari. But Amenhotep's features favored his father. He looked to have grown, for he was taller than me and had developed big muscles in his arms.

"Hello," my adopted brother said. "I came to let you know dinner is almost ready."

Paser excused himself as I changed my clothes into something appropriate for a royal meal.

"How are you feeling?" Amenhotep asked. "Better, I guess. I came by earlier to see you and you were out. Where did you go?"

"I feel much better, thanks. Rekhmire pronounced me recovered, so I went to spend time by the river."

"You could have asked me to go with you."

"I am sorry," I said. I was not sure why he lingered to talk, as our relationship had fluctuated between distant and close. Some days my adopted brother showed interest in my life. But his demeanor changed when his friends arrived, as if I embarrassed his good standing.

"I left in a hurry," I replied. When he looked at me, puzzled, I told him how upset I was about Siamun getting to command troops. "He will get men killed."

"Not to hear him tell it," he replied. "When he left a half-moon ago, he boasted that he would kill the Habiru traitors."

"He is a terrible fighter. Once the men in his command figure that out, they will not listen to him."

"Perhaps you are right, Ramose. But we can do nothing about it. Besides, that is not the real reason for Siamun's journey."

"I heard about what happened," I replied, referring to Siamun's failed attempt to rape our sister, Meritamen. "Why are they concerned with his actions now? He has raped half the servants in the palace."

"I know," Amenhotep agreed. "He acts as a common soldier. Why does Father believe someone so undisciplined can rule?"

"You look different," I proclaimed.

"You do too!" he exclaimed. "And I do not mean your illness. You seem taller and stronger too."

"Paser said I come of age soon. I suppose you will, too."

"Right, and when that happens, both of us will receive positions in government and married off for political purposes."

"Married?"

"Ahmose-Ankh and Meritamen will marry as part of the Wepet-Renpet festival. But Father and Mother will use the rest of us to shore up alliances in the region."

Amenhotep explained the ritual. Just like Osiris and Isis, the oldest son and daughter marry and ascend the throne. Ahmose and Nefertari were siblings, though she married Ahmose after their brother Kamose died. I noticed Paser working in my room cleaning up my bath listening to our conversation. I realized Harwa was correct. The servants learned all that occurs in the palace.

"Some Pharaohs take other wives for political purposes, but given the number of children in the family, I doubt Ahmose-Ankh will marry another if Meritamen produces an heir."

"But that means that Ahmose will choose my wife?"

"Yes, at least, your first one."

"Do you know who they are thinking about for me?"

"I overheard Ahmose, Rekhmire, and Balaam discussing the daughter of a Kushite chieftain for you. I heard little of what Balaam said for his back was to me. But I thought I heard him say the chief wished you to prove yourself in battle."

"Prove myself in battle?"

"Lead men. It may be why he sent Siamun to fight. He is closer to marriage, anyway. As the youngest son of Pharaoh, you provide the lowest status as an ally. He gains more influence over the other chieftains if you prove yourself powerful."

A pit formed in my stomach. Why did I need to prove myself to marry anyone? Disgusted, I changed the subject once again. "How is it working with Balaam?" I asked. Rekhmire taught me most of the time. His knowledge of magic was unsurpassed in the kingdom. While Iyov taught us fighting, I realized I knew little about Balaam.

"Different."

"How?"

"Lots of ways. He is proficient in magic, but Balaam does not like to read old scrolls or use wands like Rekhmire."

"Then how does he do magic?"

"He says with his mind. Balaam believes there is one God. He thinks we are all part of the same being. Idols help conceptualize aspects of the one, but he finds them unnecessary."

Amenhotep's words nagged at me. I tried recalling what it might be, something about how Rekhmire and Balaam perform magic in different ways. I ceased trying to remember and said to Amenhotep. When "Rekhmire said something similar to me today. He uses idols and wands to focus his concentration."

"But he believes in many gods," Amenhotep countered.

"True. Rekhmire uses the device needed when drawing upon the power of that god. He used a wand of Isis for healing and protection. But he says that magic permeates all things."

"That makes sense. Use the god or goddess associated with the power you want to evoke. Though Balaam is my teacher now, I still do not understand how he performs magic. How does he do magic at all if everything is the same in his eyes?"

Over the course of the last few seasons, Miriam, Amenhotep, and I often discussed this question. While Miriam and I sensed the interconnectedness of all things, Amenhotep struggled to grasp it. We had discussed many topics including magic, governing, and how to create a fair society whereby all have access to food and shelter. These conversations would shape many of our future laws.

"You have different parts of your personality," I said, trying a different approach. "For example, your behavior differs when you are alone with me versus how you act when Maiherpri and Hannu are there."

"What does that have to do with anything?" Amenhotep snapped, glaring at me.

"I am sorry. I do not mean to touch a difficult subject. I act differently with you than with Rekhmire. We show different parts of ourselves at various times."

"Oh. I guess that makes sense," he admitted calming himself.

Glad he accepted my explanation, I thought for a moment how to explain the existence of one god, and the story of creation that Harwa told me, of how existence pulled itself into a ball and spit itself forth. I did not understand how El Shaddai created both direction and containment at the same time. Later, at Mount Horeb, I would understand this aspect of manifesting.

"Here is another way to think about this," I said. I repeated the story of Amun-Re creating the world to Amenhotep, then asked, "What created Horus, or Osiris?"

Amenhotep pondered that for a few moments before he responded. "Amun-Re did. He existed before all else."

"And who created Re?"

"No one. Re is just Re, and all things sprang from him."

"How?"

Exasperated, Ahmose barked, "It just happened."

"Which brings us back to there being only one God."

"How?"

"Because whatever created everything must also infuse everything."

"Balaam uses that everything to perform magic?"

"That must be it," I said with more certainty than I felt. If Balaam used the ALL to perform magic, could he be doing magic without a wand or props? "Balaam worked for Apepi?"

"Briefly. He advised Khamudi during the war."

"Why did Ahmose keep Balaam as an advisor?"

"I do not know," Amenhotep confessed. "I remember Rekhmire saying he was a skilled negotiator."

"I vaguely remember something about that." Harwa once told me that Balaam possessed a remarkable ability to manipulate people. I recalled watching Ahmose changing his mind after Balaam spoke. Both times I went to the audience chamber to observe the proceedings I felt the power of persuasion.

"Do you know where Balaam came from?"

"Somewhere west, I think. Did I tell you he saw my becoming Pharaoh? He is teaching me ideas about rulership, and the divine nature of Pharaoh. Maybe that is why the idea of one god confuses me. He believes in one god one moment, but then mentioned this idea of a divine monarch."

"Not to state the obvious but for you to become king…"

He finished my sentence. "Ahmose-Ankh and Siamun both need to die. Yes, I know. I do not want Ahmose-Ankh to die. Balaam did not say how this would happen. He has been wrong before. He thought the Hyksos would defeat the Egyptians. He failed to account for Father's skill as a military commander."

I mustered a response, "Interesting," but a pit formed in my stomach. I knew my oldest brother faced danger, but I did not know how to respond. Tell him that there was a plot against him? Even if he believed me, how would he protect himself? And maybe no conspiracy existed at all. Maybe Balaam envisioned Ahmose-Ankh dying in an accident.

"Ramose, do you believe in one god?" Amenhotep asked.

"What?" I stumbled out of my thoughts. "Yes, I do. I think I believe in other gods, but they do not differ from you and me. We are all aspects of the one. Something controls them."

"But how would something control a god? For example, no one tells my father what to do."

"He does not control everything," I said.

"How does one god control everything? Does it intervene in our lives?"

"Maybe this one god delegates. The Pharaoh creates policies that others implement. At least, that is what Rekhmire told me. A good ruler always delegates."

I could tell Amenhotep wished to learn more about how to

be a good ruler. He liked to do things well. But the feeling about Ahmose-Ankh lingered with me. Balaam had not been the only one to see Amenhotep as Pharaoh. My biological sister, Miriam, foretold the same the first time she met Amenhotep. That day, Siamun tortured a frog in front of Amenhotep and me, precipitating our friendship. I said nothing to Amenhotep as the event still traumatized him. Four years after the incident, he still disliked frogs.

As I finished dressing, I turned to look at my brother. We smiled at one another, then left my room to join the other royals for dinner

15

The grand double staircase of the palace started at two different points of the upstairs before arriving at a large landing mid-floor. The two sides joined in the middle, descending as a wide stairway to the ground level. Ornate carvings of wood inlaid with gold portrayed scenes of heroism from various Egyptian stories. Guards stood at the bottom of the steps preventing non-royals from wandering into the private apartments of the Pharaoh and his family.

Amenhotep and I traversed this staircase on our way to the evening meal. We turned left, walking through the wide corridor, columns to either side of us. The pillars divided the vast space into three walkways. Painted murals of Amun-Re, Pharaohs, and other subjects of Egyptian history covered the walls on both sides. The hieroglyphic pictures lacked the same depth, colors, and sophistication of the Minoan artwork adorning the walls of the palace in Avaris. The Upper Kingdom in Waset had limited access to Minoan culture, and the palace reflected this. Ahmose removed all non-Egyptian artwork.

Arriving at the grand double doors of the dining room, two guards allowed us entrance. The dining hall expanded out from the entryway, creating a cavernous area filled. Smaller doors gained entrance to the room at the opposite end, two doors on the left and one to the far right. Servants stood at attention spaced two cubits away from each other along the walls, waiting to serve the meal. Balaam, Rekhmire, and Iyov milled together at the far side of the room from where we entered. The middle of the chamber contained a long table with place-settings for thirteen. For a moment, I wondered who the guests would be when I saw three nobles speaking with each other as were Rekhmire, Iyov, and Balaam. Adorned with a form-fitted white linen dress with gold inlaid around the neckline, Meritamen approached us as we came through the doors. Her well-developed breasts and hips swayed back and forth as she walked towards us. Sitamen followed her wearing a similar dress in tan.

"Good evening, my brothers," Meritamen said.

"Good evening, sisters," I responded.

"You both look lovely," Amenhotep said to the delight of the two women. They said nothing, but their faces glowed in response.

"Mother told me there is a surprise tonight," Sitamen said. "Though she did not say what."

"You shall learn about it soon enough," Meritamen replied.

A few moments later, Nefertari and Ahmose entered the room from the far side. Walking through the doorway, a flicker of anger still registered on Nefertari's face before her countenance transformed. She greeted the guests with a warm smile, welcoming them to her celebration of Wepet-Renpet. Though the official beginning of the holiday lay two or three days away, a feast for a small group of private friends and nobles heralded the New Year festivities. She went over to the three nobles speaking in the middle of the room while Ahmose migrated towards Balaam. Rekhmire and Iyov crossed the room to join the Pharaoh.

After a few moments, Nefertari motioned us over. "I want to introduce you four to Minmose, Inret, and Pentu. Each are nobles your father trusts."

I knew Minmose to be the father of Hannu, but knew nothing of the other two men. We exchanged pleasantries with them before Ahmose and his advisors joined us. Just as Ahmose was about to speak, a herald stepped into the dining hall to announce Nefertari's surprise. My oldest brother, Ahmose-Ankh entered the room.

Nefertari's face lighted to see her eldest child while

Ahmose's looked dark. The differences in their looks reminded me of the faces of the sphinxes at the stairs of the palace in Avaris. One black, one white, opposites of expression and attitudes about life.

Ahmose recovered and followed his wife to greet their son. While he wore a white linen frock similar to mine, his disheveled appearance betrayed a hasty change. I learned later he arrived from Buhen only a quarter of an hour ago. Nefertari greeted him with a big hug. Looking at the two of them together, it was clear she was his mother, though the masculine facial features gave his face sharper angularity. He wore the small chin beard in the style of Egyptians. He looked less like Ahmose than either Siamun or Amenhotep.

Each of Ahmose-Ankh's siblings hugged him in welcome, though Meritamen lingered in an embrace with him. She beamed at him as Ahmose addressed his eldest child.

"Why have you returned?" Ahmose accused his son.

Surprised by the tone, Ammi replied, "It is the festival season, and there will be no fighting because of the heavy rains. Also, mother told me to come at once, so I did."

Ahmose glared at his wife. "I ordered him to remain in Buhen."

"Why?" she responded with mock surprise. "Meritamen is of suitable age to marry, and he is our oldest son. They should marry this year during the festival. It is custom."

Before Ahmose could reply, Balaam interceded. "Your majesty, if I may."

"We know your desires, Balaam," Nefertari snarled.

"I do not," Ahmose retorted, "And would like to hear what this esteemed advisor to Pharaoh has to say."

Balaam looked between the two, then spoke. "Marriage to the oldest daughter signals to the gods that the groom become Pharaoh. However, Pharaoh questions Ahmose-Ankh's readiness to rule. Maybe there is another who is more worthy?"

As Balaam spoke, a strange sensation enveloped me as a quiet whooshing sound filled my head, causing me momentary dizziness. As fast as the sensation arrived, it dissipated.

"Yes," Ahmose agreed.

"Who is more worthy?" Rekhmire asked. "Not Siamun who cannot perform a simple mission of defeating a small band of tribes in the desert."

Balaam thought for a moment, his eyes darting back and forth as though looking for an idea. "Maybe Siamun needs training from his more experienced brother."

Once again, as he spoke, the woozy feeling came over me.

"That is an excellent idea, Balaam," Ahmose exclaimed.

"After our two oldest children marry," Nefertari said.

"Ankh must prove himself worthy," Ahmose screamed, dropping the Ahmose from his eldest son's name.

"Ahmose-Ankh's success in Nubian reveal his leadership skills and ability to rule. Besides, Siamun's tried to defile our eldest daughter and tortures animals. The soldiers under his command do not respect him!"

"Do not speak about my son that way!" shouted Ahmose.

"Maybe if you had disciplined him, he would be less cruel!" Nefertari yelled back. She stormed from the room, while everyone but Ahmose watched. Rekhmire's gaze lingered longer than felt comfortable.

Though the tension remained, Ahmose instructed us to sit. Not wishing the awkwardness to continue, we all took our seats while the servants sprang into action to serve the meal. When the door to the kitchen opened, cooking smells wafted into the dining hall, reminding me of my hunger. I had eaten little in the previous weeks because of my illness. The sight of the large platters of bread, dipping sauces, meats, and vegetables entering the room made my mouth water.

As each plate came around the table, I took large helpings of the offerings. With as much decorum as I could muster, I tore the thin soft bread to grab pieces of fowl and lamb from my plate. Spices of cumin, coriander, paprika, cinnamon, and saffron gave the meats a savory, yet sweet flavor. I wanted to ask Rekhmire the precise mixture of spices, for he taught me how to cook as part of my lessons. It was then I noticed my teacher's absence.

About a quarter of an hour later, Rekhmire and Nefertari returned to enjoy the meal. My mother said nothing of the earlier argument, increasing the apprehension for the assembled. For some time, everyone ate in silence until

Rekhmire spoke.

"How do things fair in the South, your Highness?"

"No better or worse than anywhere else in the kingdom, Rekhmire," Ahmose-Ankh responded.

Rekhmire smiled. "The natives are subdued?"

"There are pockets of resistance."

Balaam raised an eyebrow. "Pockets of resistance? That is not what I have heard."

"Do you have spies in Buhen, Balaam?" Ahmose-Ankh asked. When Balaam did not reply, my brother continued to answer Rekhmire. "Most fighting is between different Nubian factions. They could not unite behind one leader. Two of the chieftains have daughters of marriageable age. A marriage to one or both could solidify relations and prevent the Nubians from unifying."

"What are you suggesting?" Ahmose asked, his voice tipping towards anger. "That you should marry both?"

The sounds of eating halted as another potential fight brewed.

"I suggest nothing of the sort. I am saved for Meritamen. You have three other sons, however, two in this room of nearing marriageable age. Might they be considered?"

For the second time today, the subject of marriage arose associated with me, a pit formed in my stomach. Everyone resumed eating.

"Neither of your younger brothers," Balaam said, emphasizing younger to note Ahmose-Ankh excluding Siamun, "have battle experience. The chieftains in question require that of anyone who will marry their daughters." Again, I felt the whoosing sensation when Balaam spoke.

"I do not know where you heard that," Ammi responded. "Maybe a spell you have conjured?" My brother glared at Balaam. "The chieftains only require an overture from Pharaoh to offer their daughters. Each has approached me at different times asking for such an alliance."

"Ramose's prowess in battle precedes him," Minmose said. "My son, Hannu witnessed him vanquishing Maiherpri and Siamun in different contests."

"Is this true, Ramose?" Ahmose-Ankh asked, beaming.

"Lucky battles," Iyov answered for me. "He lost control of

his emotions fighting Maiherpri injuring him severely. Siamun told me later he did not try very hard."

Ahmose-Ankh's look told me he did not believe Iyov's explanation.

"Your majesty," Balaam said. "Might I suggest that we replace Siamun in the desert campaign with Ramose to gain experience for marriage. Siamun could continue his studies here with Ahmose-Ankh and Iyov."

"Why not Amenhotep?" Iyov asked.

"I think it would be good for the nobles to see Ramose fight near the region of his ancestors to prove his loyalty to Egypt." Each time Balaam spoke, the dizzy feeling rose in me.

"An excellent idea, Balaam," Ahmose replied.

Ahmose-Ankh and Nefertari exchanged concerned looks, while Meritamen rolled her eyes.

"After the wedding of our eldest children," Nefertari retorted.

"I want the head of Awawa or Kaa before he can marry his sister," Ahmose responded. "Kill one of them and you can marry Meritamen."

"That will increase tensions in the region," Ahmose-Ankh protested. "The hard work to create peace and stability for the last two years would be lost."

"My son would not question my decision," Ahmose snapped back. He glared at Ahmose-Ankh daring him to defy him, but Ammi said nothing.

After a few moments, Rekhmire tried to placate everyone, "There is no need to decide on this just yet. Fighting will be impossible in Nubia until late Akhet."

"You are right, Rekhmire," Ahmose agreed. "We have time to discuss our plans. We shall enjoy the Wepet-Renpet festivities. Then we can decide the best course of action."

Lighter discussions continued as Ahmose and Nefertari avoided speaking to one other. Ahmose-Ankh quietly ate while Meritamen tried to draw him into conversation. He politely responded at first, slowly engaging in the discussion and appeared to enjoy himself again. The nobles, advisors, and Ahmose spoke about various plans for the kingdom, including construction of Ahmose's tomb.

"I cannot believe the various noble families are bickering so much over where to place my tomb," Ahmose said.

"Selection brings a great honor to the family, your Majesty," Minmose replied.

"I do not believe the various factions seek an honor. Rather, they desier to line their pockets with money from visitors."

"Have you decided upon a spot, your Majesty?" Inret asked.

"I have, Inret," Ahmose replied. "I intend to build a pyramid in Abydos."

"Abydos, your Majesty? Rulers abandoned that place long ago."

"It is so far away, your Majesty," Pentu complained.

Ahmose waved off their complaints with a gesture. "There are many reasons for selecting Abydos. We must show all Egyptians that we are the rightful heirs to the united kingdom. By building there, no noble family gains an advantage while sealing my legacy as rightful ruler. Besides, the Chief of the Treasury, Neferperet found a massive limestone quarry nearby that provides the raw material. He oversees its opening now."

"But a pyramid, your Majesty," Inret said. "Who possesses the knowledge for such an undertaking?"

"Rekhmire found scrolls about pyramid construction. He gave them to Neferperet to begin the process."

"And there is plenty of labor," Minmose commented, looking my way with a sly smile.

Ahmose laughed but said nothing.

"A pyramid is a splendid idea," Pentu said. "Rekhmire, my congratulations to you in finding a suitable place of internment for our illustrious monarch."

He raised a glass of mead and drank. The other nobles and advisors followed suit, while Ahmose's family refused to partake in the toast.

The talk continued for some time, though I missed some conversations as my long day caught up with me. Minmose noticed me slumping in my chair, commenting about it.

"Your liberator of the Eastern Desert is falling asleep, your Majesty."

Rekhmire came to my defense. "His Highness is recovering from an extended illness."

"Fever?" Inret asked.

"Poison," Nefertari replied, her eyes steely.

"Poisoned?" Minmose asked. "Are you sure?"

"Very sure," Nefertari responded.

"Might it have been accidental, your Majesty?" Pentu suggested.

"His Highness," Rekhmire responded while eyeing Balaam, "had a rare mixture of blue lotus and mandrake."

"Hardly something that one ingests accidentally," Balaam agreed.

For a few moments, the two magicians, both advisors to Pharaoh, stared at each other as though locked in a fierce battle. The whooshing sound and woozy feeling coming on stronger than I experienced earlier in the evening. Balaam looked away.

"Ramose knows his plants well," Rekhmire said. "Hapi speaks to him."

"Is this true, Ramose?" Nefertari asked.

Still a little woozy from the evening and the whooshing feeling, I drank to steady myself.

"Maybe," I said. "I hear the whisper of the river. It tells me of its life and ways."

"What has the Nile told you of late?" Minmose asked, smirking.

"If Ahmose reopens the canal, the river will flow with blood."

Silence filled the room. Ahmose and his advisors looked at one another.

"It spoke to you again? Why did you not tell me?" Rekhmire inquired.

"I heard this before I was poisoned. I forgot about it until now," I answered.

"Are you sure the Nile told you that, Ramose?" Rekhmire asked.

"Yes. Why does it matter?" I asked. Many of the adults shared concerned looks, so I added, "I figured I was already feeling the effects of the poison."

"Do you remember why you came to the palace?" Ahmose asked.

"It was many years ago. I remember I fell and hit my head." I did not share that it was Miriam who heard the river, nor that

Miriam told me of the vision I had when I was little, for I feared betraying Nefertari.

"Does the river tell you how to stop the catastrophe?" Ahmose asked.

"I have not asked the question."

"The next time the river speaks to you," Rekhmire advised. "Ask it how to prevent the troubles."

"I will Rekhmire," I responded. "But I may have to wait for Akhet to pass, for the river is full this time of year. It hurries along to the Great Sea with little time to answer my questions."

"We have time," he said.

"Not too much time," Minmose responded. "The canal is vital for trade to the East."

"Do not worry, Minmose," Ahmose said. "Ramose's presence will ensure the success of this project. Senusret's canal will reopen."

Ahmose smiled slyly, and Iyov and Rekhmire nodded as though the three of them implicitly understood a secret not shared by the rest of us. Balaam's face remained blank, while the nobles looked confused. Looking between the people, I suspected what Miriam had many years ago. Pharaoh possessed a secret purpose for me.

***

Betraying no emotion, Nefertari suggested Amenhotep take me back to my room. Agreeing, my brother helped me up. We said goodnight to the assembled and left the dining hall. In silence, we walked up the long stairs back to my quarters. I heard the door close, and without thinking, started undressing.

"That was an awkward evening," Amenhotep said.

In one motion, I removed my tunic and turned around, startled to see my brother remained in my room.

"I thought you left."

"Apologies, Ramose. I needed to talk to someone about what just transpired."

Calming myself, I quickly donned my clothes for sleep. "Bizarre evening," I agreed, still unsure why Amenhotep remained.

"Did I not tell you about father seeking to marry you to a Nubian princess?"

"You did," I acceded.

"Father believes Siamun or I should marry Meritamen."

Amenhotep's mention of our demented brother surprised me, but not as much as his belief that Ahmose wished Amenhotep to marry Meritamen. Keeping my thoughts still, I allowed an answer to bubble up within me. I realized my brother felt slighted by the suggestion to send me on a mission instead of him. Maybe his conversation with Balaam contributed to this idea.

Unsure of the strength of our friendship, I asked, "Are you upset that Rekhmire advised I go?"

He looked as though he would reject this notion, but instead told me the truth.

"I am the older brother!"

"Only by a few months," I conceded while Amenhotep glared at me. Then I added, "I would rather they send you."

"You were angry when you found out that Siamun would go in your place!" he yelled.

"That is true," I replied. "But I respect you. And they ask me to fight people who may be relatives to prove to some Nubian Chieftain my worthiness for marriage! This is no honor; it is a loyalty test!"

Both of us stood there agitated, hands on hips, staring at each other. For a moment, I readied myself for hand-to-hand combat with Amenhotep. He relaxed his stance and cried.

"I have lived in the shadow of both my biological brothers. Now my adopted brother usurps my turn!"

The truth out, Amenhotep blushed and turned to leave.

"Wait!" I cried out. He stopped, turned, and looked at me. "I have no desire for the throne."

"Then why did I hear Balaam, Iyov, Rekhmire, and father arguing about a prophecy?"

"What are you talking about?"

"That you would become the most significant leader in Egypt's history? Do not deny you know something!"

"I do not know what you are talking about. Is that why Balaam told you, you would be Pharaoh?"

Amenhotep nodded. He moved to sit on the divan near the center of my room. I walked over to sit on the other side.

"If you become Pharaoh..."

"... you will take my place," he interrupted. "How else can I become Pharaoh and you be the most significant leader in Egypt's history?"

There were many other great Egyptians who were not Pharaohs. Joseph my great Uncle comes to mind. Amenhotep knew nothing of him because of Ahmose's admonishment of all things not Egyptian. Imhotep, architect of the pyramids is another. But my brother would hear nothing of this. I knew I did not wish to become Pharaoh, any more than I desired Siamun to become ruler of Egypt. Though given the choice between the two, I would become Pharaoh to stop Siamun. I knew I could say nothing to change Amenhotep's beliefs about this.

"Whose prophecy was this?" I asked.

"All three of the advisors."

"I heard Iyov, Balaam, and Rekhmire each saw a great leader arise. One saw an Egyptian child while the other two foretold a Habiru. However, I heard nothing about this person becoming Pharaoh."

"It is why they brought you to live at the palace."

"What do you mean? Nefertari told me she wanted a sixth child because five is unlucky."

Amenhotep laughed. "She lied. She knew the real reason behind it."

I knew Ahmose needed a Habiru child to help him recover the staff he coveted. Something stopped me from explaining that to Amenhotep.

"Did you feel a whooshing or hear anything when Balaam spoke tonight?"

"What are you talking about?" he responded.

As best I could, I described the dizzying sensation as if the wind blew through my head. "The noise made hearing his words difficult."

"Maybe you are still feeling the effects of the poison," he volunteered.

"Possibly," I agreed. "But why did I only feel it when Balaam spoke?"

My brother shrugged. The door opening interrupted his next question.

"I thought I heard you two talking," Ahmose-Ankh said,

shutting the door as he came into the room. "Are you two debriefing the evening?"

"Yes," I said. I filled Ammi in about our conversation without mentioning Balaam's prophecy of Amenhotep becoming Pharaoh. Something I would later regret. "Amenhotep is upset I am being asked to replace Siamun."

"You are not being skipped Amenhotep. Their reasoning has little to do with you or Ramose. Ahmose and his advisors want to use Ramose to set an example for the Habirus."

"Why?"

"The tomb that Ahmose is building? It is more than a pyramid. They have planned a vast complex of temples and monuments. Most of the workers are Habirus, who are unhappy at being forced to build a shrine to the ruler who subjugated them. There have been reports of sabotage at the building site. They believe I have something to do with it."

"How would you have anything to do with it?" I asked.

"I speak about freedoms for the Habirus and wish to integrate them into our society. Ahmose believes that my work incites rebellion. His advisors now question Ramose's intentions."

"Is that why he called you Ankh?" Amenhotep asked.

"That was bizarre even for Ahmose."

"And not wanting you to marry Meritamen," I added.

"Also strange under the circumstances," he conceded. "I am the oldest son. It is my duty and right to marry Meritamen. If something should happen to me, then the next son becomes betrothed to her."

"Even before Siamun forced himself on her," I said, "I do not believe Meritamen wished to marry that one."

"She may have no choice," Ammi said. "She will marry the oldest living brother. If none remain then Ahmose and Nefertari select someone to become Pharaoh."

"Is there anything you can do to protect her?" I asked.

Ahmose-Ankh thought about it for a few moments before a smile broke across his face. "There may be a way to protect her."

"How?" Amenhotep asked.

With a slight blush, Ammi refused to say more and changed the subject.

"Ramose, do you remember my friend Mahu?" Ammi asked. When I told him I did, he continued. "After you left, Ahmose discussed your replacing Siamun in the Northeast desert. Nefertari arranged for my friend Mahu to go with you. He is an experienced soldier and tactician. Listen to his advice."

"I will, Ammi," I said.

"He will help you with any problems you might encounter. Do not worry. I doubt there will be any Habirus you will fight."

Turning to Amenhotep, our oldest brother addressed him. "I am here for the Wepet-Renpet celebration. You will get more military training and maybe a command. Unfortunately, we must watch Siamun continuously."

"I will help however I may, Ammi," Amenhotep said.

"This has been a long day," Ahmose-Ankh began. "We should all get sleep as there will be many functions, dinners and festivals they will require us all to attend in the coming weeks."

We bid each other good night, and I crawled into bed to fall asleep.

16

"Good morning, your Highness! Time to rise!"

Paser drew back the curtains around my bed. The bright sun shining through the window marked its rising several hours ago. Paser informed me that Rekhmire expected me at my morning lesson. I stood from my bed, washed and dressed. Paser presented me with some baked sweet bread to break my fast, though the previous night's feast satiated my hunger.

"Did you hear what transpired last night?" I asked.

"I heard many things that transpired, your Highness," he said. "That Siamun struggled to accomplish his mission? He needs more time to learn."

Paser was right. Siamun's father would believe he deserved more time to learn how to lead. "You are right! If he were my child, I would give him more time and instruction. Why did Pharaoh agree to replace him with me?"

"Balaam," Paser responded.

"Balaam?"

"He manipulates Pharaoh, though I know not how. The servants who witnessed these events say he uses magic to influence those around him. His Majesty is very susceptible to Balaam's wishes."

"How do you mean?" I asked, thinking about the spinning sensation I felt every time he spoke.

"Have you not heard Balaam say something and Ahmose agree to it, regardless of how outrageous the suggestion?"

I nodded. "Did anyone ever tell you they felt a spinning sensation?"

"Spinning sensation, your Highness?"

"A whooshing. That makes little sense to you. I felt as though I would faint every time Balaam spoke last night. A sound arose in my ears too."

"Nay, my Lord. No one has told me such things."

"I must still feel the effects of the poison," I said.

"That could be, your Highness."

"Rekhmire suggested I replace Siamun though."

"Not from what I heard, your Highness. It was Balaam who suggested it."

Recreating the scene from last night, I realized Paser was correct. Why had I remembered Rekhmire suggesting it? And why did Amenhotep believe the same? I thought about the times Balaam and I were in the same room. Only three times I could recall; twice in the audience chamber and last night at dinner. All three times I felt the whooshing feeling.

"You are right, Paser. Odd I missed that."

Giving me a grave look, Paser said, "Not odd, Ramose. It is the magic Balaam uses to gain his desires."

"Why would Balaam want to replace Siamun with me?"

"I do not know, but when you go on your mission, you must be careful, for they may try to trap you somehow."

"I will discuss with Rekhmire."

"Rekhmire has," Paser paused. He started, then stopped. "Rekhmire may not be trustworthy in this situation. You must speak to Harwa after your lessons today. He will know what to do."

"What do you mean about Rekhmire?"

"I said more than I should. Please do not misunderstand. Rekhmire is an excellent teacher; he does not wish you harm. He works for Ahmose, however. And I am unsure if he is immune to the wiles of Balaam."

"I will find Harwa today," I responded.

"Yes, you will," Paser said, smiling.

I finished dressing and headed to Rekhmire's study on the other side of the palace complex. The compound comprised several colossal stone buildings surrounding a large rectangular courtyard. Covered walkways lined the edges of the yard with small alcoves where various government officials met, discussing affairs of state.

As I walked from the main palace to the administrative offices, servants greeted me, an unusual occurrence. Most were Habiru, and I could not remember any servant acknowledging me in my years at the palace. I arrived at Rekhmire's office wondering about this sudden change.

My teacher's office contained a large antechamber with several rooms adjacent. Benches and tables filled most of the interior space. The chamber empty, I walked around to see what Rekhmire planned for the day. On one table lay several amulets of different designs inlaid with gems. They contained lapis lazuli, a deep blue the color of the night sky, green turquoise, gold, and other precious stones and metals of different colors. I recognized a few of the symbols, the eye of Horus, a scarab, Bas. Others were unfamiliar. As I was about to pick up one, I heard Rekhmire enter the room.

"Good Morning, Ramose," he said, approaching me. "I see you found today's lesson. Which do you like?"

My eyes wandered over the various jewels and shapes, an onyx vulture, a gold collar, a silver ankh.

"Why does it matter?" I asked. Rekhmire's reproachful expression told me my question came out more challenging than I intended. I added, "For what purpose?"

"Oh!" he replied, relieved. "Something you feel might provide protection."

I inspected the amulets again, this time with a purpose. An intricate ornament with a three-fingered hand with thumbs on either side of the fingers, caught my attention. A small amethyst lay in the lower center of the hand and engraved in a manner to reveal an eye.

"That one," I said pointing at it.

Taking the jewel from the table, Rekhmire handed it to me and said, "An unusual person chooses a rare item." He explained the amulet I chose was meant to be a two-fingered amulet. Typically made from black onyx, the talisman depicts the sign of peace. This one resembled an entire hand.

Rekhmire pulled out a statuette of the goddess Serqet, an ivory wand, a chalice, and a rod fashioned in the shape of a cobra. He placed the four items on the table and unfurled a scroll. "Read this," he said. "Direct the words at the amulet."

As I did, Rekhmire instructed me to recite the words over the amulet.

"Conjure the goddess Isis and her son Horus to emerge from the swamps to protect you from evil. You are invoking their power to protect you, flattering their deeds and remembering their victory over Seth."

For the rest of the morning and early part of the afternoon, I practiced the incantation, trying to modulate my voice to the correct pitch.

"Ooooo settt," I intoned several times as Rekhmire corrected me. Once perfect, he directed me to recite the words of the scroll in the same tune. I repeated the words four times while holding the amulet. Then he waved first the wand, then the rod over the amulet. Taking a drop of oil from the chalice, he placed it on the amulet, instructing me to rub it over the jewel.

I did as instructed, repeating the process four times while rubbing the amulet with oil.

After the fourth iteration Rekhmire declared the process complete.

Using braided flax as a chain, I placed the amulet around my neck. The day already warm, Rekhmire's office seemed hotter because of our efforts. Believing me fatigued, Rekhmire suggested we stop for the day.

"Remember these spells, Ramose. You may need them. Tomorrow may be our last lesson for some time. I believe Wepet-Renpet will start the day after next."

I nodded before leaving wearing my new amulet.

***

Exiting Rekhmire's study, I headed to the river. Following the path through the date palms, papyrus, and pomegranate trees, I arrived at our meeting place to find Harwa sitting on a log staring at the river.

"I hope you have not been waiting long," I said, approaching my friend.

"Paser sent word you needed help."

"Did he tell you of what occurred?"

"Only bits and pieces."

I recounted the events of the past evening, including my lesson that day with Rekhmire, showing my amulet to him.

"The hand of God," he said. "An excellent choice!"

"Rekhmire showed me the protection spells I needed to imbue it with magic," I said, excited to explain the details.

Harwa listened to my descriptions, asking questions to clarify the process at various points. When I finished he stated, "You imbued magic on the amulet, but not protection."

"Oh?" I asked, surprised.

"Rekhmire showed you an attraction spell, useful if you want to get a spouse, but not for going into battle."

"Why would he do that?"

"I do not know. Tell me again what happened that evening."

"Nefertari and Ahmose argued about Ammi's and Meritamen's marriage. Balaam suggested it is premature to propose to the gods Ahmose-Ankh's readiness to be Pharaoh."

"Suggested? Why do you use that word?" he asked, concerned.

I shrugged my shoulders.

"Did you notice anything strange?"

"No," I declared.

"Come over here," he said.

I backed away scared Harwa wished to harm me. Never had this feeling overcome me. He moved towards me, making me want to run, but a sudden compulsion stopped me. Harwa raised his arm, and I flinched, readying myself for a blow. Instead, he dabbed my forehead, and I felt a weight lift.

"There was a whooshing sensation that came over me every time Balaam spoke," I blurted out. "Both Rekhmire and Amenhotep believed the poisoning still affected me. I cannot understand why I said nothing to you."

"Because Balaam placed a hex on you, and likely the others."

"A hex?"

"He placed a suggestion in you to not remember the evening."

"Why?"

"I do not know. But it could explain Rekhmire's behavior this morning."

"Is that why I felt faint?"

"In part. The whoosh you heard is the sound of magic."

"The sound of magic?"

"Every spell cast creates a sound of sorts. It disturbs Ma'at. You sensed it and felt the change."

"But I did not feel it when Rekhmire worked his spell."

"A different magic." Harwa reviewed with me the structure of the universe. Energy flows and vibrates as a vast unseen world exists beyond what is visible. Certain objects and people attract and congeal more energy than others. "Rekhmire possesses a good amount of attractive power. He invokes the Ka and Ba of the god associated with the magical request. He is an excellent scholar, pouring through scrolls and able to follow the instructions. But he does not improvise or understand the depth of his power."

"Is that why he always uses a wand?" I asked.

"Yes. Or a staff. Rekhmire believes he requires something to direct his energy. Balaam attracts well too. But he knows the force comes from within. But he tries to bend those hidden forces to his will. That is the sound you heard."

"I heard Balaam performing magic?"

"Yes. And you felt the suggestion spell he placed on you and the others."

"The spell caused us to misremember the events of last night," I said, with a sinking feeling.

"Yes. But I cleared it from you."

"How is their magic limited?"

"Both Rekhmire and Balaam look outside themselves to perform the magic."

"Is anyone powerful enough to make these transformations?"

"An individual cannot do that. But you, as part of the ALL, are more than powerful enough. If you allow the power of what IS to enter you, anything is possible."

"I do not understand," I said.

"Let us fix your amulet to protect you and I can demonstrate."

"Why do others use different forms of magic?"

"They struggle with themselves, believing it harder to be than it is. Open your heart, Ramose, see what is in there and allow the goodness to come through you. Then you can do anything."

Excited, I asked, "What do I do?"

"Take off the amulet and place it in your hands. You will build up energy within yourself, then slowly release it into the amulet. Start by sitting still, close your eyes, and feel the surrounding energy. Breathe in the manner I have shown you. Call your Sekham."

"What is that?"

"It is the power within you. Combined with your Ab or heart body they make the core power of your life."

"What about the Ka and the Ba?" I asked. Rekhmire once told me Ka and Ba animated the power of the god within the statue, allowing it to help or hinder us in our lives.

"Ka and Ba are essential parts of the soul. Rekhmire's magic uses those forces, but I am teaching you something else. From the Ab you find what it is you desire. You must know what is in your heart before you can manifest anything.

"Now, allow the energy to build up while holding the intention to bring protection to the amulet."

I did as instructed, feeling an energy build within me. A few moments later, Harwa said, "Now direct the energy towards the amulet and say a word to bind the energy to the amulet."

I said aloud, "protect," and let the energy flow from me to the amulet.

"Good, Ramose!" Harwa said. "Though saying the word aloud is babyish."

"I thought I had to say it out loud," I defended. "Rekhmire had me intone everything in a specific melody and tone."

"Oh," Harwa apologized. "He believes that the sounds of the words give them power. However, vibrations can produce modulations other than sounds. You built the energy up in your body also creating vibrations. Let me see your amulet."

I handed him the small golden hand, watching as he inspected it. "Very good, Ramose. You have talent."

"Why have none of my other teachers instructed me in such techniques?"

"They fear you, Ramose. You represent something they do not understand. Ahmose and his advisors want to control you."

"Rekhmire too?"

"Rekhmire is..." he paused thinking of the word he wanted before saying, "Compromised."

"You are the second person to say that to me today. What do you mean?"

"I would rather not say."

"What of Nefertari?"

He shot me a quick glance as though I hit a nerve. Composing himself, he said, "Nefertari understands proper teaching is the only way for you to reach your potential. Our meeting was no accident."

"Potential?"

"You know various prophecies float about you?"

I told him of my conversation with Amenhotep the previous night. "How would he become Pharaoh, while I am a great leader without him dying?"

"Leadership takes many forms, Ramose. It is true you may one day become Pharaoh, but alternate futures await you too."

"How do you mean?"

"The astrologers believe the stars imbued qualities to those born at a particular time. Pharaoh and his advisors tracked all the babies born the same day as you. They searched for the special child; one the oracles predicted to arrive that day. The divinations Rekhmire, Iyov, and Balaam cast upon you conflicted. Each saw something different."

"Why?"

"Divination is a weak form of magic and unreliable. If you want to know the future, ask El Shaddai."

"What is my destiny?"

"What do you want it to be? Part of it lay in what you choose."

"I do not know my choices," I complained.

"No one knows their path, Ramose," Harwa admonished.

"I know I do not want to marry a Kushite princess," I said.

"Then you will not! Focus on what it is you want. Use the desire nature within you to manifest what you seek. You are doing it anyway, so direct it. Your possess remarkable talent."

We sat watching the river flow. The water moved fast this time of year as the rains continued in the South. Sopdet returns in two days. For seventy days of the year, it hides. Its return marks Wepet-Renpet, the New Year. I did not understand what he was saying, and my youth prevented me from asking what he meant. Later, I would understand what he spoke about and my adopted mother's involvement in my life. Instead, I changed the subject back to magic.

"How does El Shaddai fit with this other way of doing magic?"

"By understanding the surrounding energy is the All, no separation between me and not me."

"Like you taught me a few years ago?"

"Exactly. I suspected that you could do magic because you had touched the void."

"Is that the unseen world?"

"Yes."

"Balaam can reach into it too."

"He can, but he tries to bend it to his will."

"How do you mean?"

"The form of magic Balaam practices supposes that humans are at the center of everything."

"Are we not?"

"Hardly. There are forces much stronger than any human or civilization. Look at Strongili. The people there performed sacrifices to stop the island's destruction. Then they build walls and culverts to redirect the fire river. It changed nothing."

Strongili, an island Harwa visited in his youth, lay in the Great Sea, north of Egypt. The mountain exploded, bursting with fire and rocks. The people left knowing of the danger, but returned to find everything destroyed or buried under cubits of ash. Over half of the island disappeared into the sea.

"Could magic have stopped the eruption?" I asked.

"Maybe," Harwa replied. "But at what cost? Everything is connected. Stopping the explosion might have created problems elsewhere."

"Is that why they did nothing?"

"I do not know. Things happen for many reasons, some we learn later in life, while others we never do."

"Then how do I know what I do is right?"

"Open your heart and follow what it says. At some point, you will use magic and either it will fail you, or the outcome will not produce what you expected. Then you will know that surrender to the ALL is the only way."

"How do I do that?"

"Follow your inspirations instead of your desires."
"How do I know the difference?"
"You do not. Then you do."
Harwa smiled as he did when he spoke riddles.
"It is time you returned to the palace," he said. "Place the amulet around your neck and be sure never to take it off."

17

The next morning, I awoke to bustling inside the palace. Preparations for the New Year's celebrations began, and this year I would partake in the rituals. Paser readied me for my lessons with Rekhmire. In the excitement of the festivities, I forgot about my discussion with Harwa and any need for caution with Rekhmire. The day brought no concerns with my teacher, for I spent the day learning chants for that night's ritual.

"According to my count, we should be able to see the dog star just before sunrise tomorrow morning along the horizon. When we do, it marks the New Year. Tonight's ritual welcomes Osiris back from the dead, renewed for the coming year."

Towards sundown, Paser prepared me for the ritual. Fasting began at sunset, continuing for twenty-six hours. I ate a small meal alone, Paser tasting everything before serving me. Then he prepared a bath with a small amount of salt and oils. As he scrubbed me, I asked about the scents.

"The oil smells familiar," I said thinking of my first days at the palace.

"It is cedar and myrrh used in the mummification process. Though you might remember it from your adoption ritual."

Reserved for newborns, Nefertari performed the Sebou ritual for my adoption to help Egyptians accept me into the royal family. It did not work as planned.

"You look sad, Ramose," Paser said, interrupting my

reverie. "But you take the solemnity of the day too far." He smiled.

"Sorry, my friend," I responded. "The scent brought back memories of the Sebou ritual and the cruelty I have endured over the years."

Nodding, Paser said, "You have suffered many insults over the years. However, things are changing."

"Are they?" I asked.

"You are not a powerless little boy others can push around. You are coming into your strength, and you must use it wisely. Remember your origins, Ramose."

I rose from the tub and instead of handing me a towel, he dried me himself.

"You are to do nothing. The ritual begins with cleansing. I wash and dry you. Then I anoint you with oil."

With ease and care, Paser rubbed the oil on me, describing the purpose of each. He placed a clean and fresh linen tunic over me. The roughness of the fabric betrayed its newness. He tied a braided flax sash around my waist. Then he set new sandals on my feet. Paser observed his work for a moment, adjusting my costume before escorting me to the front of the palace, where most of my family members assembled.

After waiting a quarter of an hour, Nefertari arrived. As she was the last person to be ready, we departed for the temple complex, a short walk from the palace. I suspect my memories from my early childhood played tricks on me, for I have no recollection of going to the gigantic compound before this except for the Sebou ritual. There must have been other times, but I could not recall them. Maybe the familiar scent of frankincense, cedar, and myrrh placed these two events together in my mind. Or the circumstances of this evening and the next few days fostered the connection for me.

Only the royal family, priests, and a few noble families took part in this ritual. Less than one hundred people gathered on this hot Akhet evening in front of the temple compound before we walked through the gateway in silence towards the first stop. In near silence, the procession moved towards the temple complex. In the intervening years, the complex changed. The high red walls still loomed over the white chapel in the foreground. The etchings of Amun-Re, sun god of Egypt were visible in the faint light of sunset. But the small white chapel in front now possessed a matching calcite twin to the left of the entrance. Changes abound inside the complex, too. Limestone had replaced the second wall of red brick. A gate with a portico guarded the final courtyard. In the center stood a small chapel to Isis, in front of the temple. Between the portico and the temple, columns lined the center of the courtyard on both sides, creating a corridor to the main temple.

The myth of the brother and sister played prominently in the New Year celebration. Seth, their jealous brother, kills Osiris to take the throne. The demented brother cuts Osiris into many pieces, spreading them throughout the world. Isis, Osiris' sister-wife collects the pieces and puts him back together. Osiris impregnates Isis, giving birth to the first Pharaoh, Horus, while Osiris becomes lord of the underworld.

Upon entering the temple of Isis, the gathering sang songs of lamentation, mimicking Isis' desperate search for her husband-brother. Ammi and Meritamen stood close together, almost touching as they looked at one another while singing. I stood observing my siblings, wondering about their behavior when a beautiful voice distracted me. The sound rose, a scale higher than the other singers creating a countermelody. Opening my heart and closing my eyes, I ceased singing to better hear this voice, feeling the vibrations deep within my soul. The singer came closer until I surmised she stood beside me. I opened my eyes to see my sister Sitamen wearing a sheer sleeveless netted dress made of Mitra shells and beads. While she wore a linen gown underneath, the clothing accentuated her curves. For the first time, I noticed Sitamen's beauty and felt something stir inside me I never felt.

Telling of this time of my life brings feelings of shame for what stirred inside me. The spells cast upon me and the others are no excuse for the weakness that overcame me. I do not defend my actions. I take comfort knowing the Breath that is Creation works in mysterious ways. For the events unfolded in such a manner to allow people's liberation. Still, the events of that time trouble me.

Sitamen and I were about the same age. She mirrored Nefertari. Her eyes, nose, and mouth reflected the beauty of her mother, while her face revealed little of her father.

Something about her, however, sprung from neither parent. Though dark, her skin possessed an alabaster quality reflecting the light. And her voice! The trills, pitch, tone, and modulation capabilities she possessed were unmatched by anyone else I had heard in Egypt. Only Rekhmire's ability to sing compared, and it was a pale comparison.

Sitamen smiled as she sang. My heart raced, and my knees weakened as she came closer. After standing silent and slack-jawed for a few moments, I remembered to sing. Starting again, Sitamen harmonized her voice with mine as we stood face to face as Ammi and Meritamen had earlier. Pangs of guilt rose when I noticed Amenhotep scowling. They subsided quickly.

The chanting stopped as the assembled moved in unison through the inner chapel towards the main temple. Sitamen walked on my left, Amenhotep my right. We walked in silence until the high priest start the next song. While the previous tune possessed a lamentation quality, this one maintained a more frenetic pace. The words sung reflected this frenzy as Isis searches for her dead brother's body. The rhythm repeated; notes rising and falling. Up and down the song continued as the process walked through the center of the compound to reach the other pantheon.

Once we are all inside, the music changed to sounds of relief. Having collected the pieces of her dead brother from around the world, she reassembles him with the help of the other gods. Osiris rises from dead. The siblings re-declare their love for one another, and Isis conceives Horus. I looked to see if Meritamen and Ahmose-Ankh were holding hands again, but could not find them anywhere. My search for the older siblings ceased when Sitamen's hand brushed against mine, sending a jolt through my body. Feeling a stirring in my loins, I pulled my hand away, fearing to show my manhood underneath my loose gown. Frowning at first, Sitamen laughed when she realized my embarrassment. Looking as though she might reach under my short tunic, a sudden disturbance caused us both to turn around. A noble woman fainted from the heat.

As I was about to reach down to help her, Sitamen grabbed my arm and whispered, "You are a royal! You must not touch her."

"But she needs help," I replied.

"Her family will aid her. If you touch her, you must leave the temple complex to re-purify yourself."

Responding to my puzzled look, she said, "The purity ritual made you divine. Though a noble, they do not consider her a deity."

We turned back to the high priest who started a new responsive chant. Between Sitamen's beautiful voice and my reverie, I could not describe the song. My focus shifted between her words and wonderment about what makes something divine. On different occasions, I spoke to Harwa and Rekhmire about this. Did a Habiru manservant sprinkling oil over the adopted son of a Pharaoh turn him into a god? I did not think it would. But maybe the ritual brought the divinity within each of us to the surface.

Before I could contemplate this further, a series of staccato sounds and moans brought me back to the present moment. The beautiful melody returned, and the gathered continued to sing, then replaced by the rapid firing notes and wails. Once again this gave way to the softer theme. Back and forth the music switched between the harmonious music and the wailing with the intervals coming closer and closer for near an hour until I heard only the groans of the assembled women.

After several minutes, a new, sweet harmony began. Sitamen inched closer. With discretion, she pointed towards the high priest.

"Watch," she whispered into my ear, her warm breath and scent making me woozy once again.

The high priest raised his hands to reveal a baby doll. The assembled adored the newborn god, Horus before starting the chanting again.

Sitamen again pointed to a spot high on the wall above the high priest's head. A large opening exposed the pre-dawn sky as the light rose in the east. In the center of the window, a bright white light shone through. Sopdet returned to the sky after a seventy-day hiatus. Simultaneously, a priest dressed as Osiris rose from a coffin to join a priestess dressed as Isis and take the baby in his arms.

The sweetness of the melody brought tears to my eyes as the ritual came to a close with the rising sun. As the light streamed through the opening in the wall, the high priest sang the final note to end the ceremony. In silence, the nobles parted to give space to the royal family and the priests. Somehow Sitamen took my hand in hers and we walked together back to the palace hand in hand.

18

In retrospect, the evolution of my relationship with Sitamen made sense. She and Meritamen both welcomed me when I arrived at the palace. I enjoyed time with both sisters, but neither played a larger role in my life than the other. Both were children to me. When Amenhotep and Siamun bullied me, she and I spent time together and became friends. But as Amenhotep and I reconciled, I spent less time with her.

I worried about Amenhotep's reaction given our disagreement the other night. I sought Amenhotep, but I did not see him anywhere. Paser's stiff greeting at the entrance interrupted my search for Amenhotep. I let go of Sitamen's hand as she smiled, saying she would see me later.

"Your Highness enjoyed his first Wepet-Renpet ceremony, I trust," he said, as we walked back towards my room.

"It was interesting," I said. "Some melodies were beautiful. Did you know Sitamen had such a beautiful voice?"

"Sitamen?" Paser said as he led me upstairs. "Your sister?"

"Adopted sister," I corrected.

"I did not. We must hurry."

"Why?"

"I will explain in a moment."

Entering my room, Paser closed the door. A bath waited for me to clean myself again. The cold water refreshed and awakened me.

"Serah wishes to meet you and Ahmose-Ankh. Everyone

will rest, giving us a chance to slip out of the palace unnoticed."

"Can this wait until later in the week?" The celebration lasts one week, followed by the Tekh festival on the twentieth day of the first month of the year, Thoth.

"We have an opportunity now," Paser said. "As does Serah."

"But everyone gets drunk during the Tekh festivities. Would not that..."

"You may be drunk too," Paser interrupted. "Or fighting in the desert."

Too exhausted to argue further, I did as Paser instructed. Handing me shabby clothes, he told me to wear them so I would blend in with the slaves inside the Habiru quarter of the city. Then he led me along a hidden corridor to a staircase.

"How did I not know about this exit?" I asked.

"Servants use it. Come, we must hasten."

Paser lead me to the kitchens, empty for the moment as everyone fasted to start the festival. In a few hours, the cooks would arrive to prepare the meal for the celebratory dinner.

At the back of the kitchen, a narrow door led to an alley where Ahmose-Ankh waited. The three of us traveled through the lane between the palace and the temple complex. Veering away from the river, we moved through the streets of Waset. The houses became smaller and more rundown as we moved further from the palace until we came to an area of makeshift huts and tents, some on raised mounds to protect from the coming floods.

The Habirus did not celebrate Wepet-Renpet and cooking smells wafted towards us, stirring my hunger on this day of fasting. Paser lead us along the paths between the huts knowing his way through the maze of temporary buildings. He instructed us to follow him inside an unadorned tent that looked the same as the others.

At first, the dim light prevented me from seeing much. But as my eyes grew accustomed to the darkness, I noticed the richness of the interior. The dirt floors, basic furniture, and lack of decorations typical of Habiru poverty transformed, replaced with opulent rugs, sofas with plush cushions, and a carved table with inlaid marble in the middle of the tent.

On a divan near the middle of the room, sat an ancient woman with long thinning white hair, her skin wrinkled and dried as a prune in the summer sun. Looking at her eyes, I noticed a white film over them, and I wondered if she could see through them. She spoke to us with a crackling and creaky voice that shook with each breath.

"Come in, come in. Sit. I am pleased Paser asked for this meeting."

The three of us sat down around the venerable woman. "I am Serah. Ramose is it?"

She looked straight through me, suggesting her eyesight did not work. However, she possessed vision.

"And Ahmose-Ankh. Crown Prince to the throne in name only."

Ammi grimaced. "My father's foolishness allows Balaam to remain an advisor."

Serah emitted a guttural tone, sounding like a raspy cough. Was it a laugh? "I have met whom you speak. A forked tongue he has. Why is it you wished to meet me?"

"I understand you see the future," my brother replied.

"Are there not enough Egyptian seers available to his Royal Highness?" she chided. "Why would someone so esteemed wish to consult with a poor, old Habiru slave?"

"I would not call you a poor, old slave," he replied. "Your ability to pierce the veil of time is renown."

"You come wanting to know how to protect your sister."

Ahmose-Ankh tossed multiple coins into a basket sitting on the table, then asked, "Will she?" He left the question unfinished.

He tossed another coin, making a loud clanking sound as it banged against the money he put there earlier. Only then did she answer his question. "She is safe; you saw to that."

"That is good," Ahmose-Ankh replied, appearing relieved.

"But there is still danger."

"Of course, there is."

"For your other sister, Sitamen. The beast turns his eyes towards her."

"Sitamen?" Ammi said with a concerned look.

"You must protect her."

Ahmose-Ankh looked towards me. A grin appeared on his

face.

"Not that way," Serah said, responding as though seeing his expression. "That will create the chaos you wish to avoid."

"I did not think I would..."

"He is destined for another."

"The daughter of a Nubian Chieftain."

"Another," Serah emphasized.

"Another? Who? But Rekhmire and other seers say Sitamen..."

"Ahmose-Ankh!" Serah raised her voice. "Egyptians seers are not reliable. It is why you are here!" Then she lowered her voice, only a raspy whisper emitting from her lips. "The magic of Isis veils their vision. To pierce through the mists, one must go beyond the petty beliefs of individual gods to the source of creation, El Shaddai."

"El Shaddai? That is your god, is he not?"

"El Shaddai is not a god in the sense you worship. El Shaddai is creation itself. We do not stand before idols pleading with them to make things this way or that. If El Shaddai wants us to have something, it is granted. Our supplications do not matter."

"Then why pray at all?" he asked.

"To hear our destiny and know how to proceed."

"You speak as though our destinies are sealed. Am I not part of this ALL?"

A smile broke along the broken lines of Serah's face. That guttural sound rose from her throat. It was a laugh. "He is smart, Paser. A very smart one. You are right, Ahmose-Ankh. But not everyone has enough Ruach, enough spirit; you might call it Ab, I believe. Not everyone has that strength to change the forces moving around them. Or even flow with the forces that rule our lives."

Ammi smiled and nodded as though he understood her words. "My father moves against me."

"His self-doubt blinds his vision, something true for many people."

My brother looked surprised. "Ahmose doubts himself? Why?"

"I can only tell you this. Ahmose fears you becoming Pharaoh threatens his legacy."

"That is ridiculous!"

"It is true."

"How do I counter the surrounding forces?" he asked.

"You must recognize what is within yourself. Your observation you are El Shaddai is correct; made in ITS image. My grandfather Jacob understood this to a point. Do you know his story?"

"I do not. They forbid us to learn about anything of the Habiru's."

"Bring my harp," she barked at a servant who responded by carrying the large instrument from the corner to the sofa, placing it in front of my great aunt. "Your father's imposed ignorance only weakens his goals." She began playing the harp and as she strummed, she muttered to herself as though wondering if she should tell the story. She played soothing music as we waited for her to speak again.

"There are parallels here," she mumbled, after a long silence. "Yes, similarities both boys should learn." She stopped playing and raised her voice to address us. "Ramose, listen! For this story concerns you too. Multiple spouses pose risks in families."

She began playing again. "As you know, the brothers can fight and become jealous of one another."

She looked my way, and for a moment I thought she spoke of Amenhotep. But she referred to Joseph, whose brothers of a different mother sold him into slavery. She conveyed the story Harwa told me several years ago. Ammi listened with rapt attention, not knowing Joseph once led the kingdom.

"What you may not know, Ramose, is how Jacob came to have so many wives. My father was born of Leah's maidservant, Zilpah, though I am getting ahead of myself."

Stopping for a moment, she closed her eyes, plucking the harp as if the tune and finger movements helped recall memories lost.

"Jacob fled his brother Esau after stealing his brother's birthright. Though twins, Esau came out first, followed by my grandfather. Jacob reflected both his parents' intelligence and guile. But his twin possessed none of the qualities of either parent, as though El Shaddai placed him in the wrong womb. Isaac glorified his older son's strength and hunting prowess, traits he wished for himself.

"Rebecca recognized that the spirit of El Shaddai ran strong in Jacob. She plotted with him to steal Isaac's blessing from Esau. Once done, she told Jacob to flee the land and find her Uncle Laban. Doing so, he arrived to meet Rachel."

At the mention of my foremother, the notes changed. Serah played sweet and melodious music, bringing tears to my eyes.

"Rachel's grace and beauty shone through her. Jacob recognized her immediately, both as his cousin and as the woman he would marry.

"Knowing Jacob's desires, Laban took advantage of the young man." At the mention of Laban, the notes transformed into a dissonance, matching the tone of disgust in Serah's voice. "For Laban insisted Jacob work for seven years in exchange for his daughter. When the seven years past, Laban, the vile person he was, switched Leah for Rachel. Discovering the deceit after the ceremony, Jacob asked for Rachel. Laban required Jacob work for him another seven years to marry Rachel, to which Jacob agreed.

"After doing so, Jacob and Rachel married, leaving afterwards. As fertile as the Nile, Leah kept producing son after son for her husband. Rachel, however, remained barren like the desert. When she gave Bilah, her maidservant to Jacob, another son was born. Leah then gave her attendant to Jacob giving birth to my father. The friction between the sisters carried to the sons of the different mothers."

"Rivalry between siblings exists in many families regardless of the number of mothers," Ahmose-Ankh observed.

"True enough," Serah responded as she stopped playing the harp. "But Jacob brought this upon himself. He played favorites in part because like his mother he saw into the future. He knew Joseph deserved the blessing of first-born, but did not make him work for it. Even if it is your birthright, you must earn it. Joseph's lack of understanding this inflamed his brother's jealousy."

She played again, a different tune that pierced clear to my soul. The soothing music combined with not sleeping the previous night made me soporific. I felt myself nodding off until Serah spoke again, her fingers continued to move across the strings of the harp. Each note carried her words into my very being.

"Jacob's spirit allowed him to survive the trials he faced. In fourteen years working for his Uncle, he brought more wealth to the region than Laban could imagine. My drunkard uncle's laziness could not prevent Jacob's success, as though everything he touched turned to gold."

"How?" my brother asked.

"Jacob knew the secret of El Shaddai."

"What is that?" Ammi asked.

Serah stopping playing. She looked at Ahmose-Ankh. "The secret cannot be told, only experienced. Everything comes from the All, living in each of us. Love is its currency."

She played again and spoke. "We are like each note in a song. As notes run together to make music, we integrate to make the universe. Each note must be true to its tone, as we must be true to our own divinity."

She sounded a note so wrong, and out of place, it jolted all of us. "Otherwise disharmony and chaos overthrow the order of existence."

Returning to the harmonious melody, Serah strummed the harp, saying nothing.

"Why tell me this?" Ahmose-Ankh asked.

"Because you live out of balance. Like an untuned string, you struggle to sound the right chord. However, you do not know yourself well enough to realize your discord."

"I know the difference between right and wrong."

"I am glad someone so young is so wise," she said.

"I am a warrior."

"Who does everything his mother tells him to do."

Ahmose-Ankh jumped up. "Why did I bother coming here?" he demanded. "I thought you could help me!"

"You or one of your brothers will become a great leader," Serah calmly replied. "Possibly the greatest ever."

"Surely not my demented brother Siamun."

"He knows himself and what he is. He is not afraid of using his power."

"And that makes a great leader?"

"Not by itself, no. But it is a quality to emulate."

"He tortures animals," Ahmose-Ankh argued, sitting down again.

"Power comes in many forms. Some people abuse it as Siamun. Most waste it, as you do."

My drowsiness disappeared, for the conversation reminded me of my discussion with Harwa.

"How do people squander their power?" I asked.

"You can speak," Serah teased, smiling. "I thought you might be mute. Harwa taught you well. Silence can be powerful. As can be hate. Either can be a weakness. Calling out injustice or using words of hate are both capacities of speech."

"Cannot either be used to abuse power?" Ahmose-Ankh asked.

"Of course! What do you think happened to the Habirus? Ahmose uses hatred of my people to control those who might unite against him, claiming my people harmed Egyptians, which never happened."

"I disagree with my father's policies."

"What have you done to change those policies or help Habirus?" she asked.

Ahmose-Ankh had no answer.

"Siamun plots your demise. He gathers people to kill you."

"What do I do?"

"Act!" she shouted. "Find trusted people who can protect you. Look for allies. Without them, you will fail."

"Kill Siamun?"

"I did not say that," she responded. "Though deranged, Siamun plays a vital role in this story. Sometimes, the best response to an enemy is to keep them close."

Ammi thought for a few moments, pondering her words.

"I will take him back to Buhen," Ahmose-Ankh determined. "Father wants me to show him how to administrate the outpost. Rather, Balaam suggested it to father."

Serah smiled in response. "Sometimes it behooves us to enter traps."

"How do you mean?"

"Watch yourself Ahmose-Ankh. You know the snake hunts."

"Siamun?"

"Balaam," she responded. "Siamun decides on his own, but Balaam nudges him along. He wants something."

Ahmose-Ankh said he understood the situation and would take care going forward. We thanked Serah for her time and readied to leave. Ahmose-Ankh excused himself first, leaving the tent. Just before I followed my brother, the old woman called me.

"Ramose! You have not come into your own, yet. Like Jacob, your power to manifest is great."

"Thank you," I responded, looking down, not knowing what else to say.

"Jacob learned something later in life more important than creating." She paused, looking off into the distance, though the opacity of her eyes prevented me from seeing where she gazed. "Grandfather learned true manifestation requires alignment with El Shaddai. It is one thing to want something, Ramose. It is another entirely to allow the wishes of God to work through you."

Before I could say I did not understand, she continued. "You wish to save the Habirus and stay Egyptian. You cannot any more than Ahmose-Ankh can. Soon you will face a choice. Stay in Egypt as an Egyptian. Or leave to discover something within yourself. Regardless, you are a leader."

"What if I do not want to lead?" I asked, exhausted and struggling to stand at this point.

"You have touched El Shaddai," she stated as though telling me the sky was blue. How did she know? "Not even Joseph did that. I see in you a quality I have only seen in Jacob, but more so. You cannot outrun your destiny."

She reached a thin, frail hand towards me. I pulled away, but stopped. Instead, I let her touch my face with that hand while reaching for her other.

"Ahmose will ask you to find something."

"What?"

"A staff. Though he proclaims it to be his, it is not. Do not let him have it under any circumstance."

"What do I do then?" I asked.

She moved her hand to my chest and looked into my eyes.

"Follow your heart. Not the emotional heart or Ab as the Egyptians call it, but the part of you connecting to El Shaddai. You will know what to do. Follow your heart, listen to the voice you hear. And you will find a gift more precious than all the gold, gems, or power in the world."

The old woman hugged me, sending me on my way. "Our paths will cross again, Ramose."

I left the tent, joining Ahmose-Ankh and Paser. In silence, we walked back to the palace.

19

I returned to my room to sleep for several hours. Paser told me to sleep, for there would be another prayer service before the evening meal to break the fast. It would require me to dine with the royal family and various nobles.

I changed into a simple loincloth and exhausted, fell into a deep sleep, dreaming of Ahmose ordering me to find a staff, while I played a harp. I pleaded with him; I did not know of its location. A noise stirred me from my repose. Shaking off slumber, I opened my eyes to see Sitamen standing next to the bed. She put one finger over her lips, suggesting silence. Letting her gown drop from her shoulders, she stood for a moment naked, allowing me to take in her full beauty, before slipping under the covers next to me. She put her arm around me, pulling me closer. Her scent, a mix of cedar, myrrh, and perfume I could not recognize, aroused my vigor. I suspect she had not bathed since the ritual. Or maybe I smelled the funerary oils on myself. Regardless, her fragrance intoxicated me as I felt her body against mine.

"Protect me from Siamun," she whispered.

"How?" I asked.

"By laying with me."

With a stupid expression, I responded. "Like we are now?"

By answer, she pressed her lips against mine, wrapping both her lips around my lower while touching my tongue with hers. She pulled me closer to her body, rubbing her crotch against mine. At first, I found the kissing awkward. I mimicked the movements of her lips and tongue, finding it pleasurable. We continued thus for I do not know how long. With lips locked, she removed my loincloth, taking my member in her hand, rhythmically stroking it. I pulled away from our kiss to let out a moan.

"You are circumcised," she murmured, a smile across her face as she fondled me.

In one swift motion, she pulled away from me, rolling me on my back and then sitting back on top of me.

"How do you know what to do?" I asked.

"Mother has shown me how to perform the ritual for Amun-Re. I have desired you for some time."

She moved my hand, first placing on her mound. I felt the hair there and then she moved my hand to an area of wetness between her legs. She released a squeal of delight. Then she moved my fingers inside her, moisture becoming more pronounced. I learned the pattern and performed it without her help. Then she emitted a low audible groan. Taking my manhood in her hand once again, she moved it to penetrate her, as I felt her moisture on the tip of my member. Just as she I was about to enter her, Paser burst into the room.

"Stop!" he cried. "Get off Ramose this instant!"

I groaned as my arousal remained in my loins. My adopted sister rose from the bed, displaying her nakedness.

"Put something on and return to your room," he demanded.

Sitamen stood tall, every inch of her exuding the title Pharaoh's Daughter, even as she was naked. I watched her dress before she sauntered from my room.

"Why did you stop her?" I demanded, still panting.

"They reserve you for another," Paser said.

"The Nubian Princess!?" I seethed.

"No, another. A woman. One whose power matches yours. Not a girl seeking to exalt herself."

I wondered what he meant. Paser commanded me to bathe myself. I still felt a surge of energy in my stomach.

"What is this feeling in my belly?"

"Breathe, as I showed you." It was Harwa's voice. "Breathe and imagine the energy extending along your spine."

I did as instructed, ignoring Paser's transfiguration into

Harwa. I felt the force rise along my back and towards my head.

"Now bring it back down the front of your body as you inhale."

I imagined the energy cresting the top of my head before descending through my face, chest, and back to my loins. The circuit continued as I exhaled and inhaled in a slow and steady manner.

A still and quiet voice called my name, but I continued to breathe, feeling waves and waves of peace and pleasure.

"Moses," it said. Why did it use that name? "Your power awakens. Soon you face a choice."

"What sort of choice?" I asked.

A different voice now spoke. "Ramose!"

"What sort of choice?"

"Ramose!" the voice barked.

Feeling myself being shaken, I opened my eyes to find myself in bed.

"Ramose. It is time to get up." Paser stood next to my bed. "You must prepare for the last part of the Wepet-Renpet celebration and the feast this evening."

Confused, I looked around.

"Was Sitamen in here?" I asked.

He laughed. "You must have been dreaming. Hopefully, a pleasant one."

"Until you interrupted us."

"Probably for the best," Paser said, still laughing. His face turned grim before saying, "Take care with Sitamen, Ramose. Her desires and yours may not aligned."

"What do you mean? Am I reserved for someone?"

"You may be," Paser smiled again. "But I know nothing about that. Sitamen has plans for herself that you may help her achieve."

"She wishes to exalt herself."

"Yes," he nodded.

"You already told me that." Then when he looked confused, I added, "must have been in my dream."

"May I suggest that you discuss this with Harwa?"

"Is he not gone for Akhet?"

"He remains in Waset. I will send someone to find him."

"You command others?"

"Of course! There is a hierarchy amongst the servants. I have seniority. That is why I am your manservant. But we do not have time for this discussion at the moment. You must finish getting ready and go back to the temple."

We laid a plan for reaching Harwa. I washed the myrrh and cedar from my body, removing the odor of mummification. Paser sprayed a different perfume on me I could not place. As I inhaled the fragrance, memories of my dream of being in bed with Sitamen tumbled back.

"What is that scent?" I asked Paser.

"It is a lotus based perfume with frankincense and cinnamon. Nefertem, the god of perfume-making created this for Amun-Re when he grew old to ease his suffering. We only use it for this ritual."

I said nothing of my dream to Paser, wondering if there was any way I had smelled this in the past. The scent was the same as what Sitamen wore in my dream.

I joined the royal procession back to the temple complex. Sitamen, dressed in a different formal gown than the one she wore earlier, looked beautiful. As each of her hands held bouquets, she did not reach for mine. But she looked at me with eyes of longing, and thinking of my dream, I blushed and turned away.

Coming to the temple complex, we walked straight across the compound, taking a different path than the previous evening, towards the largest temple of Amun-Re. Obelisks stood on either side of the large stone path that ended in a ramp leading down to a lower level of the trail. Smallish statues of the gods of the Egyptian pantheon lined the way.

Etchings of the life of Amun-Re reached to the top of the high walls. Statues of the god and his family lined the inside the main wall. The interior of the temple revealed tall columns spaced two to three cubits apart that buttressed the ceiling. The pillars continued down the main hallway for many cubits before stopping at a new and gigantic statute of Amun-Re seated on a throne as Pharaoh, holding a staff with a hook at the top, holding a jewel in place. How did I not notice this yesterday?

Save for the beginning, I remember little of the evening.

Sitamen, Meritamen, and Nefertari placed the flowers they carried on the altar in front of the giant statue while singing a haunting tune I had not heard. Her hands, free of the flowers, Sitamen returned to my side and took my hand in hers, setting my heart racing. Desire rose within me as in my dream. Panicking, I held my breath, causing me to feel faint.

Recalling the second part of my vision, I inhaled and exhaled in the manner Harwa taught me to calm myself. The stirring in my loins rose as I felt a tingle climb up my spine, cresting my head and continuing down the midline of my torso. The power cycled through my body, up my back, and down my front in a continuous motion. Closing my eyes, I saw colors as that of a rainbow swirling in my field of vision, twisting and climbing around a white core.

I watched the shapes dance before me as I continued to breathe. A sense of peace swept over me, and for a moment, I felt as though floating on a stream moving through the air. For how long this continued, I did not know. A squeeze of my hand jolted me. I opened my eyes to find Sitamen staring at me.

"Are you unwell, Ramose?" she asked.

I looked at her confused for a moment.

"Mother!" Sitamen screamed, holding me up as though I might fall over.

Nefertari came over to help Sitamen bring me to the floor.

"Is he going to be all right?" Sitamen asked.

"He will be fine, Sitamen. Fasting can do this to anyone, but Ramose's illness weakened him."

Servants bearing a litter came to carry me back to the palace. Instead of joining the celebration downstairs, I ate dinner in my room that night. Dejected at first for being excluded from the celebratory feast, a knock on the door changed my mood. Harwa entered dressed as a servant.

"You have been busy, I hear," he said, smiling. I ran over to greet him, glad he came. "How do you feel?"

"I do not know what happened, but I do not think fasting caused this." I told him about the breathing technique and energy movement.

"What in the name of Amun-Re possessed you to do that technique? And who taught it to you?"

"You did!"

"I did not!" he objected.

I told how he showed me to do this in my dream.

"Tell me the entire dream," he said.

Embarrassed, I blushed as I recounted the complete vision. My mentor asked for clarification at multiple points. When I finished, he looked out the window. The longer he did so, the more nervous I became. Had I done something wrong?

"Is it bad I dreamt about laying with Sitamen?"

"What?!" he said, turning around. Grinning, he said, "No, that is not unusual for a boy, nay, a man, your age. I have a different concern."

"What is that?"

"Your dream may be prophetic."

"It is?"

"Absolutely! Forget the part about Sitamen for a moment, though I believe it to be important too. You learned a breathing technique reserved for experienced Magi. It is something I may have taught you. But your vision showed you."

"How?"

"I do not know. Then you used this method during the ritual."

"And fainted."

"Not the worst thing that could have happened to you, and because of Sitamen jolting you out of your state. You reached a state of energy, called Ruach."

"Serah said it was Ab."

"You met Serah?" Harwa asked, sounding surprised.

"Earlier this morning."

"What did she tell you?"

After recounting the conversation, Harwa asked, "Ahmose-Ankh did not know Siamun would try to rape Sitamen too."

"How did he make Meritamen safe?" I asked.

"By lying with her. As you almost did in your dream with Sitamen."

"How would that protect her?"

"Siamun possesses peculiar," he paused for a moment. "Appetites. He not only wants what he cannot have, but also what is untouched by another. Ahmose-Ankh recognized this and lay with Meritamen."

"But Ammi can not do that with Sitamen?" I asked.

"Not even if he becomes Pharaoh unless Meritamen dies. Pharaoh only marries his oldest sister. They consider it bad luck to marry another."

"I did not know."

"But Sitamen does. Has she been paying attention to you?"

"What do you mean?"

"Standing next to you, taking your hand, kissing you?"

"She has not kissed me," I retorted.

Harwa smiled at my response, then said, "That is good. I suspect she is interested in you. And will try to seduce you."

"That is nonsense. Sitamen is my sister."

"Technically, she is not. They adopted you, and therefore you could marry her. She knows that."

"Marry?"

"You are both of age and are desirable."

"I am?"

Harwa smiled. "Yes, Ramose. You are young, strong, and good looking. You appear exotic to Egyptians. Based on what you told me, I guess she is very interested in you."

"Really?"

"It is how Egyptians court." He gazed at me, then added. "But there is more going on here. Come over here."

I walked over to him and Harwa gently placed his hand on my forehead. "How did I miss that?" he muttered.

"What did you miss?"

"An attraction spell. I assumed when Rekhmire showed you the wrong spell, you only cast it on the amulet. But somehow it is in you too. I do not know how I missed it."

"Rekhmire cast that on me?" I asked concerned my trusted teacher would have done such a thing.

"No. The other spell lay on top of it so I cannot be sure. It is possible that Rekhmire cast the spell without knowing what he was doing. Maybe he is under the spell of suggestion."

Though I felt a slight relief by the explanation, I still felt unsettled.

"Tell me more of your dream," Harwa said. "Try to pay attention to me and not Sitamen for a moment," he teased. "What was Paser's reaction in your dream?"

"Upset and angry," I responded. "He said I was reserved for

someone else."

"Did he say who?"

"No. Ahmose-Ankh and Serah discussed the same thing today. She did not reveal whom I am to marry. Only that it would not be a Nubian princess."

"Nor Sitamen."

"No. She was very clear about that."

"You have had a most unusual dream, Ramose, likely prophetic. In other ways, I believe you may have been thinking about what Serah said."

"Thinking?"

"In your sleep. Some dreams are like that. At least that is what Joseph explained about dream interpretation. He knew the difference between prophetic dreams and just a regular one. Yours has elements of both."

Harwa and I discussed elements of dreams, symbols, transitions, and personal versus impersonal characteristics of each. My vision had a quality of the divine talking directly to me.

"More like one of Jacob's dreams rather than Joseph's. You may be more like Jacob than you know. Heed Serah's advice, Ramose."

"About wives?"

"Yes. You may desire Sitamen, but I have never known Serah to be wrong with her prophecies. Another is destined for you."

"Is that why Ahmose-Ankh went to see her? Her vision is true?"

"I imagine it to be so. Ahmose-Ankh and Meritamen play with fire. Meritamen may be protected, but this is not over for them. And if something happens to Ahmose-Ankh, Meritamen could be in danger."

"There was one more part of the dream I do not understand. What about the choice?"

"The choice? Very peculiar."

"You will not tell me, are you?" I accused him.

"If the voice did not, why should I?" he countered. "I do not know what it means Ramose. I could relate it to Sitamen or something else."

Disappointed he refused to tell me, I let it go.

"One more thing," he said. "Do you recall from your dream what time of year Sitamen came to your bed?"

"I do not, but I felt strange when I woke up in my dream. As though I drank too much."

"As I expected! That is the Tekh festival. It comes in the middle of the month. It celebrates Ra getting Bastet drunk, so she did not eat all humanity. Everyone drinks until they pass out. When they awake, participants perform a sex ritual. Maybe Sitamen plans to seduce you then."

Though it pained me, I knew he was right. I felt I must remove myself from the palace during the festival. But how? My strong desire for Sitamen would not allow me to resist her seductions. Though I struggled against Serah's proclamation for a wife I did not yet know, I needed to avoid Sitamen for now.

"Let me discuss leaving for the Eastern Desert before the festival," I told Harwa.

"I think that wise, Ramose. You may make a good leader someday."

Harwa's words encouraged me. But I would soon learn there is more to leadership than decisions-making.

20

Though he advised me to avoid Sitamen, I forgot Harwa's advice the next morning upon waking. I found her on the terrace near the river eating breakfast with Meritamen and Ahmose-Ankh.

"Good morning, Ramose," my brother greeted. "Are you feeling better this morning?"

"I am," I replied.

"What happened to you last night?" Sitamen asked, coming over to give me a hug.

Embracing Sitamen, my knees weakened, inhaling her scent as I lingered in her touch. For a moment, my dream flashed through my head, and I almost kissed her on the lips as we had done in my vision.

"Why did you faint?" Meritamen asked, stopping me from my mindless actions. I noted Ammi's concerned look as he watched Sitamen and I arm and arm.

What do I tell my adopted siblings? I wondered. Letting go of Sitamen, I said, "Some residual poison still affected me."

"Are you feeling better?" Meritamen asked.

"Yes," I replied.

The four of us spoke for about a quarter of an hour when Ammi pulled me aside.

"Remember, Serah's words," he said. "They reserve you for another."

"Why do you think she is right?" I challenged.

"You cannot protect Sitamen in that manner."

"You shielded Meritamen thus," I argued.

"That is different."

"How?"

"I am the oldest son, destined to be Pharaoh. We will marry. Our actions only removed a threat."

"And went against Pharaoh's wishes."

"Because Balaam poisons his decisions," Ahmose-Ankh hissed louder than intended. The two women looked over at us. Then calming himself, he switched the subject back to Sitamen and me. "Besides, what about Amenhotep?"

"How do you mean?"

"The Sebou ritual claims you as a child of Pharaoh. Should you lay with either of our sisters, the people would exalt you above Amenhotep. Chaos would ensue as though Siamun raped our sister."

"Chaos?"

"Seth betrayed Osiris trying to marry Isis creating discord in the universe. No one ruled while Isis searched for the body of her brother."

Ammi explained that Seth desired anarchy more than anything else. My actions could create a similar outcome. A battle raged within me. I struggled with my desire to know Sitamen, for the feelings of my dream lingered. A force inside me stirred, seeking an outlet through her. But I shunned upsetting Amenhotep.

"Amenhotep is your friend, now," my older brother said, as though reading my thoughts. "I could see the hurt on his face seeing you and Sitamen hold hands."

Ammi's words softened my passion, for I loved Amenhotep and did not wish to deceive him.

"Very well, Ammi," I said. "I will remove myself from this situation. But you must protect Sitamen."

"Let me consider how to do that," he suggested, as we rejoined our sisters.

We talked for about half an hour, eating a small breakfast before I excused myself to seek Miriam. Servants busied themselves preparing for further Wepet-Renpet celebrations. Decorations, platters of food, and gifts moved throughout the castle.

Wandering towards the Habiru quarter, different activities ensued. I avoided this section of town because of my station. But my adventure the previous day with Paser and Ahmose-Ankh removed any hesitation. Various Habiru and Egyptian slaves worked placing barriers to protect their houses from flooding. Though only two days old, it was clear this inundation season would be severe. Huts often safe from the flood zone could become submerged in a few weeks. Near the river, people carried water-logged clothing and bedding. As I walked through the poorer part of town, people scrambled to remove the few belongings they possessed to protected locations. Anger welled inside me, seeing the disparity.

Asking a few people along the way where I might find Miriam, I arrived at her tent.

"Ramose?!" she said, surprised to see me. "What brings you here?"

I filled her in about the last two days. When I came to the part about marrying the Nubian princess, she winced.

"You cannot marry a Nubian!" she exclaimed. "They are not worthy of you!"

I refused to respond to my sister's tribalism. Instead I said, "Serah says I am destined for another."

"You spoke with Serah?" she asked. I recounted the tale. The respect for Serah's wisdom reached to all corners of the Habiru tribes. Miriam asked a few questions, but she was most curious about Ahmose-Ankh's interest in the Habiru seer.

"All know Serah's gift of prophecy. She is a remarkable person," I explained.

"Who does she see for you?" Miriam asked. "One of our people when you lead us from this desolate place?"

"She did not say. Nor did she reveal I would lead the Children of Israel from the land."

"She said you have not come into your own and to do so you must leave the land. Maybe you need to start your mission right away."

"That is why I am here," I replied. "I will speak with Nefertari and Rekhmire about leaving in the next few days."

"How long will you off?"

"I am unsure. I suppose it depends upon the state of the battles. I do not relish being in the middle of the desert during

Akhet. It is already warm here by the Nile. I cannot imagine how hot it will be in the desert."

"Truly."

"But staying here during Beshemet may be worse. Sitamen shows a passion for me."

"Your adopted sister?"

"I do not know how long I could resist her even though it would bring disaster Amenhotep, and the Habiru people."

"You cannot be with her, Ramose. It would be wrong for so many reasons."

"I know, Miriam. That is why I must go."

Miriam embraced me. "Be safe, Ramose."

***

I returned to palace incensed. The discrepancy between the lives of the royal family and my biological relatives disturbed me. I sought Nefertari to discuss a plan for my leaving before the Tekh Festival. As I walked through the royal chambers, I thought I should explain my actions to Amenhotep, though I did not understand them myself. I wanted to tell him the truth; that I felt something for Sitamen but did not know how it would affect him. Tempted by her, I wished to remove myself from the situation to protect him. The alcohol in the Tekh festival affects people in strange ways, and I did not trust myself or the others to behave appropriately.

But I spoke none of those thoughts. For when I passed Amenhotep's room, I saw Hannu, Ankhu, and Maiherpri sitting with my adopted brother. Instead of saying nothing and continuing on my original mission, I looked in.

"What do you want Habiru?" my adopted brother snapped.

Breathing to calm myself, I replied, "Can we speak alone?" My heart raced.

"So you can stab him in the back again?" Hannu answered.

"I have done no such thing," I countered.

"You held hands with Sitamen," Ankhu said. "You need to learn your place, Habiru!"

The treatment I received at the hands of the lazy nobles recalled the atrocious conditions the Habirus dwelt. My rage swelled. The energy I felt the previous day rose within me as a wave began in my arms and hands. Simultaneously, a flood of power vibrated inside my sacral and abdominal regions. I breathed, and felt the power inside me grow to a point I could direct it towards one of these nobles and destroy them.

I gathered the force, trying to determine the best way to release it at these boys. Thinking a blow was necessary, I moved towards them. A look of horror shone on their faces as I approached. The four boys scrambled to their feet to defend themselves.

Just as I came close enough to strike, I heard Ahmose-Ankh behind me shouting. "Stop Ramose!"

My oldest brother grabbed me from behind but pulled his hands from me as though shocked. I turned to see Ahmose-Ankh looking back and forth between his hands and me.

"Are you injured?" I asked.

Shaking his head, he continued to stare, mouth agape. I turned back to Amenhotep and his friends, frozen in their stances. "I came to apologize Amenhotep, and that I am removing myself from this situation. I leave tomorrow or the next day on my mission."

I turned around and walked past Ahmose-Ankh to leave the room.

"Wait!" Ahmose-Ankh commanded, coming to his senses again. I stopped at the threshold of the door. "Ramose, come back in here! Maiherpri, Hannu, Ankhu, leave now!"

The four of us moved as Ahmose-Ankh ordered, feeling his commanding presence.

"Please sit, Ramose," my older brother requested after the other boys left. My body still shook with rage. I continued to breathe to calm myself. After a few moments, Ahmose-Ankh spoke. "This needs to stop now. You two are good friends."

"He started it," Amenhotep accused.

"I did not!"

"Stop. Neither of you started anything. You had a misunderstanding. Things are moving faster, for the end of the prophecies come."

"What are you talking about?" Amenhotep asked.

Ammi sat down across from us with a sigh. "Before I tell you, I want to ensure you two are friends."

Amenhotep pouted but said nothing, so our older brother continued. "Ramose meant nothing by holding hands with Sitamen. He only wished to protect her."

"Protect her? From what?"

"Siamun. But he knows now how that could affect your standing too."

I wanted to explain Sitamen grabbed my hand, but I only nodded my head.

"Why would Siamun do that?" Amenhotep asked.

"He has unusual desires, as you know. Siamun wishes to bring chaos to the family. Father's obsession with the prophecies blinds him. Soon the time comes to deal with Siamun once and for all."

"What prophecies?" Amenhotep asked.

"There are many. But two compete against one another."

"How do you know this?" I asked.

"I have discerned this through my spying skills, listening to others' conversations, ensuring my survival. The time draws near though that one of the two prophecies will come true."

He paused for a moment before continuing. "Ramose knows the first prophecy; a Habiru child would rise to lead the people from the land. Some believe Ramose is that person and I suspect part of Father's desire to bring Ramose to the palace Amenhotep would be to show him the superior ways of the Egyptians to prevent this from happening."

"That makes sense," Amenhotep agreed.

"But another prophecy predicts a child of the pharaoh rising, of vast power. He will rule not only rule over Egypt but will be renown forever as a leader of all people in faith and virtue."

"So whoever becomes the next Pharaoh will be the greatest leader ever?"

"Perhaps," Ahmose-Ankh responded. "But I do not know. We are at momentous times to be sure. And I believe Ahmose feels he can become that great leader."

"How?" Amenhotep asked. "I mean if the prophecy is about one of us."

"I wondered too. It upset many people when father brought Ramose into the family because of the second prophecy."

"Why?" I asked.

"Because it now applies to you too. You could be that great leader, though you are Habiru. Egyptians fear oppression."

"Unless they are doing it to Habirus," I snapped. I relayed

to Ahmose-Ankh my walk through the Habiru quarter today and the abject poverty I witnessed. He nodded as though he understood. Amenhotep ignored this part of the conversation to ask another question.

"Then why would Ahmose risk Ramose being in the family?"

"He seeks the Staff of Osiris to change the prophecy with its power."

"It has that much power?" Amenhotep asked.

"He believes it to be so."

"What does this have to do with me?" I asked.

"I do not know, Ramose," Ahmose-Ankh replied. "But I suspect he will ask you to help him find it."

"How?"

"That is unclear. But I overheard Ahmose and Rekhmire speaking about preparing you for a mission."

"I remember they spoke about this the day Siamun left the lamb's leg in my room."

"I overheard them discussing it again. I think it is why they send you to the East."

"Is that where the staff lay?"

"Perhaps," Ammi admitted. "Or maybe it is to prepare you for another aspect of the mission. Do not let him get it Ramose. Whatever you do."

"Why?"

"He will give it to Siamun. That must never happen."

"What if he finds it without me?" I asked. "Will he not just give it to your demented brother?"

"I will take care of that problem," Ahmose-Ankh said, looking stern.

***

Ahmose-Ankh changed the subject and the three of us talked about lighter subjects for several hours, joking and teasing one another. Amenhotep's servant interrupted our laughter to inform us of the need to prepare for dinner.

"In case we do not talk tonight," Amenhotep said, "Good luck on your mission." He came over to embrace me for a few moments. I left, my friendship with Amenhotep repaired, thanks to Ammi.

As I walked to my room, I remembered my intent to speak

to Nefertari. Her servant led me to her as she began preparing for the evening meal.

"You wished to see me, Ramose," she said, moving about the room.

"Yes, Mother. I wish to leave on my mission earlier than planned."

"How early?" she asked, sitting down next to me.

"Before Tekh."

"It will be burning hot in the desert, Ramose."

"I know, Mother. But.." I stopped. What do I tell her? That I lust after her daughter.

"The issue with Sitamen is clear to me," she helped. "I am arranging plans to keep you separated. I do not know what has gotten into that girl."

"Harwa found an attraction spell cast on me," I volunteered.

"He did? Leave us at once," she ordered her servants. After the four women left, Nefertari implored me to tell the entire story. Starting with the amulet selection, I told her the events of the past few days.

"Show me the amulet," she demanded.

I took the Hamsa out from tunic to show her.

"Take it off so I can look at it."

"Harwa told me to never remove it."

She started to demand I remove it, but a curious change came over her face. She looked into the distance as if listening to a voice only she heard. "No, he must leave it on," she mumbled. "Danger still exists." Then turning to me, she said, "Leave it on."

She came close. I could feel her breath on me as she examined the amulet. She pulled away, sitting back in her chair. "Balaam cast that spell," she proclaimed.

"How do you know?"

"I just know."

"But Rekhmire was with me. He is the one who told me the attraction spell is a protection one."

"Rekhmire would not have done that on purpose."

"I do not understand."

"You said that Harwa removed a suggestion. Balaam placed that there. And he did the same to Rekhmire, causing him to do the wrong spell."

"How do you know?"

"I cannot explain, Ramose." She thought for a moment as though calculating something in her head. Then she said, "There is more going on here that you suspect. But I think getting you away from Sitamen might be best. Thank you for telling me about this, Ramose."

We discussed my leaving on the mission early even with the heat. She recommended stopping in Avaris for Tekh and allowing the men to celebrate.

Later that evening, the festival began with some singing and giving thanks to Amun-Re for the flooding. Ahmose-Ankh and Meritamen stood between me and Sitamen. Every time she tried to get close to me, one of them or a friend of theirs would intercede.

I sensed her frustration when we sat for dinner. Servants instructed me to sit between Amenhotep and Ahmose-Ankh. They placed Meritamen next to my older brother, followed by the son of a noble I did not know. Across from him sat Sitamen. She entertained him and another courtier sitting next to her. Both were potential suitors for marriage.

"I understand Prince Siamun returns from battle," the one across from her said.

"He struggled to bring victory to Ahmose," she replied.

"Does Ahmose-Ankh take his place?" the man across from her asked.

"Nay, my Lord," she replied. "His highness Ramose takes his place." She looked over at me as she spoke, her eyes twinkling. Neither suitor saw her face, for both looked my way as she spoke. "Let us drink to Ramose's success."

The assembled raised glasses to toast my mission. Ahmose glared in my direction, though I did not know why. Balaam, sitting next to my adopted father, smiled.

"We shall see, how the young prince fairs," the man next to her said before drinking. "Fighting in the desert this time of year presents many challenges."

"Well said Yuny," Ahmose agreed.

"Horses are useless because you must carry too much water and food during Akhet," the noble observed.

"Siamun's combat training included chariots. I believe it to be the root of his struggle."

"Is that your excuse for him?" Nefertari asked.

Ahmose glared at his sister-wife, but said nothing. He continued his other conversation with Balaam and another noble. Talk resumed around the table for some time as Amenhotep and I discussed my mission. Ahmose-Ankh tried to explain how arid the land away from the Nile delta becomes.

"You have not felt such dryness in your life, Ramose. Barren does not describe the region this time of year."

"Why does anyone live there?" I asked.

"Why indeed?" Ahmose interjected into our conversation. "We have had this discussion many times, have we not Ahmose-Ankh?"

"Yes, Father," Ammi responded, subdued.

The conversation Ahmose referred followed their typical banter about the subject of Habirus in Egypt. Ahmose believed they should either find their own source of water or stop reproducing. He did not want more foreigners in his country. Ahmose-Ankh argued Egypt possessed more than enough resources for all who wished to settle in the land. I heard the argument my first Akhet at the palace many years ago, the same day Siamun showed his propensity for cruelty as he pulled the wings off a dragonfly in the royal apartments.

"Let us not have that discussion tonight, Ahmose," Nefertari said. "We have had enough discord this holiday."

"As my queen wishes," Ahmose replied with a slight hint of sarcasm.

Ammi described the terrain, pitfalls, and challenges of fighting in the desert. Having little context, I did not understand his advice, but said nothing. Only when he described Kenite fighting techniques did I ask anything, for I wanted to know their weaknesses and strengths.

"Ramose is the bravest fighter in Egypt," Sitamen spoke, her face alight. "He can defeat anyone in combat."

"How little you know of battle, Sitamen," Ammi responded. "It is chaotic and bloody. The enemy comes at you from many angles, arrows buzzing by you from places unseen. Even the best warrior depends upon the surrounding men to guard his backside and flanks. All the while you are slashing and stabbing at others, hearing the sounds bones breaking, men crying out, surrounded by death."

The room became silent, listening to Ahmose-Ankh's description of battle. My brother's words scared me, for I knew I only practiced one-on-one combat. Sitamen would not back down.

"Ramose will rise to the occasion. The prophets foretold such."

Ahmose's face contorted with rage. "What do you know of prophecies?"

"I know what I have heard," Sitamen snapped.

"How dare you speak of something, told in confidence by the priests in the temple?" Ahmose countered.

"Let us not make a big deal about this, Ahmose," Nefertari said, trying to calm her husband-brother.

"She speaks of things she should not!"

"She knows not what she speaks about," Nefertari replied, a sly look in her eyes.

"I know Ramose will become a great leader," Sitamen responded. I was not the only person at the dinner surprised by her boldness. I did not understand her boldness as this behavior seemed out of character.

Balaam touched Ahmose's arm to calm the monarch. "Maybe Sitamen is correct, your Majesty. Let us give young Ramose a chance to prove his prowess in battle."

"What do you have in mind, Balaam?" Ahmose replied.

"If Ramose is blessed, then one company of men should be enough to fulfill the mission."

"An excellent idea, Balaam," Ahmose smiled.

"That is not enough troops, Father!" Ammi objected.

"It is for someone blessed as Ramose believes himself to be."

Though I proclaimed no such thing, no one corrected Ahmose's statement. Whether that was because he was Pharaoh or the others believed me to be so bold, I did not know.

"Father, the entire company will get killed!" Ahmose-Ankh argued. "You gave Siamun triple the men needed for success!"

"So you say."

"As did your military advisors."

"I have made my decision." Then turning towards me, Ahmose added, "Ramose, excuse yourself to begin preparations."

I nodded, rising to leave as the assembled gave their regards. Sitamen rose too, but Meritamen moved to cut her off from coming towards me.

"Let me embrace my brother," she demanded. "Let me go!"

But Meritamen held her, preventing her from hugging me.

"You are not acting yourself, Sitamen," Nefertari said. "Something inflames you!"

As I moved around the table, I saw my adopted mother glaring across the table towards Balaam, who only smirked in response. I said goodnight and left the dining hall. Ahmose-Ankh followed me, saying nothing until we arrived at my room.

"Listen, Ramose," Ammi said, closing the door behind him. "You and the others are in grave danger on this mission. Ahmose's generals estimate the mission requires three or four companies to secure the area."

"Should I not go?" I asked.

"You do not have a choice, my brother. They would view not going as cowardice or defiance. The mission presents challenges any time of year, but particularly during Akhet."

"What do I do?"

"Listen to the experienced military people under your command. They will know how to best protect all of you. Take few risks. Keep the bulk of your forces together."

I affirmed my understanding with a nod.

"One more thing to know. Given the heat, the enemy will always be close to an oasis."

"Oasis?"

"Underground water bursting from the earth fill the desert. Trees, plants, and animals surround the pools of water. Sometimes, it requires digging to find the water, but it is close to the surface. The desert peoples stay near those places, defending them, unable to wander more than a day away."

"If we find a force of them, we know we are a day away from this oasis?"

"That is correct. Waiting for reinforcements is your best course of action at that point."

"Did Siamun find any oasis?"

"I heard he kept running into ambushes getting men killed."

"I will try to avoid that fate."

Ammi embraced me, saying goodnight.

21

First light the following morning, I arose to find Mahu and a detachment of soldiers waiting. Though I had only met him once, I felt better knowing Mahu accompanied the mission. His dark complexion stressed his features. Taller than most Egyptians, his nose was longer, possessing a robust hooked appearance, and firmer jawline than his Egyptian brethren that even the customary chin beard could not hide. Mahu came dressed in his military uniform, a young officer in the army. At least a foot taller than the other soldiers, he looked even more remarkable in his suit because of his broad shoulders and well-developed arms, the right one larger than the left.

The company of men seemed disgruntled to be moving out before the Tekh festival. Judging from their appearances, they celebrated early, still hungover from their libations. In loud voices, two men, Sobi and Toruk, spoke about their grievances of the deployment during the celebratory season.

"The day is likely to be hot," I said. "We best begin our journey."

The men gathered their belongings. Not moving fast enough for my second in command, Mahu barked orders for them to quicken their pace. The formation developed, and the men boarded the boats to take us north to Avaris.

The three-day river journey north would lead us through narrow and vast parts of the Nile. The river flowed fast during the season of Akhet, and high water levels could be dangerous for boats. We distributed the extra supplies and weapons amongst the various ships.

The journey proved uneventful as we arrived in Avaris on schedule. Celebrations of Wepet-Renpet continued in the North. Though Mahu suggested otherwise, I followed Nefertari's advice to allow the men to partake in the festivities that day and evening.

Many of the recruits arrived late the next morning, delaying our departure. Mahu said nothing, but I knew my mistake. Allowing them to partake in the festivities but not enforcing a curfew delayed our departure. Even with my generosity, Toruk and Sobi continued to grumble as the hot sun affected those who drank the most alcohol.

From Avaris, our journey proceeded over land. Our movement to the area we believed the insurgents to be hiding would be arduous. That morning, we walked until the day became too hot. Then we continued after the day cooled. Even with a branch of the Nile nearby, I had never felt the heat of the sun as I did that day up to that point in my life.

I stumbled along in the heat, listening to the complaints of the assembled. We kept going as the day warmed until Mahu suggested we halt for rest.

"From here on out, we should not be moving during the heat of the day," he suggested.

I ordered the men to set-up camp in protective formation. Though relieved to get out of the mid-day sun, they assembled the tents haphazardly. Tired myself, I said nothing.

For the next few days, we marched eastward, avoiding the hottest part of the day. We left the safety and relative coolness of the river to venture into the blistering furnace of the desert. The landscape's barrenness blazed in stark contrast to the fertile Nile. Sand and rock continued as far as the land could see. The scene possessed few changes in the distance. Only the occasional plant broke up the brown color.

Changes came the second day out from the river, when my lack of experience proved fatal. The path we traveled cut through a pass between high stone cliffs on either side of us. In hindsight, I saw the wisdom of avoiding this location. The narrow area only allowed four men to walk across abreast. But instead of bypassing this outcropping, I ordered the men to continue marching through it. After we would travel through this spot, I told the men to reassemble their formation on the other side. The events that unfolded interrupted the plan.

Everything started well. Mahu and I lined up in front and passed through the restricted space, and he ordered the men to take defensive positions as the others marched through the area. Creaking noises turned into a low grown. Then I realized the mistake. A rumbling came from above as boulders rolled down the sides of the outcroppings, descending towards the men in the middle. Mahu and I shouted orders as the men in the front and back moved out of the way, while the rocks crushed several men still in the middle.

Around the sides of the outcropping, a large group of Kenites rushed us. Our forces cut in two; we hoped for the best as I readied myself to repel the assault. Only Mahu's foresight saved us as our archers loosed arrows, felling the first wave of attackers. A second group came before most of the soldiers could release another set of bolts slashing several of my men.

I stepped forward, spear in one hand, sword in the other fighting several men at once. Mahu admitted later, my fighting prowess surprised him. Reaching with my spear, I pushed back the assault of the enemy, killing several attackers while using my small sword as a shield to block blows. Mahu rallied the men on his side as we continued to defend our position. I ordered the men to create a formation to either side of me. Ignoring my orders, Toruk used his quick sword to slash through several Kenite spearmen, saving several lives. His fighting skills proved to be very good.

The attackers retreated, reassembled, and resumed their charge. Wave after wave came at us, but we repealed the onslaught. When the Kenites tried to outflank us, my men covered each other. Several times, I helped save one of my men next to me. One soldier received a severe blow to his arm. I guarded his side while he could fall back, another defender taking his place.

After the fourth attempt, the ambushers tried to retreat, but Mahu ordered the men to cut off their escape. None of them survived. I do not remember how many men I killed that day, only that the sounds and sights of the battle sickened me. My will to survive surpassed my disgust of killing others.

Remembering that they had divided my force, I ordered some men to follow me. Sorting through the dead bodies and boulders, we climbed to the other side to join the fracas.

When we came through to the other side, we found the rearguard plastered under a ledge that shielded them from boulders. They fought their attackers to a standstill. Climbing through to the other side, I led a charge to relieve them. More bones crushed, more guts spilled, as blood poured onto the desert floor. However, I gave no notice to this, lost in the moment of battle, defending my Egyptian brethren.

By mid-day, we eliminated the attackers. Besides the twelve men who died by boulders in the initial attack, thirteen men were dead or would die, with another twenty-three wounded, losing almost a tenth of my company. I looked around to see the countless bodies of the Kenites littered on the ground. Bile rose from my stomach, and I vomited.

***

Two priests, trained in medicine, tended to the wounded, comforting the dying with potions to ease the pain. Most of the injuries comprised bruises, cuts, and a few broken bones. Though my royal status did not require my assisting, it pleased me to contribute, holding men down while the priests set bones or administering poisons to those with mortal injuries to ease their suffering.

Mahu instructed the uninjured men to dig graves for the dead. Away from the waters of the Nile, their bodies would become mummified in the sun's heat. A few men in the company dragged several of the Kenite dead away from the shaded area we prepared to camp until the day cooled.

As I tended one of the wounded, I noticed Toruk and Sobi standing around doing nothing. I said nothing as I worked with the priests. Members of the company thanked me for my assistance.

As the cooks prepared the mid-day meal, I approached Mahu about our next steps. He motioned for me to enter the commander's tent.

"I led us into an ambush."

"You did," Mahu whispered.

"Ahmose-Ankh warned me about the landscape, but I did not understand. I have never seen hills and outcroppings like these."

"How would you know the dangers?"

"I hear the men complain that I got so many killed. What was I supposed to do to prevent this?"

Mahu thought for a moment. "Permission to speak candidly, your highness."

"Please Mahu! Ahmose-ankh told me to trust you. It is why I ask."

"Did you not receive basic command training? You fight well."

"I learned to fight to defend myself."

"But no military or command strategy?"

"None."

"Why would they have given you this commission? No offense intended."

"None taken."

"Why did you agree to do this? You moved up the timeline even."

I explained what happened at the dinner the night before setting off, Sitamen's unusual behavior towards me, and what she said that night at dinner. I felt Mahu's anger as he listened to my tale. Taking a deep breath, he said, "Ahmose-Ankh gave you some good advice, but we must teach you as we go. I plan to pull you aside when necessary."

"Thank you. What should I do now? The men hate me."

"They appreciate your care tending the wounded."

"Fantastic. I can lead them to near death and treat their wounds after."

Mahu laughed.

"What did I do wrong?" I asked.

"Aside from walking into a trap? We have to pay careful attention to our movements here in the desert. The enemy had the advantage of the terrain, and we marched the troops into the valley, allowing them to attack with boulders. Your rapid response and fighting skills prevented more deaths."

"What should our plan be now?"

"There must be an oasis nearby."

"That is right. Ahmose-Ankh mentioned that would be the case. He said they would be only a day away from the water supply."

"If we can take the water supply, we will render the rest ineffective."

"But Ammi warned me not to take risks."

"We cannot stay here forever, we do not have enough water. And the oasis may be behind us. Send out scouts tonight to find the spring. Then we can move our troops in secret. Other scouts will search for Kenite ambushes, so we either avoid them, or spring them along the way."

"An excellent plan, Mahu. Let us implement it."

"Before that, you need to make an example of Toruk."

"How do you mean?"

"Did you not see his behavior the last few days?"

"I have, but..."

"You chose not to reprimand him! Soldiers expect discipline. The desert requires it. Otherwise, the men will devolve into the action you have witnessed in him leading to unnecessary deaths."

"What should I do?"

"Punish him for his conduct. Disobeying orders leads to insubordination. You must keep your troops in line when in the desert, otherwise, we all could perish. Even if you have a bad plan, they need to listen to your orders."

We agreed that I should flog Toruk in public because of his brazen defiance. Mahu assembled the men to make a spectacle of Toruk. Addressing the gathering, I spoke.

"For disobeying my direct order, Toruk, and endangering the men, I will punish you," I said. "Please step forward and take your shirt off."

I reached to the whip that Mahu gave me in the tent. But Toruk stood there, defying me with his hands on his hips and a smirk on his face. The sneer reminded me of the callous disregard Siamun showed me. My anger swelled, churning for the years of taunting I received at the palace, for the anguish my brethren received by the hands of Egyptians. I am sorry to say I took matters into my own hands.

An energy surged within me as occurred in the temple the previous week. A burning force rose higher and higher within my body. Then my hands tingled and throbbed. Feelings I held back for so long burst forth as I directed the power towards Toruk. His face contorted as he clutched his throat as though he had no breath. I continued to push the energy at him as the color in his face changed from dark to purplish. I heard a quiet voice implore, "Not that way! Not yet."

An image formed in my head. Instead of taking the whip, I unsheathed my sword and in one swift motion swung. Toruk's face registered panic in the split instant, my sword buried through his neck as I cut straight through it, separating his head from his body. The headless body crumbled to the ground as the other soldiers stood in shock. My heart raced as I stood over Toruk's dead body, sword in hand, dripping with blood.

I breathed deep into my belly for several moments to calm the energy in my body, steadying myself.

I looked at the soldiers. Fear filled their faces mimicking the cold look on Toruk's dead countenance. Only Mahu watched, betraying no emotion about my act. As my heart steadied, I shouted. "Let this be a lesson. I will no longer tolerate insubordination from my troops. Am I understood?"

"Yes, Your Highness!" the men said in unison.

"Bury your fallen comrade," I commanded, pointing at three soldiers in the front. They sprang into action to follow my order.

I cleaned my sword and sheathed it shaking still with rage. Though it felt good to discipline a disobedient soldier, my anger remained unabated. Feelings of revenge continued to fester inside me as the energy within me pulsed. Deep within me, I sensed I needed to learn to control the rage that slithered into my soul, lurking closer to the surface than I cared to admit to myself.

***

The three men buried Toruk as the others finished their tasks for setting up camp. After cleaning my sword and washing up, I returned to the command tent. I felt tense and uncomfortable. I thought my actions wrong and needed to decide the next course of action. Turn myself in? Run away? Serah told me the time would come when I might need to leave. Was this that time? Fleeing now would be difficult. Even if I could escape the camp and my men, the Kenites would try to kill anyone dressed as an Egyptian soldier. Serah may be right about my need to leave Egypt, but this was not the time.

I paced the tent, contemplating my options. Runaway? Or turn myself in for murder? After about half an hour of this internal struggle, I realized that no one entered the tent to arrest me. I summoned Mahu to the tent.

"Since you are second in command, I surrender myself to you. After the mission, turn me over to the authorities."

"What are you talking about, Your Highness?" he asked, perplexed.

"I murdered a man and deserve punishment."

"You disciplined a defiant soldier."

"But he did not deserve to die."

"I disagree. Though exotic, Toruk's punishment was just. He defied a direct order from you. The men expect you to discipline them."

"But I went too far."

"No, you did not." A smile came across his face. "The men whisper that you are the crazy Habiru."

"Crazy Habiru?"

He laughed. "No one will disobey you again. Toruk was a great fighter. That you drew your sword so fast and beheaded him without him even reaching for his says something about your fighting skill."

"But the men fear me."

"That is not a bad thing, your majesty. Fear can be your friend."

"It is not a problem?" I asked.

"No. You are not here to make friends with the soldiers. Fear of you may save their lives."

Being ripped from my birth family combined with the torment of Siamun created terror in me. I wished never to impose this feeling on others. Mahu's viewpoint perplexed me.

"I need to think about this."

"What is there to consider? Living in fear is common for them. Command requires disciple no matter how you achieve it."

"Does not love and respect produce more loyal subjects?"

"Our father Abraham would have said so. But his son Isaac based his life around the fear of El Shaddai."

"You are Habiru?!" I exclaimed, surprised by Mahu's revelation.

"Did not Ahmose-Ankh tell you that my mother is from the tribe of Ephraim?"

"No, he did not."

"I tell few of my origins."

Recovering from my shock, I returned to the previous discussion. "What do you mean about Isaac's fear?"

"Serah knows more about this, and likely you should discuss with her. But Isaac's fear of the Lord motivated him. You can use that principle to command."

"Like Ahmose?"

"The people fear Ahmose, though I question how loyal the nobles are to him."

"He plays favorites to be sure."

"I recommend you avoid that. Treat everyone the same. If a soldier is out of line, deal with him as you did with Toruk. Though, maybe not lopping his head off in front of the men."

"My anger got the better of me," I admitted.

"You must not do that in battle, Ramose."

"I know."

"Did you have an experience of Toruk before today?"

Ashamed, I did not answer right away. Then I confessed to Mahu what I could not admit to myself earlier. "I took justice into my own hands with Toruk."

"How so?" Mahu asked.

"I must trust your discretion in not sharing this story with others."

"Of course, Your Highness."

"Ahmose's goal in this mission is to prove my worthiness for marriage to the daughter of a Nubian Chieftain. Before leaving Waset, I ventured to the Habiru quarter to discuss the matter with my sister, Miriam. On the way, I witnessed a man beating two Habirus for not working hard enough preparing for the Wepet-Renpet festival. It was Toruk. He seemed to delight in his cruelty towards them. I thought of killing him there and then but stopped myself."

Mahu sat listening to my tale without saying a word, so I continued.

"Have you been to that side of the city? It is disgusting how the Egyptians treat our people like animals while other Egyptians celebrate the festival. And for him to be beating those men."

"I have seen such behavior, Your Majesty. It is the reason I hid my Habiru origins from others."

"Please call me Ramose."

"Only when we are in private."

I nodded my head in agreement, then said, "I understand Mahu. I do not have the luxury of hiding that information. Which is part of my concern with disciplining the troops."

"Cutting Toruk's head off ensures that you will have no further problems with discipline."

We burst into laughter. Not from a place of cruelty. Rather we both felt relief. I looked at Mahu and realized he was becoming my first friend that was not a relative nor teacher.

22

Mahu instructed men of stealth to search for other ambushes near our position. Six pairs of men set out to uncover Kenite traps in the wilderness and the exact location of the oasis. Sleep eluded me, though Mahu suggested I lay down.

"They will not return for some time, Ramose. Now is the time to rest."

"I will stay up," was all I said. Though men died by my hand in battle, killing Toruk haunted me. I feared nightmares would wake my slumber.

Rather than argue with me, Mahu found a place to rest. I stayed up pouring over the map we had drawn in the sand. Mahu surmised six or seven locations for an oasis based on our knowledge of the area. We hoped the spies would help us narrow down the guess to one place. After some time, when I closed my eyes I saw the map instead of images of battle or Torak's head uncoupling from his body appeared in my vision. Exhausted from the day, I fell asleep. Though the map remained in my head, dreams of killing disturbed my sleep, preventing any chance of my gaining instruction from El Shaddai. Mahu woke me early in the morning when the first pair of scouts returned to give us a report. I felt more tired and battle weary than before sleeping.

The spies told of a rocky outcropping about a half league from our current location. Perched atop of the formation waited twenty men and large boulders ready to roll upon unsuspecting bystanders.

"I could lead twenty-five me up the back of the ledge in the night to take it," Djau said.

"Can we go around it?" Mahu asked.

"We could," Djau admitted.

"We should wait to hear the other reports before deciding," I suggested, not knowing why I did. But Mahu smiled, for I understood a basic tenet of military strategy.

Mahu and I marked the location of this ambush on our makeshift map, allowing us to eliminate one guess for the oasis location. Sounds and smells of breakfast reminded me of my hunger. We interrupted our discussion to join the others in the meal. The meal comprised bread, dried fruits and salted meats. I chatted with some men, learning about their lives as professional soldiers. Ahmose instituted a standing army after conquering the Hyksos. It was not a popular decision. But that morning, I learned the lives of many of these men improved with the conscription. They ate better than they had prior to joining the army and received gold and property as a reward for fighting well. Later, Mahu would explain Ahmose hoped to gain loyalty from the regular forces to counter-balance some noble families he feared might usurp his line. It was no wonder Ahmose recalled Siamun after getting so many men killed.

Over the next three hours, four other groups returned, giving reports similar to Djau's. Two sets of spies discovered multiple traps. Each wished to take twenty-five to fifty men to dispatch the ambushers. I resisted any action until I knew the situation in its entirety. Mahu and I updated the map. Given the new information, Mahu suggested the most likely placement of the oasis.

Around mid-day, the last group returned. They located the oasis very near to Mahu's guess. The scouts determined the enemy's defenses, the number of men, and assault points. Dismissing the spies, Mahu and I discussed our strategy.

"We should not split up our forces too much," I said. "But what is the best way to get that many men across the flat land without being spotted or leaving ourselves vulnerable to an attack."

"If I were them, I would use the high ground to spot invaders such as us. They must outnumber us," Mahu concluded. "I estimated that we needed at least four companies to take the oasis based on the reports of the last team."

"And Siamun could not accomplish the job with that many," I said.

"He refused to listen to the experienced soldiers, Ramose. He believed he knew better than others. Siamun lost almost two companies in the first two weeks. Ahmose liked his aggressiveness. Balaam had him pulled because he feared someone would kill him in his sleep."

"Five hundred men! In two weeks?! I know why I understand little about military strategy, but Siamun received training."

"All the training in the world is meaningless if you do not listen to your senior staff."

Many times, Harwa would tell me the same thing. Thinking of Harwa, I knew what I must do before determining the next course of action and told Mahu so. He nodded his head as though he understood and left me alone in the tent.

Sitting down, I began my breathing exercises. I thought about our predicament and wondered about listening to the advice of my scouts. We did not have enough water to take each ambush and then the oasis. We only brought enough to last a decan in this heat. Even if we took the sanctuary, could we hold it until reinforcements arrived? If we do not move forward, did we have enough water to return? Letting go of these thoughts, I focused on my breath.

I held my breath at the top of the inhale and again at the bottom of the exhale. Continuing in this fashion, I felt a little light-headed but persisted. Nausea and dizziness overwhelmed me and just as I might faint, I heard the voice as a picture came of how to capture the oasis.

I came to, unsure how long I lay unconscious, the vision clear though my head throbbed. I felt ill again. A bucket in the tent's corner provided a place for me to vomit, which I did several times.

Questions raced in my head about the dangers we faced and potential problems we might encounter. What about the water? What about being outnumbered? The plan made little sense as logic told me to turn back. I walked out of the tent to find Mahu inviting him back into the tent.

"Ready the men to march tonight. We will take the oasis at dawn."

Giving me a steady look, he said, "Your Highness, may we speak about this?"

"Please, Mahu," I said, inviting him back into the tent.

He walked inside, both of us sitting on cushions across from one another. Hesitating for a moment, Mahu spoke. "I am confused. I thought you did not believe we could take the oasis. They outnumber us, our water will be low after the battle. If we do not take the haven fast, we will be in danger of dying of thirst."

"I think El Shaddai told me otherwise."

"Oh?"

I told him about what happened. "This makes little sense to me either. I questioned this plan, but it kept coming back to me. Steading my thoughts, I let my mind be still, leaving me only with a clear vision. We can take the oasis without engaging the ambushers."

"Are you certain you are not trying to best Siamun?" he asked.

"No," I answered. "I hesitate about everything."

"The first rule of leadership is to be sure of your opinion. Doubt endangers success."

"I have..." I cut myself off, not knowing how to explain this to him. I hear a voice? See images? It seemed senseless even to me. As I was asking him to risk his life, I needed to tell him something. "They brought me to the palace as a young child because of a vision I had. I believe it to be El Shaddai who speaks to me. At least, that is what Serah told me."

"Does risking the lives of the company of men make sense?" he asked.

"Let me tell you the plan."

I outlined the strategy while he listened, asking clarifying questions. When I finished, he sat thinking.

Smiling, he said, "None have tried this."

"I know," I said. "What if?"

He cut me off with a wave of his hand. "Though it is hazardous, we must go. You have given orders the men are carrying out. Retreating now poses a different set of risks."

"And the men want to do it," I added.

"An excellent observation Ramose."

"Growing up in the palace requires the skill of assessing the mood of others for survival. We leave tonight."

"But we should dispatch a squad to the nearest outpost for reinforcements," he suggested.

"Agreed. Even if we succeed, who knows how long we can hold the sanctuary."

"Before leaving, let us discuss with the senior staff so they understand the plan too. They may have some suggestions."

"Excellent idea!" I said, as he left the tent to gather the officers.

***

Still doubting myself, I put on a brave face meeting the senior officers. Djau, Nehi, and Unas entered the tent with Mahu. Gathering around the makeshift map Mahu and I drew in the sand, I explained the plan. After finishing, they sat in silence for a few moments.

"How do we move through the night without falling off a cliff?" Nehi asked.

"I have an idea that may help," Djau said. "I learned a method for shielding lanterns."

"Will it prevent our being spotted?" Nehi asked.

"I have done it many times."

"How do you know?" Mahu asked.

Djau coughed, uncomfortable about what he would share. "A swamp person showed me this method when I was a boy. I have used this method to hunt waterfowl at night on Pharaoh's private lands."

I laughed. "You would not be the first loyal subject to do so. I care not how you learned this method if it works. Teach the men when we finish."

"Yes, Your Highness."

"Assuming we can avoid the ambushes through here and here," Unas said, pointing at the map. "What makes you think we can climb the rocky path on the backside?"

Mahu looked at me. The plan depended on everyone believing the plan could work to have any chance. Serah's words about leadership came back. "You will be a leader whether or not you want to be." But I worried. About overshadowing Amenhotep, about Harwa's words. Leading may be my doom, but I refused to usurp my brother. Our survival, however, depended on this skill so I said, "I have faith in the men."

"But..." Unas objected.

I cut him off. "I envisioned the enemy's hideout and saw our success."

Mahu smiled, knowing I heeded his advice. "His Highness' accuracy in prophecy is renown at the palace. We shall emerge victorious."

"Can you give us a sense of the path?" Djau asked.

"When we get there I will recognize it," I replied.

The officers looked from one to the next, dissatisfied with my answer, but knowing questioning me further would be futile.

"We will proceed as you say," Djau said. "But we must capture the oasis bys morning. Otherwise, we will die of thirst in the desert."

"Do you have a better solution?" Nehi asked.

"We should not have come with so few men," Unas interjected.

"That cannot be helped," Mahu responded.

"Given our options," Djau answered, "I do not have a better option. May Amun-Re be with us."

***

For most of the day, the men rested before preparations began for the night ahead. Our plan required stealth. Being spotted posed a significant risk as any delay reaching the oasis could be our death. Our advantages lay in the quality of our fighting force and the element of surprise. Djau taught the men how to shield their lanterns. Mahu suggested I walked through the camp encouraging the troops. I did, watching them prepare. It pleased me when Mahu revealed that the men respected my attention this day. I hoped they would fight harder because of my efforts. I preferred spending time with them than the nobles at the palace.

At dusk, we set out in threes, one man holding a lamp while two others stayed in a defensive position to defend the lamp holder in case of attack. We traveled in a northeast by east direction towards the sea, stopping to rest every two to three leagues so that the men would be ready to fight. The path of stone and sand proved treacherous in the dark. Many of the men stumbled along the way, receiving bumps and bruises because of falls. Fortune smiled upon us, for none suffered serious injuries.

When we smelled the briny scent of the sea, we turned south by southeast. Our path continued for another league when Mahu suggested we dispatch a reconnaissance force to explore ahead. We dispatched ten men, while the rest of the men waited. An hour later, the scouts returned.

"Prince Ramose's vision proved accurate," Djau rejoiced. "A guarded path ascends the backside of a hillside. We can only walk two or three abreast, but if we send archers ahead, we can remove the guards." He described the exact placement of the guards.

"Do we want to send men along the cliff side?" Mahu asked.

"It is still too dark," Djau answered. "The men could not climb while holding lanterns."

"Good point," Mahu responded.

Djau continued. "We can use stealth to kill the guards at the front of the path before sending the bulk of the men up the mountain. We only have about two hours until dawn."

"Let us begin," I said.

We journeyed closer to the cliffs and in the dim light, I could only make out the outline of the ridge I envisioned. We stopped while a small group continued to clear fighters in our way.

With stealth, the warriors killed the guards on the path. They continued up the hill to eliminate all defenders on our route to the top. I ordered the bulk of our force to begin the climb along the trail, stopping every so often to wait for the low whistle indicating we could continue our ascent. Waiting the third time, we heard the low cry of someone dying. Mahu whispered if anyone heard. Closing my eyes, I listened, not for the sounds of defenders moving, but for the voice. I waited a few moments to hear our next steps.

"Move!" I exclaimed. "They heard us. Archers ready your bows; dawn is almost here."

Scrambling, Mahu gave a triple staccato whistle announcing to our troops to execute the alternate attack plan. Men dashed up the trail passing spearmen, porters, and priests. The way forked at the top and Mahu and I each lead forces on the different hillsides.

At the first glimmer of dawn, Mahu on one hillside, and me on another, we ordered the men over the ridge and into the camp. We met little resistance. By the time the sun rose, our bowmen killed most of the guards, and the spearmen entered the camp slaughtering the unarmed, barely awake rebel men, capturing the women and children. No one escaped.

With the rising sun, I could see the oasis. The encampment lay in a gully surrounded on two sides by large rocky outcroppings. Towards the back of the southern ridge lay a cliff face, impossible to scale. We gathered the non-combatant Kenites into that area as a makeshift prison. Djau informed the prisoners, they would be free from reprisal if none tried to escape. Mahu suggested this as a deterrent. We had just enough men to hold the oasis in shifts until reinforcements arrived. We placed the surviving combatants and other men in a separate location with each tied up to prevent escape.

The camp secured, I looked around. The oasis' beauty contrasted with the barrenness of the surrounding desert, accentuating its grace. Bright green grass carpeted the hillside and much of the floor of the valley. A large pool of water provided nourishment to people, plants, and animals. Date and pomegranate palms surrounded the pond. It appeared as I saw in my vision.

The men rested in shifts as Mahu and I decided our next steps. Reinforcements were three or four days away, assuming our messengers reached their destination. Djau and Unas joined us to discuss the best strategy.

The Kenite attackers still in the desert concerned Djau, an experienced military man. He feared them uniting to attack us.

"They might outnumber us or not," Unas replied. "But we have the advantage of terrain."

"Which they know better than we do. Let me take a small band of archers to rout them one by one."

"You admitted they know the land better than we do," Unas argued. "And our forces would be divided."

"We are anyway. We are using too many men guarding the captives."

"Let us execute them," Unas suggested.

"No more bloodshed than necessary," I said, still feeling ill from the killings days ago. Today, the archers killed most of the enemy from afar. I partook in the battle, but little.

"It is necessary to remove a known enemy from within that could attack us," Djau responded. "We should remove the threat."

"He is correct," Mahu said. "Hori implemented that policy several years ago."

"But they may outnumber us," Unas argued. "As it is, we have accomplished our mission with only a quarter of the men required. I fear our exposure to counter-attack without reinforcements."

"All the more reason, to attack while we have the element of surprise!" Djau countered.

"Both of you make important points as both plans have merit," Mahu said, saying out loud what I was too afraid to speak. "Your Highness, what are your thoughts?"

I did not know what to say, weighing the choices in my mind.

"Let us wait it out. The reinforcements will be here in three to four days, and likely some or all of the ambushers will need water. Maybe we can neutralize them off one by one as they return."

"An excellent idea, Your Highness," Unas replied. While Djau appeared to be disappointed, he said nothing.

Mahu ordered the guards to cover their armor with Kenite robes to prevent being spotted by spies.

On our second morning after taking the oasis, we spotted a small group of Kenites approaching the camp. Guards called Manu and I down to the outpost to consult with the guards.

"Your Highness, the Kenites approach," one said.

"Your orders are to attack and kill them all," I commanded. "We cannot have them escape and give away we captured the outpost."

"Understood. But there is something that seems different about these men."

"How so?" I asked.

"While they wear robes of Kenites, their formation appears to be that of Egyptian soldiers."

"You are right!" Mahu said.

We watched them form positions suggesting they would attack the outpost. The arrangement they took revealed Egyptian tactics. And it became clear there were many more men than the spies counted in the desert days ago.

"What do you think, Mahu?" I asked.

"If those are Kenites using Egyptian tactics, we are at a significant disadvantage."

"Do any of you recognize any of the men?" I asked.

"Not from this distance, Your Highness," an officer named Maya said.

"Take one or two men closer to get a look. Maybe they are Egyptians."

"Why would Egyptians be taking an attack formation?"

"They do not know we took the stronghold," Mahu responded before I could. "It is what I would do under the circumstances."

"Very well," Maya replied. "I will go down there. I know many of the men at the garrison. If they are reinforcements, I should recognize one."

He left, wearing his Kenite robes, but stayed far enough away to prevent archers from shooting at him. As he approached the formation, we noted the size of the force appeared to grow. We could see Maya the entire time and no one molested him. Mahu and I exchanged nervous glances for the next hour, wondering what had become of our scout. For some unknown reason, Maya turned a corner around a formation that obscured our vision of him. The next half an hour proved stressful.

Just before I would give the order to assume defensive positions and ready for assault, Maya reappeared around the bend with three other men. They ambled over our way and none appeared to be in distress.

Mahu stood tall to get a closer look. "I think I know those men."

He climbed down from his position and walked forward towards the men. Soon he motioned for me to follow.

"Janu!" Mahu exclaimed, embracing the leader of the others. "Good to see you!"

"You too, Mahu! How are you, my friend?"

"Glad we do not have to defend against this many men."

"How did you take this place with one company?"

"Prince Ramose devised a plan of assault the men executed with perfection."

Mahu recounted the tale, embellishing parts to make me sound braver than my actions.

"Well done, young prince!" he said. "Women will sing of your exploits and legends will arise." Then he whispered, "How did you get the men to obey your orders?"

"That," Mahu coughed, "became easier after disciplining a disobedient soldier."

"We heard about that," Janu laughed. "Also, well done."

"Are you our reinforcements?"

"Yes, and no. I am here to bring Ramose back to Waset."

"Why?" Mahu asked.

"They have not told me the reason for his recall, only that we are to escort him back to Egypt."

My thoughts raced, for I assumed my beheading Toruk must be the reason. Calming myself, I realized that news could not have reached Waset. Mahu wished to return with me to explain my actions. He feared punishment too and wanted to ensure my safety.

I left Waset to prevent a rift between me and Amenhotep, but the success of my attack exacerbated the problem. As Janu suggested, my legend raised me above Amenhotep. Would he be angry? And what of Sitamen? Would she start her seduction again? Later that day, we would begin the long trek back to Waset to find out.

PART THREE

23

Standing at the prow of the boat, I looked out over the water, wondering why Pharaoh recalled me. Did he find out about my desire for Sitamen, my adopted sister, and he wished to punish me. Worried thoughts bounced through me.

Our trek from the oasis to Avaris proved uneventful. We encountered no struggles along the way other than the continued blistering heat of the desert. Though I did not believe it possible, the temperature was higher returning from the desert than venturing to the oasis.

Mahu approached me, oozing authority. If his men noticed his facial features and length differed from those of Egyptians, they said nothing, respecting his excellent leadership.

"He sends his mother to gain accolades for your victory," Mahu said.

"Who?"

"Ahmose," Mahu replied.

"Why would he do that?" I asked. I was naïve.

"He cannot have a Habiru seen as this successful. It will upset the narrative of subjugating our people."

"But I am his adopted son!"

"It matters not, Ramose! Pharaoh and the nobles view you as Habiru! Though Nefertari and Ahmose-Ankh accept you, others do not."

"My mother and oldest brother wield a lot of influence, Mahu."

"Not enough," he snarled.

Mahu was right. Ahmose rejected the marriage of Ahmose-Ankh and Meritamen, though Nefertari desired it. Ahmose held his eldest son in such contempt he refused his sister-wife's request.

"Why send his mother of all people?" I asked. "Why not send Siamun or Amenhotep?"

"After his foray into the region, they would not believe a victory by Siamun. But Amenhotep may travel with Ahhotep."

"But Ahmose's mother?" I exclaimed.

"She is an excellent military leader in her own right," Mahu replied. "None will doubt her success."

"Our success," I responded.

"Keep that to yourself, Ramose. We return to a dangerous situation in Waset."

Mahu leaned against the prow next to me and asked, "Are you still thinking about Toruk? If you are, he does not deserve your sympathy."

Though Mahu believed Toruk deserved severe punishment, I knew better. I was within my rights to discipline him. But my anger arose, not from his defiance, but from the treatment I received as a child at the palace. The taunting and torment of my brothers and sons of nobles pushed me to the brink. Mahu did not know the power rising within me to stay Toruk's sword. Harwa's impending reprimand stuck in my ears, for I knew what he would say. I must learn to manage my power before I hurt someone close to me.

When we left the oasis, I feared my summons related to cutting the head off of an unruly soldier. But now that sometime passed I knew of another reason.

"No," I responded. "They recall me for another purpose."

"A Habiru's success scares them."

"That may be true."

Mahu looked puzzled, so I added, "There was not enough time for them to know we took the oasis and send troops. Something else spurred Ahmose."

"Such as?"

"He needs me to find something."

"You speak in riddles, my friend."

I thought for a moment before answering Mahu, taking in

the scenery along the shore. Having lived my entire life in Egypt, I never appreciated the unique geography of the Nile. Before my journey, I knew only the river. My short time in the desert gave me a new appreciation. Flooding delivered water and minerals to seeds planted along its course. The lushness and greenery provided a stark contrast to the reddish-brown sand of its surroundings. I recalled Rekhmire's admonishment. Hapi's uniqueness to the Egyptian pantheon lay in its geography, as did Egypt's culture. Hapi could not speak to me in the desert, so I knew it was not his voice I heard.

Mahu spoke, breaking my reverie. "What does he seek?"

"A staff."

"A staff?"

"I know little of it. Some call it the Staff of Osiris and believe it to grant immortality to its owner."

"Is he not worried you will keep it for yourself?"

"I imagine he does," I responded. "Which is the reason he has given me little information about it."

"Why do you believe he seeks the staff?"

"Gleaning information through the years, listening when I should not. Others told me stories of the rod, of its power and capabilities."

"What sort of power?"

"Power to change the weather; extend a man's life. To help armies win battles!"

"Do you believe this?" Mahu asked, casting a doubtful look.

"It matters not what I believe. Ahmose thinks thus. He adopted me because he thought I could find the staff for him."

"Can you?"

"I do not know. Since we left the oasis, I have thought of nothing else. What I do not understand is why they sent us there with inadequate force."

"How do you mean?"

"If Ahmose believes I am to retrieve the staff, why would he send me on such a dangerous mission?"

"Something changed?"

"Ahmose must have received a prophecy while we were gone."

"What sort of prophecy?"

"About me and the staff."

"Again you speak in riddles. Did you converse with El Shaddai?"

"Maybe that is how I know what I know," I responded. I had not quieted my mind as I did the night prior to our assault, sitting alone in the tent using the breathing technique Harwa taught me. Though the voice had not spoken to me, I knew the reason for our recall.

"Do you know what the staff looks like?" Mahu asked.

"Ahmose does not," I responded, evading his question, remembering something I overheard him say to Nefertari when I first arrived at the palace.

"You have seen the staff," Mahu observed.

"In a manner of speaking," I admitted. "If I to find it, I would know. Ahmose could not say the same."

"And that is why he needs you?"

"That and because a prophecy states a Habiru would raise the staff for Pharaoh."

"For or against?"

"An odd prophecy to be sure. Even from Balaam or Rekhmire. But that is what Amenhotep overheard."

"Our recall was not because of prejudice against Habirus?"

"I do not believe so. Maybe another prophecy warned them about our success. Whatever the case, we head back to Waset."

"What will you do about Sitamen?"

"The Tekh Festival passed. Not getting drunk should help."

Mahu laughed. "Tekh can be a time of debauchery to be sure, though that is not the purpose of the drinking."

Tekh celebrated the survival of humanity. Seeing the evil of his creation, Ra manifested Bast, the Lion Goddess, to destroy humanity. Horrified of her destructive power, Ra relented. He fed her beer to get her drunk, preventing her from devouring all of humanity. As a ritual, Egyptian drink until they pass out. When they awake, prayers and devotion begin. I left Waset to avoid the festivities, worried that the spell cast on Sitamen combined with the alcohol would impair both my and my adopted sister's judgement.

I told Mahu of the argument at dinner my last night at the palace prior to our leaving Waset. That evening, Sitamen bragged on knowing of a prophecy regarding me, spurring Ahmose to send me to the desert without adequate troops.

Mahu and I discussed how our success may embolden her.

"Amenhotep is safe," Mahu said, as if reading my thoughts. "You have preserved his honor. And I and the others will protect you from Sitamen's advances."

"I will speak to someone about a counter-spell."

"Who would someone cast a love spell on her?"

"I am unsure. It must be Balaam, though I cannot figure out why he would do so. He must have cast the spell before that evening. She was..." I stopped as my cheeks became hot.

"She kissed you," Mahu said. "Ammi told me what occurred on the terrace during the Wepet-Renpet festival. Possibly you are correct about a spell. But you would make a suitable husband, Ramose. Though Sitamen's behavior may seem odd because she is your sister, others may seek advancement through marriage to you. She is not the only woman who may desire you. The slightest thing you say could be construed as a promise for marriage."

Marriage? I felt my chest tighten. I breathed to move through the feeling. Relaxing into the experience, I knew I would not marry an Egyptian. I asked Mahu for help. He agreed to help navigate conversations with any young women I may encounter in the next few days.

***

Our journey back to the capitol proved easy, for we arrived in Waset a few days later. In our time away, Akhet yielded to the planting season of Peret. Workers, slaves, and freemen toiled in the black soil, readying the seeds that would become the harvest of Shemu in several months.

I left Mahu and the others to return to the palace. My manservant Paser greeted me at the entrance. Whisking me upstairs to bathe me, he informed me that most of my family vacated Waset while I was away. Ahmose-Ankh and Siamun traveled south to Buhen. Amenhotep and I must have passed each other on our journeys, for he proceeded North to the desert with his grandmother.

"Sitamen, Meritamen, and Nefertari journeyed to Avaris to dedicate the new temple there, though I suspect there may be other reasons for their journey. Ahmose wished to see the progress of his pyramid. Trouble haunts its construction. I fear his frustration will bring more repressive laws to our people."

"Are they sabotaging it? Or do they not understand Imhotep's instructions?"

"I suspect a little of both, though the outcome is the same."

"If everyone is gone, for what purpose do you scrub me?" I asked, as he scoured my skin raw.

"I heard of your battle and thought you might wish to wash the scent of death from you."

"I bathed sufficiently in Avaris," I responded.

"Serah requested your presence," Paser admitted.

"Do you know why?" I asked.

"She did not see fit to tell me but sent word that I was to bring you to her upon your return."

I stepped from the tub, taking a towel hanging from the stool nearby. I wondered why Serah wished to see me, feeling apprehensive of her visions. She wanted me to take a leadership role, something I resisted.

After dressing in nondescript clothes, Paser led me down to the servants' staircase, through the kitchen and out of a door to an alley next to the palace. From there we blended into the crowd of people moving between the royal compound and the central part of town. The poverty in the Habiru quarter still struck me. Many people had nothing but the clothes they wore, though there was more space for people than the last time I visited. Ahmose forced the relocation of many Habirus to the pyramid to work on its construction. Only the elderly, infirm, and young were spared the march.

Half an hour later, Paser and I entered Serah's tent. As my eyes adjusted to the dimness, I noticed no changes from my previous visit. Lush rugs covered the dirt floor with a plush sofa and a carved, inlaid marble table in the center of the seating area. Across the table from the divan sat Serah, an old woman with long thinning white hair. Her dry and wrinkled skin reminded me more of a prune than a woman.

"Come in, Ramose, come in," her voice creaking and crackling. "You and I have much to discuss."

She excused Paser as I sat on the couch across from her.

"I hear you have had many adventures, my young friend," she said as I settled myself. "Tell me what you have learned."

I told her of my travels, of seeing the oasis and the plan to capture it. I told her about Toruk and continued to the part of our stealth through the desert.

"How did you discipline this unruly soldier?" she asked, eyes closed.

"I killed him."

"Though I am not a soldier, that seems extreme."

"He made me, Aunt Serah."

"Made you?" she questioned.

"He refused to accept my punishment!"

"How would his refusal make you kill him?"

"I demanded he remove his shirt to be whipped as is my right as his commanding officer. He stood there, smirking, daring me. I pulled my sword and cut his head off."

"Just like that? How amazing he did not defend himself," she mocked.

Tears ran down my face. "I stopped him from acting," I cried.

Serah scrutinized me before asking how.

"With my thoughts," I replied. "The anger and hurt rose inside me. I felt the power surge through me. Using a force, I choked him."

"You choked him?" she asked, perplexed.

"With my mind. Toruk moved his hands to his throat as though gasping for breath."

"Remarkable. You choked him. Until a voice told you to use your sword," she finished my story.

"How did you know?" I asked.

Serah stared at me, or so I thought. Though she possessed great vision, her eyes seemed not to function. We sat in silence for some time, her gaze unbreaking as my discomfort increased with each passing moment. Finally, she broke the silence.

"You did nothing! Except allow your anger to get the best of you again, Ramose."

"I know Auntie."

"Not well enough! You will disaster upon us all, if Ahmose punishes you."

She left the thought hanging and took a deep breath. "Only El Shaddai brings what is into being."

"But Harwa taught me..."

"Bring me my harp!" she interrupted.

I rose from the sofa, walking over to the harp. I lugged the large instrument from the corner of the tent, dragging it along the sand before it caught on the border of the lush carpet in the middle of the room. With much care, I lifted the heavy instrument over the edge of the rug, and half carried, half dragged it to a place in front of Serah. Placing her hands on it, she felt for the strings before gently plucking them. A soft, sweet, and sad song filled the tent as her fingers danced across the chords.

"You no longer have the luxury of expressing your feelings to people."

"What do you mean?"

"God responds to your prayers faster than others. That is why Toruk lost his breath when you wished him dead. You did nothing except ask for something."

"How?"

"I do not know, Ramose," she snapped. The notes rising from the harp became angry, replacing the soft tones. "I was not there. I only know what my vision reveals."

The music transformed into soothing notes as Serah calmed herself.

"A power rises in you. You are unusual not because of the ability but because you are so young to possess it."

"But you said I did nothing."

"That is true. El Shaddai does all. But you are a channel, as Jacob once was. El Shaddai listened to all that Jacob said, but manifested more slowly than you. It is why his beloved Rachel died so young."

"I thought she died in childbirth."

"She died because of the rash words of her husband."

"How can a word kill?"

The melody changed as her fingers slowed, going across the strings, sweet sounds that pierced my heart. Her face softened as she described Rachel's beauty and grace.

"It was no wonder that Jacob fell in love with her on sight. Destiny brought them together. But I witnessed her having the same effect on others, men and women. Save her sister Leah."

She stopped speaking for a moment as the tune changed to harsh notes, as though the spirit of Leah played instead of Serah. After a few moments, the melody changed back, and she continued her story.

"When Jacob led us away from Laban's home to the land of Canaan, Laban chased us for miles. Catching up to our caravan, Laban accused my grandfather of stealing idols, which Jacob denied. Laban persisted upon which Jacob swore, 'if anyone has done so may they be struck down.' If only he could have taken those words back, keeping them within himself! For unbeknownst to Jacob, Rachel grabbed the idols on their way out. Jacob came to the servants asking if anyone had dared to steal the statues. His face became ashen when his favorite wife, pregnant with their second child, stepped forward with the idols."

"Why did she take them?"

"To anger her father. She thought it punishment for their treatment at his hands."

"Laban treated them horribly," I responded. "He deserved punishment."

"Only El Shaddai may dispense judgment. Jacob knew that."

"She did not die on that spot."

"She died in childbirth."

"Because of what Jacob said?"

"Because of his curse."

"How do you know?"

"I know. I know. Words have power, Ramose. Jacob's took time to produce an outcome, but your words act on the world immediately. At least when you have the force rising within you."

"I said nothing though."

"You had the thought to punish Toruk."

"That is true," I admitted. "I seethed that Toruk treated others thus."

"Likely, it reminded you of the treatment you received too. El Shaddai listened to you and responded. Be careful, Ramose. Sometimes that anger bounces back on you."

"How?"

"The universe is mental," she interrupted. "Thought makes everything."

"What of magic?"

"Magic!" she spat. "Magic is a toy. El Shaddai hears all of

our prayers and responds. But God hears your words more clearly than most."

"The force within me..."

"Is the power of El Shaddai," she finished my sentence.

"But why does El Shaddai respond to me more quickly?"

"I do not know, Ramose."

We sat in silence for a few moments before Serah resumed playing. "Heeding the voice prevented disaster."

"How do you mean?"

"Your story confirms my vision, for I arranged your adoption by Ahmose and Nefertari."

"You? A slave? How?"

"Am I a slave?" she asked as she stopped playing her harp, looking directly at me. "Do you see me work? I have servants. I live with my people, but I am not a slave."

"What now?"

"I cannot tell, yet. What you need to know is the danger you face now is even greater than you can imagine. Ahmose will learn of your success in battle."

"His coming was not to take that credit away from me?"

"Nay," Serah replied as she stopped playing for a moment. She began again and said, "A confusing vision came to Balaam. He saw your victory and your death."

"I did not die."

"I suspect a part of you did," she mused. "But their concern focuses elsewhere. Dead you cannot recover the staff for Ahmose."

"The staff is the reason for my recall!"

"You know of the staff?"

I told her of the conversations Amenhotep, Ahmose-Ankh and I had before leaving for my mission. Each of us overheard bits and pieces of discussions between Ahmose and Rekhmire about preparing someone to recover the Staff of Osiris.

"That is not its true name," she told me. "But I have said too much already."

"What do you mean?" I asked. "You have told me nothing."

"The less you know about the staff, the better."

"Why?"

Again she stopped her playing, peering around the harp to scrutinize me. "Remember what I said about thought? Your capacity is strong but unwieldy. You have much to learn about yourself."

"What does that have to do with my power and thought?"

"Everything, Ramose!" her eyes smoldering. "Imagination begets ideas. If you do not know yourself, you perpetuate ludicrous ideas."

"That is why you are not a slave."

"That is why I am not a slave," she repeated.

"But you know this..."

"Our people have not learned of their own power," she interrupted, answering my unspoken question. She began playing short staccato notes. "One day they will learn. Maybe you will teach them. For now, they believe themselves victims of circumstance. But change stirs."

"How?"

"The hearts of some open to love and gratitude."

"Grateful for being slaves?"

"Grateful for being alive!" she reprimanded. "Gratitude that their power is hidden so they may find it. Always love El Shaddai and be thankful for Its creation."

"You still have not explained my danger."

"Should anyone learn of your budding power, you would be exiled. Or worse."

She continued playing; the tune changing to a soft, thoughtful melody. I watched Serah play the theme with one hand as she added a counter melody with the other. Her hands and the notes seemed to battle one another as her hands danced across the harp, emitting a sound as though two different instruments were played.

"The road before you becomes clearer," she said, continuing to play. "You face a choice soon."

"What is that?"

"You will learn, soon enough."

"How?"

"You will, Ramose. We may not see each other for some time. If that is the case, be comforted in knowing that I will recognize you when you return."

"Where am I going?" I asked.

But Serah did not answer my question.

24

Paser and I left Serah to return to the palace. With Siamun absent, I assumed wandering the halls would be easier, but I would soon learn my mistake. But I had no time to consider any of that, for I wished to speak to Harwa to learn more about Serah's disturbing tale. As I readied to leave for the river to find him, Nefertari came by my room.

"Ramose, How are you?"

"When did you return mother?" I asked, embracing her.

"Just now," she replied. Letting me go, she commented, "You have grown! And have been adventurous."

"Yes, mother," I blubbered.

"You are not blame for the soldier's insolence. And though Ahmose will not admit it, I understand you planned the capture of the rebel outpost."

I felt uncomfortable with her using the term 'rebel' but said nothing. Nor did I say anything of Toruk's punishment, for Serah's words still stung. Instead, I thanked her for her compliments. Changing the subject, I asked about Sitamen's behavior. The evening before my departure my adopted sister boasted of my prowess in battle. Her bizarre conduct surprised us all, for she tried to kiss me in front of everyone only to be stopped by Meritamen and Ahmose-Ankh.

"I am unsure, but I suspect she may have ingested a love potion."

"A love potion?"

"A magical drink that inflames passion and desire in the person who ingests it."

"What made her drink it?"

"I doubt she did on purpose. Someone crafted the potion and slipped it into her food or drink."

"Are you sure it was a potion?"

"That is the most likely explanation. I thought at first maybe Balaam cast a spell which he denies."

"Why would Balaam do that?" I asked.

"He has his reasons."

"When?"

"I have my suspicions."

"And in a manner that no one else drank it?"

"Yes."

"Are potions so discerning that the person who crafted it would have made her desire me?"

"I know not the potion's purpose. It may have been the person wanted her to fall in love with you or not. Few possess the skill to craft such a specific potion. To make her fall in love with you, they would require something of yours to be mixed into the potion."

"Something of mine?"

"Like hair, nails or skin."

"A hairbrush of mine disappeared for a day or two several months ago. Paser asked me if I knew where it might be."

"Why did no one tell me?" Nefertari snapped.

"The brush turned up a few days later."

"Ramose! You must remain alert to these situations." Then softening her voice, "Many people do not have your best interests at heart. It may have been an attempt to divide you from Sitamen or Amenhotep."

She hugged me again, as though trying to protect me with the strength of her squeeze. Releasing me, she said, "Do not let the love potion concern you. And Sitamen feels embarrassed by her actions. Show her kindness, when you see her next. "

"I   will."

"And we must keep your victory secret. Word of it could endanger you further. Ahmose will return soon and appoint you to a new post. The nobles…" She took a deep breath before continuing. "Many nobles fear retribution by you."

"As they should," I thought before remembering Serah's warning. Words have power. How do I clear a thought? I wondered. Another reason to find Harwa.

"What is my role to be?" I asked.

"I do not know. It is part of the reason Rekhmire and Ahmose travel."

"I thought they were observing his pyramid's construction," I retorted.

"That is an excuse."

"He seeks the staff," I blurted, regretting my words as soon as they left my mouth.

Nefertari glared at me. "What do you know of the staff?"

"Little other than Ahmose seeks it."

"Good," she replied. Lines of worry remained on her face. "Learn nothing more of it, Ramose. Promise me."

"But why, mother?"

Ashen face, she insisted. "Promise me, Ramose. Promise me, that you will not give the staff to Ahmose or Siamun."

Her eyes bored through me as though she could force my answer. I wanted to ask her why, but knew from her insistence she would give me no more information.

"I promise, Mother."

Nefertari smiled. "I am sure whatever function in government Ahmose gives you, you will do very well."

"Thank you."

"What will you do the next few days?"

"I plan to spend time by the Nile. I feel a need to cool myself in the water after being in the desert for so long."

She smiled. "I imagine you do. Be in the river, my son. Spend as much time there as possible."

"Why do you say that, Mother?"

"No reason in particular. Other than none know what tomorrow may bring. I must go to the temple now. I will see you tonight at dinner."

"Yes, Mother," I replied, and gave her a hug before she left my chambers.

After eating a snack of figs and bread, I walked down the hall to leave the palace. Hearing voices inside Amenhotep's room, I peered inside. There I saw Ankhu, Hori, Hannu, and Maiherpri talking.

"Is Amenhotep back?" I asked.

"Why do you care, Habiru?" Ankhu snapped.

"What are you doing in my brother's room?" I demanded.

"It is not your concern, Habiru!" Maiherpri snapped, rising from his chair looking menacing.

The other boys jumped up, surrounding me inside the doorway of the chamber. I breathed, trying to bring some energy up to ward them off. But nothing happened. Maiherpri came closer and shoved me with both hands in the chest. I stumbled back into Ankhu who pushed me forward towards Maiherpri who buried his fist into my gut. Not expecting his punch, I doubled over in pain. One boy hit me in the back causing me to fall to the floor.

Refusing to fight back, they kicked me several times as I lay on the ground. The beating may have continued longer had Paser come by moments later.

"What are you boys doing?" he demanded.

"Ramose fell over," Hannu assured, helping me up.

"Is that true, Ramose?" Paser asked.

I hesitated to answer. I held their fates in my hands. Attacking a royal could lead to exile or even death. These boys that taunted me for so many years removed from my life, forever. I was justified in doing so. But something held me from speaking the truth. Maybe I hoped we could become friends someday. Maybe I feared to lose control and kill them myself. Whatever the reason, I stood up and corroborated their story. I only received a few bruises to my body. But my silence would cause more pain than speaking the truth.

***

Paser treated my cuts. "Why do you protect those boys?" he asked. "They do not deserve it."

"Nor do they deserve death," I responded.

When he finished, I headed to the river. I did not find Harwa, so I bathed to clean the dryness of the desert from me. Luxuriating in the water, I let the moisture of the Nile soaked into my skin. I remember joining Nefertari for dinner that night, though nothing of note happened. I found Harwa at the same location I looked the previous day.

"Ho, Ramose!" he said. "How did you fair in the North?" He must have seen the cuts on my face as I approached, for he added, "You saw battle."

The anger and humiliation of the previous weeks spilled from me as a fountain of hurt rose from the depths of my being as I yelled at Harwa.

"How did I fair? How did I fair? I killed men whose only crime was not being Egyptian."

"War is like that, Ramose!"

"I am a killing machine." His silence and blank expression further enraged me. "Nothing stopped me! I sliced through bone and flesh. Then you made me kill one of my own soldiers."

"I did that? How powerful I am," he mocked.

"I am a monster because of you! Toruk...." I started sobbing.

"Toruk? An Egyptian?"

"I killed him."

Tears flowed as the story spilled from my mouth between sobs, Harwa listening as I recounted my actions. When I finished, he thought for a moment.

"Did you complain about Toruk to Mahu?"

So surprised I was by the question that I ceased my crying. "Maybe?"

"Think back. It may be important."

"I said nothing to Mahu. But I resented Torak's behavior." I explained the soldier's disrespect and lack of effort after the first battle. And how the memory of his behavior with the Habiru slave angered me.

"You do not have the luxury of expressing your feelings like that."

"Serah told me the same thing," I replied.

"You manifest faster than others."

"Because of you!" I accused.

"You have always been like this. Your power has spilled from you for some time."

"It has not!"

"Your power is why you are alive. The poison you ingested at the end of Shemu should have killed you."

"I thought you saved me."

"No. I only helped your recovery. You did most of the work."

"How?" My anger abated some, though I still felt uneasy.

"You have a direct connection to the divine."

"I do?" I said confused. "How can that be? I do not pray or make sacrifices."

"If prayer could control the divine and sacrifices, the Habirus would not be slaves."

"Ahmose prevents them from making sacrifices. At least Miriam believes Habiru freedom will come through those acts."

"The people of Akrotiri made sacrifices. They built structures to stop the flow of lava, which did little. The island was destroyed."

"Did the people's thoughts cause the island's demise?"

"What makes you say that?"

"Serah told me the basis of magic is our thoughts. That words have power."

Harwa thought a few moments before answering. "Not all thoughts become a reality. There is a built-in delay between thinking the idea and it becoming real. You must add emotion to the thought. And judgement."

"But I do not get that delay."

"No."

"And maybe the people of Strongili could have stopped the explosion of their island had they worked together with enough time?"

"Perhaps. Only the All knows. How did you get bruises on your face? They look fresher than anything you might have received in battle."

"I received those yesterday at the hands of Maiherpri and his friends." I told him about the events of the previous day.

"Why did you not fight back?" he asked.

"I feared losing control of myself."

"Do you remember your thoughts when you froze Toruk's will?"

"I just remember feeling so angry, I wanted to strangle him."

"You thought to strangle him and felt angry?"

I nodded.

"Maybe your thoughts and feelings are aligned with the will of El Shaddai. Events will occur that no one can control. Live life, Ramose. Follow the inner voice and hope for the best."

"I heard the voice in that moment. It instructed me to use

my sword."

"That was a good thing."

"I do not enjoy killing people."

"Sometimes it will be necessary. As is defending yourself, such as with those boys yesterday. Even Abraham battled. But you will need to learn to control your thoughts and feelings, Ramose."

"How do I do so without hurting others?"

Harwa thought for a moment. "You must learn to control your emotions. If you feel upset or angry, do not tell another person. Speak to El Shaddai."

"El Shaddai?"

"You speak to El Shaddai now. Tell El Shaddai your problems and wait for a response."

"I do not understand."

"You will. At some point, you must choose between staying in Egypt or leaving. The people see you as Habiru."

"So?"

"Many resent the Hyksos thanks to Ahmose's policies. His prejudice leads to abuse by other Egyptians."

"How do you mean?"

"If Ahmose welcomed the Hyksos, Egyptians would not see Habirus as less than human as they are now. Ahmose-Ankh understands this, which is why he wants to implement reforms to integrate foreigners into the society. But while workers would receive better treatment, the nobles would rebel."

"But when Ahmose-Ankh becomes Pharaoh, people would stop resenting Hyksos."

"If he becomes Pharaoh."

"What do you mean?" I asked, concerned for my favorite adopted brother.

"Siamun covets the throne, Ramose. He will stop at nothing to remove Ahmose-Ankh."

"Does Ahmose-Ankh know?"

"He does," Harwa responded. "But he may be powerless to stop Siamun. Others work to help your demented brother."

"Why would anyone want Siamun to be Pharaoh?"

"I do not know. The enemies of Ahmose-Ankh likely gave Sitamen the love potion."

"You know of that?"

"I recommended to Nefertari to send your sister away. The palace becomes dangerous for all of you."

"I am safe now that Siamun departed."

"Do not be a fool! Different factions move to place on the throne who they believe benefits them. You may become closer to the throne than you are now."

"I do not wish to be Pharaoh."

"That may be, Ramose," Harwa said, leveling his gaze toward me. "But your remaining in Egypt presents risks. Diverse forces move towards a resolution. It is unclear to me what it is."

"I should leave?"

"I suspect at some point, you will. You live between two worlds, cultures that have conflicting beliefs. Many Egyptians resent that you and other Hyksos live in their country. A time will come when you will need to leave Egypt."

"How will I know?"

"Trust the voice."

"Until then?"

"It is not time yet to leave. There is more for you to learn."

"Teach me."

"I am not your only teacher, Ramose. Soon I too will leave."

"Where will you go?"

"Back from where I came. Where we all are from."

"Why?"

"Your lesson will continue with others."

"Who?"

"You will learn when the time comes," he said with a tone of finality. "For now, we must teach you to better control your emotions. If Ahmose discovers the depth of your power, it could spell disaster for you and the Habirus."

He walked me through a series of breathing exercises designed to help me calm myself. I practiced for several hours, watching my breath, listening for the voice. I only felt stillness within myself, hearing nothing. The voice, it seemed, left me, for I would not hear it again for some time.

25

Farmers worked through the months of Peret plowing the fecund land for the coming harvest of Shemu. No obligation weighed on me as a royal to perform such duties. Some days, I watched my Habiru brethren toil in the fields, or with the back-breaking work of making bricks and pulling them up ramps to make whatever building Pharaoh desired. Watching them, I understood how slaves build civilizations.

I spent the season in regular studies with Rekhmire and Harwa. Each taught me what he knew of magic and the ways to access it. With Rekhmire, I learned to mix potions and cast spells. But Harwa brought my world inward, walking me through exercises of focusing on my breath and staying alert to my emotions. Was one form of magic more powerful? The contrast confused me. Harwa only explained that to know the universe, one must know one's self. This did not relieve my consternation, for Rekhmire said something similar

The days shortened as Shemu approached. Ahmose returned from his wanderings with a large army force after visiting the oasis I captured. Mahu informed me how Amenhotep and Ahhotep ventured through the Northeastern desert, capturing various oases in the North towards the land of Canaan. Egyptians would hold this area for many years.

"Ahhotep is an excellent commander," Mahu said one day we dined together. "She is teaching Amenhotep skills that Siamun did not possess."

"Why did they not send her with Siamun?"

"Soldiers rumor she refused Ahmose's request."

"That may be," I replied. "I have spent little time with her, and I hear whispers of why. She did not approve of my adoption, though she tolerates me at the palace. But she likes Siamun even less."

"That is not surprising."

"How did you hear of this?"

"Janu returned from the region. The oasis capture impressed Ahhotep. She wondered what made us attempt the assault at dawn with such a daunting landscape."

"Did Janu mention my creating the plan?"

"He had no need, for she already knew. But she told others to be quiet about it." I nodded, understanding. "She or Ahmose may ask you about it, however."

I thought it was another thing to worry about, but I saw little of Pharaoh or Ahhotep during this time. Nefertari informed me that Ahmose and his advisors debated what role to assign me.

"Your leadership and military skills are excellent, Ramose," she told me one morning while we breakfasted on the palace terrace by the Nile. "And I feel Egypt would benefit by your leading troops. But we must consider the nobles and take care not to foment rebellion."

I said nothing in response, knowing it would be useless to argue. Besides, I did not wish to be a military leader, for conquering more people disgusted me. I felt I could do more to help the already subjugated families living within the land.

As Shemu approached, Rekhmire informed me that Ahmose decided my governmental role.

"What is it?" I asked.

"You will find out with the others when you present yourself to Pharaoh. But I believe it suits for your abilities and the needs of the kingdom."

I did not care for Rekhmire's attitude. Though I said nothing, I sulked for the next few days. Then one morning, Paser woke me earlier than usual. "You must present yourself to Pharaoh, young master. For today they shall reveal your role in government!"

Bleary-eyed, I ate a small breakfast of fresh-baked breads

and fruit followed by a cool bath for the morning was already warm. My man servant laid out clothes of the finest materials for the occasion. He helps me into the embroidered tunic, the material stiff from disuse. Many years have passed since my last appearance in the Great Hall.

After I finished dressing, we walked through the hallways of the royal apartments, past the lush tapestries depicting battles hanging on the walls. Coming to the stairs, we walked down one side, its twin joining at a landing before turning back around in a wide walkway to the main artery of the palace. Paser and I turned right through the long corridor lined by columns on both sides of us. In the alcoves past the columns, people quieted as we passed. The hallway ended with tall double doors marking the entrance to the audience chamber. Today, I used the main doors, for I was both a guest of honor, and an answerer to Pharaoh's summons.

Paser adjusted my tunic, whispering words of encouragement. He stepped away as the guards opened the doors to announce my arrival.

"His Royal Highness, fourth son of Pharaoh, Ramose answers the summons of the Divine Pharaoh of Egypt," the guard bellowed.

"Bring him to me," Ahmose drawled.

As Paser had instructed, I walked a slow and steady pace towards the throne. Courtiers, nobles, and officials sat in silence, knowing Pharaoh's decision affected their lives. All of Pharaoh's sons possessed power in Egypt, but only I was Habiru and taunted by their sons. Now they feared retribution at my hands for this torment. I walked towards Ahmose, thoughts of revenge swirling through me.

As I drew closer, the lines etched around Ahmose's eyes and mouth made him appear older and more tired than I remembered. The dye in his traditional long thin chin beard black could not hide the gray facial hair peeking through his large pores on his jawline. The burning desire for conquest and power showed in his eyes, but fatigue quenched some lust.

Ahmose sat in his gold-plated throne with a lion's head carved into each arm, and lion's claws carved into the feet. He held a long staff with an ankh at the end. I knew this was not the staff he sought.

As instructed, I stopped at the designated spot five cubits in front of Pharaoh and bowed.

"Welcome, my son," he said, using an address I never heard. "I imagine that you wish to hear the role that Rekhmire and I have chosen for you."

Lifting my head, I replied, "I would your Majesty."

"I doubt you will cry this time," he said, smiling. He referred to my initial visit to the palace when I lived with my biological family before my adoption by the royal family. A laugh came from the audience. I smiled as he continued. "Your teachers report you possess supernatural knowledge about the river. Rekhmire believes you communicate with the god Hapi. That the river god speaks to you, bodes well for your character and ability. Truly, the decision to raise you in the house of Pharaoh was justified. What say you of your communication?"

"It is true, your Majesty, that I enjoy listening to the river trying to penetrate its secrets." Though I heard a voice when I lingered by the Nile, I knew it was not Hapi.

"Rekhmire states you understand the ways of Hapi, the river, and how papyrus grows on its banks. For these reasons, we give you a new governmental role. One that fits your talents, your royal upbringing, and your Habiru heritage."

Silence enveloped the chamber as the nobles waited to hear Ahmose's pronouncement.

"Overload of the Canals of Egypt shall be your new title. Our borders resettled, we can focus on commerce and infrastructure. Our first task is to reopen Senusret's canal, for it will improve trade in the region."

Murmurs of approval greeted the pronouncement. Ahmose basked in the adulations for several moments before stamping his staff on the grown to quiet the crowd.

"My forbearer Senusret built a canal between Bubastis and the Bitter Lakes," he continued. "Over the years it fell into disrepair, but with your help, we can reopen it. Once completed, we will build an entire network of canals to increase trade. The borders of Egypt extend from the Great Sea and the Kush frontier. The canal will improve trade from the Western Frontier to the East and beyond. Can you make this happen?"

With this one act, Ahmose honored and insulted me.

Though he gave me control over the waterways, at least in name, he held me accountable for the removal of the swamps by others long before my birth. He asked me the question as a way of showing respect to my gift. But I sensed a ruse. He needed my help, and I knew why.

"Your Majesty. I believe with proper preparation, we could safely reopen the canal."

"How so my son? What preparations must be made?"

In hindsight, I should have pretended the voice seized me. I could have told them not to build the canal, though I doubt that would have stopped the project.

I heard the river speak, but Harwa taught me of the swamps, telling me of the effects of the volcano, the removal of the papyrus, and what might happen if the canal were reopened. But telling them what I knew risked exposing Harwa or Nefertari. For she arranged the meetings with Harwa and Miriam.

Not knowing what to say, I blurted, "Your Majesty. Let me travel to Bitter Lakes along the canal route to observe the waters there."

"A wonderful idea, Ramose!" he rejoined. "As the details of our discussion do not concern the others assembled here, let you and I continue this discussion later in my private chambers."

"Yes, Your Majesty," I responded.

"Welcome to the Imperial Government of Egypt, Ramose."

I bowed before withdrawing from the audience chamber, silence piercing the cavernous space.

***

Though I could not be sure, I sensed my actions, and responses pleased Ahmose. He seemed excited by my answer to the question of the best approach to fix the canal. I wondered if he had little concern about opening the canal at all. Later that evening, I found answers to these questions.

Ahmose pleasantly greeted me when I arrived at his private chambers. He dismissed his guards, informing them not to disturb us for one hour. Nefertari absence was palpable.

"Ramose," Ahmose beamed. "You did well today. And exactly what I wanted."

"I did?" I responded in mock surprise.

"Yes. I needed an excuse to send you abroad, and a military mission would needlessly threaten the families that resent you. I know of your success in the desert. Ahhotep marveled at your strategy in taking the first oasis."

"Our being outnumbered required a bold plan," I replied.

"Well said! Tell no one of it though for likely I would need to banish you from the land."

"I will say nothing."

"Good. Your new position affords us the ability to send you abroad without suspicion. Starting in the East makes sense because the territory is familiar."

"What would they suspect? That you will not build canals?"

"Oh, I will be. They are needed for trade. But having you away from court is best for you."

"And you," I interjected.

"Do not be surly with me," he snapped. "The nobles dislike for you challenges us both. Remaining in Waset year-round only endangers you. You gain freedom to move around the land while performing a mission for me."

He paused before telling me my real mission, what I already knew. "You know of the staff." It was a statement, for Ahmose learned of my knowledge of this artifact.

"Why would a staff be so important?" I asked, though I knew he would not tell me his real reason.

"It is a sign of rulership, a sign of power. Crafted long ago, they have attributed many powers to it. One legend suggests a person wielding it can rule the weather, water, and lands far beyond Egypt. Imagine how we could prosper if we could control the exact amount of flooding in the river?"

"Do you truly believe that is possible?"

"No, but having the staff would solidify the power of my dynasty. Most of my ancestors in the Upper Kingdom forgot its history. But the remembrance of it remained with the Hyksos. I learned of their treachery in stealing the kingdom after finding the staff. Stay your wrath. I do not hold you responsible. The Hyksos thought their people crafted it and brought it with them to Egypt. But Rekhmire found notes of it in an ancient papyrus. We believe it to be an Egyptian artifact. Maybe finding it will bring peace to the two peoples."

"Or increase the chances of a rebellion," I thought, but said nothing.

"I have never seen the staff but have a description. A tall staff, with a loop at the top and a jewel within the loop. The gem is unknown, for different tales exist. I thought the artifact may lie near Nubia, but too many eyes watch me, making my ability to search impossible. Sending you east will throw off suspicion. Later, we will send you south. Something to do with the swamps. I am told that a man named Harwa may know something about the staff."

At the mention of my teacher's name, I felt my heart might stop as my chest tightened. Did he know of Nefertari's treachery in arranging my meeting with him and Miriam? If Ahmose noticed, he betrayed no sign of it.

"And Ramose?"

"Yes, Father," I said, steading myself with my breath.

"Tell no one of your true purpose. Not even your brothers. There are rumors that it drove the last Pharaoh insane. You may be immune to that fate being Habiru. Find it and return it to me."

"Very well, Your Majesty. I shall go East. I would like to organize a team if amenable to you."

"Please do so."

Testing Ahmose, I asked, "Do you know anything about this Harwa person? I mean, how will I recognize him?"

Pharaoh eyed me. I did not know if his spies learned of my meetings with Harwa. Was it possible that he knew all along and encouraged the arrangement? He responded nonchalantly.

"I do not know Ramose. It may take some time to find him. He may not even be alive anymore. But maybe you can find someone who knows him. Be discreet though."

"Yes, Your Majesty."

"Good luck, Ramose."

I nodded curtly and left Ahmose's private chambers. I understood his plan, why he adopted me in the first place, why he made me commissioner of the waterways. His true interest lay not in peace, but in power. Once I recovered the artifact, he would banish me forever.

26

Preparations followed for the next two days. I wanted to gather loyal men to accompany this mission. The third morning after the ritual, I arose to find Mahu and a detachment of men ready to leave. Again, our journey would take us to the former capital of the Lower Kingdom, Avaris. From there we would go by land along the length of the old canal towards Bitter Lakes. Though Ahmose's true goal was different, I wished to protect the river. As Ahhotep and Amenhotep subdued the rebel forces, we expected little resistance from any enemy in this region. The force, smaller than that captured the oasis, proved to be nimbler than a full company of men. Mahu and I discussed the mission while we sailed the Nile.

"Do you believe problems will arise from re-opening the canal? Or was that more for Ahmose's benefit?" Mahu asked.

"I asked someone else that very question a few years ago," I responded thinking about Harwa telling me about the Strongili eruption and leaving something in Bitter Lakes. He believed it was ready to bring death and destruction to the clean waters of the Nile. I did not know what I meant, but I told Mahu, "I will feel something."

"What do you mean?" Mahu asked.

"I am not sure. We will find out soon what danger lies with reopening the canal."

We arrived in Avaris three days later. Meritamen greeted us at the dock, with a few of her ladies-in-waiting.

"Where is Sitamen?" I asked, hugging my older, adopted sister.

"She is not well," Meritamen responded. "We sent her back to Waset for healing."

"She is embarrassed to see me," I responded knowing she lied to protect Sitamen's feelings.

"She cares for you. It is only...."

"She was inflamed," I interrupted.

"Yes. But she does not understand her actions."

"She ingested a love potion."

"A love potion?"

"Mother did not tell you?" I asked, confused. I wondered why Nefertari did not share this with my sisters.

"No," Meritamen responded, looking confused. "Why would Sitamen drink a love potion?"

"She did not do it on purpose," I whispered. "Someone slipped it into her drink. We do not know who. But we should discuss the rest in private."

We walked to the palace from the docks. Old feelings stirred, climbing the steps to the entrance. Though I stayed here a few seasons ago, I felt pangs of pain. Being ripped away from my family was something that never fully healed. My quarters remained untouched save for refreshments laid out for us to enjoy. Meritamen and Mahu joined me as we had a light snack.

"I thought Balaam used spells to drive Sitamen," I started, "but Nefertari insists it was a potion."

"How does she know?" Meritamen asked.

"I do not know. Why did she say nothing to you?"

"Who knows? Mother is selective with what she shares with me. Or maybe she learned something on her trip back to Waset. How did someone deliver the potion?"

"Likely a servant at the palace."

"How do you know?" she asked.

"Paser told me. The palace staff have divided loyalties."

"Divided?" she responded.

"Many servants support freedoms for Habirus. But others want to remove all of them from Egypt."

"A servant that wishes you out of the royal family?" Meritamen suggested.

"Was the potion specific to you, Ramose?" Mahu asked.

"I believe so."

"Then it could have been a Habiru servant's actions," Mahu suggested.

"Why do you say that, Mahu?" Meritamen asked.

"Because a marriage between Ramose and Sitamen would solidify Habiru legitimacy in Egypt."

"That is unlikely. Most of the staff know our ways. A second brother-sister pair would create chaos," my sister replied. Meritamen explained to Mahu that only one brother and one sister marry in the Egyptian Royal family.

"What would have happened had Ramose and Sitamen consummated their union?" Mahu asked.

"Ahmose would have deemed Ramose a usurper," Meritamen replied. "Punishment would be swift and harsh for both him and Sitamen."

"That eliminates the likelihood of a Habiru being involved. But Sitamen must have known too."

"She did," Meritamen said. "Which makes her actions curious, though the love potion may explain some of it."

"It is strange," I said thinking about it. "I did not know this could be a problem before all this happened."

"You seem friendly with your staff, Ramose," Meritamen remarked.

"A few I trust. My survival depends upon it."

"There is nothing we can do about Sitamen now," Mahu changed the subject. "There are many reasons and people who could have performed this act."

"That is true, Mahu," Meritamen agreed. "But I wonder about Teta. He lost a lot because of Ramose."

"Siamun threatened me after Ahmose stripped Teta of a few titles," I offered.

"He did?" Meritamen said. "Did you tell mother?"

"For what purpose?" I responded.

"For now," Mahu interjected, "All of you need to know of changes in flavor in food and drink. I would make sure that you each have trusted food testers."

"What is your mission this time?" Meritamen asked.

"They have made me Lord of the Waterways," I responded. "We are investigating the dangers of rebuilding the canal."

"Could opening the canal cause problems?" Meritamen asked.

"We will find out," I responded.

"How will you know?" she asked.

"I am unsure," I confessed.

"Ahmose sends you to find the staff," Meritamen said. It was a statement. When I did not respond she added, "If you find it, take it far from Egypt and away from Ahmose and Siamun."

"Why?" I asked. Meritamen was the third person to tell me this.

"It has powers, Ramose, power to make someone live a long time. Ahmose and my demented brother would do terrible things if they lived so long."

Though skeptical, Mahu and I asked questions about the staff. Meritamen knew nothing of the origins of the staff, only some of its capacities.

"Is there something about the staff that would not want you and Ammi to marry?" I asked.

Meritamen gave me a queer look, as though she wished to tell me something, but then changed her mind. "I am unsure about that. I suspect something but I will wait to say anything."

"Do you believe the staff is that powerful?" Mahu asked.

"It is why Ramose is in the family," Meritamen replied. "Ahmose risked the wrath of the nobles to recover it."

"That I do not understand," I said.

"I do not either," my adopted sister conceded.

The next morning, we said our goodbyes. We walked east towards the rising sun and the source of the day's heat. While not as hot as the last time we ventured through this region, the day was still warm. Walking along the dried and barren bed of the previous canal caused me to wonder how foliage ever grew along this route. But I felt traces of the energy of papyrus as we walked.

Late in the afternoon, we arrived at our destination, Bitter Lakes, an area of several large and many smaller lakes. Plants grew around Lake Timsah, the smallest of the lakes, and comprised fresh water. Great Bitter Lake lay just south of Timsah, and further along was Lesser Bitter Lake. Little vegetation grew around those two bodies of water because of the high saline content. Though Lesser Bitter Lake was closest to the sea, it possessed a small patch of vegetation that grew on its southern shore, but nowhere else. I suspected there might be an underground freshwater spring feeding the plants.

As the sun set in the West, Mahu and I walked along the southern edge of Greater Bitter Lake. At one time, this area teemed with Papyrus, palm trees, and other vegetation. Now it was barren, a false oasis in the desert. Human mismanagement combined with a natural disaster left the water poisoned. The Hyksos had cleared much of this area of papyrus to grow grass to feed cattle only to die because of the salty water. I felt the ground beneath me cry for moisture, though water lay next to it., I knew Harwa was correct; something lurked in the water. I felt it.

"Mahu," I said. "I will sit by the water and...." How do I explain this to him?

"Listen?" he said.

"Yes," I replied, smiling, grateful that Mahu understood my process.

I sat near the water and closed my eyes. I observed my breath, feeling my chest expand and contract to quiet myself. Images and ideas arose, and I watched them float along the river of thought. Beginning as whispers, like words brushing against my ears, hints of the danger came to me. Strongili's eruption left ash and other debris in the water, making it more stagnant. Nothing grew here because of the contamination. Flooding might clean it, but the waters of the Nile would not rise enough in this region to wash away the filth. My legs tired, I rose to share with Mahu my discovery.

"The lake is a problem," I said. "Completing the canal will harm the Nile."

"Can we prevent injury to the river?" Mahu asked. He spoke of the Nile as one does a person, a living being. In Egypt, everyone spoke of the river this way, for it brought life to the otherwise barren region. My recent experiences in the desert gave me a greater appreciation for this idea.

"Possibly," I replied. "We should plant papyrus along the canal route. Once it takes root, then we can build the canal starting from the West. The papyrus will clean the dirty water."

"Clean?"

"Maybe clean is the wrong word. I have observed papyrus for many years. Now I have seen regions of water with and without papyrus. The water behaves differently. You can trust drinking the water near papyrus regardless of how fast it flows."

"Yes, others have advised the same. Building from the river to allow the plants to take root. Close that side, then open the lake. This will allow the plants to purify the contaminated water before it touches the Nile's."

"An excellent suggestion! If we build from the lake, I sense that the lake will contaminate the Nile."

He nodded as though he understood. I stood there for a few moments surveying the land, wondering if any chance existed for our intervention of the canal. I doubted this would work but thought I should discuss with Harwa. Though Ahmose wished me to avoid discussing the staff with anyone, Meritamen's mentioning of it saved me from that. Telling him of Harwa would make the next few days easier.

"I must share with you something but promise you will tell no one else."

"You have my word, Ramose."

"I have a friend, a 'swamp person', named Harwa. An ancient fellow who has seen many things happen in Egypt, even working for the government in Lower Egypt before Ahmose conquered it. He taught me much about understanding the swamps and how they filter plants. He may have some idea of what we need to do to prevent this disaster."

"You want to talk to him before returning to Ahmose?"

"Yes. Let us camp here tonight. We can find him on the way to Waset."

"I will have the men pitch tents and prepare camp," he said. Turning around, he instructed the men to set up camp. Turning back to me he added, "The inhospitable nature of the place   unsettles   me."
"You,   Mahu?"   I   said.   "Nothing   flusters   you."
He smiled. "Almost nothing. But the stench of death permeates this   area."

"It will only be one night," I acknowledged. "We will leave first thing in the morning."

***

The wind blew fiercely that night, sending a sickening sulphurous smell towards the camp. Between gusts, I heard the whispers from the lake. Danger lurked beneath its surface. The noise and stench made sleep difficult. I tossed and turned on the hard ground, wondering if the wind would rip the tent from its pegs. In fits and starts, slept, the noisome odors permeated my slumber. Screams swirling in the breeze woke me. Jumping up, I grabbed my sword and unsheathing it; I ran from my pavilion. The wind twisted the scene as I could not be sure what I viewed. Looking as it must have come from the lake, a large beast, nearly twice as large as any man with four long arms or tentacles torn a soldier in two. Bringing half the man to what appeared to be a mouth, it began sucking the blood and moisture from the dead man as the two other tentacles lunged at another guard. Wildly, the soldier swung his sword at our attacker. Noisily, the sword disappeared into the monster as if though it were mud.

Not knowing what to do, I tried to steady my breathing. Almost immediately, I felt the current rise within me. "How do I stop this creature?" I thought. "Serah said the power lies in my thoughts." Fear erased my ability to think, but still I breathed and brought the vibration higher and higher in my body.

Finished consuming the other two soldiers, the beast turned towards me. The thought "fire" entered my mind. I began feeling a burning sensation throughout my body. As one of the tentacle-arms swung at me, a flame lit on my hand as I scorched the beast. Finding this effective in stopping it, I brought flame to my other hand and pummeled it with both fiery fists.

The fire burned the creature as I realized it comprised mud and vegetation. From where it came, I did not know. It howled with the wind as it began retreating away from the lake and towards Egypt. I stopped myself to let it be. I heard Mahu yelling, "Ramose! Destroy the creature. It will come at us again!"

"Ramose!" I opened my eyes to find Mahu shaking me.

"Ramose, it is morning."

I looked around and saw no signs of a mud monster. Relative quiet permeated the tent flaps for the tempest had broken. The only sounds I heard came from the men breaking down tents and collecting items that scattered in the night. The lakes remained silent once again.

"You woke me from the strangest dream. A mud monster rose from the lakes and began attacking our camp."

"A mud monster?" Mahu asked, smiling.

"He ate our swords and men before I drove it away with fire."

"Fire?"

"It is not important. I will ponder the meaning as we return."

"The meaning is obvious, is it not? Danger lurks in the lake."

"And if I try to stop it, it will only make matters worse," I added. Before Mahu could say anything else I added, "Get the men ready to leave."

Mahu left to carry out my order. I rose from the ground, stiff from the night. My dream permeated my thoughts. Though the wind died, the smell remained; the stench of death. Once packed, we set out towards the rising sun and Avaris. This time, we did not tarry in the former Hyksos capital. My small contingent sailed south towards Waset. Another night passed, and the next morning, I ordered the boats ashore. I told Mahu it was to look at the plants. But somehow I felt Harwa's presence.

"What are you doing then, Ramose?"

"I must find Harwa and I sense he will be here. I would ask you to join me, Mahu, but I fear he will not show himself if I am not alone."

I entered the swamps through a small opening of papyrus plants. I stepped carefully along the root formations to keep my feet from touching the water. Following the extensive system of tubers, I walked for a quarter of a mile until I found a clearing. I waited, thinking about the events of the last few months and wondering about the staff. Everything that I knew about it sounded dangerous. But not nearly as terrible as what my adopted family believed would happen if Ahmose found it first.

Within an hour, a rustling nearby alerted me to Harwa's presence. I turned to see him walking through the stalks of papyrus.

"Ho, Ramose."

"Ho, Harwa."

"You have questions about the staff." It was a statement.

I told him the story Ahmose told me.

"You mean the Staff of Melchizedek?"

I looked at him curiously.

"Despite what Ahmose told you, the staff is not of Egyptian origin. It belongs to the Habirus before its theft from Jacob. Ahmose wants it for himself, which is why I had Reuel take it as far away from him as possible."

"Reuel? Who is that?"

"On old friend of mine. He advised Apepi towards the end of his life, and Khamudi after him. But the last Pharaoh of the Lower Kingdom refused to heed Reuel's warnings."

"Warnings of what?" I asked.

"The great wave, the rise of the Upper Kingdom, and Balaam."

"Balaam?"

"Balaam betrayal ran deep. He promised the staff to Ahmose and revealed our defense plans."

"In exchange for?"

"I am unsure," Harwa confessed.

"Then Nefertari is correct. Balaam created the potion that inflamed Sitamen." I told Harwa of my conversations with my adopted mother.

"Balaam's actions makes less and less sense each time I hear what he does. What does he seek?"

"The staff?" I suggested.

"Unlikely," Harwa countered. "He could have taken it by force."

"Unless he is afraid of you or this Reuel person," I suggested.

Harwa smiled. "I had not considered that. You are learning." The compliment felt good. "But Reuel and I removed the artifact from the Lower Kingdom before Balaam could seize it."

"Where did you take it?"

"Reuel went east with the staff as I spread the rumor that it became lost near Nubian."

"Why?"

"We knew Ahmose would seek it. Only a Habiru worthy of it should receive it. For that person will lead the people out of Egypt and back to their homeland."

"Homeland?"

"El Shaddai promised the Land of Canaan to Abraham, Jacob's grandfather. Should Ahmose ask, you can tell him I know not where the staff lingers. But tell him you need to go south to get it."

"South? I thought you said he took it east."

"Your immediate destiny lies to the South! The winds of change are about you, Ramose. Events move quickly. Soon you must choose between the people of your birth and the people who raised you."

"You speak in riddles, Harwa."

He smiled. "To one with vision, there is no riddle. Only truth. You are ready for what awaits you."

"What do you mean?"

"I am finished being your teacher."

"But I have more to learn!"

"You will have other teachers," he assured.

"What of my dream?" and I told him of it.

"I think you are correct, Ramose," he responded. "Nothing can stop the danger hiding in the lakes once they build the canal. Your intervention will probably worsen the situation."

"What should I do?"

"For now, go south and explore the swamps there."

"But you said, I will only make things worse."

"There is something you must do there."

"What?"

"I cannot tell you."

"And then what do I do?" I snapped.

"That depends upon what happens you go south. Most likely you will need to leave Egypt."

"Leave Egypt? Why would I do that? This is my home."

"You may live in Egypt your entire life, Ramose, but it is not your home. Your home is here," and he pointed to his heart.

I realized the meaning of his words and I felt tears well in my eyes. I knew this would be the last time I would see Harwa.

"You will never lose me, Ramose. I am here always, for I am part of the One. We can never be separate. Give my regards to Serah and Miriam."

He walked towards the same opening of the papyrus he entered and turned around. "When you leave Egypt, go find Reuel in Midian."

"Reuel is alive?"

He said nothing, turned away from me, and disappeared in the dense foliage. A light flashed just past where he walked away, and I ran over to see.

"Harwa," I yelled. "Haarrwa!"

Silence was my only response. I saw no trace of him in the swamp. Harwa was gone.

27

Stunned, I slumped to the ground and tried to collect my thoughts. Gone was Harwa, a pillar of support most of my life. I lost my friend, advisor, and teacher who helped me navigate the pitfalls of palace life. For some time, I cried, not sure what to do next. I sat there, tears rolling down my cheeks. Too numb to move, I stayed still for at least half an hour before I remembered his words.

"Soon you will face a choice."

Serah spoke the same words the last time we met. How would I know the choice? How would I know when this happens? My road lies south, he said. But Reuel is in Midian to the East. This made no sense to me. And what actions must I take in the South? Find something related to the staff? Though I knew Serah had answers, I suspected she might withhold them from me. Nevertheless, I sensed I must confer with her.

I washed my salty face in the water and set out to rejoin Mahu. When I found him later, I told him we needed to return to report to Pharaoh.

Mahu leveled a curious look, but said nothing in front of others. Instead, he ordered the men to prepare for our departure.

Boarding the boats once again, we continued our journey.

"You found him," Mahu said as we stood alone at the bow.

I nodded. "He said to go south..." I stopped. Should I tell

Mahu of this choice? What if he influenced me to make the wrong decision? Or tried to stop me from leaving? For now, I would say nothing. Instead, I spoke words I did not understand, "I must go south. I do not understand why. But I can observe the swamps there. Maybe we can find someone that knows how to transplant the papyrus plants."

"Will that delay the project?"

My head swirled thinking about what Harwa said, about the staff and my leaving Egypt. Steadying myself, I answered his questions.

"We must delay it. Abandoning the project makes the most sense, but I doubt Ahmose would do so. The lakes reek! You smelled them. But replanting the papyrus might work, though the area around the lakes is likely too barren and dry to grow anything. Whatever the plan, I doubt Ahmose will approve of anything."

"I do not disagree," Mahu replied. "But talk to Pharaoh about it. Tell him about Ma'at. Will he not understand that?"

I thought back to a conversation long ago. Ahmose screamed at us that day, lecturing us about Ma'at's purpose to allow the priesthood to control workers. If you want balance, truth, and harmony take it for yourself boys. Saying nothing about that day, I told Mahu, "For an Egyptian, he has some strange ideas about Ma'at."

Before Mahu could ask about it, a sailor informed us we would arrive in Waset in a few moments. Going below deck, I went to retrieve my belongings and found my bag open. I remembered closing it and searched the contents to be sure nothing was taken. After a few moments of going through it, I found nothing missing. As Mahu and I disembarked, I said, "I must meet with someone else before we talk to Pharaoh."

"How long will you be?" he asked.

"Only a few hours."

"Word will arrive to Pharaoh that we have returned before long."

"Can you stall? Or better yet, ask Paser to do so."

"Very well. I will find Paser then plan to meet you in your quarters in two to three hours."

"Thank you, Mahu."

***

He nodded and turned away while I headed away from the river towards the Habiru quarter. People cowered as passed, though I did not know why. Reaching Serah's tent, one of her servants recognized me.

"Is Serah expecting you?" he asked, concerned of my presence.

"I doubt it. Unless she has seen my return," I quipped. Scowling, he slipped inside the tent. People glared at me as they walked by while I stood outside the tent. Then I realized I wore my military uniform. Serah's servant came out of the tent with Sitamen and Meritamen. Seeing the look of surprise on my face, Meritamen exclaimed. "Ramose! What brings you here?"

"I could ask the same thing," I responded. They both looked surprised.

My adopted sisters exchanged nervous glances before Meritamen spoke. "We found a Habiru baby floating in a basket on the Nile. We wanted to find the parents."

I saw that Sitamen, looking very tired and worn, held a newborn child in her arms. Sitamen moved the blanket to uncover the child's sleeping face. From my quick glance, I could not know his tribal origin, though it appeared he may have Egyptian features.

"That is terrible! Why would someone do that? Did Serah know who the parents are?" I asked.

Meritamen and Sitamen exchanged nervous glances. "She did not. But Serah wondered if he comes from a union of an Egyptian and Habiru couple."

"She and Miriam are discussing finding a wet nurse for the child, though," Meritamen added.

"That is good," I responded.

"I thought about naming him Moses," Sitamen blushed. "Not after you!" she added. "I meant because I too drew him out of the water."

"I doubt Ahmose would allow you to keep that name anyway," I said, trying to reassure her. She smiled, but said nothing. So I added, "Nefertari told me about the love potion that affected you. I need to tell Serah about a friend of hers who died. But I would like to spend time with both of you before I leave on my next mission."

Sitamen smiled. When she said nothing, Meritamen interjected, "We would like that."

The two went on their way I entered the tent, needing a few moments for my eyes to adjust to the dimness. When they did, I saw Serah sitting across from Miriam as the two spoke in quiet tones.

"Ramose," Serah's gravelly voice greeted me. "You return with news and questions."

"I do, Aunt Serah. Hello Miriam." I sat next to my sister, who smiled. "You are helping Sitamen find a wet nurse for the Habiru child?"

"Is that what she told you?" Miriam responded.

"Miriam," Serah whispered. "I know you must know those who can help."

"Yes, Auntie," Miriam responded, rising to leave.

"You should not have come in your uniform, Ramose!" Serah scolded. "You compromise my standing by doing so. Not to mention that it frightens the people here."

"Harwa left," I blurted.

"What do you mean left?" Miriam demanded.

Looking out past both Miriam and I, Serah mumbled, "The time nears." Then she barked at Miriam, "Finish your tasks."

"Yes, Auntie." Miriam took some towels and wrapped them around other soiled towels and garments before placing them in a large basin. Then she left the tent.

"Start from the beginning Ramose," Serah commanded.

I told Serah of my visit to Bitter Lakes and the dreams I had near there. She asked for details of the dream and I recounted as best I could.

"Who were the soldiers killed in the dream?" Serah asked. When I told her I could not recall she said, "Think! Were they nobles? Farmers?"

I thought for a moment. "One came from a peasant family and one from a noble family."

"As I suspected," she said.

"What does it mean?"

"You are correct. Your efforts to stop the danger will only make it worse. And the effects will be broad reaching and not distinguish between rich and poor. Whatever lays at the bottom of that lake comes for all."

"That feels right," I said.

"And what of Harwa?"

"He disappeared in a flash."

"He is done with incarnation. But he told you to go south and then east?"

"Yes. To find Reuel. But I do not understand why I should go east."

Serah looked out, lost in thought for a few moments before mumbling, "So you think he is the one?" She looked as though she listened to someone respond. After a few moments she asked under her breath, "And the other? The one just born?"

"Think who is the one, Auntie?"

She turned towards me, eyes ablaze for a moment before softening. "I am sorry, Ramose. I was speaking to someone else." Her gaze returned to starting into the distance as though conversing with a disembodied person.

"Very well," she said after listening for a few more moments. "We will do it your way. You have yet to disappoint me old friend. And my judgement is cloudy today."

Serah looked at me again. "Do as Harwa suggests, Ramose."

"Why go south?"

"I do not know. But Harwa saw something. Go south. Then the path to the East will become clear."

I was about to ask another question when Miriam walked in. "He is gone?" she asked near tears. I nodded.

"Did you dispose of everything?" Serah asked.

"Yes, Auntie."

"And a wet nurse?"

"I found someone who will do," Miriam replied.

"Good. This burden should not be the Habirus alone. Pharaoh should support the child given it has Egyptian heritage."

"Yes, Auntie," Miriam agreed. "They should!"

"Do not just criticize Egyptians," Serah snapped. "It is time for our people to grow up."

"But we are only slaves!"

"That excuse is no longer valid. We must bear the responsibility, too. A time comes for us to be a light upon all nations."

"A light to all nations?" I asked.

"Have I told you the story of how Rebecca came to the family?" When both Miriam and I shook our heads, Serah pointed to her harp, which I brought over. She began playing as if attempting to summon memories out of the instrument. Sounds rose, filing the tent with a sweet ambiance. I felt, rather than saw, a shimmer arise between the harp and myself. I realized the harp provided an extension of her, as though the music gave life to her memories. Serah began her story.

"My namesake was Abraham's first wife, Sarah. After her death, Abraham realized that he must find a wife for Isaac if his lineage would continue. I met neither Abraham nor Isaac. Both were long gone by the time of my birth. But Jacob kept their memory alive, just as you both must do the same."

She changed the notes as if to emphasize the command. Then she continued the original melody and her story. "Sarah lived a rich life. But she kept her son close to her until she died at 137. Abraham purchased a plot of land with a cave to bury her. Abraham, Isaac, Jacob and Leah are all buried there too."

The music conveyed a sense of grief as Serah's thoughts drifted with the notes. After a few moments, the cadence transitioned to a more upbeat sound as she continued her story. "Abraham instructed his servant to go find a wife for Isaac. He did not want his son cavorting with the Canaanite population. I do not believe he trusted them. But Jacob told me it was because of another reason.

"'You shall be a light unto all nations,' he said long ago. 'My grandfather Abraham knew that this land belonged to us. But only if he and his descendants remained faithful to the One God. He wished to prove his faith in El Shaddai by not marrying Isaac to anyone in the region that could lay claim to the land. It is also why he only purchased only a small plot.' That was many years ago, Jacob and I spoke of such things."

"Why could he not marry a Canaanite? Miriam asked. "Because that would dilute the claim that El Shaddai has on the land. Abraham wants us to test our faith. He did not want anyone to be able to declare it was not the power of God. He bought the property for the burial for the same reason. And he wanted a transactional record so the bodies would not be removed   later."
Serah paused. If not for her fingers dancing across the harp and

the music coming from it, I would have believed her to be asleep. Then she continued.

"Abraham placed his faith in others by asking his servant to go forth to the land from which he came to find a wife for Isaac. The servant asked El Shaddai for guidance, though he did not understand how to hear the voice of the Lord. He envisioned a test. He would find a well. Once there, a woman would offer him and his animals water. Then he would know this woman is destined for Isaac. He found the place, he saw, and a woman offered him water first and then as much as his animals desired. The woman was Jacob's mother, Rebekah. They dealt with Laban, her brother, and they returned to the land of Canaan.

"Rebekah knew what she was being offered. She knew her role as a foremother to our people. And after Esau married two of the local women in the region, Rebekah conceived of the plan to provide Jacob the birthright. I have told you both that story."

She stopped playing and looked at us. "That is why I know our people are to be a light upon nations."

"How?" Miriam scoffed. "We are oppressed!"

"Have you not paid attention to our lessons? El Shaddai answers our prayers."

A barky hoarse laugh escaped Miriam's lips. "Answers our prayers with more affliction?"

"Freedom will not just happen! El Shaddai sets the conditions. It is our job to listen to the guidance. But faith in the One is key. Just as Abraham's servant trusted the One."

"That is why he sent him?" I asked. "Instead of going himself?"

"Yes. Our forefather's faith in El Shaddai rubbed off on all who came near him. The time nears for our return to the land given to us. But we will not just appear there. We must use our legs to walk the way, and arms to swing swords to conquer the land. Then plow the fields to grow food to eat. But we must trust in the One to bring us there."

"I have asked for freedom, Auntie," implored Miriam.

"One must cultivate desire, while releasing judgement of the results."

When Miriam said nothing, Serah added, "Say goodbye to

Ramose. It may be awhile before you see him."

"You are leaving too!"

"Most likely to the South for some time. After that..." I trailed off. "We shall see where El Shaddai takes me." But in my heart, I knew.

***

After saying goodbye to Miriam, Serah provided me with robes to cover my Egyptian uniform. I removed them once I left the Habiru quarter. When I reached the palace, Paser took me upstairs to make me presentable to Pharaoh. My servant scrubbed me hard. Mahu had told him of our journey and the filth of the lakes. As he washed me, I realized that I had not washed since being in Avaris prior to walking the canal. The stench I realized had lingered until now.

Once cleaned, Paser let the guards know I was ready. We waited and spoke for some time before Pharaoh summoned us. Then Paser escorted me downstairs to the foyer in front of the audience chamber. We waited once again for Pharaoh's summons. Mahu stood still, showing no emotion, while I paced the hall trying to think of something to tell Pharaoh in front of others. I felt my heart skipping beats and my chest tightening. My mouth became dry. I knew what he needed to hear to allow me to travel south, and it had nothing to do with swamps or a potential disaster. What could I say before all the nobles to not arouse suspicion? A quarter of an hour later, the guards opened the doors to the audience chamber and announced our arrival. Ahmose inclined his head, motioning us forward.

"Ramose!" Pharaoh exclaimed as we approached. "You returned sooner than expected."

"Greetings, Your Majesty," I responded with a bow. "We bring news," I stammered. My mouth remained dry as the words sputtered from my lips, worried that I would say the wrong thing. "Danger lurks in the lakes. Bitter Lakes is more desolate than we believed," stumbled from my lips.

Did Pharaoh give me a disapproving look? "Is this your assessment, Mahu?" he asked.

Mahu loosened his at attention pose for a moment. "Your Majesty, once the region teemed with life, but no more. An ill wind blows through the region, spreading reek and death to even the wild grass in the region. Ramose feels something wrong in the water as though Ma'at itself had been disturbed."

"You felt this Ramose?" Ahmose asked.

"Yes. There is a system that exists between man, the water, the river, the animals, and the plant…"

My father interrupted me. "We know what Ma'at is, Ramose. I do not need a sermon." Laughs erupted from some nobles.

"Forgive me, Your Majesty. I meant no disrespect. I do not understand the cause of the imbalance."

Having found my words, I continued speaking, though my voice cracked and wavered.

"I think the pyramids, the palaces, the new construction. It is affecting Ma'at. We need to rebalance the system before rebuilding the canal. This project will only add to the imbalance."

"Are you suggesting that we stop construction of all of Pharaoh's great projects for Egypt?!" a courtier snickered.

"Of course not, Dharmu," Ahmose remonstrated. "Even if Ramose is suggesting such a thing, I will not allow it. Are you saying that we want to explore replacing the swamps to our south, Ramose?"

Ahmose believed the staff lay south. That is why he wished me to travel there. Harwa told me to go there too, so I replied, "Yes, Your Majesty. We must take action immediately. Otherwise, disaster could strike and the river will run with blood."

"Are you threatening His Majesty?" Balaam leered.

"I do no such thing, Balaam!" I barked. As the other times Balaam spoke in my presence, I felt a whooshing sensation. Pausing for a moment, I brought up an energy, and imagined flicking it away. The feeling stopped, so I added, "I would rather prove me wrong after taking action than proved right."

"Understood, Ramose," Pharaoh replied.

"What would we need to fix the swamps in the North?" Rekhmire asked.

"Replanting the swamps in the region could reduce the impact. Otherwise, we risk poisoning the river with the water from Bitter Lakes."

Murmurs of disbelief erupted from the audience, dotted

with derisive laughs now and then. Ahmose stamped his staff to silence the crowd.

"Please continue, Ramose," Pharaoh commanded.

Already feeling nervous, the snickers and comments left me tongue-tied again. Finding my voice, I spoke what Harwa told me to say. "Replanting the papyrus should help. But I need to observe some swamps that have been untouched to know for sure. Maybe Hapi will reveal to me the secrets to the solution to our problem."

"Very well, Ramose," Ahmose said. "Go South and figure out a way to solve this issue. But I am only giving you one moon to do so."

"Your Majesty?" Rekhmire said.

"Yes, Rekhmire," the Pharaoh replied.

"A merchant ship leaves tomorrow. Maybe Ramose and the soldiers can escort that ship to Buhen?"

Ahmose frowned at his advisor. "An excellent idea, Rekhmire," Ahmose said. Then turning to me. "We have reports of a Nubian uprising that your brothers Siamun, and Ahmose-Ankh are handling. But to be safe, take the detachment of troops with you and guard the merchant caravan that leaves in the morning."

"As you wish my lord," I replied, before Mahu and I withdrew from the chamber.

28

Dismissed, Mahu and I left the audience chamber. Showing no emotion, we walked through the hallway until we found a quiet alcove where I pulled my friend aside.

"Thank you for your help in there," I blurted, as I collapsed against the wall.

"You are welcome," he replied. "We both better get packed again. This journey will be longer. Buhen is at least a week away."

"I know. This is long overdue. I may want to spend some time with Ammi."

Mahu agreed, for he and Ahmose-Ankh remained good friends. We parted as I left to find Paser and prepare for the journey. But instead of finding Paser, Amenhotep sat in my room when I returned.

"Apologies," Amenhotep said, standing up from the settee in my room. "Paser told me it would be fine for me to wait for you here."

"When did you get back?" I asked.

"Two days ago. Our paths must have crossed. You were at court?"

"I hate speaking there. I feel demeaned by the nobles."

"You must not take their words and actions to heart, Ramose."

"I know," I sighed. "But most of my life, they have treated me as a second-class citizen, though I am royalty. I am expected to present myself in court, but am mocked when I do."

"I feel the same," he said.

"Do you?" I challenged. "You are a blood relative of Ahmose whereas the courtiers consider me a pretender. I live in two worlds, Amenhotep. Viewed as a noble by some, but dirt by others!"

"It will change."

"Not if Ahmose continues prejudiced policies. He encourages the discrimination."

Ignoring my comment, Amenhotep asked. "Why did Father summon you?"

I explained to him my new role in government managing the waterways. "I leave again in the morning to inspect swamps in the South."

"Can I go with you?"

I must have given him a look of surprise for he added. "I do not trust Siamun after what I heard in the desert."

"Oh?"

"I overheard talk about Siamun trying to kill you."

"He has already tried," I said casually.

"This is different. I think some of his people were in my company. Siamun wants to become Pharaoh."

"He need not kill either of us to do that." Amenhotep's disregard for my feelings about being at court left me annoyed.

"If he believed you might protect Ahmose-Ankh, he would."

"I can handle myself." When Amenhotep looked disappointed, I added, "It is a simple excursion. I must see how the plants grow, collect some, and come home." I did not tell him that Ahmose had sent me on a hunt for the staff. Or that Harwa told me to go East.

"Be careful in Buhen."

"We are escorting a caravan to Buhen, but then head to the swamps. I do not know if either of our brothers are there. Why are you so concerned now?"

"Balaam said something disturbing the other day. I thought nothing of it until you came here to tell me that father wants you to go south."

"What was that?"

"He said that Siamun should be Pharaoh." Amenhotep told me he and Balaam were discussing how to negotiate treaties and be an effective ruler, when Balaam criticized Amenhotep for being too kind.

"What?" I exclaimed. "Siamun as Pharaoh?"

"Then he had a look of panic on his face and said, 'I meant to say Ahmose-Ankh will be a good king one day.'"

"That is odd," I said. "Siamun would be a terrible king."

"He is too self-absorbed. He manipulates people, not caring what the true outcome is, other than helping himself. Why cannot Father see this?"

"Not to mention, he is cruel and likes to torture animals. Ma'at cannot allow the imbalance to last long. My guess is that he will come to a sudden end."

"Stay out of his way, Ramose, or you may come to a sudden end."

I smiled at his attempt at humor and replied, "I will."

A knock at the door interrupted our discussion.

"Yes," I responded to the knock.

Ahmose's personal secretary opened the door. He informed me that Pharaoh wished to see me right away. Amenhotep gave me a quizzical look. I shrugged my shoulders in response and followed the secretary to Pharaoh's personal chambers.

"Ramose," Ahmose said, when I walked in. "Come in and sit down."

I did as he commanded.

"Did you find Harwa?" he asked, expectation shone on his face.

"Yes, your Majesty."

"Good, good." He smiled rubbed his hands together a mix of anticipation and greed. "What did he say?"

I took a deep breath and thought for a second. I repeated what Harwa said about the staff going south.

"Do you think he was telling the truth?"

"Why would he lie?"

"Siamun says that he cannot lie to you. Is that true for others?"

"I did not know that about Siamun." Ahmose looked surprised for a moment, then continued.

"I am depending upon you to recover the staff, Ramose. It

is critical…"

Ahmose stopped. He did not want to sound desperate. I could tell he was hiding something. Did Ahmose also have trouble lying to me?

"Be careful not to let any of your brothers know about the staff. In fact, it might be well to avoid Buhen all together."

"Yes, your Majesty."

"If you find the staff, hide it. Do not let anyone see it! That is crucial to the mission Ramose! Do you understand?"

"Yes, Your Majesty."

"Bring back something to replant the swamps either way. This will help allay any suspicions of your real mission. Have you thought what you will tell Mahu?"

"I already have told him that Harwa said we should go south to find more plants and seeds. We need to find a swamp person to help us who knows how to do the replanting."

"Send a message if you find the staff. It needs to be in code. Send something vague though."

"And if I do not find it?"

"You can return, and we can discuss. One more thing, Ramose. The staff is Egyptian. You are not born Egyptian. I do not know what will happen if you try to use it. You need to be very careful." I knew he lied for I felt the dishonesty in my bones.

"If I find the staff, my message will be, 'the merchants have been delivered safely'."

"Excellent!"

I knew I would never send that message for the staff lay far out of his reach. I left to finish packing and found Amenhotep still awake in our room. Our conversation lasted for several hours, discussing various mundane topics. Neither of us knew, it would be many years before we met again.

***

We departed early the next morning aboard boats made of papyrus. For something humans could not consume, papyrus proved extremely versatile. Paper, ropes, sails, and boats were some items made from the plant. The boat comprised thick stalks tied together using rope made from the fronds of the plant. Sails too came from the same reed, a requirement for this trip. Though the river flowed north, the winds blew south. for the river flowed north. I pondered the irony of my assumed mission of sailing in a vessel made of the plant I was to collect and bring back to the north. But I knew the papyrus was only a ruse for my real mission.

The week-long journey south along the river would lead us through narrow and wide parts of the Nile. We would meander along the route but in a few locations rapids or bends in the river, made portage easier.

We stayed on the boats the entire time the first two days, heading south, sails flapping in the wind, passing large swaths of papyrus grew in plumes on the banks of the river. Beyond the papyrus and date palms, I could see people working the land. By the third day, many plants appeared unfamiliar, for they only grew in the area south of Waset. That night, we camped along the shore because rocks lay ahead in the water. The experienced sailors suggested coming ashore to prevent the boats from getting caught amongst them. Navigating in the morning would be easier.

Mahu greeted me as I finished eating a morning snack the next day. "We had some visitors last night."

"Oh?"

Motioning me to follow, we walked past the camp to a clearing where soldiers worked burying bodies. My quick assessment suggested about ten.

"Nubians tried to sneak into the camp last night," Mahu reported. "The guards killed them easily. Maybe they roamed north to escape the fighting. We need to make a report when we get to Buhen."

"Very well," I replied. I thought about what Ahmose said before I left and avoiding Buhen. "But we cannot stop until we go to the swamps. Pharaoh ordered me to finish that business first. He wanted me to avoid Buhen if possible."

"We must stop there to drop off the merchants and caravan, anyway," Mahu argued.

"I forgot about that. We can inform the authorities there upon our arrival."

"You do not want to see Ahmose-Ankh?" he asked.

"I do. But I must finish the mission. I feel pressure to succeed."

Mahu nodded. He knew the real reason for Ahmose

agreeing to my going south, but said nothing else in public.

Warmer temperatures and higher humidity heralded our entry into the jungle. The foliage grew denser, encroaching upon the river, creating a more swamp-like feel as palm trees and papyrus dominated the landscape. In some areas, the reeds grew ten cubits high. The lushness of the countryside stood in stark contrast to my journey in the desert. But being here helped me realize how civilization and development took away the wild and lush feel of the northern swamps. Ahmose could blame my people for the destruction. But his construction projects are just as damaging as Joseph's. My forbearer saved lives, at least.

All journeys south along the Nile require an answer to a question when approaching the big bend. While the wind allowed the use of sails when traveling south, the big bend turned the river back on itself, rendering the sails useless as the wind is at the fore of the boat. To pass through this point, one must row, a very labor intensive endeavor, or portaged across land. As commander of the caravan, it called me to decide. Land or water?

Under most circumstances, crossing over land makes the most sense. Only a few people can row to power the boat against the current. Portage allows for more hands to carry the goods and the boats. But exposure to an attack on land is a risk. With only a small contingent of soldiers defending in the swamp presents challenges. A good meal and a night of sleep would help my decision. I ordered us to camp.

Soldiers stood guard on the edges of our encampment as members of the caravan pitched tents, while others gathered wood, caught fish, and started fires.

"Mahu, tonight I will cook for you and the soldiers."

"But Your Highness…."

"I insist," I said, interrupting his protest. "I enjoy cooking and it helps clear my mind. After the meal, I will listen to the river for advice. We have only a little further to go, but I sense dangers exist with either route."

"Very well, Your Highness. I will send Nefer to help you. She is my personal cook."

I smiled, suspecting that Mahu's concern lay with the quality of my cooking more than a royal performing work.

Ignoring his concerns, I prepared a simple meal of fish and vegetables. I rubbed the fish with a mix of sea salt, thyme, and a pinch of dill. Then I pan fried it over the fire. Everyone enjoyed the results.

"This is very good, Your Highness," Mahu said as others agreed.

"You were nervous about me cooking?"

He had a wry smile on his face, and we all started laughing.

"How did I not know about your culinary skills?" Mahu exclaimed.

"It is one job Rekhmire taught me, likely the most useful. No opportunity presented itself for me to cook during our other excursions."

"I guess that is true," Mahu admitted.

"Let us discuss the plan for tomorrow. I sense there is a lot of danger ahead."

The regular soldiers rose to clean up, while Mahu, Djau, and Janu moved closer.

"Sir, Your Highness," Janu began saying to Mahu and I. "I suggest an over ground approach because there are reports of pirates in this part of the river."

"Pirates?!" I exclaimed.

"They have always been a scourge of the great river," Janu admitted. "But their activity has increased of late because of the war. Various tribes, Swamp people, Nubians, and others, rob people along the way."

"They attack smaller parties," Djau responded. "We are a large enough group that likely they will avoid us."

But Janu voiced concerns about a water approach. "The wind is stronger than expected. Rowing slows us and makes us vulnerable to assault."

"Did we not plan for this prior to our leaving?" I asked.

Mahu and Janu exchanged nervous glances before Mahu spoke. "The reports we received from the South suggested that the entire area, including pirates, was under Egyptian control."

"What...?"

"Siamun," Mahu interrupted. "Ahmose wants people to believe he is an effective administrator, so he forged the reports. Janu sent scouts to speak to villagers. They tell a different story. Pirates are very active in the area and raiding villages too. But we are a large and armed party."

As the officers debated amongst themselves the merits of land or water, I realized Siamun's influence on my missions continued. We faced danger because of lies to protect his incompetence. Water required soldiers to row the boats, whereas going by land posed risks because we the terrain was unknown. Mahu and Janu suggested that if we go over land, we could use scouts to help with finding any ambush. Djau suggested that some in the caravan could row if they attacked us.

"What are we going to do?" I asked.

"Your Highness, it is your decision," said Mahu. "But if I may, I think we have a better chance over land. It should be faster in this area and will allow us to scout ahead to find any ambushes. Reconnaissance is impossible on the water. We do not have enough boats."

"Could we have men on the ground and everyone else in the boats? That way we gain the advantage of the scouts without having to portage the boats and goods?"

"We could do that, your Highness," Janu said. "But our forces would be split. And neither group could help the other."

"Very well," I said. "Let me hear what the rivers suggests."

Excusing myself, I walk to the water's edge to clear my thoughts. I scanned the area for crocodiles, for they were plentiful in the region. Seeing none, I sat on a rock and closed my eyes. I took easy breaths through my nose, filling my lungs and then exhaling for twice the time. As I sat there, I fell into a trance, and a vision came to me. I saw the party walking on the land carrying the boats and goods. The way proved easy until near the end when three companies of pirates attacked our caravan, killing everyone in the party.

My eyes opened with a start. Closing them again, I took a few deep breaths. "We should go by water?" I asked, waited and listened. "Go by water," was the response. I sat there for a few more minutes breathing as I did at the beginning. No other guidance came.

I stood and shook my legs. I walked back to the camp to discuss with Mahu.

"Let us go by water, for the land here is dangerous," I said.

"Very well, Your Highness," said Mahu. "But might it be

prudent to have a detachment of soldiers on the banks to warn us?"

I thought about this and my vision, but I did not receive a sign. Feeling the weight of leadership, I wondered what gave me the right to make these decisions that effected so many people's lives. What if I made the wrong choice? My sense was that we would be safe without the soldiers on the shore. But logic suggested that we have soldiers on the shore to protect the greater number of people.

"Very well, Mahu. Have a small group of six soldiers be ready on the shore." I regretted saying it as the words left my mouth, feeling in my heart it was the wrong choice. But I let it stand and went to my tent to sleep.

29

I awoke the following morning to the sounds of people disassembling the camp. After conferring with my senior officers, we set out. Six soldiers remained ashore while everyone else returned to the boats to row upstream.

We rowed east for several hours before turning north, then east again. For most of this journey we could see the men along the shore. The plan was simple. One soldier would come close to the shore every fifty cubits to let us know everything was clear. We continued in this manner through the bend and neared the rendezvous location when a soldier waved his arms in a fast and slightly disorganized manner. He called to us but we were still too far from the shore to hear his words. Out of nowhere, a spear exploded through his chest protruding from his ribs. The momentum of the projectile carried him forward into the water, only the butt of the spear remained visible.

"Did you see where that came?" I exclaimed.

"From the jungle over there," Mahu responded, pointing.

"Row faster," I ordered.

Arriving at the point, Mahu and I disembarked with a detachment of soldiers. We fanned out to create a wedge of paired soldiers to enter the papyrus grove. The denseness of the jungle required us to move with care as we searched for the person who threw the spear. Though the thick foliage prevented projectiles from reaching us, we carried our spears overhead to knock down anything from hitting us.

Attempting to surprise the pirates, we crept through the hot and dense vegetation. Sweat streamed down the sides of my head and along my back. After some time, we heard sounds of fighting, the clash of steel on steel, and men shouting. The noise grew louder until we came to a small clearing. We spied three of our comrades fighting around twenty-five men dressed as Egyptian soldiers. With great stealth, my men enveloped the area to prevent escape. Using a low whistle, Mahu synchronized our forces entry into the clearing.

"Stand down, we surround you," Mahu shouted. Ignoring his order, the men kept up their assault.

Mahu, a few soldiers and I ran towards the attackers to break the siege on our men. Seeing us, the pirates turned to defend themselves. One lunged towards me. I parried the thrust with my spear in my left hand, while I stabbed the man through the belly with the sword in my other hand. Another fighter attacked me, but I overcame him with ease for my larger frame and long reach provided me with a distinct fighting advantage.

Recognizing Mahu and I, the leader of the group started shouting. "Stand down, stand down. These are not the men we seek!" Our attackers threw down their swords giving us time to look around. Mahu recognized two of the men and realized they were not pirates. They were Egyptian soldiers. We had killed ten of the twenty-five men.

"What are you doing attacking soldiers of Pharaoh?!" Mahu said, incensed.

One of them stepped forward. "Apologies! We thought your men were the traitors we sought."

Puzzlement and disgust crossed Mahu's face. "How and why would we be traitors?"

"Forgive me, Ramose, that you must hear the news in this manner. Someone murdered your brother Ahmose-Ankh in his sleep three nights ago. We suspect there was a small group of Nubians dressed as Egyptian soldiers that slipped into Buhen and killed him. We were pursuing them to bring them to justice."

I slumped to the ground hearing the news. Anger gave way to shock. My favorite brother was dead! Ahmose-Ankh protected and comforted me. Overwhelmed, I could not hear what the others were saying. I tried to see with my mind's eye how this happened, but my vision failed me as tears streamed down my face.

I came to my senses a few moments later. Now was not the time for grief, as my anger returned. I stood up and listened to Mahu speaking to a lieutenant named Pram who continued to apologize. "The bloodshed was an honest mistake." But the more he apologized, the angrier I became. Mahu betrayed the slightest amount of annoyance as he questioned Pram.

Stepping forward, I asked, "What makes you think the perpetrators were Nubians dressed as Egyptians?" Pram appeared uncomfortable as I approached.

"I am very sorry to have to be the one to tell you about your brother. We all admired Ahmose-Ankh," Pram responded. Under the circumstances, 'admired' seemed an odd choice of words.

"Soldier," Mahu started. "Answer the question."

"I do not know, sir!" he pleaded.

"Who told you to chase after the traitors?" I asked.

"I do not know, sir."

The energy I felt with Toruk began rising within me and I wished to hurt Pram. Doing so, served no purpose, so I took a deep breath and said, "You thought to chase after the traitors on your own? I do not believe that. On whose orders are you tracking the perpetrators?"

Mahu and I looked at each other, knowing that Pram did not wish to answer. As Mahu turned to ask Pram another question, Pram looked at him. My anger found an outlet as I swung my fist into Pram's stomach. Pram fell to his knees, doubled over in pain for he was unprepared for the blow.

Mahu stood over him and spoke with a cool tenseness. "His Highness does not tolerate insubordination, or have you not heard what happened to the soldier Toruk. You are lucky to still have your head attached to your body."

"Did that jog your memory soldier?" I asked.

Pram coughed and sputtered. "No."

"Are you the commander of this group?"

"Yes, Sir."

"I will ask again, who commanded you to search for the traitors." Mahu asked, still very calm.

When Pram refused to answer, Mahu kicked him in the ribs. Pram rolled in pain on the ground for a few moments while Mahu stood over him.

Regaining his breath, Pram squeaked, "Siamun told me to find them," stopping to cough, spitting up some blood. "He believes Nubians infiltrated Buhen. He did not share the evidence."

Mahu pulled me aside. "What do you want to do?" he asked.

"Get everyone ready to leave at once," I said. "Gather the dead for proper burial. I need to sit again."

Mahu nodded in acknowledgement as I walked back to the river. I heard Mahu ordering the men. I closed my eyes and breathed through my nose. How was my brother killed? Pram knew more than he shared. I watched my mind race with questions, letting each go, one after the other. "Who would have killed Ahmose-Ankh?" I breathed and let that go. "Why did they want him dead?" I let that question go too. "What is Pram hiding?" I inhaled and thought, "How did Ahmose-Ankh's murderers get pass his loyal guards?" I exhaled.

As each thought rose, I let each go to float away. My thoughts became clear. I felt the edges of the dark void, similar as I did years before. This time I watched without resistance, welcoming the enveloping darkness. In the blackness, an image formed. I watched it evolve and take shape. A face with a twisted smile gazed upon me. I knew who killed Ahmose-Ankh.

***

Mahu interrupted my reflection to inform me the men completed burying the dead, and we were ready to depart. He could not find reason to detain Pram further and allowed him to return to his boat. As he and I walked back to our boat, I said, "Let us return here when our job is complete. The plants were ceding some of their secrets to me." Though Mahu agreed, I sensed I would not be returning this way.

As we were the last to board the boat, Mahu and I pushed off to resume our journey to Buhen. We stood at the prow in silence. Heavy thoughts about Ahmose-Ankh weighed on me. I did not notice the scenery or the wind blowing from the North. Sounds of men shouting and sails flapping filled the air.

A light breezed brushed against my back as the stream carried us against the river's current.

"Buhen is a mighty fortress," Mahu said, breaking the silence.

I sensed he thought about Pram's story and Ahmose-Ankh's murder.

"It is difficult to penetrate?" I asked.

"Very difficult," he replied.

"How did Ahmose capture the fortress?"

"His Majesty is an amazing strategist, Ramose. Pharaoh captured Buhen by cutting off the supply lines, isolating the fortress. A cataract lies further south that keeps it protected. But it also prevents supplies from arriving from that direction."

"It sounds as though you admire Ahmose." It was a statement, almost an accusation.

"As a military leader, I do. He has brought stability and peace to the region."

"And enslaved many people. Your family has enjoyed his rule, have they not?"

"Some of my family has, but not others. Though my mother is Habiru, Ahmose rewarded my father for siding with him. My uncle, however, sided with Khamudi. I no longer see that side of my family."

"I am sorry to hear that, Mahu," I responded.

"Regardless of who won the war, the family might have split. Tyrants ruled both kingdoms."

"You are a realist," I teased.

"True enough," he replied. "But I have spent most of my life in the military. I have learned to follow orders without question. But you would have to have a different system of governing if you wanted to change everything."

"Is there a government that could be fair for all?" I asked, not expecting an answer. I pondered what laws could exist to allow freedom for all. In that moment, I missed Miriam for she and I spent many hours discussing that question.

"Pram is hiding something," Mahu said, ignoring my question. "Stealing uniforms and sneaking into the citadel is a plausible explanation. But why not just come out and say that?"

"How would Nubians get to Ahmose-Ankh? Nubians look different from Egyptians. Finding Ahmose-Ankh inside the citadel without being spotted would be difficult. I am told there are over three thousand soldiers stationed there. How would they get close enough to kill his guards?"

"Not to mention that they send Nubian slaves north and Habirus south to serve in garrisons," he responded.

"Exactly!"

"What if it was Habirus that killed him?" Mahu said. "They have been stirring rebellion in the North. It would also explain Pram's hesitancy to discuss with you."

"Let us assume you are right for a moment," I said. "They still have the problem of getting close enough to Ahmose-Ankh to kill him."

Mahu looked at me as he thought about my question. "It would not be easy. Ahmose-Ankh was an excellent fighter. And like, me, he selected the men in his unit, trusting they would not betray him."

"How could anyone other than Ahmose-Ankh's personal guard get close enough to kill him and then escape?"

"I agree it makes little sense," Mahu replied. "But we will be in Buhen soon enough." I nodded agreement then he added, "I do not trust Siamun. No disrespect to you or your family."

"None taken," I said, putting my hand on his shoulder. "Siamun is an interesting character."

"That is an understatement," Mahu agreed. "There is a cataract ahead that requires portage of the boats."

"Is there a swamp around there?" I asked.

"There are swamps everywhere in this region."

"You and I should inspect it while the rest of the troops and merchants move the boats and cargo."

"Great idea, Ramose!"

I did not know why I suggested the idea for I suspected replanting would never happen now. Would I even return to Waset?

We heard the cacophonous flow of rushing water before the cataract came into view. White water rushed over rocks towards us, the speed appearing to increase as it flowed past the large boulders. This required us to pull the boats from the water and carry them around the rapids. Though the river flowed fast, mosquitos, large black flies, gnats, and other insects were copious in this area. To stop the biting of the insects, we smeared mud on our exposed skin.

Various plants grew along the shore rising almost 20 cubits in the air creating an imposing green wall. While I did not recognize some plants, the familiar papyrus grew with bright-green stems that waved in the wind. The tops had feathery plumes that appeared as tiny umbrellas. But I could not see those plumes from the ground as they were so high in the air.

Swamps can present multiple problems for combat. The arid climate of the north allowed the Hyksos to overrun Egypt using chariots. But in the swampy areas, chariots sink into the mud. The foliage allows for hiding and ambushes. Though Mahu and I were experienced in swamps, neither of us had seen anything like this. We cut out some rhizomes, placing them back in the boats to return to Waset. Sniffing the air, I surmised Harwa's theory of papyrus filtering the water was correct. We knew the Nubians defecated in the river upstream. But we found no signs of raw sewage this far downstream. Harwa taught me insects would not be a problem inside the swamp, for they preferred its fringes. The interior created too much heat and humidity for most pests.

"Do you think we need to go into the swamp further, Ramose?" Mahu yelled over the sound of the rapids.

"I think we do. At the very least, I could find more plants to move North. But if we could find someone, maybe they could show me the best practices of replanting."

"Do you think there is one that would go with us?"

"Maybe. But we would need to give him free passage and likely return him here afterwards. The coming war may have scared everyone away."

"I must remind you that the area may teem with pirates. And your capture could lead to a large ransom."

"Understood. The only chance we have is if only one, maybe two people go."

"I do not like the risk involved. Pram lied about many things but the dangers in the swamps is real."

"You and I can venture inside but plan a check-in. I can hide our route and if we are not back in two days, they can send a search party."

"Very well. If we need to go further than a day out we should return and let them know. We can move the base camp closer to our path."

"Right. I hope that even if we do not find anyone I can get some sense of how the plants grow."

Mahu and I returned to the boats to explain the plan to Djau.

"I dislike this approach," he argued, yelling over the sound of rushing water. "Both of you are the most important people in the group."

Mahu tried to allay his concerns. "There is no other way to fulfill this mission. We need to find a swamp dweller to help Ramose. With our group this large, they will run if all of us stumble through the brush. Most of the soldiers have no experience in swamps. We need to run scouts and Ramose is the most experienced with swamp movement and I am the best fighter in the group." That I only trusted Mahu to accompany me went unspoken.

"I cannot argue with that logic," Djau conceded. "But make a trail for us to follow in case you do not return."

"Here is an idea," I replied. "I can make small papyrus ties like this." I tore some papyrus from a plant and created a braided strand with the shaven leaves. Holding it up I said, "I will tie these in the middle of papyrus plants stalks as we go along. You should be able to spot them, but others will not. This edge," I pointed to one end of the asymmetrical strand. "Will point in the direction that we headed."

He nodded to acknowledge he understood.

"Djau can handle this Ramose! He is an experienced officer."

"Very well, Mahu. Djau. You are in charge. You know the plan. We will see you guys in no less than two days."

"Yes, Your Highness."

***

Using our short swords, Mahu and I chopped through the foliage. As we moved further into the swamp, the dense vegetation quieted the sound of the cataract. But the heat and dampness pushed on us. The noise of bugs abated, for the increased temperatures inside the swamp drove away the insects, frogs, and birds. Every so often, I tied papyrus strips along the plants as I had shown Djau. The ties might prove to be our only track out of the denseness.

We walked for several hours without seeing, or hearing anyone until we found a section of trampled foliage.

"We should avoid going too far into the swamp," I said, breaking the silence. "The swamp people are hunters and fishermen. They will follow birds and fish."

"Someone has been through here though. See the tracks?"

"I do," I said. "But I do not think they are a swamp person."

"What do you propose?" Mahu asked.

"Let us turn north to see what we find. The river bends to that side, so the swamp likely extends that way too."

"This is like finding a tiny seed in a large mound."

"More like looking for any tiny seed out of a handful in a large mound," I corrected, smiling. "But I agree, our odds are low. Let us walk for a few more hours and then set-up camp somewhere."

Sometime later, we found a clearing that would provide shelter. We set-up camp, ate dinner, and took turns to sleep in shifts. Mahu woke me several hours later so he could sleep. He fell asleep right away, while I struggled to remain awake. The heat of the night coupled with my own emotional state almost undid me. I stood to stay alert, moving around the tent.

Nocturnal creatures roamed the swamp, but most were not dangerous. Had we been out in the bush, we would not have risked being out just the two of us as leopards, hyenas, and honey badgers roam at night. All three animals killed people traveling alone. The biggest danger in the swamp was another person.

Before first light, I woke Mahu so I could sleep a little more. After breaking camp, we continued. Rounding a bend, we spied a man cramped low. He appeared focused on something and did not hear our approach. Using hand signals, Mahu and I communicated to move in opposite directions to surround the man. Moving with stealth, we closed in from our respective sides.

Getting closer, I spied a man with a mix of Egyptian features, coupled with the beginnings of a beard. He wore no shirt, only covered by mud on his torso and wearing a tattered armored skirt of an Egyptian soldier. He appeared to be plucking feathers from a bird he killed.

With a steady and slow hand, I pulled an arrow from my

quiver, strung my bow and aimed at the man. Mahu then approached him from the front. Getting a clearer view of the scene, I saw the bird in his left hand, its head and feet dangling on either side of his palm, while he pulled feathers with his right tossing them aside. He must have killed the bird recently for trickles of blood appeared with each feather plucked.

"Hello, friend," Mahu called. The stranger jumped as though to run. I suspect he might have fled if he were not so hungry. "Friend, there is a bow trained on you from behind. Do nothing that makes my friend shoot. We just want to talk to you."

The man put his hands up to show he would not reach for his weapon. He did not let go of the bird.

Motioning with his sword, Mahu instructed the man to unbuckle his sheath. The man did so allowing his sword and scabbard to fall.

"We just want to ask some questions," Mahu started. "We are hoping to find someone who can help us with some information about swamps."

The man relaxed a little with that explanation. But I put the pieces together of his actions, looks and reactions. This was not a swamp person. Somehow, he was involved with my brother's murder.

"What do you want to know, friend?" the man replied.

"We want to restore the swamps in the North," Mahu responded. "Would you know or know someone here that could help with that task?"

"How would you do that?"

"We thought you might know. Do you know anyone that could help?"

"Let me think about that for a moment. There may be someone I know."

I signaled to Mahu my intention to walk closer. He nodded agreement. When the man looked back at me, I had my answer. If Mahu suspected anything, his face revealed nothing.

"I know of a man who lives near here. I could take him to you if you would like. His name is Harwa."

"What does Harwa look like," I asked.

"He is nondescript. He has a beard, tall like you."

"Any distinguishing marks?" I queried, feigning innocence.

"Not that I recall," the man responded. Mahu looked at me.

"You are lying," I accused. "You have never met Harwa. What do you know about Ahmose-Ankh's death?"

Fear crossed his face before he regained his composure. "What are you talking about? Ahmose-Ankh is dead?"

"My friend," Mahu said. "The man over there is a little tense. His fingers itch when people lie to him. Do not test him. Or you may lose something vital."

The man gave each of us a nervous glance. "But I am just a common soldier," he stammered.

"Very well, 'common' soldier. What is your name?"

"Bebi. I was a guard for the crown prince. 'How easy would that be?' I thought to myself thinking of my good fortune. He is an excellent fighter and could take on multiple soldiers at once."

"You guarded my brother?" I blurted out. I realized my mistake when his eyed widened. But my rage needed an outlet. I began gathering my power to strike at him.

"Tell us what happened," Mahu intervened. I began breathing to calm myself. "Maybe the Crazy Habiru will spare your life."

My reputation as the 'Crazy Habiru' lingered from beheading Toruk. Though I regret killing him, Mahu used my reputation to our advantage.

Bebi took a deep breath before telling his tale. "They murdered your brother, Your Highness, though I did not witness it. I was on guard duty, but became ill after dinner. I went to the toilet to relieve myself. When I came back towards the hallway, I heard shouts and fighting. I turned the corner to see most of the guards dead. A solider from Siamun's crew, pointed at me and yelled 'there he is'. Since I did not understand what was happening, I ran. I escaped Buhen and made for the swamps."

"How long were you gone?" Mahu asked.

"About a quarter to half an hour is all."

"Does anyone else know about this?" I asked.

"Possibly. When I fled Buhen, I took a boat part way with soldiers I knew. One told me what was going on."

"What was that?" Mahu asked.

"He claimed that he was being reassigned. Over the last year, soldiers were being replaced in my unit one by one. I thought nothing about it until the last few days. Siamun found soldiers loyal to him and had them kill Ahmose-Ankh and the remaining Ahmose-Ankh loyalists. Siamun wants the throne and nothing will stop him."

"Are you headed to Waset?"

"Why would I? To get killed? Siamun is spreading a lie that it was a group of Nubians dressed in Egyptian uniforms killed Ahmose-Ankh. They hunted down and killed most of the soldiers loyal to Ahmose-Ankh. I am no help to anyone if I am dead."

"I would have to agree with that," Mahu said. "We have a detachment of soldiers with us. We can help you get back to Waset safely and then we can deal with Siamun."

"No," Bebi snarled. "Are you sure that your group is free of Siamun supporters? I believe he has them infiltrating every level of society."

Mahu and I looked at each other. We both knew of Siamun capabilities.

Bebi continued talking. "Some believes that even Balaam is under his sway, the master now servant. Balaam suggested Siamun come to Buhen. Not to learn from Ahmose-Ankh, but to murder him."

Mahu looked at me, wide-eyed. I had told my second-in-command of the dinner at Wepet-Renpet. Ahmose seethed at his oldest son for no obvious reason. Having failed his mission in the North, Siamun appeared to be given to Ahmose-Ankh for tutelage.

"Does the name Pram mean anything to you?" Mahu asked

Bebi's face went pale for a split second. "He is the commander of the group looking for me. He is a Siamun loyalist. Please do not tell me he is your friend."

"No," I said. "Friendship is unlikely after I sucker punched him."

"Ramose, this is serious," Mahu admitted. "Buhen is not safe for us."

"Your Highness, nowhere in the kingdom is safe for you. There are spies everywhere. You and Amenhotep are in grave danger. Ahmose may be too. Siamun wants the throne for himself. And he keeps talking about a staff."

"A staff?" Mahu asked.

"He thinks it will make him immortal."

Did Ahmose know that Siamun too sought the staff?

"Siamun wants the kingdom for himself. Your father may be in danger too for all I know. Who knows what reports Siamun will send to Pharaoh?"

I nodded agreement to Bebi. Had he underperformed in the desert on purpose? It was clear he coveted the throne and had planned this for some time. How deep did his tentacles run? Balaam could not be trusted, but could Rekhmire? At the moment, I had other concerns.

"Bebi," Mahu said. "I would like to bring you back to the rest of our team. We told them we would meet them back by tomorrow at the latest. Ramose, I think the swamp project is not a priority at the moment. We must deal Siamun with foremost."

"Agreed Mahu." Then turning to Bebi I said, " I think Mahu is right. We need to get you back to Ahmose. He needs to know the truth about what is happening."

"Can you protect me? Siamun has eyes everywhere. Will Pharaoh believe me?"

Will Ahmose believe that Siamun is trying to usurp the throne? Siamun was a ruthless, manipulative, liar. Everyone in the family saw it, but Ahmose. Should I bring Siamun to justice? How would I even do that? Confront Siamun? He would have me killed just as he killed Ahmose-Ankh. Amass a force to fight Siamun? Even if I could do that, it would look as if I was trying to usurp the throne.

"I need to contemplate my choices for a moment."

Mahu nodded, knowing what I was doing. I heard him explaining to Bebi as I sat to consider our limited options. My mind raced for a few moments until I calmed myself. Then the possibilities came. I watched them float by one-by-one without judgement. After a few moments, I returned to Mahu and Bebi.

"Confronting Siamun now would be ludicrous," I said. "Ahmose needs to be informed, though we risk not being believed."

"Pharaoh does not see Siamun's true nature," Mahu agreed.

"But even if he sees the truth," I continued, "He would have to lay siege to Buhen."

"Siamun likely has support from some local Nubian princes too," Bebi interjected.

"Yes," I agreed, "that occurred to me. Siamun knows how Ahmose conquered the citadel and could defend it. There would be many lives lost in this war. We cannot confront Siamun while we visit Buhen either."

Both men agreed that it was not the best approach.

"What are you proposing?" Mahu asked. "That we go to Buhen and pretend we are on our current mission."

"I do not see an alternative. But I am unsure how to get him back to Waset." Turning to Bebi, I asked, "Would Siamun recognize you?"

"Unlikely. But any of his men could."

"What do we do with Bebi in the meantime? We cannot tell anyone about him, Mahu. I do not want to risk them revealing something by mistake. You and I know what is happening but let us keep this from the others for now except maybe a few your senior people. We still have the journey back to Waset."

"Agreed," Mahu said. "What about Bebi?"

"He can follow us from a distance. If we get Siamun out of Buhen, he will have a contingent with him. Someone might recognize Bebi. We could send two people we trust with Bebi."

"Your highness. I would feel more comfortable just following you guys, for I trust no one. I came to the swamps to find a swamp person. Harwa in particular. I have never met him....."

"We know," Mahu laughed.

"I wanted to see if I could live out here."

"Harwa left," I said. Bebi looked shocked.

"We cannot worry about that now," Mahu said. "Let us have you stay here for now. We can meet back here in a few days." Turning to me, Mahu said, "Let us return to our group and tell them we found someone who will help us with the papyrus transplanting. We must go to Buhen to finish the merchant delivery. Maybe we can convince Siamun to return to Waset with us."

I thought about Mahu's plan for a moment. It made sense. We had a reason to return here. Bebi could wait here for a few days without a problem. We had left markers around, so we knew how to return to this location. Bebi agreed to wait for seven days for our return.

293

30

As the sun set, Mahu, Bebi, and I camped in the same clearing we did the previous night. With the first light of dawn, Mahu and I prepared to depart.

"Staff will be the codeword at our next meeting," I said to Bebi.

"So be it," he replied. "I will wait for seven days."

I nodded acknowledgement.

"One other thing you need to know. Ahmose-Ankh knew of Siamun's threats to him. He arranged countermeasures."

"Countermeasures?" Mahu asked.

"I overheard him say that Siamun can have a taste of his own devices. But I tell you because there may be people you can trust."

"Thank you, Bebi," I responded.

Mahu and I walked through the small opening we walked through two days before. Though we could follow the trampled path in most places, there were many places the markers I left were helpful. Twice we nearly lost our path back. But several hours later, we heard the rushing sounds of the cataract. Djau greeted us as we approached.

"You are back early," he said.

"Yes," I said. "We found what we sought. Including a person who can help us. We planned to meet him in about one week. He will travel near us, but not with us as for he fears strangers."

"Very well," Djau laughed. "Strange people the Swamp folk are."

"Very," Mahu said.

The men broke camp as we returned to the boats for the journey to Buhen. In private at the front of the boat, Mahu and I discussed what had transpired.

"Do you believe Bebi?" I asked.

"I think I do. Does it surprise you that Siamun might want you and Amenhotep dead too?"

"That does not surprise me. But I keep having this feeling we do not know the entire story."

"Like what?"

"I am not sure. That maybe Siamun is not the one controlling the situation." Mahu gave me a skeptical glance. "Do not misunderstand me. I believe he might do this on his own. He can fool my father without a problem. But others see his conniving ways. How is he getting away with this with others watching?"

"Maybe he does not see his lack of intelligence."

"Siamun is smart, cunning like a snake."

"What other explanation is there?"

"What if Bebi is lying?"

"About what?"

"What if he works for Siamun?"

"Why would he implicate Siamun then?"

"Good question. Maybe he is the person Siamun ordered to kill Ahmose or Amenhotep?"

"That is a possibility. He escaped Buhen and avoided the search party this long. Neither are easy."

"Agreed. He said, he left to go to the bathroom because he did not feel well. They killed the other men, and he heard nothing? It makes little sense."

"I did not sense he was lying, did you?"

"No, I did not. And what if Bebi is wrong about Balaam? What if Balaam is controlling the situation somehow?"

"To what purpose?" Mahu asked.

"He covets the staff."

"If I believed it could make me immortal, I might covet it too."

I mulled the possibilities of who might be behind Ahmose-

Ankh's death besides Siamun, when the citadel came into view. The glory of Buhen revealed itself as we drew closer. Stacked stones rose high above the water to form thick, impenetrable walls. Columns decorated the walls, spaced ten cubits apart except at the main portcullis where they were closer to twenty cubits apart. Those columns were thicker with balistraria for archers. The gates opened to docks on the river.

Archers stood high on the walls, readied to shoot anyone on the dock below. Siamun's involvement otherwise, tensions lingered after Ahmose-Ankh's death.

I thought about my limited options. Closing my eyes, I breathed, trying to see if the voice would reveal to me anything. Even if I exposed Siamun to Ahmose, a war would ensue. Siamun could defend Buhen for many years. Little else came to me.

"Siamun is behind this," I said. "And Amenhotep is in grave danger."

"How do you know?"

"I feel it," I stated. "But what can we do about it?" When Mahu said nothing, I continued. "I pose no threat to him. He believes me unworthy of leadership. And someone needs to take Ahmose-Ankh's body back to Waset."

"What are you proposing? Pretend we plan to take him back to Waset for the funeral."

"Yes," I said. "That is exactly what we need to do."

"Can you determine his thoughts?"

"According to Ahmose, Siamun cannot lie to me."

"That is odd. He lies to me all the time. Are you certain?"

"I know. Amenhotep says the same thing. I do not understand it."

"If Siamun knows he cannot lie to you, we cannot risk you confronting him about Ammi's death. Otherwise, he will kill us all if he is."

"Or we need to wait for the right time to ask," I defied.

"If Bebi is correct," Mahu began, "We should leave the entire company on the boats. We may have Siamun loyalists in the unit."

"I had not thought of that."

It disappointed the men to learn that Mahu and I planned to leave them on the boat. I realized they wished to sleep in regular beds after our long journey from Waset.

"Do not be concerned," I told them. "We need to get back to Waset so we should not tarry long."

Mahu and I disembarked and walked to the locked gates. A guard standing on the ramparts above bellowed down to us.

"Who requests to enter the great city of Buhen under the command of Siamun, Crown Prince of Egypt."

"That did not take long," I whispered.

Mahu shouted back, "It is Ramose, the fourth." He stopped and corrected himself, "Third in line to the great Ahmose, Pharaoh of Egypt. I am Mahu, Commander of the third Infantry and number two to his Royal Highness."

"What business do you have in Buhen?"

"I come to discuss with Siamun, my brother, about Ahmose-Ankh's death," I answered.

"You are not a legitimate prince," he spat. Just then someone behind the guard shoved the man off the roof. He landed about ten cubits from us with a loud splat.

"You are already creating some trouble," Mahu whispered.

"Siamun is planning something. They killed the soldier because they do not wish to alert us to our danger."

"Apologies, Ramose," a man yelled down. "I am Captain Nehu. You and your number two shall enter. Wait there. I will escort you to His Highness."

"Please send men to help unload our cargo too," I responded. "We bring supplies from Waset."

The captain climbed down and ordered the gates opened. He gave instructions to unload the cargo and house merchants as needed. With his underlings following his directions, the captain motioned for us to follow.

Passing the gates, we entered a world I have never experienced. While I grew up in a city, Buhen felt different from anywhere I had lived. Tall buildings lined both sides of the already narrow streets, giving the sense of enclosure and not expansiveness. Unlike other cities, the streets curved and flowed in a serpentine fashion. The noise of the people and animals reverberated off the walls, making conversation impossible without shouting. The captain lead us through the windy streets, turning this way and that. We came to a nondescript building where two men stood against a wall guarding a door. With a nod, they admitted us into the quiet hallway.

"Buhen is a loud fortress," he apologized. "You will acclimate soon enough."

Captain Nehu led us down a narrow hallway, our footsteps echoing in on the quiet stone floors. At the end of the corridor, a soldier guarded a large door. He stood aside and opened the door as Nehu led us into the chamber.

"Your Highness," the captain said, bowing. Siamun sat on a makeshift throne. "May I present His Highness, Ramose and Mahu Commander of the third infantry."

"Thank you, Captain," Siamun said. "Dismissed."

Nehu exited without turning his back to Siamun, closing the door behind him. I studied my adopted brother's face to determine his intentions. If Siamun suspected we knew anything, he showed nothing. He left himself alone with the two of us, unworried that we might attack him. Though he feigned happiness in our presence, his smugness made me want to kill him. For now, I stuffed my anger.

"Ramose, Mahu. How are you two? Was your swamp search successful?" he asked, smiling with a stiff expression.

At first, I did not understand his question, thinking he thought we too were searching for Nubian traitors, until it occurred to me that father must have told him about the canal.

"Yes, Siamun," I said, mustering my reserves of grace and charm. "We found many plants and will go back for them before we head back to Waset. I think I understand how to do the transplanting too. With Hapi's help, we can avert any problems that may arise from the reopening of the canal."

"Wonderful, Ramose! Father's wisdom in your appointment may save Egypt grief. I must admit. I do not understand the issue. But I have other matters to attend."

"That is what we understand," I replied. "That is why I am here. Did you send Ahmose-Ankh's body back to Waset yet? If not, we would like to bring him with us."

"A kind gesture that I can grant."

"Are you planning on returning to Waset? For his funeral I mean?"

A moment of panic crossed Siamun's face. Though there were risks, I wanted Siamun to return to Waset with me. There would be no other way to contain the chaos he sowed.

"I had not planned on it because of the situation here," he admitted. "The Nubians are responsible for Ahmose-Ankh's death. It is sad they repaid his kindness by murdering our unfortunate brother." He looked down at the ground and covered his eyes. "The Nubians are creating more trouble for Egypt than we expected. I suspect, you would like to be at brother's funeral too?"

"It would be nice to support Ahmose. Plus, Ahmose-Ankh and I were close."

"Of course," Siamun admitted. "Buhen requires leadership, however."

I knew it was an excuse. Buhen possessed many people who could lead. He needed time to consolidate his base and continue his search. Remembering the encounter with Pram, I realized Siamun did not seek Nubian traitors at all. Before I could organize my thoughts, my brother spoke.

"Mahu is the most senior officer in the region," Siamun said, his voice chill and possessing the slightest bit of challenge. Then, with a feigned concern, he asked, "Could you spare him while we journey back to Waset? I should return in a month."

The question hung in the air as a challenge. We sprung Siamun's trap to separate Mahu and I to make us an easier prey.

Before I knew how to respond, Mahu spoke. "Your Highness, though I too wish to go to my friend's funeral, I will remain here so that his brothers may attend."

"I require a few days to prepare for the journey. Bring your men ashore where they will be more comfortable. Besides, Ahmose-Ankh's body it is not ready for transport just yet. The mummification process requires two more days. Does that work for you Ramose?"

"Very well," I said. "We can stay here for a few days."

"Excellent!" Siamun responded. Then turning to Mahu he said, "Let us plan to meet later this evening. There are a few items we should review before I depart Buhen."

Siamun pulled a cord that signaled for the guards. They arrived to escort us from the room as Pram entered. Mahu raised an eyebrow and turned to Siamun.

"Your Highness, might it be useful for me to stay with you

to learn the concerns regarding Buhen?"

Siamun pondered for a moment and said, "This meeting is more of a disciplinary hearing. Please go make preparations for your stay here and we shall meet back just prior to the evening meal."

"As you wish, Your Highness."

Mahu and I left the audience chamber to return to our boat, meandering through the streets, some were quieter than before. Though the streets curved and turned back on themselves creating a maze like feel, I sensed the right direction. We traveled a path very different from the one that led us to the outpost. Mahu marveled at my ability to navigate the winding streets when we arrived at the entry gates. My sense of direction would allow me to escape later.

After complimenting my effort, Mahu asked, "What of Siamun?"

"Smooth," I replied. "Like a snake's skin."

"True. Did you want me remaining here in Buhen?"

"Under the circumstances, your response made the most sense. If you had refused, he might know we suspect him. Besides, someone needs to handle the insurgency and you are the logical choice."

"There is no insurgency, Ramose. He fabricated the entire problem. And he may have left someone behind to kill me for all we know."

"Let us have Djau and Unas stay with you," I suggested. "Jana can remain with me on the boat. Speaking of which, I think we need to bring the men ashore."

"Agreed," Mahu admitted. "Maybe we need not worry about Siamun until you return to Waset."

"What do you think he plans?" I asked.

"Who knows? But he seemed a little too quick in his desire to go there."

"I thought the same," I acknowledged. I could only think of one reason Siamun wished to go to Waset. "Why would Siamun wish to kill Amenhotep?"

"I do not know. He has done many things to both of you that were disrespectful, dangerous, and mean. Siblings have strange relationships. They know us best and know our weak spots."

"True enough. But that cuts both ways," I replied thinking about my next move.

31

Shouts of joy came from the boat when we informed the others the plan for everyone to come ashore. While the men grabbed their belongings, a squad of soldiers marched right towards the boat. Mahu's and my hands went to our swords, for both of us thought Siamun changed his mind. Our concern proved premature, for the troops arrived to escort my company to sleeping quarters inside the citadel. Most of my men knew members of the regiment. As they exchanged greetings, Unas told me that many of the men fought together in the Northeastern Desert.

A tall man with a trimmed beard approached Mahu and I. His skin color and features seemed mismatched. While his skin color looked Egyptian, his nose, chin and brow told something different. His eyes were rounder. His graceful movements and elegance belied a royal upbringing.

"Good day, Your Highness," the man said. "I am Semqen, steward of Dignitary House. They have instructed me to be your host for the next couple of days. May I help you with your luggage?"

"Thank you Semqen," I said, handing him my bag. "Is that a Canaanite name?"

"Yes, my Lord," he replied. "I am a Hyksos, though not Habiru like you. My people migrated to Egypt because of a famine in Canaan around the same time as your forbearers."

I understood why he looked as he did. He belonged to a

tribe of Canaanites that resembled Egyptians, and likely his relatives once ruled the Northern Kingdom.

Semqen led Mahu, Unas, Djau, and I through the gates and back into the citadel. He took us along a different route than the captain. Crowds of people walked through the streets, making conversation difficult. Merchants, traders, workers, and soldiers flowed through the road around us doing business or speaking to friends. Voices echoed, giving a more crowded feeling to the streets. Though loud, I overheard snippets of conversation, almost all related to the death of my brother, a mix of sorrow and concern about what would come next. Some people spoke as if Siamun were already Pharaoh.

We turned down a road where fewer people walked. Semqen led us around a corner onto another street. As we wound to the right again, an extensive stone structure loomed across the road. Sheer walls rose high into the sky, announcing that this building was important. Yet, a simplicity exuded from the structure. The façade comprised simple etchings of unrecognizable images as though an unfamiliar language. An unadorned stone staircase about five cubits wide lead up to a large wooden door in the middle of the wall.

Semqen led us up the stairs, where a guard allowed us entry into the building. Quieter inside the house, Semqen told us the history of the building as he led us upstairs. The wide staircase split at a landing halfway up before continuing to the next floor.

"This place housed visiting dignitaries," Semqen told us. "Ahmose-Ankh, may his soul find peace, reopened this house for a similar purpose. Your brother treated us well. Curse his murderers!"

Mahu and I looked at each other.

"He believed," Semqen continued, "in integrating the Hyksos, Egyptians, Nubian into one society. We all had a purpose in a united kingdom. And why not? I was born in Egypt. This is my home, too! My family has lived in the Upper Kingdom for many years. We were free people and now we are slaves to ethnic Egyptians."

"He wanted to bring people together for the greater good of Egypt," Mahu said.

"Yes, he did. I am sorry Master Ramose about your brother,"

Semqen said.

"Thank you for saying so Semqen. I appreciate that. Ahmose-Ankh and I were close. I hope the crown prince finds the same sensibilities," I said.

"As do I, Master Ramose, though he dislikes all non-Egyptians regardless of the land of their birth. I wonder if the Nubians killed the wrong brother."

Ashen faced, he begged forgiveness. "I wish no harm on Siamun."

Mahu spoke soft words to Semqen. "We appreciate your fondness for Ahmose-Ankh." Semqen became more relaxed as Mahu smiled. "But what do you mean, Semqen?"

"I meant no ill-will towards his Highness, Master Mahu. The elder prince treated the Nubians with kindness and respect. He had outlined a plant to integrate them into Egyptian society while still fighting the rebel factions. His Highness, Siamun, butchered entire villages of Nubians during the war. Men, women, children, killed and tortured for no reason. It just seemed odd to me that the Nubians would kill the gentle brother."

Mahu looked at me with a raised eyebrow.

"Semqen. I understand your concern," I said. "Siamun is a more, shall we say, a divisive ruler, regarding foreigners. May I suggest to you though, not to share these thoughts with others."

"Thank you, Master Ramose. I know this. I think I am still in shock about what happened to Master Ahmose-Ankh. He stayed here the night of the attack. Siamun insisted that Ahmose-Ankh stay here, the nicest of the houses."

"He did not stay at the palace?"

"There is no official palace in Buhen. Egyptians built the citadel as a military installation to manage the mines. King Ahmose intended it for the same purpose. Senusret planned a palace before the Shepard King incursion, but never started it. The Nubians built this place."

I understood why I did not understand the glyphs outside. They were Nubian. Nubian symbols differed from those of Egypt. Semqen opened the door to our spacious room containing four canopied beds, one in each corner. In the middle of the room sat two couches facing one another with a low-set table in between. A window with a balcony provided a view to a courtyard with a small garden of palm trees, shrubs, and flowers. The refreshing scent of flowers rising from below reminded me I had not bathed in some time. I was about to inquire about a bath when Semqen answered my unformed question.

"There is a shared bathhouse downstairs. I wanted to show you your room first and set out a change of clothes for each of you before taking you down there. Shall we go?"

Semqen placed my bags in the room, and the others did the same for their own luggage. Then he led us downstairs. Behind the foyer, another staircase went down another level. As we descended, I felt the cold moisture on my cheeks, for deep in the earth there had been dug a bathing chamber. Warm air and steam hit us as we passed through a door and into an enormous room.

The bathing room, as Semqen called it, was a full bathhouse, typical of Northern Egypt. Columns lined a large pool in the center of the room. Stairs on two sides allowed entry to the warm, shallow water. The pool deepened towards the middle of the pool.

"I thought a bath would be in order after your lengthy journey, your Majesty," Semqen explained. "Do you need anything else from me?"

"No thank you, Semqen. I think we have what we need for now," I said.

"I must excuse myself then and make dinner preparations."

Semqen left the room and the four of us stripped down to bathe. I entered the bath feeling the warm water relax my body. After the arduous journey, I appreciated the soak in the quiet. My muscles released the tension of the past few weeks. I thought about my dead brother and his vision for Egypt. It differed from Ahmose's. While Ahmose wished to curry favor to friends and nobles, Ahmose-Ankh envisioned a society based upon equity, cooperation, and free trade between the parts of Egypt. He cared not about ethnic background, noble birth, or how much money one amassed. He wanted everyone to have the same opportunity for success and happiness. We would talk about how there would be no reason for wars. Food and resources were plenty. He wanted to work with the

Nubians to create a plan for a fair exchange of gold. Ammi felt that the Hyksos and Habirus could govern too.

"Ahmose-Ankh abhorred slavery. I wonder if that got him killed," I whispered to Mahu.

"Without knowing who killed him, we cannot know a motive. We are assuming who it may be, but it could have involved others. Ammi created more enemies with his ideas for Egyptian society than friends."

"True. Siamun would be a terrible ruler for everyone in the kingdom, not just the Habirus and Nubians. He does not understand how to run the country! He thinks his job is to show off, kill people, and torture those he dislikes."

"Siamun would not be the first bad Pharaoh," Mahu said.

"True. But he might be the last."

Tightness in my chest informed me something was amiss. At the edge of my awareness, I sensed an idea for me to consider. Mahu edged closer and whispered.

The tightness in my heart lifted when he spoke, indicating to me, he was correct. Still I asked, "What makes you say that?"

Mahu laid out his arguments. "We will need to uncover the other conspirators."

"Agreed," I replied. "But let us not think about this at the moment. We deserve a rub down after our journey. Who knows how long we will be on the road back to Waset."

Soda ash and tiny bottles of oil rested on the ledge of the pool. I scrubbed myself with the soda ash, rinsed myself of the suds, and rubbed oil into my skin.

A large Nubian man approached me, towel in hand, as I climbed out of the bath. He led me to a cool spot, instructing me to lie down on the marble. The attendant poured other essential oils over me, a mixture of frankincense, sandalwood and musk. He rubbed the oils deep into my back and shoulders. I realized how much tension my body was holding. Popping noises emitted from my back as he pressed into my spine in various places. When he finished, he applied a lotion of oil, donkey milk, and honey to rub into my skin. The mixture helped protected against the hot climate.

***

I lay there for a few moments languishing in the complete release of my body. The cool marble felt good after the heat of the bath. I knew I must return to the others and face what lay ahead. The others waited for me in the antechamber to the bath. Semqen sent another servant to escort us to dinner. As we proceeded up the stairs, Siamun's personal secretary interceded with instructions for Mahu to join my brother. Mahu showed no emotion about the summons, but I felt a twinge of anxiety. Mahu left us and I and the others continued up the stairs.

Djau, Unas, and I entered the dining hall where some men from Ahmose-Ankh's personal guard greeted us. Each offered condolences to me before returning to their places at the table. I sat across from Hepu, a friend of my dead brother, and the captain of the guard. As the men started taking food, I asked what had been on my mind since I heard of Ammi's death.

"How did he get killed?" I said.

Silence ensued as everyone stopped their actions for a moment. Hepu looked around the room. With hands moving in an upward motion, the captain gestured for the others to continue talking. His men responded with louder than necessary voices as the cacophony made hearing Hepu difficult. He leaned across the table and whispered, "The walls may have ears, if you know what I mean."

He raised his hands so the others to quiet the others. Then in a louder than regular voice he continued, "Siamun believes some Nubians stole uniforms from dead Egyptian soldiers and broke into the palace. None of us were on duty when the attack occurred."

"The theory sounds plausible," replied Khay, Hepu's first lieutenant. "Some of our soldiers have been soft and allowed workers who should not be in the citadel."

"How many guards died in the attack?" I asked.

"They killed all six men on duty," Hepu said. "All good men. As was your brother." Then Hepu lifted his glass of mead and said, "To Ahmose-Ankh!"

The rest of us all said in unison, "To Ahmose-Ankh!" and we all drank. There was a familiar taste to the mead, though it tasted different from its Northern counterpart. Maybe the manner of brewing in Nubia differed from Egypt.

Hepu signaled for the others to continue speaking loudly. Hepu, Khay, and I whispered.

"The official story is thinner than papyrus paper," Hepu admitted. "The six men who died were excellent fighters. Their wounds were inconsistent with battle injuries."

"How do you mean?" I asked.

"A battle like that would have seen at least one of their men killed. They may have dragged that person away, but we found no signs. A fight in a narrow space causes marks on walls from swords. The killed men showed no defensive wounds. No cuts on their hands, arms, or face. Do you understand? It was like there was no battle and died sleeping."

"They were not asleep," I said. "They were already dead."

"Dead? How?"

"How much blood of the soldiers was there on the floor?" I asked.

"Some."

"As much as you would expect given the battle?"

Hepu thought for a moment. "No," he said, surprised. "Now that you mention it, they did not. Their skin seemed to have a pinkish tone."

"The men who died? Did they complain of feeling ill that night?"

Khay thought for a moment before answering. "Yes. Five of the six men said they felt ill after dinner. But they thought it would pass and that they could perform their duty that night."

"And the one man who did not have that problem was the one who had defensive wounds on his hands?"

"Yes! How did you know?"

"Someone poisoned me when I was younger," I explained, describing the results of the blue lotus and poison mixture. "I became very ill. I would not have been able to fight off an attack, I felt so weak."

"The murderers stabbed the others to make it looks like a fight," Khay added, after listening to my story.

"That would explain how they overcame my men," Hepu responded. "We must say nothing because we do not know who was involved."

Mahu entered the dining hall, and the others stood to greet him. Mahu gave Hepu a hug in response. Servants entered to serve the next course, placing large trays of meats on the table and removing the previous course, which I missed eating because of my discussion with Hepu. Once the servants departed, the men spoke continued speaking in loud voices allowing Khay, Hepu, Mahu and I to continue our conversation.

"Does the poison taste like anything?" Khay asked.

"It has a bitter almond flavor. If you pay attention, there may be a burning sensation too."

The others spit their food out. Silence overcame the dining hall. I tasted the food and immediately recognized the poison.

"Please continue your discussions," I said using hand gestures to show loud conversational tones.

"Staying here makes little sense," I said to Mahu.

"After my meeting with Siamun, I believe sleeping on the boat is the best choice."

"You spoke to Siamun alone?!" Hepu exclaimed. "What did he say?"

"Siamun believes that Amenhotep is behind the attack. And Ramose has been helping him."

"What?" I exclaimed.

"He thinks you used your connections with the swamp people to have him killed and wants to arrest you. Siamun questioned me to understand your whereabouts and how you came here. He is spreading a rumor that you came to take back Egypt for the Habirus."

"That is outrageous!" I huffed.

"Of course it is, Ramose. Had you wanted to lead a Habiru revolt, you doing so from the North would prove easier. You could have done that when we fought in the desert."

"Is there evidence?" I asked.

"Only that he heard that Amenhotep replaced some men in Ahmose-Ankh's guard with people loyal to Amenhotep. This allowed them to sneak in and kill loyal soldiers."

"When he tried to poison me, he was complaining of stomachaches and headaches at the same time. Rekhmire thought he was trying to get attention. Maybe he is using the same strategy. Deflect attention to him by accusing his adversaries of the same behavior."

"How do you mean?" Khay asked.

"Siamun accuses others of the very thing he is doing. He accuses his opponents of treachery when it is he who committing treason. It draws attention away from him as a suspect."

"Did anyone get replaced?" Mahu asked.

"You guys are in the unit. How many people were replaced?" I asked.

"All the men killed were Ahmose-Ankh's men."

"This makes little sense. Why make this up?" Mahu wondered.

"Agreed!" Hepu said. "Unless he is trying to get rid of us by saying our loyalty lies with Amenhotep."

"How did the assassins get into the house?"

"Khay and I were on duty in front of the house that night. No one came in or out. Unless they passed through the walls."

A tightness rose in my chest. I closed my eyes and steadied my breath to calm myself. I knew how the assassins entered the house.

"There is a secret entrance to this building," I said.

"How do you know?" Khay said.

"He knows," Mahu responded. "We must search for it."

"It allows someone to escape the citadel too," I added, as the others looked around the dining room. "That is how they attackers escaped too."

"Where is it in the house, Ramose?" Mahu asked.

"Check the kitchens," I suggested. "For now, I must speak to Siamun."

"Is that wise?" Hepu said.

"Probably not. But now I must confront him!"

I left the dining room and went upstairs to don my armor. Mahu followed me upstairs. As I dressed for battle, he tried to talk me out of my plan.

"I will go with you," Mahu said.

"No! You gather the men to leave. Have them go in small groups and only take men loyal to us. The others should search for the passageway."

"But..."

"Siamun is leading Egypt towards a civil war. You heard him! He is accusing me of crimes. Confronting him now is our best opportunity to stop him."

"But he may kill you!" Mahu insisted.

"I have defeated him in combat before. But you must leave

Buhen, for only you can convince Rekhmire and Ahmose of the truth. I am tainted. That is why he wants you to stay here and have me return to Waset."

"I will take the men," Mahu agreed.

I hugged Mahu and then strapped my sword to my waist. Throwing my bow over my shoulder, I turned back to him and said, "I intend to kill Siamun. If I am not back by midnight, leave without me."

***

Mahu left my room to do as instructed. Several moments after, Semqen entered the room.

"Your Highness," he started, as I clipped the last clasp on my armor. "I must tell you something before you visit the beast."

"Be quick Semqen," I responded, grabbing my sword and spear.

"Siamun murdered Ahmose-Ankh."

"I know."

"We intercepted a letter from Amenhotep to Siamun."

"What did it say?"

"'With Ahmose-Ankh out of the way, you are next'"

"How do you know it was from Amenhotep?"

"It had his personal seal on it," Semqen responded.

"That means nothing," I protested.

"We have deduced…"

"What do you mean by we?" I interrupted.

"Ahmose-Ankh knew of Siamun's designs on the throne. He created a network of trusted servants and nobles in various places. He recruited Habirus and Nubians to help. We united in preventing Siamun from becoming Pharaoh. Once Ahmose-Ankh died, we knew Amenhotep was the lesser of two evils."

"What do you mean?"

"We have solved the problem," he said, holding up an empty vial.

I stopped what I was doing, staring at Semqen, attempting to understand his message. "We did not eat the food, you served," I said, pointing my spear at him.

"I am not sure what you mean," he stammered.

"You poisoned our food," I accused.

His face blanched as he blurted, "Someone poisoned your

food? How? I tasted it myself? Siamun has many spies here. You must leave Buhen."

Then I realized what he meant by showing me the vial. He had not poisoned us, someone else did that deed. "You poisoned Siamun?"

"Yes," Semqen whispered. "The vial arrived on your boat for this purpose."

"Do you know who sent it?"

"Our spy network. The note gave instructions, saying it was impossible to trace."

From Semqen's face, I knew my visit to Siamun was unnecessary. Still, I asked Semqen to show me a secret way there, which he agreed to share with me.

"Listen," I said. "What do you think will happen when Ahmose discovers someone poisoned his favorite son?"

Semqen's face turned pale as he realized Pharaoh would blame the Habirus and begin the purge only Rekhmire stayed.

"They will slaughter us," Semqen gurgled.

"They will round up every Habiru and Hyksos."

For a moment, I felt panic. I breathed as Harwa taught me so many years ago. I calmed myself as I allowed the tightness in my chest to subside. Quieting my thoughts, I heard the words.

"Leave Egypt, Ramose! Leave! Though you will return one day, now you must flee!"

The clearness of the Voice told me the truth of the situation. I heard it in my ears and felt it in my very being. Though Serah and Harwa both told me I would one day need to leave Egypt, I had no desire to do so.

"Get Mahu," I ordered Semqen. "And be sure that no one can listen to our conversation."

"Yes, Your Highness," he replied, as he left to follow my direction.

When Mahu entered the room, I told him all that Semqen reported.

"This is unfortunate," he replied in his understated manner. "Ahmose must not learn of this."

"No," I agreed. "The Voice told me to leave Egypt. But I do not wish to go."

"You must listen to it."

"Why?" I argued. "I am an Egyptian Prince! I have a right to stay."

Mahu gazed at me as one might an impetuous child. "Why would you not heed it now?"

"How will I help our people if I leave?"

"How will you help our people if you stay?" he countered.

"Ahmose will listen to me," I insisted.

"No," Mahu said. "Ahmose will accuse you of deceit. Siamun knew what he was doing by accusing you of this treachery."

"What do I do then?"

"You leave Egypt as the voice instructed. But before you leave, you must pay Siamun a visit."

"Why? He is already dead."

"That may be," Mahu said. "But there is something you must do for my plan to work."

In a whisper, Manu told me the plan. We agreed no one should know the truth behind my actions. Then we summoned Semqen back, who instructed me how to reach Siamun without detection. I followed his directions and when I arrived at the throne room, I knew Mahu was correct. Siamun's treachery was complete. My only option was to leave Egypt.

My father stopped.

"What was your plan?" I asked, eager to hear more of the story.

"I took the blame for Siamun's death. Amenhotep knew the truth."

"But you did not know that before you returned to Egypt? Why did you go?"

"I had faith in the One. And your mother."

"I remember you and mom arguing at an inn on the way to Egypt."

My father laughed. "I had forgotten about that day."

"What did you fight about?"

My father pointed behind me, so I turned around. So enthralled was I with the tale I did not notice the day passed. The sky turned reddish-purple in the West as the sun sank behind the hills. But I wanted to know what happened next. Did he escape Egypt? What happened when he confronted Siamun? My father smiled.

"Was the Balaam who advised Pharaoh the same…"

"As the one we dealt with years ago?" he finished my question, then answered it. "The same person. He would play a role in our people's redemption from Egypt."

"What did he do?"

"That is a long tale," he said.

"So you killed a man in cold blood for beating a Habiru slave."

"There is some truth to that story."

"But what happened right after you left Egypt?"

"I met your mother," he answered. "Surely you have heard that story?"

"I have not. I remember little of that time living with grandfather. And I know nothing of how you came to be there."

With a wry smile, my father looked off into the distance. He thought for a moment before saying, "I will share that story another day."

This ends the first book of The Lost Books of Moses. The story continues in book two of the Lost Books of Moses.